ICE

ULLA-LENA LUNDBERG

TRANSLATED FROM THE SWEDISH BY

THOMAS TEAL

Sort Of Books, PO Box 18678, London NW3 2FL

Typeset in Book Antiqua to a design by Henry Iles

Printed and bound by
CPI Group (UK) Ltd, Croydon CR0 4YY

Distributed in all territories excluding
the United States and Canada, by
Profile Books
3 Holford Yard, Bevin Way, London WC1X 9HD.

448pp
A catalogue record for this book is available from the British Library

ISBN 978-1908745477
eISBN 978-1908745422

The paper this book is printed on is certified by the © 1996 Forest Stewardship Council A.C. (FSC). It is ancient-forest friendly. The printer holds FSC chain of custody SGS-COC-2061

FILI FINNISH
LITERATURE
EXCHANGE

Sort of Books gratefully acknowledges the financial
assistance of FILI – Finnish Literature Exchange.

ICE

ULLA-LENA LUNDBERG

TRANSLATED FROM THE SWEDISH BY

THOMAS TEAL

PART ONE

Chapter One

No one who's seen the way a landscape changes when a boat appears can ever agree that any individual human life lacks meaning. The land and the bay are at peace. People gaze out across the water, rest their eyes, then look away. Things are what they are. In every breast there is a longing for something else, and everything we long for comes by boat. It's enough that what comes is me, Anton, with the mail, for I might have anyone at all in the cabin. Expectation sweeps across heaven and earth when they first catch sight of me. The landscape is no longer quiet, there's movement everywhere when the news goes round. Some are already running, shouting, "Here they come!"

It's the same with those who, ancient and invisible, exist beyond our range of vision. When a human being approaches, the air grows tighter, you feel how they crowd forward and want to know something about you, though you suspect that they no longer understand what it means to be human, that they are no longer human, that the shapes you sense no longer resemble us. All the same, you feel their insistent desire to find out who you are.

Even though I have the throttle at full speed, we move slowly. Restlessness everywhere, as I can see from the way people move. I know they're waiting and trying to stand still while they do, and I come as I come, steady ahead, cut the engine when I should and glide in towards the dock. Kalle stands there with the hawser, his foot out just in case he has to fend us off, but as usual I barely graze the edge, and so we land. The passengers have left the cabin, people call out and talk from boat to land, and the world looks very different than it did when we were out in the bay by ourselves and the people ashore were unaware.

Today, for a change, I am landing at the church dock, because we have the new priest aboard. Which is why they've been watching for us a little more keenly and why they came running as soon as we were spotted in the bay. It's the verger who kept watch and the organist who saw to it that the boats they and the others came in were all pulled up on the rocks so that we could reach the dock. There is warm smoke rising from the parsonage chimneys, for the women have made fires and have food on the stove. The wind is perfectly calm at this hour of the morning, in coldest May, but oh how glances and thoughts fly through the air. What's he like? How will it go? But no doubts are visible, for they must receive him heartily and without fear, as if getting used to a new pastor was the easiest thing in the world.

The priest has stood out on deck for quite a while, though his wife has tried several times to pull him in and told him he'll catch cold. But he stays outside, and when he sees his church climb the hill, signalling to him with its red roof, he grows solemn but wears a broad smile, and when we finally pull into the cove he looks so happy that everyone decides it will all go well. He waves from a long way out, and they wave back and shout "Welcome!" He shouts, "Thank you!" and "Here we are!" and "You good people, you've had to get up in the middle of the night to welcome us!"

He has been here once before, so he knows the organist and the verger and Adele Bergman, who is on the vestry and is mightily supportive of the church and the priest. But it's different now that he is the acting pastor and is going to settle down here with his wife and child. He's made a good first impression. But when he's about to step ashore, the boat glides out a bit as if the sea wanted to take him back, and a cold breeze draws across the bay. What that might mean I don't know.

* * *

Adele Bergman knows very well that guests out here are always easy to please. If they're coming from Åbo, they've been travelling for at least twelve hours, not counting the time it took them to get to Åbo in the first place. They've been thrown about in all sorts of weather and covered with spray. And when they finally stagger ashore, they have sand in their eyes and cold, damp clothing twined about their bodies. They're hungry but seasick, shivering but sweaty. They snap at each other and wish they'd never come.

This is the basis of the widespread reputation for hospitality that the Örland Islands enjoy. Human beings are put together in such a way that it takes them only half a day to grow hungry, bored, and tired, so when they finally get a roof over their heads and are presented with a hot stove and warm food, they truly believe they have been snatched from the brink and cannot adequately thank those who have taken them in. Of course the people of the Örlands have been showered with gratitude many times over, but the feeling is always sweet, and they have enjoyed firing up the kitchen range and tiled stoves even though it shortened their night.

They stand there looking pleased — Adele Bergman and her Elis, the organist, the verger and the verger's Signe — for rarely are people so much appreciated for such a relatively modest effort. It is always a pleasure to observe new arrivals, and now, moreover, these five people constitute an official ecclesiastical

11

reception committee with every reason to stand on the dock and inspect the newcomers and take them under their wing and guide them up to the parsonage.

And guide them into the parish, because it might not be such a bad idea to give the pastor a hint or two about certain tensions within the congregation. This fellow is young, and his wife is even younger, and for the sake of his future success, one can hope that they're smart enough to learn from others.

The priest is happy. For young people, the trip feels endless because they can't move and there's so little to do, and now he's happy because he's arrived and can go ashore and shake hands and see to the baggage and shake hands with the mail carrier and thank him for landing at the church dock with all their things. But he's happy in another way as well, because it's in his nature, and because there's a fire burning in his breast, fed by everything he wants to experience and accomplish in his life.

How nice it would be, Adele Bergman often thinks, in her heart of hearts, to have a Catholic priest who would come by himself and belong more to us alone. In our Lutheran church there has to be a wife and children and furniture tying him down and making demands on his time. People almost think there's something wrong with a priest who doesn't have all that, and so the wife gets terrifically friendly looks from everyone as she steps ashore and sets down a child so small it's a wonder it can stand on its own two feet. It's a girl, in a cap and coat slit up the back. "A real little parsonage lassie," says the organist, who is gallant and loves children and who greets her personally. "Welcome to the Örlands," he says, and the child doesn't start crying but gravely returns his gaze.

The pastor's wife is small and quick. She doesn't realize that the boat will stay at the dock until it's been unloaded but glances angrily at the priest who stands there talking, with the child on his arm, while she scurries about carrying ashore valises and boxes and rolls of bedding and asks what they intend to do about all the furniture lashed to the deck. "Petter, come here!" she finally shouts.

The priest hands the child to Signe, as if he understood how she longs for children. He hurries over to the railing and the others follow. The skipper and Kalle are on their side of the railing, talking, and then they quickly heave ashore the large and the small sideboards and chests and tables and chairs, which now stand newly awakened on the dock.

"Ready to move right in," says the organist. "Sea view and high ceilings."

Two beds and a crib follow, then a kitchen table and benches and a dresser and a commode and two bicycles, and finally the household appears to be complete. The pastor's wife counts and checks while the pastor dandles the child, who squirms in his arms and wants down. Adele looks into the cargo space and wonders how much merchandise the skipper has brought from Åbo for the Co-op, the islands' only store. "Not so bad," he assures her. "Things are starting to get back to normal, bit by bit." Which in truth they all have a right to expect, a year and a half after the war.

The skipper and Kalle will take the boat over to the Co-op's dock to unload its goods before they can head home, and now they look at the pastor's wife and wonder if they've got everything off. She thinks they have, and the skipper looks to the engine and Kalle loosens the moorings and the priest thanks them once again. The boat starts to leave, but on the dock they all stand around talking, though they ought to go inside where it's warm and get something to eat. As usual, it's all up to Adele. "Can't you all see these people are done in?" she says. "Now let's put the most important stuff in the cart and go up to the parsonage."

They amble through the morning dew up towards the big red parsonage, the air above the chimneys quivering with warm air from the tile stoves where the reception committee have built roaring fires. In the kitchen, there are saucepans and a teakettle dancing on the stove. The porridge is warm in its pot, and there is bread, buttered and waiting, covered, by the milk pitcher.

Just as they should, they stop to catch their breath. "My goodness, such lovely warmth! And we thought we'd be coming to a cold, damp house and wondered where we'd find the key!" And, "Is it possible? Is this for us? My dear friends, you're too good!"

"Do sit down and help yourselves," say the reception committee in various voices at practically the same moment, taking their own advice and sitting down. Adele has brought cups in a basket, along with enough ersatz coffee for everyone. Bread too, though the idea was that some should be left over for the pastor's family.

"Oh, oh, oh, so good," they say. "What bread! And butter! Look, Sanna, Papa's putting a pat of butter on your porridge. Now a big spoonful! Wasn't that good? Now show us how you can drink milk from a cup. And what wonderful coffee! Hot enough to warm my toes. I don't know how we can ever thank you or pay you back!"

And much, much more. It's lovely to hear, the kind of reward everyone deserves for a job well done. The reception committee sit and talk, though they know that the newcomers need to get themselves organized and get some rest. Such a long way they've come and how nice it is to be here at last and get such a warm, hearty welcome. Here they mean to stay, for they'll never find a better place.

The priest asks what villages they're from and wants to know if these are distant. The organist, with whom he'll work most closely, comes from farthest away, but he waves that aside — what does it matter when he has a boat? The pastor has only to call on the telephone and he'll come. The verger lives close by and has only a narrow channel to row across to get to the church, so he'll be glad to come and help out. As will Signe, who now thinks she'll head for the barn and milk the cows.

The pastor's wife pricks up her ears, for she and Petter have taken over the former priest's two cows. She brightens with interest and wonders if she can come along but then changes her mind when she stops to think of everything she has to deal with this morning. It will have to be this evening. "Signe, if you would be so kind as to do the milking today too, then maybe we can go together this evening. Starting tomorrow, I'll take over."

They look at her. Pastors' wives don't usually enter the cow barn, but this one says she comes from a farm and has a special interest in animal husbandry. "So it will be a lot of fun to have my own cows, even though there are only two of them," she says, and the priest looks at her proudly. "She's good at all sorts of things, my Mona," he says. "We've certainly come to the right place, because we're going to like all the farm work, in addition to the church work, I mean."

He turns again to the organist, who is chairman of the vestry, and smiles and says they're going to have a lot to discuss. He hopes it won't intrude too much on his time if he suggests that they get together informally this week and go over the parish routines, and the organist readily agrees. Adele can see that he likes this priest already, likes him even more than expected. He would have been equally obliging, though somewhat more guarded, towards a priest he liked less, but now he's looking forward to adopting the new man and supporting him. As he's done with a number of people he's close to, whether or not it served him well. As he did with Adele, although, to her quiet sorrow, he was already married when she came to the Örlands.

The priest's wife says she thinks she'll send Petter to the store this very day, when he's rested a little, and so he is given directions. He can put his bicycle in the skiff and row across the little inlet, and from there it's only five kilometres to the store. "It's nice you've got roots in Åland," says Adele. "It's been a great source of amusement to watch some of the priests from the city try to row a boat."

Petter laughs heartily and says how fortunate he is to have already made the acquaintance of the Co-op's manager, who looks like she might become a friend in need. Adele tells him he'll be very welcome at the store, and she'll look forward to his visit. He sits there at the table as if he had all the time in the world, but his wife has grown restless and gets up with her wilting daughter in her arms and looks for a place to put the child down. We ought to get our things into the house, she thinks, and get the essentials in place as quickly as we can.

Adele watches her restrain her irritation at them for not having the good sense to go home, filled to bursting as she is with all the things she wants to do, and she notices quite unexpectedly that she likes the pastor's wife too, and quite a lot. Because they're both cut from the same cloth, industrious types, called to step in if anything is going to get done. They look at each other and smile. Mona has also taken the measure of Adele Bergman. Adele stands up and says, "All right, my friends, I think we should let the pastor and his wife put their house in order! Thank you so much. And, once again, welcome to the parish. The men can carry up your furniture from the dock, and then we'll say thank you for today and hope to see you soon again."

People in the villages like to say that Adele is bossy, but for many it's a relief that someone takes charge. The organist and the verger and Elis deliver their thank-yous and head happily for the dock, and Petter runs after them and says for heaven's sake he can help to carry his own belongings. Four men take care of it all in no time, and soon enough everything is assembled in the parsonage parlour.

Goodbye and thank you and thanks again. The verger and Signe head off to the cow barn and Adele and the organist and Elis walk down to the church dock, happy as children, true friends of the church. Light at heart, for this has gone well.

Chapter Two

IT IS PLEASING TO IMAGINE that the young priest and his wife turn to each other and embrace, now that they're alone and about to begin a new life in their own parsonage. But it is hardly certain. There is much to do in a life, and unless they get a move on they won't have time for more than a fraction of it all.

There will be little rest, for where will they find the time? To begin with, Sanna, who's fallen asleep on the floor in her good coat, must be put to bed, but first the bedclothes must be unrolled, and the child's mattress and blankets must be warmed against the tile stove before the crib can be made up and the child tucked in. And as long as they're at it, they might just as well carry in the other beds and unroll the bedclothes and get that out of the way. And now that everything is so inviting, why not take a little nap themselves, since it's only eight o'clock and they have the whole day ahead of them? It is the priest's wife who makes this wise suggestion, considering they've been travelling day after day and have had far too little sleep. But the priest is wound up and says he's too restless, there's so much to see and do.

"We'll get plenty of sleep in the grave," he says brightly, but a laughing voice replies, "That's no way for a priest to talk!"

It's Brage Söderberg, from the Coast Guard, who in keeping with local custom has walked right in, especially since the door stood open. He has promptly demonstrated the proposition that Mona Kummel will repeat bitterly and triumphantly again and again in the years to come. "If you even think of lying down for half a second, for once in your life, for the first time in months, someone will walk in."

He has undeniably walked in, smiling benignly, radiating a geniality and good humour that both Petter and his wife find indescribably captivating. Unembarrassed, he stands there in the midst of the crates and boxes, grinning. Also in keeping with local custom, Brage Söderberg has not introduced himself. They get his name later from the verger. He greets both of them heartily and welcomes them to the Örlands and says he has the Coast Guard cutter at the church dock and if they're thinking of going to the Co-op for all the stuff they surely must need, then it would be no trouble to take them because he's headed there himself to take on fuel.

"Thank you!" Petter says. "What a welcome offer, but are you sure it's no trouble?"

"No trouble at all," says the Coast Guardsman. "When you live on an island, you've got to chase your chances."

To the Kummels' ears this sounds wonderfully original, for they haven't yet learned that this saying is a part of the standard local idiom. It's a way of articulating the obvious nature of neighbourly help, a way of expressing any number of independent measures and creative solutions that do not always fit strictly within the limits of land-based law. The priest picks up the scent of an independence he has longed for all his landlocked life, and it ignites a great feeling of friendship towards the still nameless Brage Söderberg. He has come on the wings of dawn and made a laborious expedition seem weightless as a feather.

But the priest's wife gets a jolt. She jumps up and pulls a sheet of paper from one bag and a pen from another. Standing at the sideboard, she writes frantically, stamps her feet and calls out apologetically, "Just another few seconds!" Brage Söderberg looks surprised and Petter begins to suspect that there's maybe no need for such a rush. But his wife has no time to reflect on that possibility. The urgency that she believes must motivate the Coast Guardsman drives them off at good speed and, nearly running, she tells her husband all the things he must remember to buy, ask for, and place on order. She has certainly forgotten much, she cries, waving the list in the air, so he'll have to use his wits, summon up all his common sense, think for himself. Now they just need to get moving, get a move on, away, and does he have the ration coupons? No, dear heaven! "Sorry, I'll run," and she runs back up at full speed.

"Wow!" Brage Söderberg does not know them well enough to comment, but Pastor Kummel, a little embarrassed, says his wife is afraid they're intruding on his work day. She'll calm down once they get organized a bit. While they wait, he inspects the Coast Guard cutter with genuine interest and the two of them discuss horsepower and seaworthiness, and the priest hopes he may ask for advice when he has the means to buy a motorboat, something he eagerly anticipates doing. But by then his wife is already back, a little short of breath, her cheeks red. She gives him not just the ration cards but also, triumphantly, his wallet, which she has found lying on the kitchen table. In among the dishes! Must he always unburden himself of his wallet as soon as he enters the house? Couldn't he just leave it in the pocket of his coat, thin as it is? Anyway, thanks to her attentiveness and presence of mind, he will not have to shame them by asking for credit on his very first visit to the store.

But now get going! And as the boat growls away across the sound, it seems to move more slowly than Mona Kummel, who steams back up to the parsonage one more time. But when she's out of sight up on the crown of the hill, she slows down just a bit. She is alone, although there's a roaring in her ears from all the engine noises and all the talk and the lack of sleep these last twenty-four hours, and she allows herself to catch her breath and gaze out at the church, which stands there red-capped in a hint of spring greenery against a blazing blue sea and bright sky. Beautiful, she lets herself think. Fresh air, though a little raw. I'll need to bundle up Sanna properly until midsummer!

She also thinks about how they now have a house and a home and a life of their own, and with joy in her heart she goes into the parsonage and starts dragging the furniture into place and unpacking their belongings. But first, in her own kitchen, she reaches out her hand and takes the last slice of bread, heavy with butter, which maybe she should have offered to the Coast Guardsman, although she didn't think of it at the time. From now on, she'll churn her own butter, bake her own bread, do everything one does on a small farm. She sees that the verger's Signe has carried in a pail of milk, still warm, and if Petter can get some flour, she'll make pancakes, and if he brings home some potatoes, all will be well. This evening he can row out and lay a net by the dock, because they bought the old priest's boat and his perch net at auction. (Where their agents were Petter's much too chatty and therefore inattentive and easily cheated relatives, but disappointments of that kind are only to be expected.)

Mona Kummel loves her husband. Love between young married couples is hardly uncommon, but the glow in her breast is something more. It's hard to hold inside her chest, hard to keep it from breaking out like a welder's flame and singeing the hair and eyebrows of everyone who comes near and encroaches on his time and on the space that is rightfully hers. Because the priest is so often away or occupied with church business, she uses industrious activity to control the flame.

Sanna, who is now awake, knows she's better off sitting quietly in her crib than chasing out into the whirlwind now rushing through the house. Mama dashes past the open door and sees that Sanna is up. "Sleep, go to sleep!" she calls. "Mama's here." There's a scraping and squeaking as she shoves the big sideboard into place in the parlour. A momentary pause while she judges the distance between the two corners of the wall, then another scrape and squeak so it's exactly in the middle, to the centimetre. Then the table and chairs are put in place. The boards of the packing crate break open with a crack, and she begins to unpack and fill the sideboard. The sounds move farther away and Sanna cries in her loneliness. Mama is so far away in the strange house that she has to cry as loudly as she can and stand up in her bed and scream "Mama! Mama!" at the top of her lungs before Mama finally hears.

"Hush, Sanna!" she says. "There's nothing wrong with you. Do you want to get up?" Quickly she lifts Sanna from her crib and carries her through the parlour and the dining room into the kitchen. She feels the back of her pants and is pleased that she's managed to get out the potty and plant Sanna on it before she's had an accident. "Good girl!" says Mama, and suddenly Sanna is sitting on her throne and looking around. She's seeing many things for the first time, and there is much to remark upon, but she doesn't know the words. "Beh" maybe, or "Deh". "Deh! Deh!" she says and points. "Yes," Mama says. "Window! We'll get curtains when we can. Paper curtains are so tiresome, I think the kitchen will have to wait until we've got some fabric."

"Deh!" Sanna says. But Mama is lying down looking for signs of mice on the kitchen cupboard floor. "You never know what to expect in an old house like this with big cracks between the floorboards," she confides to Sanna. "So we'll need to get a cat right away. Would Sanna like a kitty?" "Deh!" says Sanna. "We'll get one," Mama decides. She has her hands full, because she wants everything to be ready when Petter gets back, so he'll just stand there open-mouthed. As she scampers back and forth on her very nimble feet, she wonders if, as usual, he's letting himself be talked to death so he'll never get away, and simultaneously she hopes he won't be in too much of a hurry so she'll have time to get everything in order.

She's hungry, too, because no one can work for hours on end without eating something. There's milk in the pitcher, but not even Sanna lives on milk alone. She's crying now, tiny and thin as she is, and soon she'll be crying inconsolably, while their supposed protector, for whom Mona has left a salaried position, is off in the village making himself popular with the locals. Mona fills a pot with water the reception committee carried in and gets a fire going under it. There's a good draught in the kitchen stove, but then there's a good draught on this whole blustery island, not a tree to windward of the chimney. Out here, she instructs Sanna, you can't open the damper more than a crack or the firewood will get pulled right up the chimney!

"Wah," says Sanna, and Mama takes out the box of cold food. She's not so dumb and inexperienced that she's let herself be transported to a desert island without the wherewithal to throw up a barricade against trouble and want. There's tea, which she and Petter will enjoy at the table in the parlour this

23

evening, and sweet rusks, one of which she moistens with a little milk that she's warmed on the now hot stove and feeds to Sanna. "Good!" she commands, and Sanna eats and stops crying. "Papa will be home soon, and then we'll make some real dinner. Then Mama will go out to the barn, and tomorrow will be just an ordinary day."

Just an ordinary day is what she longs for most of all, after the years of war, after Petter's first assignment as a substitute preacher, housed in one room and kitchen with wife and newborn baby. A routine of their own is the loveliest dream in the world for people who have had to adapt to all manner of changing circumstances, all of them out of their control. Every family in Finland is calling for a home of its own, and this one has come sailing along and landed right here at the end of the Baltic Sea. And now it's furnished. In a couple of hours, Mona Kummel has made it habitable, and the only thing missing is the honest smell of cooking food. Mona cannot relax. With Sanna on her arm, she wanders from window to window and looks out. She has water boiling like mad in two pots so that whatever he brings home can be cooked without wasting a moment.

"It's awful how fast the time goes!" she says to Sanna. "It'll soon be time to do the milking and I haven't even started on the food. Where *is* he?"

"Geh," says Sanna. "Papa-papa-papa."

"He'll be here soon," says Mama. And when she's said that a number of times, in he comes, knees buckling under the load, while the Coast Guard heads back to base. Mona had thought they'd make a tour of the house, but when Petter has picked up Sanna and begun to express his admiration, she cries out that they haven't time, they need to eat something. Signe will be there any minute, and then they have to do the milking. "Well, what were you able to get?"

Petter is pleased with himself. Praise God, what a provisioning it's been. "If I weren't married to you, I would have proposed to Adele Bergman," he says. "What a woman! She sits there on her throne like some higher being that everyone looks up to. Guess what she did! She called me into her office and invited me to sit down. I realized right away that she would talk and I would speak when spoken to. She said she imagined that we needed practically everything in the way of groceries except milk, and so this morning she'd set aside some things for us. Because otherwise it would all be gone! 'It's astonishing,' she said, 'the way people grab stuff just because certain things are no longer rationed. When they needed coupons at least we could estimate the rate of consumption.'

"I sat there stunned and thought to myself that when they ran out of everything, then Adele Bergman still had a secret little reserve that she portioned out to specially deserving people. And now we're among them. I have flour, Mona. I have sugar. I have rolled oats and semolina. I have powdered eggs. I have peas. I have herring for this evening, and then we'll fish for ourselves. I have salt. I have crispbread until we can do our own baking. I even have a loaf of fresh bread as a welcoming gift. That wonderful woman had even arranged for a sack of potatoes from the village until we can find some closer by."

"Give!" says Mona, and a number of potatoes are energetically scrubbed in the kitchen basin and dumped into boiling water, followed by a shower of salt. "Twenty minutes!" she shouts. "Where's the flour? I'll make a white sauce. I brought pepper with us. Put that jar of herring on the table! What wonderful flour! I'll make pancakes, we're famished. Oh it'll be so great to have a real meal. Can you wait? Take a piece of crispbread!" She works frantically, whips the batter, makes the sauce, throws plates and knives and forks on the table, starts making pancakes in the little frying pan. "If only we had some jam," she says, and her husband smiles to himself and pulls out a little jar of apple sauce. Apple sauce! The first commercial apple sauce since the war. My goodness!

No one who's seen Mona Kummel dash about would ever suspect that she can actually sit still—and longer than you might think, once she's got the food on the table and the family in place. They eat herring and good potatoes with white sauce, and they wolf down the pancakes with sugar and apple sauce. They eat a great deal for such a small family. So much that they go on sitting when they're done, in the gentle intoxication that a hot meal can offer when it's several hours late. Sanna wears a melting smile, with a border of sugar and apple sauce around her mouth. Mona asks Petter about the people he saw at the store, what they looked like, what they said, and he tells her how polite and friendly they all were. Everyone shook his hand and welcomed him and spoke to him so freely and easily that it was a joy. "People are easy to talk to here," he says. "What good people! And what a day we've had! My head is spinning. Hard to believe that it's just one day since we stood on the pier in Åbo wondering if the boat would ever get under way."

He glances in towards the parlour and on towards the bedroom that lies beyond, for now he wants to see what miracles his wife has performed. "Well why not? Come on, although I'm expecting Signe any minute and I would have liked to clear the table before she got here. But come."

Papa picks up Sanna and they go on their tour of inspection—everything in its place, everything put to rights. "How did you find the time? How did you manage? My dear, you shouldn't have moved the sideboard and the table by yourself! Here I'm away just a few short hours and when I come back—order from chaos."

"Well, well," his wife says. "The book boxes still aren't unpacked, because you'll have to use the boards to build a bookcase. And your suitcase and office things, I've just put them in your study. You can unpack them yourself while I'm milking the cows. Where *is* Signe? It's almost six o'clock."

She looks out the window, towards the water and towards the land, and the priest follows her gaze and sees how pretty it all is, naked granite and a light green cloud like smoke between the hills this early May. Evening sun, and the church roof glowing with a subtly different shade of red than it had this morning. In the churchyard, black and white crosses, an entire congregation.

"Do you think she doesn't dare come in?" Mona wonders.

"Of course not," Petter says. "We've already met them, and they know we don't bite."

"Well, yes," Mona says, "but we should have said a time. There are all sorts of things I should be doing, and here I am just going from window to window." But as she goes, she clears the dishes from the table and pours wonderfully hot water into the dish tub. "So I guess I'll just get started," she says. "Maybe it's a way of getting her to come, as soon as I'm up to my elbows in the dishes."

"I'll fetch some more water," he says. "And if she really doesn't dare come in, I'll see her. The well is down there by the garden somewhere, if I remember rightly." He goes and comes back without seeing any sign of Signe, but the water is soft and sweet with a lot of meltwater, golden brown the way well water often is in the spring.

Mona finishes the dishes and puts Sanna on the potty for another session, and still Signe doesn't come. "If they weren't so friendly, I'd be really annoyed," she says. "Do you think she misunderstood me? Do you think I should go to the barn by myself? But of course then she'll be hurt that I didn't wait for her. What a nuisance! I so wish we could be on our own."

Mona Kummel is dying to go out to the cow barn. In the beginning, the congregation is going to think her enthusiasm for the two cows and three ewes is play-acting, to show that she's trying to share their everyday lives in every way, but in fact there is no one on the Örlands with a more fanatical partiality for livestock than the pastor's wife. As a child on her family's farm, she liked the creatures in the barn and the stable rather more than the ones in the house, and even now that she's got her beloved husband and, through him, a family of her own, she still loves the animals that first made her human. But this is not a sentimental attachment or romantic nonsense, because Mona Kummel sends animals to slaughter, punishes those that misbehave, and never says that she loves cows. She just keeps them with a passion. Rational and realistic as she is, she loves animals for their contribution to self-sufficiency and because these cows guarantee her family a life of its own.

She can't rush out to the cow barn now, because she's agreed to go with the verger's Signe, but how is it possible that the verger's Signe doesn't show up at the hour when all of Finland, yes, all of Scandinavia, milks its cows?

"Maybe they milk their cows later here, since they don't deliver their milk to a creamery?" says her husband, who sometimes shows evidence of a practical intelligence that amazes his wife. She admits that he may be right, and says it might be just as well to put Sanna to bed now. On the other hand, she needs to be washed first. There's warm water on the stove, which it would be a shame not to use, so maybe after all . . . "If Signe comes you'll have to take over."

There is time to wash Sanna and tuck her in and give her a good-night blessing before Signe arrives. And not just Signe but the verger with her. They come in quite calmly, with no apology for being late, which in their own eyes they are not. The verger asks how the day has gone. He supposes that they're tired and says that he and Signe can go to the barn by themselves so they can rest a bit.

"Out of the question!" Mona says. She is ablaze with anticipation. "It will be great fun to meet our cows. I saw that the pails had been washed — thank you so much, Signe — so let's just grab them and go!"

It's possible that the verger and Signe had in mind a somewhat longer prelude to the milking, but they adapt smoothly and follow her out into the passage where she makes an energetic racket with the milk pails and the strainer and grabs a package of cotton filters. "There's soap in the cow barn?" she says, and Signe nods. The pastor explains that he'd be happy to come along but that someone has to stay inside with Sanna this first evening in case she wakes up and is frightened in her new surroundings.

Mona leads the procession to the cow barn. She's wearing a milking smock from the old days, and she's slipped into a pair of old, worn shoes in the passage, but on the inside she's dressed for a ball. She opens the door and steps straight into the cow barn, no milk house of the kind she's used to. Two stalls for the cows, an empty calf's crib, and against the far wall a sheep fold with three ewes and a partition full of butting heads and wobbly legs that add up to a total of five lambs.

The cows turn their heads and moo. Signe introduces them. The bigger, older, dark red cow is Apple, and the smaller one with the lighter coat and gentler disposition is Goody. Both are pregnant and will calve in June.

Too late in the year! Mona thinks. And Signe says that the covering kept getting postponed. The old priest and his wife knew they were leaving and neglected the cows a bit. Now they're going dry, but they're still giving a litre or so every morning and evening, and of course even that much milk is always welcome.

Mona claps their flanks with a firm, practised hand and examines their udders, which are relatively small and firm, Goody's in particular. They sniff at her cautiously and moo again to remind everyone of food. And yes, the haymow is attached, with a door between. There's almost no hay left, but on the other hand the cows can soon be put out to pasture. The villagers who've run out have already done so.

"And so have we," the verger adds. "Keeping them in hay over the winter is really a struggle. There's not a lot growing right now, but they eat leaf buds and reed sprouts along the shore."

Mona scratches around with the pitchfork and pulls together a clump of hay that she forks up in front of Apple, then Goody gets her own dusty, meagre share. In the whole cow barn not a trace of fodder grain. Apple and Goody both have tight round bellies around their pregnancies, but their hipbones stick out like knobs, and a woman from the hay barns of Nyland can see that they're too thin.

"Spring is coming not a minute too soon!" she says. To herself, she's thinking that the former priest took miserable care of his animals, but she doesn't want to criticize. She searches around with the pitchfork and finds some dried leafy twigs for the sheep. Then she finds the dung fork and starts mucking out, in spite of the verger's offer to do it for her. It's easily done. These bony cattle have produced small, firm pancakes that stay in one piece, and this primitive cow barn actually has a drain that carries out the urine through a hole in the stone foundation. The verger shows her that the well in the corner is full of meltwater now, in spring, and he gets in ahead of her and pulls up a couple pails of water that he empties into their troughs.

The cows mumble peacefully and sweep up the dry hay while Mona and Signe wash their udders and sit down to milk. The next day, the verger and Signe are able to tell everyone that the priest's wife milks better than anyone they've ever seen and that she has a way with animals that takes your breath away. Apple and Goody turn around to look and then turn around and look again, because in a cow's life this is quite sensational. They don't release a lot of milk, but still enough to produce a good stream when Mona Kummel sets to work.

"Good teats, firm udders," she declares. "All they really need is a little fat on their bones. We have a lot to look into — the cow pastures and the hayfields."

To judge by conditions in the haymow, there is every reason to fear that they haven't enough meadowland, but the verger, who takes an interest in such things, starts in at once on a long report about the church's lands. "You'll always have hay, I think. And the church crofters will help with the haymaking, they owe you that for the land they use."

"You can't mean that the church still has crofters, not these days," she says, and the verger agrees that she's right. Legally, they own their land, but they need a little more pasture and they work off the rental.

"I see," she says, seeing complications down the road. She is quick enough to understand that their neighbours compete hard for grass. She wonders how things stand with the parsonage pastureland, and the verger replies solemnly that there is always plenty of pasture for the parsonage cows on Church Isle. But the erstwhile crofters have a harder time of it. He shouldn't tell her, but he will anyway, that they have sometimes let their fences get into such a state of disrepair that their cows get through and stuff themselves with the pastor's grass.

"Oh, my," she says. Complications indeed, for she has already made up her mind to secure ample pasturage for Apple and Goody. She pours the milk in the strainer and claps the cows one more time so they'll understand that now she's in charge. In their eyes, the verger's Signe vanishes in the mist. Now other powers rule.

Mona asks Signe about their cows, and yes, they have two. There's Gamlan and Gamlan's heifer that's going to calve for the first time this spring. "The hay harvest will decide if we keep her over the winter or send her to slaughter this autumn," the verger explains, sounding pleased, and she knows that no matter what happens, the heifer and the heifer's calf and the summer's milk will be not insignificant assets.

"I'm glad we've got to know you," Mona says sincerely. "There's so much we need to ask you about. The sheep, for example. What shall we do with them? We can't put them to pasture with the cows, there isn't any fence that will keep them in."

The verger explains that the priest and his wife are very fortunate, because the two large islets beyond Church Isle are sheep islets for the parsonage. If they shift their sheep from one to the other every few weeks, they'll have pasture all summer, so that's no problem at all.

"If you look in the haymow, you'll see we should move them out there tomorrow!" she says. "Maybe we can borrow a boat in the village?"

"Ours, for instance!" the verger suggests, for he's not insensitive to the fact that she's clever and pretty and can put in a good word for him with her husband.

32

"Thanks!" she says. "You can decide the day and time with Petter. I hope you'll come in and have some tea with us now that we're done in the cow barn."

Friends already, they walk back to the parsonage. The verger shows her how the ropes work in the well so that she can lower the pails and cool the milk overnight. Then she'll separate it in the morning and get the cream. Petter's father bought the separator at auction and it now stands in the passage. Mona washes the milk pitchers vigorously, blows life into the fire in the stove, heats water in a saucepan, and sets out some food—rusks and fresh bread with apple sauce!

Nothing comes of Petter's plan to set out nets, because the verger and Signe sit and talk and are in no hurry to leave. But he does raise the subject of fishing, and then the verger slaps his forehead. "Oh good heavens! I brought a mess of perch with me, a meal for tomorrow, and I left it on the steps. Let's hope no animal's got into it!"

"You were reading my thoughts!" Petter says. "Thank you so much! But from tomorrow on, we'll manage on our own. All this friendly help will spoil us completely. What a day we've had!"

He can't help it, he can't suppress a colossal yawn, and then his wife yawns too, like a cat. And then the priest has to yawn again, so hugely that all the movable parts of his cranium creak audibly. The verger and Signe look politely away and chat for a few minutes more, but then they get up and Signe says they have to get home to milk their own cow. It's ten o'clock, and Mona leaps up. "No, you don't mean your cow has gone unmilked because you came to help us! That's terrible!"

"Not at all," Signe reassures her. "She gives so little milk now that it wouldn't matter if I didn't milk her till morning!"

But Mona won't let it go. She thinks it's so dreadful that Signe's cow has had to suffer that Signe's own conscience begins to bother her. And when they're finally gone, the pastor and his wife are so tired they're cross-eyed. They mumble and slur their words and can hardly make their way to the outhouse or find their faces when they try to wash up before finally collapsing into bed.

"I'm so grateful you made the beds," Petter says. "We couldn't have managed it now. I don't think I've ever been so utterly done in. Or so happy."

Like a clubbed burbot — and like a second clubbed burbot — the pastor and his wife spend their first night in the parsonage. The last thing each remembers is that the other has fallen asleep.

Chapter Three

SHE CAME TO FINLAND on foot across the ice, through the forests, tied to the underside of a freight car, in a submarine that surfaced for one short moment by the outermost skerries where a smuggler's speedboat waited. She jumped into the Carelian forests by parachute. She changed clothes with a Finnish military attaché and rode to Finland first class on his diplomatic passport. Once over the border, cars with dimmed headlamps waited on secret forest tracks. Signals were flashed. Finally—Papa! General Gyllen, without whom there would have been no hope.

Well and good. The more versions the better. How it actually happened, no one will ever be told. Except for Papa, the names of the people intentionally or unintentionally involved will never be revealed. The fact itself is momentous enough—in 1939, Irina Gyllen was the only known case of a former Finnish citizen managing to flee to Finland from the Soviet Union.

If any other human being is ever going to do it again, it is of the utmost importance that no one ever finds out how it all took place.

Irina Gyllen sleeps alone. If she has to spend a night among other people on a boat, she doesn't sleep. When she goes to bed, she takes a pill. Which makes her hard to wake up when she has to deliver a baby. The Örlanders know this, it is one of her peculiarities, along with the fact that her medical licence is Russian, so she cannot practise in Finland until she has taken the necessary Finnish examinations. In the Soviet Union, she was a gynaecologist. In Finland, she took a course in midwifery and has now taken this job on the Örland Islands while she studies for her Finnish medical certification.

The Örlands are safe. Mama and Papa have spent their vacations there and know that the locals have boats that can get to Sweden in any weather. They also know that no stranger can slink in unseen. Persons that Irina Gyllen has reason to fear never come ashore without the islanders reporting on their every movement. For much of the year no one comes at all.

It is quiet. You can hear your own heart, your breathing, your digestion. All in good condition though she's already into her second life. She lost a lot on the other side, she hardly looks like a woman any more. Tall and angular without any visible softness. A sharply sculptured face, feet that have walked and walked, hands that have worked and worked.

Her body has smoothed over the fact that she has given birth, but people on the Örlands know that Irina Gyllen has left a child behind. A son.

When she wakes up, she takes a pill. Her hand is then steady, her mind adequately dulled, her memory manageable. It is then she works, writes, and keeps her records. She lives in the Hindrikses' little cottage while the community builds a Health Care Centre with the help of a Swedish donation. The people are good—friendly and considerate—but they make no attempt to treat her as one of them. They call her doctor, although she assures them she is not one, and they do not gossip about her in the village. It is only much later that she realizes the reason they don't is that their silence implies that they know things which can't be told.

The Hindrikses are good people—happy, talkative, lively. Being always greeted with friendly smiles, always getting an analysis of the weather before she goes out, being praised for having the sense to dress warmly, eating her meals with the family and not forgetting to thank them for the food—all of it helps to keep other things at a distance. There is nothing to see on the surface. Or is her closed expression striking evidence of unnatural self-control?

Of what, exactly? Of the terrible desire to live that forces people to sacrifice everything. As a doctor, you have no illusions. Early on, you notice the hope in dying patients, see how they take note of the slightest sign of improvement, refuse to admit that it's only a matter of days. The will to live is stronger than any pain or affliction, even medical students make that sober observation. It adjusts to any reality if it means that life can be augmented by one small measure. Just a few more moments, during which salvation may appear.

In theory, Irina Gyllen had understood the situation precisely. In practice, the feeling ambushed her and knocked her senseless. All she could think about was saving her own life. They took her husband first. For the boy's sake, she did what they had agreed on. Repudiated him, filed for divorce. Continued to work, because the regime always needs doctors, doctors are not something they could afford to discard. Except he was a doctor too. Yes, but surrounded by informers and jealous men. As if she wasn't. Born in Russia, father a Finnish general.

Working isn't enough. Even the best disappear. There is no way out except Finland. Even that exit is closed because she has given up her citizenship. But Papa has connections, contacts, and she can still be in contact with Papa through the Finnish legation. Which in recent years she has not dared to visit. But there are employees whom, with her heart in her throat, she can run into on the street.

Papa Gyllen is also a former officer in the Imperial Russian Army. The reason she will be arrested, that she should already have been taken, even before her husband. Will he be pressed to inform on her? Just a matter of time. No.

You live out your final days, you prolong them, if you can hold out, one more day, a week, then something may save you. You think only about saving yourself, everyone else can be sacrificed. It's why people become informers. The only reason Irina Gyllen doesn't become an informer is that she doesn't want to draw attention to herself.

In order to save yourself, you can also abandon a child. You don't even take him to your husband's parents and entrust him to their care. You just run over to the neighbours, whom you hardly know, and ask if he might stay with them for an hour while you run to the hospital. In his pocket he has a slip of paper, fastened with a safety pin, with the address of his paternal grandparents. It's like pushing him out onto the Nile in a basket of reeds. Maybe he'll be sent to his grandparents, themselves deeply compromised, perhaps about to be arrested. Maybe he'll be put in an orphanage where his identity will be erased. Maybe they can be reunited quite soon. Through the Red Cross, now that the war is over.

He was eight, understood a great deal. Had stopped asking about Papa, knew that was best. Don't think about what he's going through now. Above all, don't think about what he's thinking and feeling. Think instead about how adaptable children are, how they manage to adjust to every new situation. Remember how they're able to find pleasure even in small irrelevant things. Don't forget for a moment that they can so easily grow attached to new people, that they forget. Don't forget that they forget.

Don't think about the fact that seven years have passed, half his life. That he is now a difficult teenager, nearly an adult. All further contact impossible, grandparents unreachable, evacuated during the war, gone. Broken diplomatic relations during the war made all efforts impossible. But now that there's peace, there's hope. The Red Cross, new personnel at the legation, sooner than you might think.

Yes. But Papa Gyllen is old, retired, so too are his contacts. The new people look at them with suspicion. You have to hurry slowly, arm yourself with patience. If the boy made it through the war, he'll make it now, in peacetime. Become an independent person. Do what he likes. May not want to have anything to do with her. Entirely understandable. But there must be some way to find out where he is.

But what if he is not? A helpless child dying alone in an epidemic hospital, frozen, starving, not even thinking "Mama". Then she takes a pill. It's quiet on the island, everyone is friendly, the women giving birth are brave and capable, she likes her work. It was a piece of luck that someone told her about this job. Nice that Mama and Papa, who've grown so old during the war, like it so much out here and rent a place every summer. Everything has worked out much better than she might have feared.

She saved her own skin. An odd expression. It makes her think of skin and bones, which is all she is — tall and gaunt and stiff. Her skin and her bones are the crutches that keep her going, and it's going well, it's all going very well. The main thing is that you have something to keep you busy. Of course she gets called out as a doctor sometimes, though she's always careful to point out that she has no medical licence and no right to treat patients or make decisions that should only be taken by a licensed physician. Yes, yes, they say, we know, but doctor, if you would just please come, it's impossible to get to the hospital in Åbo. Well, all right, she supposes she can come and have a look, maybe give some advice, a bit of help, as long as it's understood that it's unofficial, the way old women through the ages have helped those who sought them out.

That's an argument they understand. Yes! That's the way it's always been. The previous midwife, who'd never been to medical school, was a thousand times better than the nearest doctor! Suddenly she's swamped with effusive stories about the previous midwife's miraculous cures. And she herself? She does indeed answer their calls, and soon the stories about her own deeds begin to make the rounds. They are seldom difficult things — cuts and wounds that need stitches, broken bones that need to be set and splinted, simple remedies for pneumonia and catarrh, medicines for pain. She sends thrombosis to the mainland, and when she finds cancer, she persuades them to take the boat to Åbo. They have an operation, come home and eventually die. Good practical experience for Irina Gyllen, who plans to be a general practitioner. She gets daily practise in diagnostics, and the stories they tell in the villages confirm that she is always right.

She treats a relatively rugged population, sheltered from epidemics by the islands' winter isolation, surprisingly well-nourished during the war years thanks to their healthy diet of Baltic herring, their mental state robust. When she sometimes commends them for eating sensibly and not coddling themselves, they are as pleased as punch.

But they cannot understand why she has such a strong Russian accent and often has trouble finding the right Swedish words, although General Gyllen speaks fluent Finland Swedish and even her Russian-born mother manages well enough. Why does Russian cling to her speech although she wants to forget it? Why can't she find her way back to the language that was her father's native tongue? Why does she have such a frightful accent, even though she spoke Swedish as a child? Why do the Russian words come more quickly than the Swedish ones even though she lives in a completely Swedish environment? As soon as she opens her mouth, Russian jumps to her lips and renders her monosyllabic and abrupt.

Of course people speculate. For example, that maybe she's not Irina Gyllen at all but a completely different Russian, a famous spy smuggled into the country perhaps, or a defector, a female scientist that Russian agents are looking for, a person whose head is full of Russian state secrets! Someone who's taken Irina Gyllen's identity, with General Gyllen and his wife standing surety. Because does she really resemble them? No, not a bit. Papa Gyllen is a head shorter and stout, Mother Gyllen is taller and thinner but not like her in any other way. There is definitely *something* fishy, because "Irina Gyllen" speaks Swedish like a Russian.

Undeniably. But whoever she is, she has a good name on the islands, and whoever she is, the Bolsheviks have been outsmarted and taken it in the chops. Which is excellent and makes people proud and protective. Not that she can't take care of herself, if it comes to that.

Yes, she can and does take care of herself, and she works hard at being normal, although it doesn't come naturally. Out here you're supposed to be full of fun and jokes, and that's the hardest part for her. The loss of her sense of humour is perhaps the most striking evidence of everything she has left behind. Large parts of her are missing as she moves among the people and tries to generate interest in the local chatter, at the moment all about the newly arrived pastor and his wife. Eye-witnesses have seen him at the Co-op and shaken hands, and the Coast Guard has seen her on Church Isle — a woman with get-up-and-go. They also mention that there is a one-year-old among the household goods and give her a meaningful look, warning her in good time that she may have another expectant mother to attend to. Now every last one of them will be going to church on Sunday to hear him and have a look at her. There will be several boats going from the village, and Doctor Gyllen is heartily welcome to ride along!

A difficult point, this. She who's been saved from the God-less Soviet Union is supposed to throw herself into the arms of the church. Of course she's thankful to be in a country with freedom of religion. And if she really was a stranger who'd taken on Irina Gyllen's identity, she would be a devout member of the congregation. But Irina Gyllen doesn't believe in God. On the contrary, she sees what has happened to Russia as proof that a benign Divine power does not exist. Truth to tell, the very young Irina Gyllen was a free-thinker even before the revolution, and what has happened since has not given her any reason to reconsider her views.

Religion is an opium of the people. The Örlanders go to church. Irina Gyllen takes a pill. Opium is what all of us need. So in essence, perhaps, she's a friend of the church. Here, where she lives very visibly among the people, she will stand out less if she occasionally goes to church on the big holidays or, like now, when the new priest is going to be closely examined right down to his buttonholes. She's going to have a lot to do with him, for the pastor is usually the chairman of the Public Health Association. And the priest's little daughter will be coming to have her regular check-ups with her mother. So why not, yes of course, she'll go. There will be a lot of people, and she likes that better than when the pews are nearly empty and everyone looks around at her to see if she sings along and reads the general confession and how she reacts to passages that they imagine will be painful to her.

"Yes, thank you," she says. "I think if you have room in the boat, I'll come."

Her Russian accent thickens whenever she's conflicted. That doesn't escape them, but they look at her sunnily and say there's always room for the doctor, and she's heartily welcome to ride along.

Chapter Four

IF THE PRIEST WERE NOT in such a howling rush, he'd be seriously nervous about his first sermon on the Örlands. He remembers it intermittently and tells himself he must take some time with it. Early in the morning. Late at night. Maybe a little while after lunch. This first time, he needs to be well prepared. Calm. Everything on paper in case he loses his way.

But how can a person get up early when he's gone to bed so awfully late? And how can he retreat to his study after lunch when he is responsible for so many things that have to be mended and assembled and put away, and then when an unexpected visitor comes wandering up from the church dock? That means talk, and it's nice to have such a talkative congregation. He wouldn't dream of sending away anyone who needed to speak to him.

Two more days, then one. Then he begins, in a state of desperation, early in the morning. Slumps in his armchair like a dead fish and tells himself that if he digests the material thoroughly now, then his brain will work on it during the day and he'll be able to shape it into a passable text in a few hours this evening. All day he leaps anxiously from one task to another so he will also have time to go through the procedures in church. The verger and the organist describe the traditions of the congregation and the signals to be used when necessary between the organist in the loft and the priest before the altar. The verger explains the ins and outs of bell ringing in great detail and when he mentions the priest bell, the pastor pricks up his ears.

"The priest bell?" he asks. "What's that?"

The verger tells him that they observe the ancient custom of ringing the small bell when the priest arrives at the church. "Not before a quarter to and not later than ten to. I stand in the belfry and keep watch, and when I see you leave the parsonage, I start to ring the bell, and I keep ringing it until you're through the church door. Then I climb down and come to help you get robed."

Both the verger and the organist look at him uneasily and the organist adds, "It's the way we've always done it."

He sees that they're afraid that because he's young, he'll think this custom is old-fashioned and set himself against it, but he smiles and says, "Of course. If that's the way you do it, then that's what we'll do."

They look relieved, and when they rehearse the key points in the Mass with the organist at the organ, the pumper working invisibly at the bellows, the verger in his pew, and the priest at the altar, a kind of exhilaration and good fellowship spreads through the building. For when the organist gives him his note and the pastor frees his voice and sings, "In the name of the Father and of the Son and of the Holy Ghost, Amen," the organist and the verger can hear that this priest can truly sing the Mass. The organist's playing acquires life and reverence, and the Mass goes brilliantly while the verger does his work smartly, turning the hymn numbers for the congregation, opening the altar rail for the priest, and following him to the sacristy when he will change from his robes into his cassock during the pre-sermon hymn.

Petter recalls that this congregation is often described as a singing congregation, and the thought makes him happy. He has already heard that the last priest's greatest failing was that he couldn't sing the Mass. There will be no problem in that area for Pastor Petter Kummel, who sings more readily than he preaches. The final liturgy goes swimmingly, and he feels a little chill when he remembers that when he does all this for real, tomorrow, he will already have delivered his sermon. He can only hope that he won't be dying of shame.

"The old priest couldn't sing, the new priest can't preach," is what they'll say. And what with one thing and another, even though Mona makes an early supper and gets Sanna to bed and tries to steer him to his study, it is dreadfully late when he sits down to work.

And sits and sits, deep in self-contempt, thinking how much he needs someone to guide him through the key points here too, the verger and the organist, so that there will be a sermon. What is the matter with him? Why is he pleasant, collected, and wise when he has other people around him, and why does he feel only emptiness and panic when he sits down by himself to concentrate on writing a sermon?

And sits, in a kind of panic-stricken hubris, his need to be dazzling, brilliant, unforgettable an impediment to his preaching. As if the purpose was to show off Petter Kummel rather than the Word. Which it is his duty to administer and expound.

The Word, the Word, Pastor Kummel reminds himself over and over as the minutes pass. He looks at the texts yet again but has so little time that he can't manage to read them carefully. There's nothing wrong with the lessons. It's the lead-in that's lacking. And the payoff, the elegant conclusion. And the brilliant discourse in the middle.

Would he have become a priest had he known how nerve-racking it was to preach? Not a chance. When he wrote his practise sermons at the university, he thought they would flow automatically once he was free from all the supervisory eyes and acrid comments. Once he could "speak with his own voice". So he'd believed. Word for word.

So now here's your chance, Pastor Kummel. Your own voice. But there is silence. He can picture himself climbing up into the pulpit, praying a little prayer and looking out over the congregation, people who are five times as critical as the theology faculty, people who have spent so much time in church that they know at once that he's on thin ice. He opens his mouth and hopes that something will come out, but nothing does. Then he reads the day's lesson, and when he's done he closes his mouth. He opens it again, but nothing comes out. Then he reads the notices and gives a signal to the organist for the collection hymn. It starts up a little sloppily. There is a great agitation in the church. His first sermon — silence.

Mona looks in. "How's it going?"

"It's not."

"You're too tired. We have to start going to bed in the evenings. We're running ourselves ragged."

"It's not just that I'm tired. I can't do it. I've got no talent for it. I'll have to resign the post."

"When we just got here? Don't talk nonsense! Use your sermon from last autumn. Nobody here has heard it."

"That's real bankruptcy, a priest recycling his sermons."

"It will give you an idea. It's here in this box somewhere. Read through it calmly. Then go to bed, and during the night it will all come together. Tomorrow morning you'll know what you're going to say."

"What would I do without you?"

"Don't be silly. Thank heaven you keep your papers in order. Here it is."

"Thanks, I'll look at it. Go to bed now. I'll be in soon."

He hopes she'll fall asleep quickly, tired as she is. She's been cleaning furiously, and baking. The whole house smells good. They're going to have the parish council and the vestry for coffee after High Mass. How is he going to be able to look these intelligent people in the eye after his fiasco? His fiasco — there he goes again, thinking only of himself and the impression he'll make. Instead of what he was put here to proclaim: the Word of God.

It's not about his own brilliance. It's about conveying the Word, which is without blemish, the support and bulwark of every second-rate preacher. But the introduction, the personal touch that puts the text in a new light? Something to make them listen? Something from their own world, which they understand and take an interest in?

In this specific instance, it's the new pastor they're interested in, however much he tries to convince himself that his own person is of no importance. Is it then wrong, is it simply ingratiating to say things they want to hear, to talk about his first impressions of the parish?

This thought fills him with strong, clear pictures and he knows what he will say. And he is calm, not deceptively calm, but calm enough to sleep. He looks at last year's sermon with new eyes, sees that he can use bits of it after his new introduction. It's going to work.

Almost unconscious, he staggers into bed. Mona is already asleep, clearly not as nervous as he. It is soothing that she seems to think he'll manage. It's far too late for him to get up early, but he'll still have time to think through the text and get it under control.

Or so he thinks, the simpleton. Because in the morning, Papa has to mind Sanna while Mama does the milking, and Sanna is not the kind of person you can just dump in a crib and close the door. On top of which, Sanna is irresistible when she has Papa to herself. She smiles and chirps and puts her cheek against his, and he thinks that he must be allowed to spend a few minutes every day with his daughter. What does it say about his Christianity if he won't let his own child come to him?

Then Mona comes back in a rush, changes clothes and bangs about setting the table. No miracle occurs in his study. He gathers up his prayer book, the parish announcements, his old sermon, his new ideas jotted down as notes. He'll have time to glance through them before it's time to go, he thinks, but then there's a commotion in the passage where someone has wrenched open the swollen door. Because the church handles all vital statistics and the parish record-keeping, people bring their administrative business to him right before the Sunday service, since Church Isle is a bit out of the way and now here they are anyway.

Perfectly understandable, and once you're aware of it, you can make allowances, but this first time it's unexpected. He hurries to his study door and meets the man with a smile, because he can hear that Mona is not very welcoming. "Come right in!" he says warmly, although she's in the act of saying this isn't a good time. And when the matter has been dealt with—and the good cheer and the high hopes—it appears that the clock has taken a jump and it's time to put on his cassock and collar. Mona helps him, proudly. The cassock was tailored at considerable cost and fits him very well! He's told her about the priest bell, and she keeps a close eye on the clock so she can send him off at a quarter to. She'll follow along with Sanna a bit later. Of course she wants to be there for his first High Mass and to see the congregation. She's more nervous than he knows. It's important that he should see her calm and without misgivings. If only he could organize his time so he was better prepared!

The church bells have already rung at ten-thirty, a lovely racket in the clear air. At a quarter to eleven, they see the verger climb into the bell tower again, and so he takes his Bible, his prayer book, papers, and notes and gets ready to go. Faint-heartedly, he prays a silent prayer that all will go well, a schoolboy's timorous prayer for help in a fix for which he can blame no one but himself. Sanna whines and wants to go with him, and Mama is angry. "Hush, Sanna! You can't come to church at all if you can't be quiet!"

It feels like when the first Christians were driven out into the arena, except they were heartened by confidence and faith. He is fearful and timid, a poor servant of Our Lord. Unworthy of his calling, he opens the door and walks out onto the steps.

Such a lot of people already gathered in the churchyard! He stands for a moment on the steps and sees a steady stream of people walking up from the boats past the parsonage. When they see him on the steps, they leave a space for him, and he moves out into it. The priest bell starts to ring.

Only the small bell, as the verger said, and it tolls more sparely than the rich sound of the two bells swinging together. As the pastor walks and the bell rings, he becomes another person. He lays aside Sanna's screaming and Mona's scolding. Mona's nervous silence, her hopes that it will all go well. He sets aside his ego, his fear of inadequacy, of making a fool of himself, of being criticized and mocked. He is no longer his own imperfect self, he is the congregation's shepherd, who unravels mysteries for them and provides them with the means of grace. He walks towards the church the way priests on this island have been doing since the Reformation, maybe even in the days of the cloister.

He reaches the gate and walks up the gravel path, and although there is a great crowd of people, he is always surrounded by open space. As long as the bell rings, no one speaks to him, and he stops to speak to no one, smiles just slightly, and bows his head. The church door is open, and as he steps across the threshold, the bell tolls for the last time.

The church seems larger now that it begins to fill with people, the ceiling higher, the choir loft farther away. The air inside is so thick that he feels he must push his way through. The verger has left the door to the sacristy ajar. The priest puts his books down on the table and sees that his robes are ready — a white alb, a purple chasuble with a cross embroidered in gold. The verger hurries in followed by the organist with fresh sea air in his clothes. They greet him and speak to him differently than on Saturday. They look at his collar rather than make eye contact. Today they treat him like a priest.

"It's going to be full today," the organist says and rubs his hands, perhaps with delight, but maybe just because they're cold and he has to play the organ. In low voices, they exchange words about the different parts of the service — that they'll have to start the collection hymn over from the beginning if the verger can't finish in time, and that they'll have to be prepared for at least two settings of the Communion table. The priest asks the Lord to bless their devotions, and the organist goes to his loft, very nervous, as the priest notes to his surprise. He is so young that he thinks that he alone is tormented and uncertain, whereas all the others must surely be calm, confident in themselves and in their duties.

The verger really is calm, always ready to offer support and to explain how things are done in this parish. The priest puts the wide alb on over his head and the chasuble on top. Silently, the verger hands him a comb so he can smooth his hair. They look at the clock and the verger peeks out — full. And more coming up the hill. He notes that the ones who live closest to the church have the most trouble arriving on time.

It's almost time, and the verger goes off to ring the congregation to the service. Now both bells are working together beautifully, and the sound is powerful and seductively bright. He must remember to tell the verger he rings the bells well. And when the bells have been tolling for several minutes, the organ starts to play. He can hear the bellows pumping all the way into the sacristy, the hissing and wheezing before the machinery has warmed up and the organist has laid his hands on the keyboard. He begins with arabesques on the processional theme, variations from the hymnal, soothing, enveloping, while the coughing and rustling continue down in the church. But when the verger starts to sing "Praise, My Soul, the King of Heaven", everyone joins in.

Never has the priest heard such song. Suddenly he understands why churches have vaulted ceilings — to make room for the singing that lives in a congregation's breast. They sing in full voice, with good support from well-trained diaphragms, they sing from expanded chests and open windpipes. They sing powerfully, and they sing slowly, and there is a wonderful tension between the men's sonorous rumble and the women's voices, so dangerously high they fling defiance in the face of death.

The priest can hardly stand still, but the hymn has only three verses so he can go in at once. He tries not to bounce but to walk with dignity, in through the altar rail, catching sight of Mona and Sanna in the first row — Sanna's face lighting up, both arms in the air, her mouth forming the word Papa! — but he can't hear a thing for the singing. He places the chalice on the altar and genuflects. Tries to pray, but the singing fills his world. And when you sing, you become a different person, more certain, happier. They finish reluctantly, as if they wanted a fourth and a fifth and a sixth verse, and he turns around. Prayer book in hand, he sees the organist's attentive back, hears the note the organ gives him. Responds, a resonant trombone, "In the name of the Father, and of the Son, and of the Holy Ghost."

It's clear that the congregation likes his voice. They respond with a lingering and wholehearted "Amen".

The liturgy is the product of difficult schisms and agonizing committee meetings, but now it lies there polished and shiny like a gift from God. It has been formulated for him so that a priest need never fall short and be faced with his own imperfections as he works to establish a direct relationship between the parishioners and the Divine. He leads them through the service, singing, reading, and they answer him with song. He is not vain, merely relieved to see that he has won their affection because he can sing. Thank you, God! He sounds happy, certain that he's made contact when he reads the General Confession with its "I call unto Thee from the depths, O Lord" and then the Absolution, from his heart. He sings "Lord have mercy upon us" with the congregation, which roars and drags and forces him to take it slower despite the organist's attempt at compromise up in the loft. And then pure joy when they stand and sing Laudamus: "We praise Thee, we beseech Thee, we laud and honour Thee", a difficult medieval melody that they sing with the utmost confidence. Their voices carry through even the extreme registers, so grandly that he, singing along at the altar, feels chills run down his spine. He adapts to their singing and drags out the ornamentations the way he realizes they've been dragged out since the days of the early church.

He no longer holds the service in his hand, the service has instead gripped him and has him firmly in its grasp. The congregation creates the service, and he feels himself in its keeping, without responsibility, like a child, and then in a flash he remembers his sermon. It will simply have to do, because now he is reading the Epistle, and, after the next hymn comes the Creed. Hardly a murmur is heard from the congregation, and he realizes that when they sing they are completely involved, but that when they speak they hold something back. Like their shepherd, alas. He turns towards the altar and the organist begins the sermon hymn. It's long — "O that I Had a Thousand Voices" — and he is glad for the respite as he walks to the sacristy, followed by the verger, who will help him remove his chasuble and surplice and put on his cassock. Arms into the sleeves and buttons buttoned while they sing inside. The Bible open to the text, sermon underneath, announcements at the bottom. All set, and he's ready to go, but the verger shakes his head. One more verse, and only then does he send him out.

A straight line from the sacristy to the pulpit. No sidelong glance at Mona's anxious, encouraging face, straight up the little staircase. Bows his head in prayer, which is nothing but black terror. Help me! While the congregation sings a convincing "Should earth and heaven cease to be, Yet shall I find my joy in Thee." Simultaneously a creaking from the number board, which the verger sets swinging to signal them to stop.

The church grows quiet, and the priest stands alone in the pulpit, no longer protected by his prayer book. He raises his head from his simulated prayer and looks out over the congregation. Nothing but friendly, solemn, interested faces. Now he knows what to say.

"Dear friends, brothers and sisters in Jesus Christ. We are gathered for worship in our own church. For me, it is the first time, and I will never forget my first meeting with this church on the bay. As you know, the journey out here is a long one, and during the night a person can almost lose his courage and regret coming. But the journey's end comes into view with the morning light. All of you know the joy you feel when you see the church and the bell tower begin to take shape in the distance, and you know you are almost here. It was so beautiful, I was so delighted, and so happy. And I thought, in the words of the Bible, This is none other but the house of God, and this is the gate of heaven."

The church is silent, but he hears a slight, friendly murmur, as if his words were being well received. He goes on, as if speaking in confidence to good friends. "Let us pray. Dear Lord. You look deep into our hearts and see us as we are, imperfect and inconstant. But you also see our hope and our toil. Thank you for your mercy towards us, your compassion and your forgiveness. Thank you for allowing us to turn to you today and all other days. Amen." And then he reads the text from the Gospel of John, "ask, and ye shall receive, that your joy may be full." And the wonderful final verse, "In the world ye shall have tribulation: but be of good cheer; I have overcome the world."

The priest is moved and inspired and he thinks that last year's sermon on this theme is not so terribly dreadful after all. With certain embellishments and additions it will be like new, which in truth it is for this audience, and, carefully, he moves into his text, which does have its moments. His voice is cheerful, and he allows himself to look out over the congregation and feels he has made contact. They are with him, even the ones who are asleep, old people who have heard all the sermons they need to hear and now take a blessed pause in the heavy air of a full church.

Yes, they're going to say that he sings better than he speaks, but on the other hand, he sings better than many others! As the sermon of a young priest at the beginning of his career, it isn't half bad, and, exhilarated, he rounds it off and turns to the announcements: a thanksgiving for the life of an old man who has died and a reminder of next week's service.

Finally the collection, which this day will go to the Evangelical Society. Lord bless our offering. The organist's baritone takes up "Jesus, lead my steps, I pray" and the parishioners shift in their pews, dig into pockets and purses, snap open or shut their pocketbooks, and begin to sing "To follow in Thy blessed way". The verger emerges from the sacristy and begins making his rounds with his collection bag. The priest comes down from the pulpit and pulls off his own cassock and puts on his robes and surplice for Communion and the closing liturgy.

They sing and sing, and the verger moves solemnly from pew to pew. The collection bag is passed along to those sitting closer to the wall, and it all takes time. They sing slowly, and the hymn is long enough. During the eighth verse, the verger comes in and checks to see that the priest is presentable. Prayer book and Bible in hand, he goes out into the church, which has gone so quiet that he can hear Sanna whining and whimpering. He knows Mona is holding her arm hard and hissing at her to be quiet. It's been a long service for such a small person, and there's a lot more to come — some lovely antiphonal song, the Invocation to Holy Communion, the Our Father, a trembling "O Lamb of God". The invitation, "Draw near with faith."

But no one comes. They look sullen, stare at the floor or glance at one another, need to be urged as if they were at a party. Wasn't it the organist who tried to hint that they didn't like Communion? If only the Sunday service could consist entirely of singing! Then they'd be the most Christian people in the world, but now it's apparent that they shrink from an individual commitment, from surrender, from the requirement to seem pious.

What if no one comes? The organist has to play, and the verger has his duties. Mona is sitting with Sanna, they agreed on that. It's unpleasantly quiet. No one looks up, but then he hears someone stand up in the middle of a row. It's Adele Bergman. She looks negative and distant, but someone has to. She crowds her way past those sitting closer to the aisle, who shift out of her way reluctantly, certainly not about to follow her example. Adele's gentle husband follows her, and then things start to loosen up in the rest of the church, the vestry and the parish council perhaps. But all of them hesitant and shame-faced, unwilling to meet anyone's gaze.

They curtsey and bow before the altar, and genuflect. So few come, and there is no second setting of the table. The priest himself is trying to get used to Communion, which he would like to see as a symbolic act. The problem is that wherever he goes there is someone who will argue with him and insist that he, as a priest of the church, must believe that the wine is actually transformed into the blood of Christ. When he explains that we drink from the chalice in memory of the blood shed for us, the person in question grows indignant and accuses the priest of lack of faith and heresy. He still likes best the Sundays that have a service without Communion. Here on the Örlands, that means three Sundays of four, and that suits him fine.

The organist plays beautifully and the priest passes out Communion wafers and follows up with the chalice, drying the cup with a linen cloth after every sip. "Shed for thee." And then, bowing and curtseying, relieved, a little happier because it's over, they walk back to their pews. The priest takes Communion himself, and when he drinks he notes how thirsty he is, and he still has the closing liturgy ahead of him.

The organist plays, and the priest sings the Anthem of Praise with the congregation and reads the blessing. And now the congregation kicks into life, forgets its ill humour and sings the closing hymn, " Like Shining Sunrise in the Spring", with such a will that he realizes that in future he needs to pick longer hymns. When the three verses have been sung, they would like to go on, but the verger has scurried away on tiptoe to ring the bells, and the organist sets to work on his postlude, which the priest recognizes as Cappelen's "Prayer" (adagio). The organ has a lovely, bright sound, which breaks down once or twice when the pumper pauses at his work.

It is over, and he is back in the sacristy. Off with his gown, the alb over his head, and back into his cassock. People are on their way out of the church, coughing and talking quietly as their feet move towards the door, leaving behind them a cloud of cough drops and naphthalene. The bells are still ringing, but soon they stop and the verger returns, along with the organist, who comes nimbly down the steps from the organ loft, warding off with his hand a corner of the upper floor that seems designed to knock an intruder senseless. They all look pleased, and the priest thanks them warmly. "And how they sing!" he adds. "I'm going to be really happy here."

He can hardly wait to go out and speak to those who are still in the churchyard, but the verger reminds him that the collection must be counted in the presence of witnesses and entered in the account book. There are a great many small coins, and it takes time, but finally it's all locked in the chest and at last they can go outside. The sun is shining the way it can in May. Many are on their way to the church dock, but many remain, in contrast with other parishes where people hurry away when the pastor appears. These people stand still and smile warmly, and when he greets them and shakes their hands, they wish him welcome. None of them give their names, and in the end he starts to ask, for he wants so very much to get to know them by name as well as by face. A little group gathers around him, people who want to say hello, and they're all in such a good mood after all their singing that it's a joy to be with them.

He almost forgets to look for Mona and Sanna, but then he catches sight of them at one side of the churchyard, isolated in a struggle, with Sanna twisting and screaming and Mona holding her tight and looking angry. They're fighting bitterly, and big tears are rolling down Sanna's cheeks. The pastor is still standing there talking and smiling but he feels a pang of depression. Must she always? Sanna has been angelically quiet and good during the service and slept a little during the sermon. It's only natural that someone so little is now worn out and cries and squirms. But he and his wife have sworn each other a solemn oath that they will be consistent in raising their children. Whatever one of them says will be supported by the other, and no child will get a no from one parent and a yes from the other. Because where would that lead? To a tyranny of the children, Mona has declared, and he has wholeheartedly agreed — they will show firmness, unity, and cooperation.

But he feels sorry for Sanna, who ought to be getting praise, not reproach. "Excuse me a moment," he says. "I see Mona, who would also like to say hello." He rushes off. "Now, now, Sanna! You've been such a good girl. Come to Papa!"

Sanna raises her arms to him pathetically, her face streaked with tears, her mouth contorted, but Mona pulls her back. "Careful of the cassock," she hisses. "She's wet!" As if that were a terrible disgrace in a fourteen-month-old child. Mona is very proud of the fact that Sanna is already almost completely potty trained at home and can be plunked down as soon as she wakes up and after every meal. Now it's been too long, and after her nap in church it happened. So Mona is angry and scandalized and Sanna is inconsolable. Petter is on edge, but he has no choice.

"I realize you want to go home, but come over anyway and say hello. I promised to come and fetch you."

Mona bristles. "Did you have to drag me into it? Couldn't you see what was going on?" But she follows him as she promised, for better or for worse, and manages a smile when she arrives with the wet, whimpering Sanna on her arm.

"And this is my family," he introduces them. "Mona and Alexandra, but we call her Sanna." The little group greet them warmly and bid Mona welcome, and they all remark on how incredibly quiet and well-behaved their little girl was in church. They all pretend not to notice that she's wet, but Mona mentions the chilly breeze and says she needs to get home and change her before she catches cold. "And then too, we're having the vestry and the parish council for coffee."

She's just leaving when a tall, angular person steps forward from the group. She doesn't smile but stretches out her hand towards Mona and says, with an odd accent, that she would like to introduce herself. Her name is Irina Gyllen, and she is the midwife on the Örlands.

Mona almost curtseys, and Sanna is quiet. The priest collects himself and presses her hand warmly. "So nice to meet you! Thank you for coming! I've heard so many good things about you from my predecessor, and I'm looking forward to working with you on health care."

"Thank you," says this brown person. "I wish you good comfort on the island. Now I should go, there are so many who want to speak to you." As she turns away, she glances at Sanna and Mona, who is ill at ease. "Sweet little girl," she says. "Maybe we will see you at the surgery? Goodbye."

She heads off for the gate and the Hindriks family follows. They very pleasantly fall in with Mona as they walk and chat, and when they reach the parsonage, Mona says goodbye and the rest of them stroll on towards the dock. Doctor Gyllen lives with the Hindrikses, they have explained to Mona, and she's an excellent woman in every way.

The only people left in the churchyard are now the members of the vestry and the parish council. The priest shakes all their hands and learns their names and which villages they come from. Fortunately, the organist and Adele Bergman are among them, for he already views them as old friends. He looks with interest at a tall, slender woman wearing a long black velvet skirt, a tailored jacket and a hair net — Lydia Manström, teacher, married to a farmer fisherman in one of the eastern villages. She radiates . . . well, what is it she radiates? Great self-control and originality, perhaps? Not easy to say what she'll be like. She has a teacher's authority, of course, and he hopes that Mona will get along well with her and make a friend.

They begin to drift towards the parsonage, and he notices that Adele Bergman and Lydia Manström hang back. They're trying to give Mona as much time as possible, whereas the men are thinking of coffee and sandwiches and push ahead. When they come into the passage, Mona, warm and red, meets them and welcomes them and asks them to come in. She ground the coffee, buttered the bread, and set the table before they went to church, and when she came back she quickly lit the fire in the stove before changing Sanna and putting her in her crib. Now she has also brought out her freshly baked rolls, and the coffee water is simmering on the stove. The pastor needn't have worried. She may have a hasty temper, but she also has an admirable haste when it comes to practical activities.

Adele Bergman looks around appreciatively. "If I didn't know better, I'd think you had a maid, Mrs Kummel, who prepared all this while we were in church," she says, warmly, and Mona is happy to get praise from such a capable woman. "Please do sit down," she repeats. "The coffee will be ready in a minute."

She goes into the kitchen, but the vestry and the council are still on their feet and need more encouragement before they'll sit down at the table. They inspect the furnishings, which they've already heard described by the people who were on the boat, and the priest looks embarrassed and says that Mona received a small inheritance from an aunt, without which they would have nothing but a kitchen table and some spindle chairs. He nods towards the table and says, "We got our china the same way. And now we're going to use it. Please do sit down!"

But they are still standing, shifting their weight from one foot to the other when the pastor's wife comes in with the coffeepot, and they let her fill their cups before they'll approach the table. They only sit when she commands, "Please! If you don't sit down your coffee will get cold!" Then at last they take their places and begin to relax and grow cheerful, pass around the sugar bowl and carefully pour big dollops of thick, yellow cream from the pitcher. The sandwiches look delicious. The pastor's wife has baked bread like they have on the mainland, churned butter from cream she's saved up all week, sliced cheese from the Co-op on half the sandwiches and put sausage on the rest and garnished all of them with parsley from the kitchen garden that has survived the winter. The food is good and plentiful, and the rolls she serves with the third cup of coffee do her credit. They are all appreciative, and the conversation runs freely and smoothly. The pastor has many questions to ask and they are happy to answer them. It will be some time before he realizes that there are two factions, equal in strength, and that they have seated themselves by village groups. The two blocks communicate only amongst themselves, but he doesn't know this yet. He sees them only as incomparably friendly, easy to talk to, altogether excellent people.

"I'm absolutely overwhelmed by such a warm reception," he says yet again. "To think that so many wanted to come to church today. And such singing!"

"Well of course everyone wanted to come and see the new priest," Lydia Manström points out. "And they were pleased with what they saw. We can hope it will mean an upswing in church attendance."

It's almost like a little meeting of the vestry as they go through items that the next real meeting should take up. They also enlighten him about the customs of the parish. It's good that he doesn't want to change everything, the way certain previous priests have done. They do not raise any immediate problems. That will wait until they all know each other better.

This is only a first courtesy visit, but they take so much time that the pastor's wife begins to wonder if they're expecting further refreshments. They must realize that almost all food is still rationed, and that the two of them have already used way too much of their allowance. If they're to go on at this rate, they won't make it. Adele Bergman at least must understand, she thinks, and looks at her in desperation. Adele Bergman gets the message and understands, has already calculated the approximate expenditure of coupons and wonders how they're going to manage. Although they've got cows in the pasture and fish in the sea. She gives the pastor's wife a friendly look and hears the little girl complaining in the bedroom.

"May I come say hello to the pastor's daughter?" she asks, following Mona into the bedroom. Mona lifts Sanna from her baby bed, feels her backside and determines that she's dry. "But now I'm going to the kitchen to put her on the potty before she has another accident."

Exactly as Mona had thought, Adele Bergman has used Sanna as an excuse to get a look at the bedroom. But be my guest. It too is very proper. Two beds with light brown bed-spreads, each with a chair as a nightstand, and a bureau. Still a bit bare, but they'll have time to acquire a variety of things. A little crucifix hangs above the bureau, and that pleases Adele Bergman. This young priest seems thoroughly Christian every day of the week, and God knows that such a priest is what this parish needs.

She helps to get the vestry and the council up and out, and just as she'd calculated, the organist offers her a ride in his boat and promises to put her ashore at the Co-op dock, since of course Elis took their boat home much earlier. "It's been a good day," she says confidentially, both to the organist as they sit talking pleasantly above the clatter of the engine, and to Elis when she gets home.

Chapter Five

IT FALLS TO THE ORGANIST to carefully instruct the priest about the divisions within the parish. He treats the subject lightly, as if it were only a question of a little good-natured rivalry between the two equal halves of the community, and as if he himself stood above the whole struggle and looked down on it with amused condescension. But he grows more serious as he speaks, the furrow between his eyebrows deepens, and his face darkens.

"There are people in the east villages who wouldn't pull a west villager from a hole in the ice if they were drowning," he says.

"It can't be as bad as all that!" says the pastor, trying to laugh it all off. "And if it's an east villager who's fallen through the ice? What would the west villagers do?"

But the organist, who had stood above the fray, now says "we". "We'd probably pull him out, most of us. But you never know. There's so much personal rancour in a place like this. Real hatred, to tell you the truth. Only a few. But it can poison a whole community."

"How does it express itself?" the priest asks, hesitantly.

"Indirectly. So the divisions are passed down from one generation to the next. The local council consists of two equal blocks, which makes it almost impossible to get anything important done. The chairman has the deciding vote, and pity the poor devil who gets elected chairman. There's always pressure, not so much from the other side as from his own side. Same thing in the vestry. I'm the chairman there," he adds, and now he smiles as if he couldn't stand to look serious. Here on these islands, everyone wears a happy face. That much the priest has already learned.

The priest smiles too. "I'm sincerely happy to hear it," he says from the heart. "I'm glad you told me all this. What do you think it will mean for me as pastor?"

The organist considers. "You're different from the man we had before. He was older and more cunning, if I may use that word. Over the years, he grew very adept at playing off one side against the other. He knew what to say to get the outcomes he wanted. Don't forget that in the parish council, you're the chairman, and you need to chair those meetings forcefully. As for the vestry, it would be a good idea for us to talk things over in advance so I know where you stand."

The priest is not as dumb as he may look. He takes the hint, amused and interested. "So you can explain the hidden tensions and intrigues to me and help me figure out what I think. Thank you. Yes. You're a great help, and I hope we can work together in future, too, and talk to each other frankly."

The organist is pleased by the priest's appreciation and confidence. "I'm telling you this also because you need to know that there's always a terrible tug of war for the pastor. Of course the church is supposed to be neutral, but this isn't about politics. It's personal. If you can make friends with the pastor, you can draw him to your side and get his ear."

"Oh, my," the pastor says. "I can see that I've already been drawn towards the west villages. You and your family and the estimable Adele Bergman and Doctor Gyllen and the Hindrikses. And the verger and Signe, although they live so close to the church that we can almost count them as neutral. But it can't be helped. I don't intend to sit here like a hermit and treat both sides with suspicion. I mean to go out and meet people in all the villages! You know, I didn't pick up any of this when the council and the vestry were here for coffee. Everyone was so nice, and I liked every one of you."

"Of course you did," the organist says. "There's nothing wrong with us one at a time, we're all very 'nice', as you say. That's why this division is so deplorable. Because it divides people who could be best friends. Instead we have to be cautious and on guard. It's a shame."

This has been a lot for him to swallow, the organist can see that, but the priest is looking ahead. "It's good you've told me all this," he says. "But now in the beginning I think I'll act as if I didn't know a thing. Even though you've told me, I'm sure I don't yet understand all of it in depth. First I need to get a bit closer to people."

"You're off to a good start," says the organist warmly, which gives the priest time to formulate what he's feeling.

"You'll probably think I'm childish, but I already like it here so much that I don't ever want to leave. Do you think you could stand me for the next forty years?"

The organist laughs, as if the divisions had never been raised. "Sounds wonderful. That will be the news item of the year—a priest who isn't on the lookout for a richer parish."

As friends, they set to work on what looks to be a long collaboration. Even in a small parish—or especially in a small parish—there are a host of questions to be aired at every meeting of the vestry. There is already quite a pile of official post. They read it together and the organist sifts through it with an experienced hand and decides what needs to be given to the vestry and what the priest can deal with himself. This one sits with pen in hand and looks capable of sending off letters in a steady stream. He seems almost eager, as if his fingers were itching to get started, and the organist is happy at the thought of working with a priest who respects the way things have always been done and doesn't immediately want to make changes.

The priest himself looks on the organist the way a young man looks on an experienced older man, with almost childish confidence. As they sit there in his study, working, glancing at one another appreciatively, the pastor feels an uninhibited pleasure in having an older man as support, guide, and friend. Almost a father figure, if the organist had been a little older. He is in fact only fifteen years older, but he has life experience and practical skills, which the priest well knows do not necessarily come with increasing age.

He thinks of his own father, and how different his life could have been if he'd had a father like the organist, who could have given him guidance in difficult matters and taught him useful lessons. Instead, he's had to figure everything out on his own, by trial and — especially in his youth — by painful error. He has had to learn carpentry, construction, and repair, for Leonard, his father, is unable to do any of these things. He has suffered shame and fled from this same father's high-blown declarations, such as "I know what people are like!", although anyone following his advice would have met with misfortune. All his life, he's had to rely on learning from experience, and now he sits here opposite the organist and thinks what it might have been like to have had a father who was sensible and just.

Petter is the oldest of three brothers and it happens that the organist too has three boys and, even more remarkably, a beloved and spoiled daughter, exactly like the Kummel family's adored Charlotte. The youngest of the sons is the family's sunshine child, just like the Kummels' Jösse, forever twenty years old in his hero's grave, whom Petter still thinks of with a curious distaste and . . . shame?

The similarities are striking, and it is with great interest that he makes his first visit to the organist's home. Where he is amazed to see that this incomparable father figure doesn't seem to have a very good relationship with his sons. On the contrary, they avoid him, always seem to have important things to do that drive them away from the table and out the door as quickly as they can manage. To have such a father and to shun him, that surely indicates that no son can have had a good relationship with his father, at least not once he's entered puberty.

It sometimes seems to Petter that biology has an answer for almost everything that happens in a human life, but there is no explanation for puberty. He can understand the importance of liberation and the development of an independent personality, but why must this period last so long and the alienation be so profound? Why must people reject the value of learning and actively oppose the acquisition of knowledge during the very years when their capacity to internalize instruction is at its height? And why do human beings see themselves as hopeless, ugly, and miserable when in fact they are at their most attractive age? What is nature's purpose with puberty, which is as cruel as death?

Although when you look at the three adolescent organist sons, you have to admit that if they're feeling ugly and miserable, they hide it well. They're just a bit reserved because they're sharing a dinner table with the pastor. In their different ways, they're as shamelessly attractive as their parents, well built, with a startling loose-limbed elegance. But no camaraderie between them and their father, no visible trust, no understanding, only a barely discernible smile of ridicule whenever the organist tells a story. To his horror, Petter recognizes certain glances he himself exchanged with his brothers when father Leonard got going. Otherwise there are few similarities between the wise and capable organist and the sadly foolish Leonard Kummel, who is such an embarrassment to his sons. All they have in common is fatherhood, which a son must turn away from if he's to become his own man. This is what the organist's sons dream of, just as the teacher's sons once did. But still, these boys' highest aspiration — to become unlike their father — is much harder to understand than that of the Kummel brothers!

For his part, Petter would be happy to adopt the organist as his father, if such a thing were possible. He feels a warmth of spirit, as if for the first time in his life he stood under someone's protection and was not required to be the oldest and wisest, a model for his siblings, a support for his mother, and an ideal schoolboy. A beast of burden collapsing under the weight of hopes and demands. A dried herb in a plant press of expectations.

Now, at last, he sits side by side with a man in whom he has absolute confidence, a man who says, "This is the way we do things here." A man who expects nothing more than that he be young and ignorant and in need of help. A man he has already impressed with his pragmatism and common sense. A man who is easy to talk to and whose replies show that has listened and understood.

Giddy as he is from all the friendship he feels, it will take a while for him to realize that the organist is not universally loved here on the islands. Many bear him a grudge. His payment in kind is a thorn in their flesh, especially during the hay harvest when he drives home the yield from the splendid hayfield that belongs to the church and is reserved for the benefit of the parish organist. Later, he learns that the organist was a hated customs officer during Prohibition. There are those who consider him self-righteous — in his own eyes a head higher than everyone else — and who therefore think he needs to be cut down to his ankles. They bide their time.

This is a side of island life that lies in the shadows when people show their smiling faces, but the priest is young and learns quickly. He does not regret the respite he enjoyed when he first arrived, believing he had come to an ideal community. It was what he needed so that love and loyalty could take root for all time.

* * *

He has ridden through the villages on his bicycle, on roads with a strip of grass down the middle and lots of gates. Sometimes he has to stop and ask, but he's already learned the names of many farms. The bicycle is a good thing to have, but all the houses face the sea where the real traffic is. Spanking dinghies, thumping herring boats, creaking skiffs. Out there is where he would like to be, and he's been talking to the organist about getting a motorboat, which he could use both for fishing and for getting around.

Mostly for getting around, although he loves the idea of putt-putting about in his own boat, free and independent. He reviews his assets under the friendly eye of the organist. His salary is small and his student loans large. Unlike the local people, who spend big when they've had a good fishing season or sold seal oil to the government and then later live close to the bone, the priest has little chance of acquiring a large sum of money. But it will work itself out, and he now tells the organist proudly that he learned to sail when he was still a boy. The skiff that goes with the house has a hole for a mast in the thwart, and there's an old spritsail. He's going to fix it up and use it. But in the future he's going to have a motorboat so he can move about in all kinds of weather. If the organist hears of any good deals, he should let him know.

The organist is happy to find the pastor so open and trusting. Maybe too much so, he thinks fleetingly, knowing that there are those who would exploit those qualities. Of course he does need a little guidance, and when it comes to figuring out how to organize their lives on Church Isle, he is ready to help in word and deed.

As if to confirm this thought, and to make both of them jump, the phone rings. It is Adele Bergman, who has heard that the priest cycled by. It was easy to guess where he was headed, and now she wants to say that if he'll stop in at the Co-op on his way home, he can pick up the paint and thinner he ordered. Some good brushes have also come in, and some coffee biscuits if he wants to splurge.

The priest smiles when he gets this message, for here is another person who will support him in word and deed. "Whether you like it or not," the organist says, who nevertheless is an ally of Adele Bergman's and chairman of the Co-op board. "We wouldn't have got through the war half so well without Adele," he adds quickly. "When you live as far out as we do here, it goes without saying that we're last on the list, and when the Central Co-op got to our order, there was never anything left. But Adele didn't take it lying down. I've heard her talk to them on the phone. 'Our Co-op members are just as valuable as those in the city, and according to the Co-op bylaws, we have the same rights. As a Co-op manager, I won't bend an inch, and I demand that we get the deliveries we're entitled to. Without delay. Because we're farthest out, we should get our deliveries first, since the small amounts we need are hardly noticed.' And so on. She never let them forget us. It was a lot easier for them to carry our orders down to the boat than to try and explain to Adele why we weren't going to get them. When things got really bad, 1944 for example, and it was simply impossible to get your hands on any boat fuel at all, she went to Åbo herself and got her hands on two barrels of petrol, which she had them carry down to the boat with her. Then she stood there and guarded them until the boat left, and then at every stop along the way. Word got here before Anton did, and when the boat arrived in the wee hours, there was a crowd of people on the Co-op dock with canisters. And then things got really hot. 'The store will open at eight o'clock and not one minute earlier,' she told them. She must have been dead tired, but there she stood at eight o'clock on the dot and measured out what everyone had a right to. Adele gets more done than a man. People laugh at her, but they count on the fact that she'll get her hands on what we need. When we went to the herring market in Helsingfors after the peace was signed, everyone from here was astonished at how little there was to buy in the shops—compared to what Adele could plunk down on the counter for us if she thought we were worthy and had earned it."

The pastor and his wife are unquestionably among the worthy. Even if you specifically refuse all privilege, it's impossible to refuse Adele's goodwill. And a good thing, too, because the locals find all sorts of things in their sheds and boathouses that they can make use of when things get tight, whereas the pastor and his wife have to start with two pretty much empty hands. God helps those whom Adele Bergman helps, he thinks, laughing, on his way home, heavily burdened. A poor man would have an easier trip home.

* * *

He has fixed up the skiff and raised the sail and heads off. Not slowly, either. The boat hisses through the water and there's spray from the waves when he turns.

He learned to sail when he was still a boy, he says, and he's always liked to sail as close to the wind as he dares. To press ahead before you come about, that's life. Of course he's turned over on occasion, but that's no big deal. And he suspects that he'll do it again a few times before he gets the hang of the skiff.

I catch him in the act, you might say. I'm approaching the bay when the priest comes streaking out behind the point. He shoves the rudder over so hard that the boat just lies down, the way you might blow down a house of cards. The priest is in the water, swimming like an otter with the sheet firmly in hand. Though it's heavy going with the boat in tow, he drags it onto a skerry and turns it over easy as pie and wraps the painter around a stone.

He's standing there wringing out his clothes when I come up, cut my motor and throw out a grapnel. "In God's name," I start, but I have to laugh when I hear myself, for that's usually the priest's line. He laughs too and cries hello. "Are you all right?" I call.

"You bet," he says. "I've got to test the limits a bit and see what the skiff can do. She needs coddling, the little dickens."

My own skiff drifts towards the skerry as far as the grapnel permits and there we sit and talk, I in my boat and he on land. He spreads his clothes out on the granite and then sits down himself on a dry spot. "I'll just have to sit here until everything's dry. Otherwise I'll be in trouble when I get home."

He makes it sound like a great joke, but it's easy for me to believe that his wife would give him a dressing down, and he deserves one. He sails like an idiot just because he's young and strong and swims like a fish.

"You need to be careful till you know how the winds twist in among these islands," I warn him. "They're nothing to play with, the sea and the weather, and it doesn't always end this well."

It's then he says that stuff about having turned boats over lots of times. And then he says, "You must have done the same, you've lived your whole life on the sea."

Then I really have to think. I'm taken aback when I have to tell him the truth. "No, not that I can remember. I've always kept my feet in the boat, even if the rest of me hung out over the gunnels."

He sighs but then laughs again. "I guess that's the difference between doing this for a living, like you, and doing it for fun and excitement, like me."

"Yes," I say. "And there aren't a lot of us who can swim, either. They figure it just prolongs the suffering if you go overboard in open water. What'll happen to you if you turn her over in a big bay and you're not up to swimming ashore?"

"Maybe I'll have the wits to make my turns a little wider," he says, and I understand why people like him, because he's not cocky, however foolhardy he may be.

He's funny too, sitting there drying out. Even if I don't intend to say anything to his wife, I haven't made any promises to keep my mouth shut otherwise. We've always kept an eye on our priests and talked about how they behave. If it's something hilarious, so much the better. We have the post office in our home, and when I tell the story to Julanda the news will spread quickly. For we forward the news from a laughing mouth free of charge, without ink and envelopes and stamps.

Chapter Six

THE CONGREGATION SEES HIM SUNNY. Smiling, interested, eager to learn. Friendly, unaffected. Full of energy. Unassuming and appreciative, always with a good word for everyone. Full of fun, once you get to know him and realize that there is more than gravity beneath that cassock. So charmed by everything the parish has to offer that everyone melts. He likes the landscape: bleak, improbably beautiful in all its moods, fresh breezes and open vistas. The people: indescribably appealing. Charming. Intelligent. Handsome, lively, quick-witted. Knowledgeable, amazingly well-informed. Talkative and articulate. Exceptional. His new life as an island priest: a gift from God.

So cheerful that you might think he's never suffered a setback, that what lies behind the delight that wells forth is a lack of deeper life experience or an inborn naiveté.

Nothing about him indicates that he comes from the great affliction. The endless war. An intense aversion to himself and to everyone who ran after him with their senseless expectations. A Christianity rendered stiff and almost dumb. A greyness and brownness drawn across all of existence. In spite of it, people's terrible will to live, and, as if to mock them, death's endless variety and the cycles of disease, anguish, and loss that everyone is forced to pass through on their way to death.

She draws a short biography from him, Lydia Manström, who takes it in and only passes along such things as will cause no one embarrassment. What she retains within her tailored velvet jacket with its braids and trimmings is this: the oldest son of an overly ambitious teacher and an unpredictable father, forced to start school a year ahead of his own age group, always teased and excluded. Unable to honour his father, plagued by his mother's overblown expectations. At the age of fourteen, stricken with tuberculosis of the stomach and the knees, a year in hospital, in the tear-filled eyes of his mother, dying. In an adult ward, among repulsive men with indecent stories and suggestions — the poor nurses! — and no reservations about his innocence. And then to see how they died, suffocating in their obscenity, drowning in their slime. How he prayed and promised to serve the Lord with joy all his life if only he could escape the hospital alive and make a life of his own. How he recovered, became a star pupil in school, took up sports to get into condition, graduated, and began to study theology. Studied and studied, often with distaste and without pleasure. The war that broke out. His stricken conscience at being exempt from military duty while brothers and friends were dying at the front, his resolve to be always ready, without complaint, to help those who needed him — Mrs Vale O'Tears, Miss Gloomquist, Mr von Woe. Food supply commission, Home Guard, fire brigade, war orphans. His studies like wading through tar. Debilitating anxiety, despair at the alliance with Germany and Finland's unfortunate invasion of East Karelia. Pangs of conscience like a fire blanket over his rebellious spirit. Should I or shouldn't I? But yes! You must. Always.

And then the things that Lydia Manström can calmly pass along: Mona, who saved him, her teacher's apartment that made it possible for him to complete his studies. His ordination, his brief service as an army chaplain, his first appointment as temporary pastor in a parish that had lost its priest. The birth of Sanna. And then across the water to a life that is open and bright and fantastic. Ten times better than he had humbly hoped for as an unattainable future goal. Freedom. Openness. Warmth. Beauty. And the word he avoids saying for fear of losing it, the word that nevertheless insists on making itself heard like a paean—Happiness.

And now he gets effusive, talking about how theology itself has suddenly burst into bloom, how he sees that beauty in nature is an analogy, a metaphor for God's love, for life in Jesus Christ. That we can celebrate the beauty around us because that affirmation is a recognition of God's love. Christianity is not gloom and doom. Christianity is an affirmation! He means to preach this message.

Yes. A little embarrassed at being so emotional, but still very happy. He smiles at Lydia Manström as they sit catching their breath after his first parish catechetical meeting in the east villages. "And you yourself, Mrs Manström? How did you come out here?"

"Across the water", she says evasively, although he has a right to a confidence from her after all he's told her about himself. He waits, feeling a bit snubbed. Surely he hadn't been that pushy? She has to go on. "We met in Åbo. I came down to the boats. He sold fish. Then I came out here and gave a class in weaving. When it was over, we were engaged. Simple as that."

It sounds as if she would rather have a tooth pulled. It's clear that you don't ask personal questions of Lydia Manström. It's a different story with her husband, Arthur Manström, a man of wide experience, who is always enthroned as the central figure in the tales he tells. He now comes sweeping in, impressive, Roman nose, velvet voice like a lover. Lazy as a god, courted and admired, he claims proudly to be a farmer fisherman but lives on his wife's salary as a teacher. The foundation of it all is eloquence . . . indeed, when eloquence was passed out, Arthur Manström stood at the head of the line and helped himself.

The priest is a bit overshadowed here, although he too has a beautiful voice and can both sing and talk. But Arthur can talk the sparrows off the roof, he draws people's attention like a wood sprite, he scrapes and smiles and flatters and bows. Once, he lured the chaste Lydia from Åbo to the Örlands. Knew that he couldn't let her return a virgin, because it would then be too easy for her to reply evasively to letters, to make other plans, to be sadly unavailable when he wanted to visit. A secret engagement would not do, either. No, he needed to speak calmly, smoothly, fluently, back her into a corner, down onto the floor, in under her skirts, a calm voice through all the No! No! while his hand makes its way past waistbands and openings, into position. Accomplished. And then she can only become engaged and marry him, for in Lydia's world if you lie with a man then he's the one you must marry.

There is much gossip, and it will eventually reach even the pastor's ears. There was only one child, now the adult heir apparent, today in the process of fathering his own children. What everyone would like to know: Did he tire of her once he had her? Is she perhaps revolted by the act of sex? Was she injured so severely in childbirth that she is incapable of . . . ? But on the other hand she isn't sickly and in pain like women with uterine prolapse and a damaged urethra but rather energetic and full of drive, with good posture, a slim figure, a rapid gait, and she's a real disciplinarian at school. Active in the

Martha Association and People's Health, a leader in the food supply commission during the war, a promoter of adult education, practical skills and handicrafts. Writes letters to their member of parliament and the county council and lobbies for the interests of the Örland Islands. Writes "we" in her letters, but is absolutely "she", an outsider. Silent as the grave when it comes to personal matters.

Arthur reigns in the masculine world of the farmer fishermen without overexerting himself, rests up at home when Lydia is at school, has all manner of errands and activities in the afternoons that require him to be out once school is over. Appears in Lydia's company mostly at the table and especially when they are invited out. He then leads her by the elbow, smiles and speaks like a seraph, with a heavenly sweetness. He has many names for her: my better half, my consort, the mistress of my house, my treasured companion, my wedded wife. She calls him Arthur, which stamps her as an outsider, because on the Örlands, women call their husbands "himself".

Arthur, well, here he is. He sits down beside the priest on the Åbo sofa in the parlour, his bass voice purring with pleasure. He has eaten his fill and has had some real coffee. Perhaps, too, he has fortified himself from some bottle of two- or three-star cognac, because those who can't stand his flash and twinkle will hint later to the priest that he hasn't a sober moment. If so, we are viewing genteel inebriation at its most appealing—he's a kindly and communicative fellow with a broad register and converses about Church Isle in the Middle Ages and tells stories about the former priest who preached in his Home Guard uniform. Once as he climbed into the pulpit, his revolver fell from its holster, and when he bent down to pick it up, the church's famous acoustics picked up someone whispering clearly, "Duck thy heads, for now he reloadeth."

"There are many such stories," the silver-tongued Arthur adds, and the pastor laughs and says that he's sure there are. It's like being taken by the hand and led through the steps of a dance—you nod and smile when you get the signal and are then swept away across the floor. The pastor glances around surreptitiously and notes that Lydia is no longer present. Somewhere in the great convivial flow she was washed towards the kitchen, where she clearly has much to do now that dinner is over. The dishwater steams and there are towers of pots and bowls and plates. Arthur holds forth, and the priest, who learned at home to regard his father's conversation with a certain scepticism is nonetheless charmed and seduced. Arthur must have sold his soul to be able to talk this way! Lydia still has hers, a hard pod in a vault, a petrified dream deep inside an active and laudable sense of duty. The priest has revealed some of his to her, and she has observed it without asking a single question, but in such a way that he's been led to reveal still more.

Mona has been at home with Sanna, which she all too often has to be, and when he finally gets home after this long day and would simply like to read the newspapers, he wanders around with Sanna around his neck and tells Mona about everyone he's met, intelligent and well-spoken every one, but the prize goes to Arthur Manström. He repeats a couple of the anecdotes he can recall and adds, "Lydia is a different story. Probably smarter than all the rest of us put together but discreet as a spy ring. I believe she's the least gossipy person I've ever met."

Mona gives him one of those penetrating looks that make him look away. He knows more or less what she's thinking. He should watch his tongue and not quite so frankly reveal his innermost thoughts to anyone and everyone. A person needs to button up and caulk his hull. Things said in confidence sound entirely different when shouted from the rooftops. This is what she's thinking, among other things, and she's right as usual.

But. It's not true that he babbles indiscriminately. It you expect candour from others, you have to open the door to yourself a bit. If you want to reduce people's reservations, you have to thin out your own. And yet it's something of a problem for Mona that he sits there chatting with people as if he had all the time in the world. Time that ought to be hers. Theirs. Of course it's fun and exciting to have a new priest who's young and full of fun, happy and accommodating, of course everyone wants to talk to him, sit there and bask in his attention and waste the time he ought to devote to so much else.

While the priest lingers in the village, eating party food and drinking coffee until his belly is stuffed, talking and singing hymns, his wife has done the milking and washed the dishes, put the laundry in to soak, cranked the separator, scrubbed the kitchen floor where he has thoughtlessly tracked in mud, built a fire in the bathhouse to heat laundry water, hauled up water from the well, washed clothes with a will, fed herself and Sanna at appropriate intervals, chased off the tenant farmer's cows which had broken through the fence, pounded in some posts ostentatiously with a stone without attracting any attention whatsoever from the tenants, who do not show themselves in any window. And when she looks inside, there is not a living soul. It's like the *Mary Celeste* — a fire in the stove, food warm on the plates, sails set for a light breeze, but no life. Back in the parsonage, there's no end to it. If she has a free moment, there are clothes to be mended, letters to be written. Food must be prepared — though he'll hardly be hungry when he gets home — and kept warm in case he comes late, as usual. The evening milking will have to be done soon, and Sanna will have to go with her because there's no one else in the house. She's sensible for her age, but you still have to keep an eye on her so she doesn't get covered with dirt or go too close and get stepped on. Gnats and mosquitoes enough to drive you crazy. Sanna screams and cries, and the cows throw their heads and stamp their feet — they'd step right into the milking pail if she wasn't careful. It takes forever even if she hurries, and then she has to stand there and filter the milk and lower it into the cowshed well. The warm milk warms up the well water, and the whole thing is an inefficient joke for someone from a real dairy farm with a basin and ice stacked under a layer of sawdust. But you have to be grateful to have milk at all, so she can't complain. "Come, Sanna. Now we can finally go. Good girl."

Yes. Sanna. It's not right that he so rarely has time for his own daughter. His own family. Of course he has to do his job, but shouldn't he have some time for himself? But then he has to write his sermon, and study for his pastoral exams, and read through the endless pile of correspondence from the diocese. He has to stay abreast of the local news, and the world news, otherwise he'll be hopelessly out of touch, and then there are all those theological journals. He has to write letters to his mother, all too often and all too detailed, and she immediately responds with dreadfully long and closely written replies. More's the pity, because then he has to write again promptly, also closely written and at length, and sympathize. There's no end to it.

The parsonage is on Church Isle, isolated from the parish, and in human terms it offers a haven of peace for the priest when he finally gets home. And it certainly looks peaceful for a moment or two when he comes jogging up the hill from his boat. The wind dies at dusk, and the evening air is raw and damp. He takes the steps in a couple of bounds, lifts the latch, smells the fire in the stove, opens the door. A scream of joy and Sanna throws herself into his arms. Mona, angrily, "Sanna! Go straight to bed! Once you're there, you stay there!" She takes Sanna by the arm, hard, and Sanna yelps and clings to him tightly. Strict loyalty a requirement, but he must be loyal to his child as well, and he holds Sanna close and says, "Just a little while. I haven't seen her all day."

No indeed, but he hasn't seen Mona all day, either. Mona, who sees him mostly when he's worn out and dog-tired and still has lots of work to get through even though it's already late. The parish never sees him that way, whereas she . . . But what is she thinking? The husband she loves has come home at last, and she ought to be happy. And of course she is happy. She's only irritated because she can never have enough, because she's jealous of the parish that gets such great gulps of him while she gets him back when he's dead tired and should just be allowed to go to bed.

"Sit down," she says. "We'll have some tea and you can tell me about the catechetical meeting. What the food was like, and who you talked to. Sanna can stay up for a little while, but then to bed." With Sanna's arms around his neck, he starts to tell about the meeting — how well they read, how openly they answered his questions. How the organist is clearly on his guard in the east villages. About the baked pike and about Arthur Manström and his lawfully wedded wife Lydia. About the way his head buzzes with all the talk and the singing. How nice it is to be home. How absolutely wonderful it is to come home to his two girls. He never in his life expected to feel such happiness.

They sit there a bit dizzy with exhaustion, drink their tea and know a little more about the nature of happiness than they did when they were even younger. Then Mona had taken their relationship for granted. Later events made her terribly jealous and put her on her guard. Not that he would have been unfaithful or allowed himself to be tempted. It was rather that he behaved as if he lacked a sense of self-preservation and believed that he was some sort of Jesus put on earth to bear the world's sorrows.

In plain language, Mona had to murder a whole religious movement in order to save him. This was the Oxford Movement, an intellectual and theological renewal of faith, with great ethical demands, which had a powerful influence on Petter and his closest friends during their studies at the School of Theology at Helsingfors University. During those same years, the movement was hijacked by the Americans and transformed into Moral Rearmament, MRA. In Petter's second parish, where he served temporarily as assisting pastor, MRA had a solid foothold among a leading group of parishioners. A person with as much common sense as Mona had only to look at them as they greeted Petter to hear alarm bells. Unrealistic dreamers, the whole bunch, who managed to monopolize him in no time and pull him into endless evening meetings that fairly reeked of confession and tormented self-examination. So persuasive were they that Petter got the idea that it was his duty to stand up in the pulpit before the entire congregation and confess the erotic missteps of his youth as well as the vice of self-abuse, a plan averted only when Mona threatened to beat him senseless with a cast-iron frying pan rather than let him leave home for church, and when Uncle Isidor made an emergency visit. In the course of this private conversation, Isidor stressed the fact that a priest must by all means be truthful, but that he must also be an example for his congregation, as prescribed in his clerical oath. What kind of example will he be if he stands in the pulpit and wallows in youthful sins, no longer of any consequence. If a priest could . . . well then, couldn't anyone? That's what many will think. Others will laugh at him behind his back and he will lose all his authority and, worse, his legitimacy as a priest. Does he want to be relieved of his office? Has he lost his mind? Has he thought this through all the way to the bitter end? Think of Mona and his little daughter. Think of his mother! Who has already suffered such grief.

It does not help him to cite the Oxford Movement's four absolutes: absolute purity, absolute honesty, absolute unselfishness, absolute love . . . ("Absolute idiocy!" Mona calls from behind the door) . . . because those are abstract concepts, even if they are a distillation of the most beautiful thoughts in the Sermon on the Mount. But we live as best we can here on earth, where our actions have consequences on a social plane. Think, dear Petter. Think. And if you won't think about those consequences, then think instead about the four absolutes. Which of them did Our Saviour place first? Yes, love. And if you want to be absolutely honest with yourself, who is it that you love most? Yes, Mona and your little girl. Your mother. You have no absolute right to cause them such distress.

All that is bad enough. Even worse is that in the overheated atmosphere of those evening meetings, when Mona must of course stay home with Sanna, there are romantic young women who confess their wicked thoughts and, weeping, throw themselves on the priest's breast. And the priest, who stands for absolute love, what is he supposed to do? Unable as he is to see through their cunning, he tells himself that it's all pure spiritual anguish when in actual fact it's an irresponsible effort to captivate a married man and father. Moreover a priest and a model for the parish. Where is he supposed to put his hands? What is he supposed to do when they cry, "God! I cannot go on like this!"

They. Well, one. Who is so terribly in love that she can't stand it but comes rushing to his home in her despair. Right past Mona as if she were a simple servant girl, no one who mattered. Straight to the priest. "Oh God! Help me! Pray for me!"

His face a picture of masculine helplessness. She is about to push him into his study. She doesn't see Mona, doesn't reckon with her, she is meaningless, a person lacking spiritual life and love in Christ, a person who in a deeper sense has no right to him. She, Mona, with a teaching degree, steps forward and takes the overwrought young woman by the arm, hard. "Calm yourself!" she commands. Miss N stops in her tracks. Her tears freeze on her cheeks. Her hand halfway to his breast. Her thought cut off in midstream.

"Forgive me," she says. "I didn't mean . . . I don't know why I'm here."

"So it seems," says the pastor's wife. "I suggest that we drink a cup of coffee in the kitchen and then maybe you'll feel better."

She bustles about in the kitchen. Angry as a bee, Petter sees, but frighteningly polite to the fervid young woman, who sits at the table and shrivels, without a sob or a sigh. "Here you go," Mona says, and Miss N dares do nothing but drink her coffee. Looks at no one, least of all at the priest, who stares into his cup. He can think of nothing to say, although he's the one licensed to preach, and his wife is forced to continue.

"To my way of thinking, MRA has gone way too far. Its demands are terribly exaggerated and people get all worked up and overwrought and lose their heads. I can't give you any advice, but I can't help thinking you'd be better off staying away from those meetings. And I'll give the same advice to my husband, who has many duties here in this parish without MRA trying to draw the last drop of his blood."

Now Miss N looks at Mona, eyes wide, and draws a breath almost like a mortal sigh. "Yes," she breathes. "Thank you. I hardly recognize myself. It's like a dream."

"Yes," Mona says. "Reality is different. Work, for example." She looks at her husband, the priest, a penetrating gaze. So blue, so powerfully blue. So indescribably, incomprehensibly, powerfully blue. The fifth absolute — blueness. "Yes," she concludes. "And now I have to get on with mine. Perhaps you'd like more coffee?"

"No thank you," she breathes. "I have to go. What you said about the meetings is right." She says goodbye to them both, and no one who sees her go can help feeling sorry for her, the way we feel sorry for any young person who has lost her faith and hope. What passes later between the priest and his wife occurs in private, but we can presume that it is not the priest who emerges triumphant.

"How could you be so blind?" she cries, for example, after he's assured her, scandalized, that there was of course no physical attraction on either side. "Everyone must have seen it but you! Don't you understand anything? What would you have done if I hadn't managed to stop her?"

He looks like a schoolboy, not like the beloved man she married. "I suppose I would have prayed with her. You know in the Movement we talk a lot about prayer. About its power to change our lives."

"Ha! She threw herself at you! She was this far from a declaration of carnal lust."

"Then naturally I would have calmly talked sense to her. Explained that we're brother and sister in Jesus Christ. Nothing more."

"I wonder if you really don't realize how overheated the atmosphere gets at those meetings of yours. Your demand for honesty has pretty much the same effect that pornography has on a dirty old man. There are thoughts and inclinations that people are better off keeping to themselves. A little common decency never hurt anyone. You encourage simple, unbalanced souls to vent the feelings that they'd keep under wraps in a more sceptical atmosphere. Has it occurred to you that you're acting like a sect, though you belong to the church?"

He can hear how weak he sounds as he admits that there is much in what she says. That it takes someone with her analytical ability to put a finger right on the sensitive point. Yes, people's feelings ran away with them. Yes, the atmosphere was thoroughly overheated. As a priest, he should have realized that they expected leadership from him, not simply a confirmation of their surging emotions. What she says about sectarianism is perfectly true. Distressed as he is, it's still interesting to see how it starts. You think it's just an internal revival, and then it turns out that you stand at the forefront of a little group that is distancing itself from the rest of the congregation. It's not healthy, she's absolutely right about that.

By and by he also agrees to decline to attend any further evening meetings. Doesn't intend to make excuses but means to be absolutely honest when he informs Westerberg that he is taking this step because he has grown increasingly dubious about the overheated atmosphere within the movement. It is becoming too naked and intrusive. It's becoming sectarian, he will say, and then add that he would also like to spend more time at home with his wife and newborn child.

They talk and talk, though neither one of them has the time, and of course the result is that, both of them in tears, they reaffirm their love and agree that he naturally never and that she naturally never thought.

The priest stops going to the meetings, which gradually die a natural death when one after another of the little group stops coming. Some internalize the absolutes and continue to have them as lodestars in their personal lives. Others remember the whole episode with shame. In any case, the movement does not recover. Across Finland, a few faithful enthusiasts support it for a time, but it wavers and fades and eventually gives up the ghost.

She who murdered it feels a certain triumph at first. Then doubt and unease as well. That he could actually be so naive. That she has to act the policeman. Save him from things he should have the sense not to stick his nose into. That she has to get so angry in order to make him see what's going on.

This background made it easier for her to support his decision to ask for an appointment to the outermost outer islands. Here they will be isolated from the whole world's Christian cliques and coteries. Here they will have more time for each other and be able to live a life of concord and true love.

In truth, it is hardly possible to find a congregation less given to sectarianism than the people of the Örlands. The prevalent, cheering belief out here is that the church is one, and that that one church is the Örlands' church. Its priests are the object of healthy interest and indulgence — the way they sometimes behave! But they are theirs, for better, for worse, as long as they have them. Often they serve with a wandering eye, on their way to richer pickings, and are quickly forgotten. But this one says he wants to stay and meets their interest with great candour and goodwill.

There is something special about him, which his wife is the first to acknowledge. That's why she loves him, why she married him. But wherever he goes, he attracts people like a magnet, she might almost wish he were a little less attractive. As it is, there is no one who doesn't want to talk to him and bask in his glow. He himself is unaware of this magnetism and is astonished that people are so friendly. Extraordinarily friendly, he keeps saying. A little less would be plenty, his wife thinks. Moderately cordial would be just fine. So that he could do what he needs to do, hold his meetings and functions, and then come home!

The pastor's wife is no clinging vine. Wherever you plant her, she sends out strong stalks and leaves. She handles herself with the greatest competence, organizes and manages and keeps an eye on her domains. She is happy to work alone, for then everything stays on track. But of course she listens for him. And of course she goes from window to window sometimes and wonders if he's never going to come. What kind of a marriage would it be if she never wanted him at home?

Of course she understands that the church and the congregation are his primary responsibility and that he's never really off duty. He gets up from his supper with a smile, he closes his textbooks and comes out of his study happily, delighted to be disturbed. Come right in! Talks at length about the weather, which out here is a subject of life and death, asks about family members, whose names he's already learned, discusses boat connections and the fishing prospects, compares notes about the hay. Lets people take their time before getting to the point—some kind of certification from the parish register, as is often the case, or a christening or maybe even a wedding. Then both parties grow exhilarated, for the priest can recommend marriage warmly. So now at last! He sounds so enthusiastic that it warms their souls. If they have doubts, they forget to mention them.

It takes time, like everything else he does — a simple trip to the post office, a visit to the Co-op. He might as well announce his schedule from the pulpit, the crowds could hardly be larger. People stand waiting for him on his way home. If he catches up to someone on his bicycle he stops and chats. Every cottage asks him to look in as he passes. The church is one and the priest is one, but he ought to be eight people, so there'd be something left over for his wife.

Smiling, he tells her it will be like this only briefly, as long as he has the novelty of newness. Now, after the long winter, they're eager for new people, but it will be different when summer comes. Then they'll start with the hay, the children who work in Sweden will be coming home, and there will be sailboat visitors and summer guests. In August, they'll start on the autumn fishing. They'll be busy. This is only a honeymoon, the workaday world will soon begin.

The pastor's wife had no honeymoon. They got married during the Continuation War, at the Helléns'. That evening they were driven by horse carriage to the school where she was substituting. In the morning, she went down to her schoolroom while he studied exegetics in the teacher's quarters. This is the way she usually describes the unromantic beginning of her married life, concealing the fact that there were also oceans of shyness, tenderness, and bliss.

As a result, she doesn't really like it that he can compare his feelings for the Örland congregation with love and marriage. Of course she ought to be pleased at his lively interest and strong feelings. She can't admit even to herself that she wants those feelings reserved for herself alone. It's obviously a good thing that he's put himself on such a solid footing with the congregation right from the outset. Naturally she's proud of his ability to capture people's affection. She notes proudly that he's just as good at making friends as his father ever was, Leonard the famous chatterbox. But in contrast to him, Petter has substance and an unaffected manner that goes straight to people's hearts.

Here on the Örlands they can work side by side. His salary is meagre, so their little farm is of the greatest importance if they're to pay off his student debts and buy a boat and a horse. Much of it is in a sorry state, but it also has great potential. They can enlarge the kitchen garden, dig up a new potato patch, and clear bushes and undergrowth for an extra fairly good-sized hay meadow. They will also have to build a new fence and clean out and rebuild the cow barn. By next year, the whole place will look very different.

The priest is interested in farming, his wife is an expert. She is already looking ahead to the end of the summer when she will be leading two bountiful cows and a heifer into a freshly limed barn with a loft full of fragrant, nourishing hay. They're going to get a household pig and three hens. They need to get some seed potatoes as soon as possible, although Petter says that no one in the villages would ever think of planting potatoes when the ground is still so cold. They do it closer to midsummer. "Not here!" says Mona, who has already dug a couple of furrows in the kitchen garden and planted parsley, dill, radishes, lettuce, and carrots. Onions and beets, peas and beans will follow as soon as the soil is a bit warmer. And she hasn't forgotten flowers. She's brought seeds for columbines, daisies, and marigolds, and she can dig up some sod with cowslips and wild pansies from the cow pasture and transplant them to her flowerbed. Later in the summer, she can collect all sorts of seeds from the churchyard and set out tulip and narcissus bulbs in the autumn. As early as next year, everything will be more the way she imagines it—blazing flowerbeds, a

well-tended vegetable garden. If the pastor is to be a model
for the community, then the parsonage should be one too, and
the pastor's wife goes to work with confidence.

They work for their common future, and Mona thinks that
when they're old they'll be able to look around and agree that
these hardworking years were the best of their lives. They will
then be old and weak and lack the urgency and the briskness
of youth. Now they are young and healthy and can deal with
anything. Even if it seems overwhelming, there is little they
can't accomplish—and they have time.

Chapter Seven

He says it's fun to be on the move and happily jumps aboard and comes with me to visit the priest at Mellom, his closest colleague. The engine thumps along and we stand and talk while he looks around and asks me to repeat the names of the islands in the order we pass them, because that will be useful to know when he gets his own motorboat and can make the trip under his own power.

He's already good friends with Brage Söderberg and is very impressed with what he knows. "You've got to have unbelievable concentration if you're going to make it through the islands in fog and darkness the way Brage does, using only a clock and a compass, and be certain that you're exactly where you've reckoned you ought to be. That's what I call competence. It's almost uncanny. Of course you have to have grown up out here."

"Yes, you only learn that from experience."

"But not from experience alone. It takes a special focus, I think. I'm sure you'll agree that not everyone can learn to do it. You can live your whole life out here without the slightest idea of how long it takes between islands at whatever speed you're travelling."

"A lot of people are good at that. Not many as good as Brage."

"I'd go anywhere with him. And with you, too. I hear you've pretty much seen it all."

"Well, I've seen a bit. But to tell you the truth, before I go out I can see how it's going to be. When the bays are frozen, for example, I see where the ice is rotten and where the currents are running. I've never fallen through the ice, not yet. Because I go where I've seen the ice will hold, and I come home all in one piece."

He sounds, how should I put it, reverential. "You mean you know these parts so well you can see the tricky spots ahead of you?"

"That, too. But also that I can see how it's going to be."

"Do you have what they call second sight?"

"Yes, nearly everyone does in my family. There's nothing special about it. You see what's going to happen. You can't change it. I knew my old lady was going to die. Signs and warnings everywhere, but nothing I could do anything about. When I'm going out on the water it's a little different. Then it's more active, like a collaboration. I keep my eyes open and I'm told how things are. Then it's up to me if I pay attention to what I've seen or just do what I want."

Reverence again. "You mean it's like a higher guidance? Like a guardian angel?"

"Yes, you could say that, yes. I don't doubt there are guardian angels. But I can tell you that there are powers out here that were old when Jesus was young."

"How do you mean?" he asks. Not the way you ask in order to keep the conversation going but because he wants to know. We can both see out, so it's perfectly natural that we don't need to look at each other, and the watches are long out here so you don't have to worry that you'll run out of time.

"I see it like this, that when Jesus was young and out on the Sea of Galilee, there were powers out on the lake that were ancient. The people who'd grown up there knew about them and had run into them in certain situations. Jesus was an outsider. When he saw where his disciples should cast their nets, he thought it came from God, but it was from them, out on the lake. They realized that this man was *something special, and they let him see. And he was the sort of man who saw. And who do you think it was who let him walk on water? It wasn't God."*

The priest stares straight ahead. The bay is as smooth as glass, and the thumping of the engine echoes between the islands. "Have you ever felt their presence?"

"We all did, back in the days when we sailed. Back then, you couldn't use your engine to outrun the weather, you had to keep your eyes and ears open. The whole world was full of signs. They told you when you should run for home before the storm caught you. They showed you where the fish were. They woke you up so you didn't oversleep. They were there all the time, but you had to interpret them and understand them."

"Have you seen them, ever?"

"Yes indeed. Old codgers dressed in hides who stand up on land and signal you to make it home as fast as you can. They warn you about storms. At first you think it's some old guy from some other village, but when you sail around the island you don't see a boat anywhere, and the old man has vanished so completely that you think you dreamed it. Nodded off and dreamed it. But several times I put the helm hard over and sailed for home leaving my herring nets to their fate, and every time the seas nearly swamped me before I was back in the lea of my own island."

The priest looks deep in thought about something, but I go on. "It often seems to me that the ones you can see, they're among the very youngest. They're like human beings, and they know what it's like to be unprotected on the sea when there's a storm lurking. They know how we live, and they help us. There you've got your guardian angels, almost. But the much older ones, they're more difficult. They don't understand you, because they've been in their world such a long time that they don't really know what it's like to be human any more. They're curious, and you can tell they're all around you, as if they'd really like to know what it would be like to be in your shoes, but they don't always understand that you're about to get yourself in trouble. Sometimes they do nothing, although they could have reached out a hand and saved your life.

"I remember one time when I was out with my herring boat at night. It wasn't exactly a storm, but there was a heavy sea. Pulling and sucking like mad. I wasn't worried because my motor was running like a sewing machine, and I was keeping a good distance from those steep cliffs on Klobbar. But there was a terrible power in the waves, and even though I was steering seawards I was being drawn in steadily towards the land. It was pitch-black, but I could hear the way we were getting sucked closer and closer, that horrible gulping sound from the cliffs and the short rattling echo of the motor. I could feel in my gut how the cliffs were pulling me in, in spite of my steering away at full speed.

"The whole time, I felt there was someone right behind me. Curious as hell, the way they are when something's up, as if he thought it would be interesting to see what happened when we were driven onto the rocks. You can't talk to them, because I think they come from a time when they didn't talk like us. They don't understand what you say, so you have to get them to respond on some other level. I was thinking so feverishly that it wasn't just language but a cry so primitive that anything could understand it, 'Now you've got to help me to get round that point!'

"Then I could feel how he gave me a push so the boat picked up speed and we made it around Klobbar by a hair and out into open water. 'Praise and glory!' I said, but I don't think they understand stuff like that. The next time I passed that way, in full daylight, I went ashore and put half a loaf of bread on the rocks. I've learned from experience that there's nothing they're as wild about as bread. The smell of bread is the best thing they know, because it reminds them of something they once loved dearly. That's what I believe.

There's nothing they like better than bread, and if you want to stay in their good graces, then leave some buttered bread behind when you sit and eat your lunch on some skerry."

The priest mumbles something about gulls and terns. "Of course," I say. "Naturally they take those shapes, you can understand that. It's like in dreams when white birds hover like a cloud above swarms of herring. When they show us where to fish, they take the form of white birds."

"I don't know what to say," the priest says, but I like quite a bit what he nevertheless does say. "What you're saying is incredibly interesting. You and Brage are the most skilful, most competent boatmen I know. The only conclusion I can draw is that there's another kind of wisdom than the one we learn about in school and at the university. Call it another kind of sensitivity if you like. Anyway. I respect it and esteem it."

"I know that a lot of people call it superstition," I say, gently.

"Not I," he says. "But all that was a lot for a fairly green priest to swallow. Some time I'd like to continue this discussion, but right now I'm most interested in how you're going to navigate in to Mellom. The channel goes between two islands that look like just one. Tricky!"

* * *

From one world to another. Handshake with the postal-boat skipper, quickly up onto the dock at Mellom, a smiling face for the Mellom priest, who has come down to meet him. A rare chance for a meeting with a colleague, a great joy!

Fredrik Berg is only a few years older than Petter Kummel, but he's had his pastorate for two years and is wise and disillusioned. Soon enough, this young pastor will wake up to his congregation's less attractive sides. There will be feuds, discord, obstinate silences, letters to the newspaper, ugly messages to the diocese. Just wait. But at the same time he can't help finding Petter's enthusiasm infectious, as is the friendship he immediately offers. "I was hoping for that!" Petter says when Fredrik, the older of the two, suggests that they should call each other by their first names, even though they've never met before. Fredrik studied theology in Åbo and Petter was at the University of Helsingfors. Nevertheless they have more in common with each other than with anyone else in the archipelago — two young priests strolling from the dock to the parsonage in lively conversation.

They are both nature lovers, it turns out. The beauty of nature makes up for a lot, Fredrik acknowledges, and Petter makes comparisons. The smell is different because of the pines on Mellom; there are no conifers out on the Örlands. For a moment, the scent of pines and their deep green reflection on the water make him nostalgic for the security of the inner archipelago, but at the same time he's as proud as a child of how wild and salty and windswept the Örlands are. Never green reflections on the water, only dark grey-blue and silver and ash grey, or a bright blue glassy surface like today. "I'll never tire of that. I'm thinking of staying on the Örlands my whole life," he declares.

Fredrik Berg has a penchant for sweet-and-sour smiles, but he can't quite pull one off as he says to his new friend, very cheerfully, "Just wait till autumn. And winter."

"Oh I will!" Petter says. "I'm looking forward to it!"

They saunter towards the parsonage, two men at leisure, in no hurry, but so young that even a slow walk covers a lot of ground. Soon they're walking up the parsonage steps. Fredrik looks a little uncomfortable when his wife comes out the door. She is nervously eager to make a good impression and fears she has already failed. "Welcome," she says. "Did you have a good trip?"

That stops him for a moment as he thinks back. "A good trip? Well, yes, I suppose so. Anything can happen out here. You go out on a little boat trip and get a lecture on pre-Christian thought into the bargain. Post-Anton is unbelievable." He shakes his head. "Excuse me, that isn't what we were going to talk about."

"They're so fantastically superstitious out here, they all believe in ghosts. There's hardly a one would dare walk past the churchyard after dark. But now come in, both of you, and sit down at the table. Come in, come in!"

She waves them into the dining room and goes into the kitchen herself. A child peers at them from the stairs, another from behind a door. A third is screaming from the bedroom. The table is set, and Mrs Berg comes in with potatoes and boiled carrots, then comes back with a baked pike, resting golden and beautiful in its own juice. Petter looks at his colleague with interest. "Do you fish?"

"With the greatest pleasure. I caught this one on a spinner. But mostly I fish with nets. I wasn't raised on it, so I've had to learn by experience. Fortunately, there were people happy to teach us when we first came. What about you?"

"Yes, indeed. Papa was from Åland and I've been laying nets with him since I was six. And my brothers and I pulled spinners so fast in a rowboat that everyone thought we had a motor. When we got here there were some nets in the boathouse that we'll set out when we've got the time. Big holes. If my highly esteemed predecessor had any that were better, I believe he must have sold them."

Fredrik laughs heartily at that. "I think you've got his number. Our friend Skog never misses a bet. Did he manage to sell you his generator?"

"My uncle Richard bought it at the auction. You mean it doesn't . . . ?"

"Nope."

"Good money down the drain! Oh my. There are so many holes I could have mended with that money."

Fredrik is just glad it didn't happen to him. In a good mood, he calls in the two self-propelled children and has them say hello to Pastor Kummel. They look at him critically, one curtseys and the other bows. Petter is fond of children and talks to them and asks questions, they twist and writhe and let Mama answer. She urges them to eat before the food gets cold. Petter is hungry, and he can't praise too highly the island custom of stuffing hot food down the craw of anyone who's come a great distance. "And this is delicious! Thank you so much for your hospitality." He looks around discreetly for the salt, but they do things differently here.

There are many conventions to follow, many questions they must ask him, and much for him to report. How they're getting along, if Mona likes the place, about their little girl and whether she tolerates the constant breeze on the island without getting ill. About their impression of the congregation. "Old scoundrels and cocky youngsters," Fredrik Berg sums them up. "How are things going?"

Petter, earnestly: "I don't know what to say," and then, as if he'd been awarded first prize, "But what a parish! What a joy to work with such people."

Fredrik is about to say, "Just you wait!" but controls himself. "Well, yes. But I was thinking of the vestry and the parish council."

"Excellent. Though the organist tells me that the divisions in the community are serious. That's not really news. All parishes have factions. I think I won't let on that I know anything but just play it by ear from case to case."

"Good luck with that," says the Mellom priest, who decides to wait with his examples until the two of them are alone. The meal is being cleared away, it looks to be a beautiful day outdoors, and both men long to go out. Kummel's thoughts are already racing as he thanks his hostess. They make their escape with ease, leaving Mrs Berg with her pots and pans. She looks the way Petter recalls that his mother often looked, and fleetingly he wonders if Mona will come to look that way. But Mona's industrious and strong and a completely different sort of woman!

To begin with they walk with their hands behind their backs, but gradually they loosen up and Petter actually begins to gesture a bit with his arms. "A whole world!" he says. "There's no branch of science, no academic area that couldn't find subject matter in such a place. Oddly enough, I've grown much more interested in my studies out here than I ever was at the University."

He observes the plant life with interest, subtly different from that on the Örlands. Pines predominate, even on the south side facing the open sea and the Örlands. Out there the granite is bare, with stripes and grooves from the ice age, great boulders that tumbled from the glaciers and have worn depressions in the granite where they've lain for thousands of years. The two men move from botany to geology, an area both know something about. The words "weathering" and "gneiss" are mentioned, and Petter has already learned that parts of Paris were built with granite from the Örlands. Fredrik grows more relaxed the farther they get from the village, even though he did exchange pleasantries with a couple of fishermen they met among the boathouses. But when they're alone again he says that they're nice enough face to face, but behind your back they say other things entirely.

Petter thinks about this and says that the important thing for him is that they're friendly to his face, it creates goodwill and makes all transactions so much easier. "Of course I realize that there will be occasional confrontations, but then it's good to remember that their faces are normally so friendly. For the time being, until I've got a clear picture of the battle lines, I'm going to assume that all the friendliness is genuine." He stops and adds, abashedly, "Call me naive if you like, but I really believe it is. The same way my friendliness is genuine. What would I have to gain by ingratiating myself with a lot of grinning?"

"Quite a bit," Fredrik thinks, but he says, "It's not a question of their ingratiating themselves. It's more about a frightening desire to question. To object. Delay. Resist. Obstruct. Stall. Conspire. Betray. Deny. As if all of that was so much fun that it's impossible to resist — practically the meaning of existence. Even the ones you've come to know as wise, temperate, experienced, fair-minded people. Even them."

They stand looking out to sea, in the general direction of Petter's islands to the south, not visible now but sometimes appearing above the horizon like a mirage on a hot summer day. He struggles with the thought that Fredrik wants to spoil his devotion to his congregation, which in Petter's case includes even their weaknesses. It also occurs to him that Fredrik's remarks are not general observations but rather the result of personal disappointment, maybe even bitterness. He smiles. "It sounds like you speak from experience."

In the face of such sunniness, the priest of Mellom melts once again. He smiles back and suggests that they find somewhere pleasant to sit down — out of the wind, with a good view and a nice rock ledge to sit on.

And then he says, "As you've certainly noticed, we're alone out here. No fatherly dean to ask for advice. We have the theological authority, although we're young and green, whereas the old men are polished politicians to a man. You can't let them see you're inexperienced. You're the one who can read canon law. You're the one who understands the instructions from the cathedral chapter. You're the one responsible for seeing that the rules and decrees are followed. If you show any uncertainty, they're like wolves. And if you give as good as you get, then suddenly they present a united front."

Petter waits. It's about Fredrik's parsonage. In winter so cold it's almost uninhabitable. The curtains blow right out into the room. The rag rugs ripple in the draft through the floor. Raspberry bushes are forcing their way between the floorboards in the parlour. The tile stoves have been condemned, the brickwork is cracked. The water buckets are covered with ice in the mornings. The children would be better off in an igloo, which would keep them warmer even in the Arctic. But the crux of the matter is this: the decision was made to build a new parsonage back in his predecessor's days. The place was chosen, and the plans were drawn. The church's Central Fund came through with its usual contribution. The minutes of the parish committee show a decision to provide the congregation's share in the form of lumber and labour. But the execution of this decision is a joke! Nothing has been done. Nothing is being done. And because the decision's been made to build a new parsonage, no repairs can be made to the old one. Every meeting of the committee is a battle. Every meeting ends with postponement. If he weren't their opponent, he'd be impressed by their delaying tactics. Such calculated infamy! Such insinuations! The members of the congregation have to pay for their own labour and materials when they build a house, but the priest wants to put others to work so he can lounge about in the finest house on the island.

"It's not about me!" he says. "I mean, it's not my house they're going to build, it's the property of the parish and it will benefit every priest who comes here. They refuse to see that."

"Goodness!" says Petter. "I haven't even given a thought to next winter. We're going to have a draughty time of it ourselves."

"A decision has been made. It's right there in the minutes. There are letters from the church's Central Fund. It's my official duty to see that a new parsonage is built. I'm neglecting my duty if nothing happens. I mean to stay here until the new parsonage is almost finished, then we're going to move. They'll realize it wasn't for my own sake I pushed the project through."

Petter greatly admires all this determination. "Moving is the last thing I have in mind," he says. "I'm only afraid that someone else will go after the post before I've taken my exams and can apply to be permanent vicar myself."

That sends Fredrik Berg into gales of laughter. "And who would that be? They haven't had anything but temporary pastors out there since I don't when."

"But there must be other people like me," Petter says. "I won't rest easy until I've got the paper in my hand. But how I'm going to have time to study with everything we have going on is more than I can imagine. I'm only one person, although I need to be at least two."

Fredrik Berg is also studying for his pastoral examination — not, however, so he can stay but so that he can find a post somewhere else. They agree that the paper is a good thing to have, because it gives them more room to manoeuvre. But they also agree that it's a real nuisance having to prepare for yet one more examination, and pull together a dissertation, while at the same time struggling on as a lonely priest in a remote parish where you can only laugh hollowly at the thought of finding textbooks in the local library. Those books are going to cost a pretty penny, but the lack of time is even worse.

"Most of all, the lack of blocks of uninterrupted time," Petter expands on the theme. "Of course I'm used to that, but somehow I thought it would be different when you controlled your own time. How dumb can you get?"

Fredrik Berg sounds resigned. "You said you had only one child so far. We have three. And we're careful not to have more. I never thought, either, that life could be so stressful. Wife and kids is the most natural thing in the world, I thought. Human beings have lived in families for thousands of years, you think the routine is built in. I simply couldn't imagine how chaotic it would be."

Petter laughs, what else can he do?

Fredrik Berg looks happy, too, but he means what he says. Petter has a moment of terror—what if the demands on his time never lessen but only increase? How will he deal with it? But on the other hand, it's different with Mona and Sanna. There's no one quite like Mona. And he couldn't live without Sanna. There's no chaos with them. An oasis. Life. Quickly he returns to the subject of the pastoral examinations, picks up the discussion of the heavy volumes they have to plough through, the dissertation topics they're considering.

"It frightens me," Petter says, "that out here, theology seems less relevant than a lot of other academic subjects." Fredrik agrees. Amazingly little of what they studied is of any use to them in real life. For their work as pastors, they should instead have studied finance and had someone really good teach them how to manage with minimal resources.

"Like Mona," says Petter with a full heart. "She studied home economics and keeps books that take my breath away. When it comes time to discuss the annual budget in the vestry, I'm going to ask her for advice. And of course I'll look at what they've done before."

"They'll like that," Fredrik says. "If you try anything new, your life won't be worth living."

"Yes, I know," Petter says. "Don't get me wrong. I'm no reactionary, but in this case I really don't think it's necessarily an improvement to replace customs that have evolved over a long time and worked out their kinks with new ones, just because they're modern and up-to-date." He looks a little embarrassed and goes on. "Take the liturgy, for example. It's taken a thousand years to polish it, and I doubt I could come up with something better in an afternoon."

He gives Fredrik a friendly little box on the shoulder—just kidding. But at the same time, he thinks fleetingly of Post-Anton and it occurs to him that the customs on the Örlands may date back further than he can imagine and that if he violates them he will be defying not only the living but also people long since dead. "I'm glad I've got my organist," he says. "He's a wise man, very experienced, very diplomatic. He'd do very well wherever he was. It's really a tremendous waste of talent that people as strikingly intelligent as many of the people are out here get no education beyond elementary school."

A shadow passes across Fredrik's profile. "Like the war," he says. Lightly, but with feeling.

Petter draws a quick breath. Is it possible that Fredrik thinks the way he does? "I'm glad you brought it up!" he bursts out. "For years I've been thinking about all the ones who never got a chance. Full to bursting with talent and special knowledge. Full of hopes and expectations. Shot, maimed. Tragic on the personal level, a terrible waste for the nation economically." He pauses, cautiously. "I suppose you were in it?"

"Yes. As a chaplain. I was ordained just in time for the outbreak of the Continuation War. I happen to know that you were a chaplain as well."

"Only at the very end, when the war was already over, and even then only with the troops on Åland. A real sinecure, compared with what you fellows went through." He feels compelled to add a few words about his illness as an explanation. "I had a medical exemption during the war. I had TB when I was in middle school and it was there in my papers. So I was in the Home Guard and the food supply commission and the fire brigade instead. I'm sure it saved my life. I managed to finish my studies, with delays, of course, and I was ordained in 1943. I often had a bad conscience because I thought Hebrew and exegesis were so boring, but of course a lot of men at the front would have given anything to be in my shoes."

Fredrik looks at him with sympathy. He's been feeling a slight superiority simply because Petter was never at the front. That experience gives you a sharpness and a vigilance that Petter lacks. "As for me, I was in Eastern Karelia first, then on the Isthmus. I can tell you, it tests your faith. And as if you weren't wrestling with your own doubts, the boys see to it that you're really forced to confront your beliefs. For example, I led prayers with the ones who wanted to pray before going out on patrol, and of course I prayed for success in their work and asked God to send them back in one piece. Immediately someone shouted, 'What kind of a priest are you who doesn't pray for our enemies and those who persecute us?'" Fredrik pauses for effect, and Petter obliges.

"What did you say?"

"I said he was right to put his finger on one of the most important points in Christianity, a fundamental principle that we find difficult in times of war and calamity when our existence is under threat from an enemy pursuing an unjust cause. Maybe our Lord didn't mean that we should pray for our enemies' success but that we should think about their welfare and pray that their hearts might be enlightened so that they cease to make war against us and persecute us and agree to a just peace."

"Well said," Petter says.

"Some of them laughed and a couple of guys from Öster-botten shouted 'Amen!', but there was one man in real distress who said, 'Many of the Russians we're shooting at are here because they have to be, not because they want to attack us.' 'You're right,' I said. 'That's why we put our cause in God's hands. It's he who can see the whole picture. We've been put here to do our duty as soldiers. And as soldiers, we have every right to pray for help in doing our duty successfully. If we can also pray for our enemies' enlightenment and conversion, so much the better.'"

He drops his slightly preachy tone and goes on. "I guess you never struggle harder with your conscience than you do in a war. Do the things we've been taught really hold up? What do we actually know about God's plan for the human race? How far does our loyalty to the state go? For me, it was terribly ominous to cross the old border during our advance in 1941. Nevertheless, I had to publicly thank God for our progress. I was appalled by what the Germans were doing down in Europe, but I still had to pray for our comrades in arms. Then in 1943, I was convinced that we had to make peace in order to save whatever could still be saved. But as a chaplain I was nevertheless required to do my best to instil courage and optimism in boys being sent straight to their deaths by the men commanding the army, who could see everything was going to hell but still didn't have the guts to start negotiations."

The genial Fredrik Berg has set his jaw and doesn't look at Petter. His expression says it doesn't matter to him in the least what Petter thinks. But Petter has straightened up and seen a community of thought. "You mean you sympathized with the peace opposition? So did I." They turn and stare at each other with real pleasure. What good luck that they've been placed in adjacent parishes! Two young priests with such similar values! They talk at length and from the heart about the war and the terrible choices Finland faced, and about their own agony. It is almost unbelievable that now, after all of that, they sit and speak openly in a free country, when things could have turned out so very much worse! They talk about the everyday happiness of living in peace, with young families and realistic hopes that their lives will get much better.

As regards the larger situation of the church, they cannot avoid talking about the increasing secularization and godlessness and, almost with nostalgia, about the powerful trust in God that people felt during the war — so quickly pushed aside in the material strivings that have followed it. But here, alone together and in almost identical circumstances, they can put such thoughts to the side and speak instead of the pleasures of peace and the joy of believing in the future.

The advantage of being an island priest is that you control your own time and can make up neglected duties later. Petter will return to the Örlands with Post-Anton that evening, so they have the whole day to themselves. The early summer weather is beautiful. They take a turn to the parsonage and have afternoon coffee, then out again and have time to wander across all of Mellom while they continue their conversation and lay the basis of a lasting friendship. When they were in school, Fredrik would have been an older boy with the right to snub and make fun of a little kid like Petter. But childhood comes to an end. As adults, they can be equals, share experiences, discuss career, family, life, books, open themselves without being mocked or isolated.

Perhaps Fredrik is not always so pleasant and full of smiles. When they stop by the parsonage, his wife says, "It's nice to see that Fredrik's found a friend and colleague he can talk to."

"And that I have a colleague like the priest at Mellom!" says Petter warmly. "I feel much better knowing we can talk on the phone any time we like. I think I'm going to need that."

"It's so far to the dean that we'll just have to get along without him. So here and now let's create our own Archipelago Deanery. We'll confer and make our own decisions. What do you say?"

"Brilliant!" Petter agrees. "We're going to have to elect you dean for the time being — until I've grown into my clothes a bit and can run against you."

They laugh, two rogues who have found a means of diversion, and Fredrik's wife looks a bit less nervous, as if she knows that she won't be criticized when Petter has gone. Now the two men go out for another walk and manage to cover the Mellom pastor's entire domain and all its villages and harbours, woods, hills, and beaches. All the same, not as pretty as the Örlands, Petter thinks, with considerable secret pleasure. He delivers his thank-yous with warmth and sincerity, asks the children to forgive him for monopolizing their father all day, assures Mrs Berg that he will long remember her hospitality with deep gratitude. It's hard to know when Post-Anton will appear, but he means to go down to the dock and read the newspaper until the boat arrives, for it's now high time for life in the parsonage to return to normal!

Fredrik would like to go with him to the dock and sit there all night if it came to that, but he has office work to do, and when he's at home it's his job to read the children their bedtime stories. "Now don't forget that we're going to stay in touch," he admonishes Petter almost anxiously.

Giddy from all this friendship, Petter wanders down to the steamboat dock. It's already getting colder, and naturally he forgot his sweater on the boat. Before sitting down in the lea of a boathouse wall, still warm from the sun, he stands looking out to sea, white as ice in the failing light. There are streaks of gold, violet and black in the sky, and they draw grooves of darkness and gold across the smooth surface of the water. It is utterly quiet, if by silence we mean the absence of human activity. Far out, there are strings of eiders clucking and ah-oohing. As if the entire space before him was actually populated by powers and spirits alongside those that are visible.

Post-Anton comes precisely when he sees in his mind's eye that the priest, whose sweater is lying on the hatch cover, has begun to shiver and wrapped a newspaper around his shoulders. Petter hears the thumping of the diesel for quite a long time but thinks it's a larger boat farther out. He stands up to look, and it is Anton, now with passengers on the boat and a lot of freight that he's picked up in Degerby for the Co-op. The passengers have climbed down from the Stockholm boat in the Degerby roads and are on their way home to the Örlands after spending all winter in Sweden. They are talking and laughing, full of anticipation, and the priest is finally a minor figure in the crowd. No chance to continue this morning's conversation with Anton, and that may be just as well. On thinking it over, he realizes that it dealt with experiences for which he has not quite got the words.

Chapter Eight

THE PASSENGERS IN POST-ANTON'S BOAT are a sign that the summer season has begun. The priest is right that his congregation now has other things to think about. By comparison with the newcomers, he is already naturalized, a familiar figure on his bicycle and in the pulpit. Everyone greets him heartily, but conversations are brief. The hay is what everyone thinks about now, hoping they'll get enough rain to keep the grass from burning up where it stands and that it will then stop raining so they can get it in before it mildews and rots. They present their wishes clearly, and of course their priest knows enough to stand in the pulpit and pray for good weather and the growth of the soil.

The crops are of great interest at the parsonage as well. The pastor's wife is especially attentive. She grasps things quickly and is aware that out here you have to fight for every blade of grass if your cows and sheep are going to have enough fodder to get them through the winter and spring. For the moment, her crew of animals is doing well. Goody has produced a heifer that they mean to keep, and Apple has had a bull calf that they'll fatten over the summer and slaughter in the autumn — cash in hand plus a little meat. After the calving, the milk and butter situation is brighter, and Mona cranks the separator happily, saves the cream and churns it while the family drinks buttermilk and skimmed milk and soured milk. She looks forward to the haying, a clean, fresh outdoor labour at the prettiest time of summer. She and Petter working side by side to produce visible and lasting results. It smells good, and it is very satisfying to fill the barn with good, fresh hay while threatening rain clouds line up in a row.

It is always a mistake to anticipate pleasure, because naturally she and Petter are not left to work in peace. Even before midsummer, the first small sailboats arrive from Helsingfors. During his school years, Petter looked on people with the flag of the Nyland Yacht Club on their boats as indescribable snobs and bullies, but when they glide in to the church dock to tie up and jump ashore in their white sailing trousers, they are pleasant and talkative and full of admiration for the beauty of the journey and of the Örlands. Of course they are welcome to tie up at the church dock, it's a pleasure to have them! And yes indeed I'll show you where the well is. They invite him for coffee in the cockpit and are neither scornful nor pitying when he turns down the cognac. Together, they celebrate the fact that they can finally move about freely and sail among the islands again. While they're talking, another boat sails into their little bay, and they call from one to the other. The new arrivals sit on the edge of the dock and are given a mooring brandy. Lovingly they look at their boats and trade survival stories — how close the boats came to being destroyed in some bombardment, how sadly leaky and corroded they were when they could finally begin to restore them, the sails mere mouldy rags. How hard it was to get hold of what they needed. Who'd have believed you'd have to buy linseed oil and varnish and canvas on the black market? They exchange the names of dealers and contractors while they caress the railings and admire the shiny hulls, red as gold in the evening sun.

A couple of them even go to church on Sunday and sit there benevolently, like white men among the natives. After the service, they talk with the pastor about the local sights, and before he knows what's happening he has agreed to give a guided tour after lunch. True, he and his wife usually rest for a while on Sunday afternoons, the only day of the week they have the chance, but he can make an exception. They will enjoy themselves, he assures them. "I rarely have time to get away, and I'm as eager as you are to see everything!"

It really is a great pleasure to show them around. The distances are not as small as people tend to believe when the see the Örlands as a collection of fly specks on the map. It takes half a day to see Church Isle and the hills west of it with their stone labyrinth and ancient hiding places from pirates and Russians, their newly excavated bronze-age settlement and, as a contrast, their recent artillery emplacements blasted out of solid rock for the Continuation War. Also the greatest sight of all in the eyes of the Örlanders — the little lake in its crater of grey granite that all visitors must be dragged out to see. "All fresh water, all the way down!" the Örlanders explain proudly, blind to the whole great sea which lies heaving all around them, even in the calmest summer weather, and which is the source of the sailboat people's enthusiasm. Someone is interested in plants, so they stop to botanize. Yes, indeed, there are a number of odd species to be discovered among the stones! Others look at birds. Someone else recalls the proud history of the Örlands during Prohibition. My goodness, yes! They gaze meaningfully at a couple of the larger houses in the west villages, which can be seen from the hill, and they chuckle.

Several stories suitable for the ears of a pastor make the rounds, about smuggled liquor and restaurants in Helsingfors.

The weather is wonderful, and it's a fantastic luxury to be free from work and out of doors in pleasant company. Looking at the time, he draws a deep breath and declines the offer of an evening snack, says goodbye and hurries home. He can't understand how it's grown so late, and he appears at the parsonage feeling guilty. "Forgive me, I had no idea it would take so long. Has anyone called?"

Mona can put up with the sailboats. It's fun for Petter to socialize with people from Helsingfors, and they're pleasant enough and, on the whole, take care of themselves, stay on their boats, in cabins where they can't stand up straight, sleep in bunks where they can't even sit up, and live on canned goods they've brought with them and on fish and bread they buy in the villages. But all the relatives and friends who come to visit are another thing entirely.

It's no exaggeration to call it an invasion. They come like outright raiding parties, and primarily of course it's Petter's rabble that can't stay away. Petter stands on the steamboat dock and receives them with a warm smile and a hearty welcome, while he timidly wishes there was a custom that required parents to keep their distance during the first few years of a child's marriage. For his part, he takes boyish delight in showing them his church and all the villages and people in his parish, his cows and sheep, his sailing skiff and his nets, but he is keenly aware that Mona is not happy, although she controls herself. "Two weeks!" she cries. What did she expect? That they'd make that long journey merely to turn right around and head back?

"You know they're unpretentious, don't ask for much. They want to get to know Sanna and see how we're getting along.

Mama will be happy to help with the housework if you'll let her."

Mona snorts. As if she'd want to have her mother-in-law pottering around in her kitchen! She cleans frenetically before they arrive, sure that the old lady will criticize and complain about everything that's not absolutely perfect. She'll inspect and examine and scrutinize. Nothing Mona does will be good enough for her eldest, idealized son. Mona is angry, angry, angry before they come, takes Sanna by the arm, hard, "Not a peep!", snaps at Petter when he comes in with water buckets so full they splash over the sides, lies awake at night foaming and steaming. When he's fallen asleep, she lies awake repeating quietly to herself, "And here I'm supposed to be their servant and cook their meals and take care of them from morning to night. Not a moment's peace all day long while you can at least take a rest now and then and have a really good time as their guide in this beautiful weather! And I slave on, have the coffee poured and the meals ready whenever it pleases them to saunter in. All you have to do is sit down at the table. Cook, maid, hired girl all in one, but their chamberpots they can carry out themselves!"

And so on. Her exhaustion black as night. But she also has a motor that shoves her out of bed when the alarm clock rings and it's time to go out to the cows, which have all of Church Isle for a pasture but usually come when she calls. "Come bossy, bossy! Come!" Apple first, the lead cow, ploughing her way through the bushes under protest, gentle Goody in her wake. As a teacher, you can't have favourites, but with cattle it's allowed. Gentle Goody following temperamental Apple because it's her sweet nature.

Cows calm and comfort people, or anyway they do Mona. She milks them promptly, feeling almost happy, talking to them a little when no one can hear. But she hurries — strains the milk, carries the can to the well, peels off her dairy smock on the steps, quickly in through the door. Petter has built a fire in the stove. Sanna is up, they're eating breakfast. Happy, at this stage. Thank God they'll be arriving by cargo boat this afternoon, not in the middle of the night. But they will soon have that experience too, for who arrives in the following wave but Petter's brother Frej and his wife Ingrid. Then a long series of Petter's cousins, and when they've all been placed, yet another one shows up unannounced: "I figured I'd surely be able to find a room in the village in case you have no space for me."

"Church Bay Inn", it should say on the door. "Free food and lodging, first-rate service" in smaller letters underneath.

In a family, there's always something. The worthy Kummels show only a cursory interest in their granddaughter and in Petter's domains. He remembers what he got when he was a boy and showed them something he had made — a pat on the head. They've other things on their minds. They arrived worn and harried, and both of them take him aside for endless conversations he doesn't have time for. Petter is twenty-eight years old but has never yet felt free of his parents. Papa has to be kept in good humour, Mama needs help and sympathy. Now that he's an adult himself, he has to be their marriage counsellor. They're over sixty — in heaven's name, why can't they accept the fact that they're married and stop having all these crises?

They've been belabouring the present problem for years, with all its branches and offshoots. Papa is retired and has gone to ground on Åland with no intention of returning to the schoolhouse on the coast of Finland, which he has come to loathe. Mama stubbornly continues to teach there, despite the fact that she now has the right to retire. He thinks she ought to move to Åland and take care of him. She is hurt that he has abandoned their conjugal home in Finland and allows her to struggle on alone, without his help. Now, when they come out to the Örlands, they haven't seen one another for nine months, and they are not happy to do so now.

Mama suffers from her famous sense of duty, and both she and Petter know how it will end. But not right away. Not with some kind of smiling resignation. First there must be a great deal of talking, sympathizing, commiserating, soothing noises, and the speaking of quiet words of wisdom. While more and more time passes. Mama is aware that Papa, in frail health and completely impractical, will have a hard time getting through another winter alone. "It was awful," she says, "to come into the house and see the way it was, as if he'd been living in a lumber camp. Burned food stuck to the frying pan, indescribable rags in the bed, the whole place messy as a den of thieves, soured milk in the pitcher, everything to make me feel as bad as possible. I know I can't leave him like that for another winter."

Her certainty makes Petter's compromise proposal sound almost welcome. "How about this? You live in peace at the school for one more year. Then you can get your pension and move to Åland. If this is a long, hard winter, Papa can live here for six months, let's say from November to April. The Örlands are still part of Åland, and new faces would make a little change for him. What do you say?"

While Mama is thinking it over, Petter speaks cautiously to Mona, who is surprisingly agreeable. She likes her father-in-law better than her mother-in-law, and why not? The parsonage attracts a lot of visitors, and if father Leonard entertains them, maybe Petter will get a chance to work on his pastoral examination. Papa is immediately keen on the arrangement, always happy to sit down to a good meal. Mama needs to carry on a good deal longer about her duties and about everything she will have to leave behind — relatives, friends and clubs, villages and the landscape itself, Helsingfors with its shops and cultural amenities, but it is clear that she finds the suggestion attractive. Much can happen in a year. Of course she cannot wish that Leonard, sickly, nervous, impractical, might be called to his forefathers, but some great intervention from above is nevertheless not beyond the bounds of possibility, and a year, which has not yet even begun, seems at this stage a satisfying length of time.

With all these complicated negotiations going on, and with all the time-consuming emotions they engender, there is still the hay harvest to plan, in all haste. Mona has been looking forward to it eagerly, under the verger's supervision. The Holmens, who lease one of the church's meadows in the western villages and do a couple of days' work each year in payment, usually get called upon when it's time to make hay. "Of course they'll come. They've been waiting for this since the day you arrived! It's always been done this way." The verger promises to come himself and help with the mowing but is surprised when Petter sticks his head in one evening and suggests the next morning. "This early?" he wonders, almost shocked. "No one starts haying here until sometime in July."

"The sea level's dropped and there seems to be a real high pressure on the way. And Mona says we should cut the grass when it's still juicy and full of nourishment. I count on her completely."

"Well, maybe," says the verger doubtfully. "If you've got enough grass. Here we let it grow as long as it will get, and even then it's barely enough."

When it comes to church customs, the pastor sticks to the local traditions. When it comes to agriculture, he sticks to

Mona. The Örlanders are part-time farmers. In season, the fishing is more important to them. Mona is a farmer's daughter from the grain fields of Nyland. She knows better than anyone on the Örlands when to cut the grass and harvest the crops. For example, her potato tops are plump and ready to blossom when the last of the Örlanders are still planting their last seed potatoes. No one questions her expertise, not even the verger, who is a born traditionalist. On the contrary, he is pleased that there will be no collision with his own haymaking or the Holmens', since the pastor clearly means to have his cut and into the barn before it's time for the rest of them to mow.

The pastor's wife may think that the vicarage's hay meadows are on the small side, with poor soil, but in fact they have many advantages and lie enviably close together on Church Isle. For the villages in general, hay meadows are spread out all over the map. Farmers have their land in the village, in outlying fields, and on the larger islands. In some cases, fishermen with one or two cows have no meadow at all but have to gather grass around their cottages and out on the islands where the farmers don't harvest the meagre sedge that grows among the rocks.

Mona gets Petter to sharpen the scythes that evening, and early the next morning the verger arrives and has coffee. Mona goes out to the cows and the men to the meadow, still wet with dew, which is how it should be when the mowing begins. They decide how to proceed. "Best you go in front," says the pastor politely, but before very long the verger gives up. The pastor works like a mowing machine, long sweeping strokes, a supple back, good stride. During the midday meal — pike and potatoes with white sauce, fruit cream — the pastor explains that he used to work as a summer boy on his uncle's farm on Åland. Cutting grass is something he's been doing since he was eleven years old. Naturally he's developed a certain technique.

Mona is never sunnier than in haying season. It's the best time in a farmer's year. The workers need to be kept well fed and in good spirits. But much is done differently on the Örlands. For example, they don't stack the hay on pikes but let it dry on the ground in long windrows, which are turned in the sun till the grass is dry enough to store. If the weather is good, you take in first-class hay with this method, but if it rains and the hay gets turned too many times, its quality declines dramatically. Mona figures that the farmers on the Örlands have transferred their fishing mentality to farming — it's all a question of luck and the weather gods. If the fishing goes well, so much the better. Getting in the hay before it's lost its vigour, well, that's another piece of good luck.

She looks at the pasture grass, where no one has ever sowed a seed of clover or timothy and thinks that drying pikes would stand quite far apart on these fields. But when they've been mowed and she goes out to do the evening milking she is met by a fragrance without compare. "Petter, come here," she calls. "Bring Sanna!" They stand on the steps and breathe. The smell of the grass is strong and sensual. Every plant gives off its aura and essence, building an atmosphere that awakens waves of longing and desire. Sanna sits perfectly still on Petter's arm, and he puts his free arm around Mona. "That there is such a thing in the world!" he says. "I'll put Sanna to bed. Come as soon as you can."

The next morning they decide to go out with their plant book and identify every plant growing in the meadow, but the telephone rings, and a new flock of sailboaters tumbles in. They've sailed all night and are filled with the beauty of the experience. Water, coffee cream, directions to the Co-op, general chatter, it all takes time. Off on errands, but some of the fragrance lingers, reinforced by memory. Every day it changes a bit—more hay, less grass—but what hay! The sea level is still low, the sun shines, there is a light breeze. A dry spell so perfect that Mona ventures out after only two days to start turning the windrows, in the afternoon when the hay on top is completely dry. The windrows are so light and fine that it's a joy to let the breeze help as she turns them with her rake. At times the windrows seem to turn themselves. She walks beside the verger's Signe, who works the neighbouring row. It's not heavy work and they talk as they go, about the animals and their hope that the weather will hold and folks will finish their haymaking well before they start getting ready for the herring fishery. Signe tells her how it used to be, when they all went off to the fishing camps and stayed until well into September. She talks more than she could have in the verger's company, and before the day is over, the hay is turned and the smell has changed—more barn, less heaven. Both of them are pleased and sweaty. "Almost makes you want to jump in the sea, if it weren't for all those sailboats," says the pastor's wife. But Signe says that you jump in the sea if you want to kill yourself. Otherwise you wash in the sauna!

For the next few days, Mona is deeply nervous. She runs around doing her chores and suddenly stops to look at the sky. This strangely beautiful weather can't last, it's only natural for the sea level to rise a bit at the shore, it's starting to get cooler and there are banks of clouds above the outer skerries. Everyone who came to church on Sunday was astonished that the pastor's hay was already mown. If it rains on the hay now, everyone will say that they were in too great a hurry. She passionately wants to show them that this is the time to cut grass, not when the hay is overgrown, and with all her might she tries to keep the clouds away. "Stay out there!" she commands them silently. "Don't you dare come in over these islands!"

The verger, who is her friend and admirer, states with all his authority that the granite is now so warm that the rain will go around it. "Even if it rains at sea, that doesn't mean it will rain on land." He is wise and experienced, no nonsense about God's will. Why would he want it to rain on her hay! She walks down to the meadow one more time to check. If it doesn't rain, it needs only one more day. At least one, because the humidity is higher now and the hay is drying more slowly. She noticed that with the laundry she hung out.

The pastor's wife is far too experienced to hope for beginner's luck, but the pastor is entitled to believe in a miracle. Although a little rain drifts in during the evening and, in mourning, she gives up the hay for lost, there is no great downpour. In the morning there is a damp mist in the air, but no more rain. Towards evening, the sun peeks out, the water recedes a bit from the cliffs, and the breeze freshens and blows away the mist.

Just one day late, they phone for the Holmens and Brage Söderberg's horse, who comes swimming across the inlet behind Brage's boat. "A sea horse!" says the pastor. "Now I've seen everything!" There is a dilapidated hayrack in the parsonage shed, and Brage, aware of conditions on Church Isle, has brought some harness, and soon they have the sea horse harnessed up and ready. Brage cannot stay, but he can see that his horse is in good hands. The pastor handles it well, and his wife chats easily about all the horses she grew up with. Meanwhile, unnoticed, the Holmens have arrived in their boat and wandered up to the meadow with a pitchfork and a rake. They greet the others warmly, and the pastor is once again charmed by members of his congregation. There is intelligence in these two smiling faces and a lively interest in their clear eyes and in the expressive words from their lips.

It goes so well it's as if they had worked together always, with Mona and Tyra raking up and Petter driving and tramping down and Ruben loading. No friendships arise as effortlessly as those formed at work. Like old friends, they throw themselves down by the barn and drink coffee that has stood in glass bottles wrapped in thick wool socks along the south-facing wall. Cheese sandwiches and rolls have been inside in the cool darkness. The food is good, just right for haymakers, and their conversation is just right for four pairs of ears. But of course that's precisely when a couple of the sailboaters come wandering by and ask if they can help. Since the war, the whole country has learned to smell its way to coffee and fresh-baked bread, and Mona has to go back to the house for more cups and to butter some more bread. They certainly don't need their city help. They just confuse things and fail to see what needs to be done. Petter puts them in the haymow in the barn, which is already nearly full, and asks them to tramp down the hay so there's room for more. They're willing enough, but it's harder work than they'd imagined, and sweatier, and itchier, and hard stalks push right through their deck shoes.

Unnecessary extras that need to be humoured. Things never turn out the way you think. The next time someone asks if they don't get lonely out here, they're likely to get a punch in the nose!

She looks around. They're not going to get in all the hay this evening, but if all goes well they can finish the next day. If so, the hay will be of very good quality and will last a long time. They can collect leafy twigs as a complement for the sheep, but leaves aren't plentiful either, and the cows eat the reeds as soon as they stick up their heads.

"The way we have to work for fodder!" Tyra says. "We're so happy to have the church meadow. I don't know how we'd manage otherwise." She tells how they used to go to the outer islands when she was a girl and rake up a little grass here and there. "After Easter, our cow had to eat moss and twigs. Every day Mama went to the barn to see if the cow was still alive." Mona realizes that she's been afraid the pastor and his wife would take back the meadow for their own use, since they've shown themselves to be such serious farmers. And it had been a close call. If the organist hadn't explained that the church meadows beyond Church Isle have always been leased in exchange for work. "There are those who could hardly manage otherwise," he'd said, and the pastor gave in.

Tyra goes on. As nice as the weather is, they'll surely get their grass cut and into the barn before it's time for the fishing. The meadow isn't so big that they'll need to borrow a horse. Ruben can carry it in on his back, she can tramp it down, and the children can rake.

"An admirable desire to stand on his own two feet," the priest says later to the organist, but the organist looks uneasy and says he offered his horse, but Ruben has a hard time accepting help. He'd rather break his back with a tumpline. "The worst part is that everyone needs to get in their hay at the same time. So the fishermen have to wait, and then it starts to rain on the dry hay before they can get it under cover."

Although the pastor and his wife see themselves as small-holders and active farmers, putting new land under cultivation, they have a privileged situation. No matter how collegial they try to be, there is a gap between them and others. They can always fall back on his salary, the others must depend on what a capricious Mother Nature can provide. It sounds cheerless, but in fact the Örlanders are like the fish they catch, quick and glittering. They smile as they talk about the toil of the autumn fishing, how hard they work, how little sleep they get, how exhausted they are. It is something they look forward to as they labour at the haying. The pastor's wife has her hay literally high and dry when the weather grows unsettled and the Örlanders start cutting. Every time Petter has been in the village, she asks him how the hay harvest is progressing. Surprisingly slowly, he has to admit. No one likes haymaking, it's heavy and boring, they tell him, and Mona is amazed. It's fishing that's hard work! Not boring, but still hard. Night work, cold and raw, deadly dangerous in a storm, expensive nets that can drift away if luck is against them.

Yes, but people are full of stories, the fishing is what life is about. It's where they find their identity and their self-image and the pictures that describe their lives. They value variety and risk-taking more than security and routine. Standing on a safe piece of meadow, turning wet hay, is deadly dull. Struggling in rain and wind in an open boat, that's life! You're thrown around like a rag doll, but you come ashore weighted down with herring.

They still come to church on Sundays and make little detours to look at the pastor's well-raked meadows and to peer through the cracks in the overstuffed barn and stare out across the potato patch that seems to flourish somewhere far to the south of the Örland Islands. What they have to say about all of it is not so clearly heard, but when the parsonage cows come strolling along, blooming matrons, they remark loudly that, well, for those who have good grass . . .

For his part, the pastor has paid close attention to the popular mood at the prospect of the autumn fishing and in his sermons makes many allusions to the fishing in the Sea of Galilee and to the fact that the disciples were fishermen, recruited beside their boats. The congregation picture their own shores and boat-houses, and after the service, the former verger tells the pastor straight out that if you didn't know they were Jesus's disciples and became apostles and evangelists, you'd have every reason to think it was very wrong of them to just wander off in mid-season and leave all the work to the poor women and children.

"And the boats lying there to dry out in the sun!" he adds disapprovingly, aware that the Lord moved in a warm, dry climate.

"Yes indeed," says the pastor. "I'm sure everyone on Galilee agreed with you. But that's what's so remarkable about Jesus — that he gets us to drop everything and follow him."

Silently, to himself, he's thinking what a tough battle it would be if Jesus were to appear and ask Mona to abandon everything and follow him. Petter could burst out laughing when he thinks how successfully she'd struggle. "Impractical," she'd call him, with reason. "Visionary. Dreamer." And Petter himself, trying to mediate between them, with nothing but weak arguments in both directions.

He's in the process of acquiring a little kingdom on earth, with brimming barns and root cellars. An example for the parish, which, however, has its eyes firmly on the sea. The Örlanders work hard at the autumn fishing, up before dawn so they can be out at sea when the sun comes up and raise their nets, gut the fish, rinse them, pack them in barrels in neat rows, salt them, then rest in the afternoon, if they have the time, before heading out again with their herring nets. A long trip out to the fishing waters, a long way home. From Church Isle, you can see dark boats far in the distance working their way through rain and waves.

Several people have mentioned how important the church is to them when the weather's bad and it's hard to see. Even though they know the right heading and know where they are, when the church appears on the top of its rocky knoll it's still a reassurance that they're headed right and will make it home this time too.

"Can you explain it?" they say. "When we come to church it seems like she sits in a hollow, but when we're out at sea, we see her up on a hill, as if she were keeping watch. It's like a miracle. She stands up on the hill and looks for us, and when we come up from our boats on Sunday she stands down by the churchyard and welcomes us."

"Like the Holy Mother of God, as we'd say if we were Catholics," he says. "It's a beautiful thought."

"It's not a thought, it's the way it is," the old verger says. He's hurrying after the others, who are on their way to their boats, moving faster than they do in summer. They'll eat and rest and be ready to go out with their nets as soon as the Sabbath is over at six o'clock.

The summer has turned on its heel. The sailboats are sparse in the bay, and one day the last of them has gone. The guests at the parsonage have thinned out too, and soon they'll be alone in the house. She and he and Sanna, who's run wild and been spoiled by all the attention. "Now we'll need to tighten the reins a bit," says Mona, "and pull her back into shape."

Chapter Nine

Still August at its most beautiful, but the evenings are dark and there is a cold breeze. The parish around them is very hard at work, and days go by without anyone setting a foot through the parsonage door. It's quiet at the store and the post office. There is time for heartfelt conversations with Adele Bergman and Julanda at the post office, well-informed and full of goodwill. She knows a lot because she asks questions—for example, if they won't soon be expecting a little one at the parsonage—and she gets him to lay out his Åland family tree back to Adam. In return, she tells him how the fishing is going: not too bad, though the fisherman has never been born who would admit that it's going well. By the middle of September, they should have taken what they need, so they'll have time to salt down their herring and get ready for the autumn market.

The organist has a farm and his organist's salary, so he isn't dependent on the herring catch the way the fishermen are, but he fishes by tradition and so that his boys can earn a little money of their own. He comes rushing to church on Sunday mornings without having rehearsed, his fingers stiff with cold, and doesn't play as well as he does in the spring and summer; this too is a tradition. The congregation yawn and sleep discreetly during the sermon, an indulgence no one begrudges them. Then they fly away in their boats, and the verger is left in the church, pottering about and chatting with the priest, who basks in the peace and quiet like a cat. Young man that he is, surely the rush and bustle of the summer has not worn him out? Of course not, but this calm is now a welcome part of existence. Perhaps he's become too materialistic, he tells the verger, and it's high time he thought about the spiritual side of his work.

But as soon as he says this, he starts laughing and has a story to tell the verger, whose cow grazes on the other side of the narrow inlet separating Church Isle from the main island. "Early this morning I was sitting in the sacristy thinking about my sermon. The light wasn't good, and suddenly it got even darker. I thought the sun must have gone behind a cloud and I looked up at the window. And there I saw a large, dark, unmoving face with big eyes staring straight at me. I was as frightened as a child, and all sorts of thoughts went through my head. I thought of the devil, though I've never imagined him so substantial, and the expression 'God sees you' occurred to me, though I'd never pictured God looking like that either. Staring, dark. Myself, I just stared back, without moving a hair, and then I blinked and looked again. Do you know what it was? It was Gertrude, with her dark face, who'd swum across to Church Isle and now stood there staring in at me through the sacristy window. Probably as terrified as I was, and just as incapable of understanding what she saw."

They both laugh, but the verger is uneasy that his cow has invaded the parsonage's pasture. "She's a dickens of a cow for wandering off," he says. "We've run the fence clear out into the water, but she swims around it, the old devil. I assume Mona sent her packing."

She had indeed. Armed with a big alder switch, she came dashing up and drove the blasted cow back across the island and out into the water. As if it wasn't enough that she had to keep an eye on the tenant farmer's animals, now she's also got the verger's cow to watch. There is nothing to eat on the verger's land, grazed bare, so of course she swims over. And the tenant's cows stretch the barbed wire till it breaks in order to get at some grass, but that's no reason for the pastor's cows to suffer. They've both been properly covered and can now graze on the meadow where fresh growth has exceeded expectations because they cut their hay so early and the dew has been rich and also the evening mist.

It's as if they were closer to the primitive forces of nature out here, and Petter observes that they work in harmony with the primitive forces in Mona, who has acclimatized astonishingly well. If he asks her if she likes it here, she snorts and says she doesn't have time to think about it. She has so much to do, and when you've got a lot to do, you're happy!

Sanna is one and a half years old in September and has started to talk like a grownup. Petter falls head over heels in love. "She says 'summer people', she says 'salt herring'. Isn't that fantastic?" he says. He can't get enough of his daughter, who acts silly and writhes with delight, and Mona gets angry. "Such nonsense!" she says. "Don't encourage her! She has to get it through her head she's not the queen of the castle."

She lifts Sanna from her Papa's arms and Sanna screams and cries because Mama is mad. "Shame on you!" Mama says. "What a way to act! Now you can just sit in the bedroom till you can be good!" She whisks her off and puts her down in her crib with a careful thud. "No one feels sorry for you!" she says. "The way you carry on. Now you can sit here and calm down."

She closes the door and goes back to Petter, who looks sheepish and unhappy. Poor Sanna! She wails in despair. Why shouldn't she be queen of the castle now and then? But he doesn't dare say so to Mona, who is absolutely convinced that children should be kept on a short leash and not allowed to believe that they were put on earth to be courted and indulged. Discipline hurts, but it's necessary if the child is not to become a pest. Sanna has been spoiled by all the summer guests and given an altogether exaggerated sense of her own importance. They have to take that out of her.

Mona gives her husband a piercing look. "It's high time she had a little brother or sister, so she's not ruling the roost alone!"

They've talked about it before and considered and planned. The best time for a new baby would be after the haymaking, when the worst of the work has been done and it's still summer and warm. The end of July, to be exact. She counts on her fingers. "Middle of October. We can start then."

She makes it sound like one more job, but she looks bashful and turns away, puts her hands to her face and smiles between her fingers. He's up from his chair and takes her in his arms. She writhes like Sanna. "Not yet! First two weeks of pastoral work till late at night."

This is the way the pastor and his wife practise birth control. Work their heads off so they get to bed very late and then collapse as if they'd been clubbed. And in the day, anyone at all can walk in at any time, which promotes abstinence and chastity.

* * *

The time is well chosen. The herring market in Helsingfors begins the second Sunday in October, and large portions of the congregation head off well in advance. The last Sunday they're at home, many of them come to church. It's like a thanksgiving celebration for the completed fishing season. The pastor prays for those travelling to the market, and they sing a hymn about the changing seasons, "As Transformation Overtakes the Brightest Summer Day". You can hear that the voices are hoarser and less exuberant than they were in the summer. The wind roars in the roof, and draughts make the candles flutter. Mona has put clusters of rowan berries in the altar vases since there are no longer any flowers. When the congregation heads off for home, the following wind is so strong that the boats' exhaust fumes blow forward. When the verger has gone, they're alone. For three weeks, so many people are gone that it no longer pays to plan gatherings of any kind. Complete tranquillity reigns.

They look at each other and then look away. He stretches out his hand, and she backs off. She takes Sanna by the hand and walks with small birdlike steps. He follows closely, gently exultant, his body as warm as liquid bronze despite the storm. Into the parsonage, off with his kaftan. And?

Barely past noon. Potty time for Sanna. Sunday lunch on the table. Petter can hardly stand to watch the spoon going in and out between his wife's lips. Sanna fusses. She's usually so good and now she's difficult, whining and complaining for no reason. He doesn't want to hold her, even though she's reaching out for him in tears. Mama takes her arm hard. "Now you be quiet! Time for your nap!"

Normally, Sanna takes a good long nap in the great quiet of a Sunday afternoon, but getting her to fall asleep today is like pulling teeth. She bounces up and down in her crib and cannot rest. Mama gives up trying and goes out to the kitchen to wash the dishes. "Let her fuss for a while," she says to Petter, who throws himself down with a three-day-old newspaper and tries to read. When it's quiet in the bedroom, he looks up. Mona looks out through the kitchen door and stands still, listening. "I'm just going to . . ." she says, finish up, or whatever it was she meant to say, but just as he hears her throw the dishwater quickly into the slop bucket, Sanna gives a howl from the bedroom. There doesn't seem to be anything wrong with her, except that she senses that they desperately want her to fall asleep. And sleep long and deep. Not on her life!

It gets later and later, and for the first time ever when Sanna doesn't want to take her nap, Mama gives up. Mama always wins, but now she looks at the clock and goes into the bedroom and picks up Sanna from her crib. "If it doesn't suit you, then you can just please stay awake until tonight!" she says angrily. "Otherwise you'll never get to sleep this evening!" Sanna hiccups from fear. When Mama is this angry, knowing a lot of words and whole sentences doesn't help. The only thing to do is cry, and Papa has taken shelter and pretends not to hear.

Sanna, usually so bright and curious, always finding something to do, is now nothing but unhappy. Tired, despondent. When it looks like she might be wilting, sitting on the floor and rubbing her eyes, Mama gives her a shake. "It was you who wanted to stay awake, little lady, so now just be so kind!" she says. They drink their afternoon coffee, and Sanna won't drink a drop of milk or chew on some bread, she just sobs. The evening is so far off that it's hard to imagine the day will ever end. Mama is mad and in a terrible mood and Papa doesn't dare say a word.

"Do we really want another one?" she says to him. He laughs timidly, cautiously, maybe not understanding what she means any better than Sanna. Only that she's angry and won't ever forgive her for not taking her nap.

Then finally she goes out to do the milking, and Papa takes Sanna in his arms and they read the paper together. Much has happened on Åland and in the world, and Papa's voice rumbles so pleasantly when she leans her head against his chest. She almost falls asleep, but then Papa moves and says, "Well, well, Sanna, we'll eat as soon as Mama comes back, and it's a good idea for you to stay up. Then you can go to bed right after supper."

He says it nicely, but she is so tired that she starts to cry again, and he's sorry. "Sweetheart," he says. "Darling girl. Believe me. This will pass. Tonight you'll sleep like a log and tomorrow morning you'll be happy again. Come, we'll get everything ready so we can eat as soon as Mama comes in."

They go to the kitchen and Papa puts water in the saucepans and gets the fire going in the stove, and then he sets the table. There's fish soup to warm up, and he slices the bread and puts out the butter and sets out plates and silverware and glasses and Sanna's cup. Mama should come now, but she doesn't, and again they don't know what to do. Papa can't leave Sanna alone in order to go out and see what's keeping her, and if he takes her along on his arm, Mama will be angry because she's crying.

They wait, Papa more nervous that he will admit, and finally she comes. Rips open the door, closes it with a bang. Clatters angrily with the milk cans, tears off her coat, slams her boots against the wall. Papa looks cautiously into the hall. "What's wrong? We started to worry. I would have come out, but . . ."

"Confounded cows! First I couldn't find them anywhere and they didn't come when I called. I was up on the hill to see if I could spot them, and then I went down towards the tenants', and that put me in such a rage I almost had a heart attack. This time it was our cows that had flattened the fence and gone over to their cows. Wretched animals! As if they didn't have good grazing on our own meadow even after we cut it, at least compared with the tenants. Their cows are grazing on bare rock. And I had to go in and beg their pardon. You can't imagine how painful that was. Here I've complained to them so, because they let their cows come over to us, and now it was ours that went over to them. You can imagine how smug they looked! I could have . . . Anyway, I chased them out of there quick as a wink, and when we got to the milking place, Apple wouldn't let me tie her up. She balked and knocked into Goody, who also started to run away. If I'd had a gun, Apple would have got a bullet between the eyes! I'm not going to put up with it! Tomorrow I'm putting them in the barn. They've been out too long already, and we've got plenty of hay. You'll have to fix that fence the first thing you do in the morning!"

All the pastor can manage is an occasional "Oh my." Sanna sits paralysed on his arm. "Supper is ready to eat," he says timidly. "The soup is warm. Come in and sit down and catch your breath. You must be done in."

She gives a loud snort. Clearly she's not going to calm down right away. She's going to be angry all evening, it's going to be awful. She's been out so long that it's already pitch dark. The oil lamp stands cosily on the table. Within its cone of light, a little family could be happy together. But not tonight. Mama gives in and takes her place at the table, and Papa serves the soup and tries to feed Sanna. He spreads the soup thin in the bowl to let it cool, but it's still too hot when he tries to give her a spoonful and she jerks her head aside and hits the spoon. "Oh no! Sanna!"

Mama flares up. "Hush! What is all this constant whining! You're impossible! Stop it!" She jumps up and grabs a dish cloth, wipes up the soup with big swipes of the cloth, swiping Sanna's face as well, who is now wailing. There is nothing here for a natural conciliator like Petter Kummel to do, only draw in his head and hope that the storm will pass.

"Now eat!" Mama commands. She shovels soup into Sanna, who doesn't dare do anything but swallow. Papa can see that she'll throw up before the evening is over. The day that began so well with church and best wishes for a good journey for those travelling to market has gone off the rails and overturned in a ditch. Sanna is the scapegoat, just one and a half years old, not old enough to understand that she should get out of the way and let her parents reproduce.

Papa stands up and lifts Sanna from the table. "I'll go and put her to bed, and then I'll wash the dishes. Just sit and rest for a few minutes. Have you even opened Thursday's paper that came yesterday? Darling, don't be so angry."

Mama stands up also and snatches Sanna away from him. "Potty! And then she has to be washed! Put her to bed, indeed!" she snaps.

In fact, Papa knows the routine, but when Mama is mad he suffers a kind of paralysis and loses a good deal of his common sense. "I can do all that," he says.

But just as Mama taught Apple and Goody a lesson earlier this evening, she must now teach Sanna a lesson as well. Nothing is easy. She demands submission, but neither of them knows how. Papa sits in the parlour and pretends to be deaf while Mama is severe with Sanna, who tightens up and produces nothing in the potty and who screams and struggles when she's washed and sure enough throws up on the kitchen rug.

"Yuck!" Mama cries. "For shame Sanna! What a mess!"

Papa looks in horrified. "How's it going? Can I help?"

"Stay away!" she shouts, and Sanna's defender retires. She is alone with a force of nature that Papa sometimes tenderly calls his wife. Her distress is stretched to its absolute limit before she is finally dumped into her slatted crib. The pastor advances to perform his calling and read the evening prayer, but he is sent away. Mama delivers a "Now I lay me down to sleep" as if it were a call to battle, and rounds it off with "Not a sound! Now go to sleep! Good night!"

Blows out the lamp, leaves Sanna in the dark and goes. There's a light in the parlour, and Sanna can hear them talking, but she is utterly forlorn and cries and cries. Then falls asleep.

So the pastor's wife is hardly in the mood, and the pastor feels inhibited and inadequate. Still, he wants to show his goodwill, so he puts his arm around her shoulders and tries to turn her towards him. She pulls free energetically and snorts as only she can. "After a day like this, it'll be exegetics for you," she says. "And a letter to dear mother," she adds sarcastically. "And I need a bath. Where will I find the strength to deal with it all?"

Now is not the time to say that if anyone can find the strength, it's she. He wishes he had some errand in the village he could retreat to. A sudden call to a deathbed or some other watertight reason to disappear. Too late, it occurs to him that he could have started doing the dishes while she put Sanna to bed. Now she's already in the kitchen, banging around, the door closed to the hall and his study in order to save heat. No fire in the study, where it's a bit cold and raw, but at this late hour it doesn't make sense to build one. Shivering, he sits down at his desk, his books within reach, church law completely lacking in insights into the vacillations and miseries of ordinary human beings.

There is reason to fear that the whole reproductive scheme will get badly sidetracked, but fortunately the couple's youth makes it possible for them to make a sudden change of course. A night's sleep works miracles, and had it not been for Sanna's waking up early, something might have happened that very morning. Sanna has a baby's short memory and wakes up free of last night's abysmal unhappiness. She smiles and coos when she sees her beloved idol and says "Papa morning" and, for the sake of fairness, "Mama morning". She is happy and good all day and falls asleep that evening without a murmur.

So the pastor and his wife lift her slatted crib into the study and return to the bedroom. "Wow, it's cold! Get in quickly! Oh, your feet are freezing."

While the market folk are away and the Örlands catch their breath after all the hectic activity, the parsonage is steaming hot. Mona's passion is as powerful as her rage, and Petter has good health and staying power. Even before the market boats have returned, weeks later, the pastor's wife can say with certainty that she is with child.

Chapter Ten

BY THE TIME THE MARKET TRAVELLERS RETURN, autumn has taken a great leap forward. They have done well. Post-war Finland cries for salt herring, hazelnuts, wool yarn, everything. Lovely wads of cash warm their breasts, the men are dressed like gangster bosses, with padded shoulders and, here and there, the gleam of a new gold tooth. The children's cheeks are puffed with goodies, the women have dress fabrics spread across their kitchen tables, scissors poised hesitantly above the patterns pinned to the material. There are new oilcloths, cooking pots, two or three battery-driven radios, shiny shoes, winter coats, nylon stockings. Solvency soothes them, the fishing is over, there is no rush.

He sees new sides of his beloved parish constantly, so many expressions on their graphic faces, so many words in their mouths, the pastor takes joy in every reunion. People stay ashore and are sociable and content and go happily to parties and Bible study in the villages. The Public Health Association holds a members meeting about the Health Care Centre, which will be built partly with donated money, partly with the labour of the Örlanders themselves. The membership consists of the pastor (chairman) and Irina Gyllen (secretary) plus thirty members, most of whom are also members of the local council and the vestry. Among them are the organist and Lydia Manström and a carefully balanced selection of worthy persons from the two halves of the community. Plus the manager of the Co-op, Adele Bergman, a key figure as the person who requisitions building materials and furnishings.

The organist has told him that the two blocks are equal in strength. The priest himself and Doctor Gyllen are the wild cards. Before the meeting starts, the villages count their troops and a noticeable unrest is discernible. The east villages have fifteen members present, the west villages the same. Doctor Gyllen will vote strictly in accordance with the best interests of the Health Care Centre, not specified in advance, while the pastor is thought to lean towards the west on account of his close friendship with the organist. If both he and Doctor Gyllen vote on the west side, things will go badly for the east villagers. Gustaf Sörling is seen to stride to the telephone, turn the crank and ask to be connected to Erik Johansson, the only member of the steering committee not present. Something that sounds like an order is discharged into the receiver. Gustaf Sörling rings off and walks to the rostrum, leans forward and wonders if the meeting might be delayed for a short time so that Erik, who's had some trouble with his horse, can get to the meeting.

"Yes of course, by all means," the pastor says, knowing that everyone will welcome the opportunity for further intrigue. It takes a good long time for Erik Johansson to appear, wearing a suit jacket thrown over everyday clothes, and with a bad cold. He slinks in on the east side and gets his instructions from Gustaf Sörling, who then nods to the pastor.

He looks out over the assembly. They are all of them older than he, and they know how everything is to be done, but they look at him with friendly faces when he sits down at the table and thanks them for their trust. "We are all friends here," he says, "so just tell me if I make a mistake or miss something important." He turns to Doctor Gyllen. "The key person sits right here. We can count ourselves fortunate to have our real expert on hand. Doctor Gyllen knows better than anyone what the Health Care Centre should include in order to serve its purpose as effectively as possible."

"It is a great help that our foremost donator is also doctor," Doctor Gyllen says. "He has sent a drawing. I send it around. We see here thoughtful plans. Practical. First floor — hallway, two small patient rooms. One examination room. Small operations can be done. Larger if crisis. School health care, vaccinations, doctor. Little kitchen for sterilizing, maybe cup of coffee to pep up. WC. Upper storey — office space. Small kitchen, WC. Flat for nurse. Cellar — furnace room, large kitchen for cooking food. Dressing room. Storage room. WC, sauna, laundry. Well planned. I recommend."

The drawing is passed around. Like a whole little hospital, unbelievably well equipped. What a fantastic thing for the whole community! Everyone agrees on this, and it is a happy thought that a part of the cost will be borne by the Örlands' own successful son.

Adele Bergman studies the drawings with particular interest. The financing is all arranged! she thinks triumphantly. Cooperative Central in Åbo will now get an order that will shut their mouths. Calmly, slowly, methodically, she will call in her order, then complement it with a neatly typed list, sent by post, detailing each item. The largest order ever to come from the Örlands. Yes, we're building a Health Care Centre out here. Cement mixer, cement, bricks, sheet metal, lumber — for starters. "Yes, a cargo boat will be hired and sent to collect the materials when they're ready. Thank you! Goodbye." Sweet.

"I venture to say", she says solemnly, unable nevertheless to suppress a smile, "that as far as the Co-op is concerned we will manage the requisitions and deliveries. We can handle most of it through the Co-op Central Office. We have contacts for the remainder. The most important thing right now is to form a building committee to find a contractor in Åbo or Mariehamn who can estimate our materials requirements and oversee construction. That we can do with our own labour, with the exception of a plumbing contractor who knows central heating and can lay water lines and water closets."

The members look at each other in wonderment. Central heating! Water closets! Uttered calmly by Adele Bergman as if they were the most ordinary things in the world. She ought to be chairman, the pastor thinks. What a woman!

"Thank you," he says. "It is reassuring that we have Mrs Bergman's expertise and business contacts to fall back on. The next step is to establish a building committee. You, my friends, know much better than I who among you has the necessary experience and is best suited to be on the committee. I call for suggestions. Or, ah, perhaps we should have an informal discussion first."

He has noticed a meaningful glance from the organist. He and Adele Bergman are in a huddle — the two of them have long been in general agreement on communal issues. The organist has a seat on the Co-op's steering committee and both of them are members of the vestry. The organist is also on the local council. They confer quietly for a moment. A certain uneasiness spreads through what the pastor now knows to be the block representing the east villages. Sörling clears his throat. "Mr Chairman!" Petter nods.

"I would like to point out that in this community we strive for a fair distribution of representatives from the two halves of the parish." The east block nods and murmurs its agreement.

"A commendable goal. You need only make nominations. The usual thing is a committee with four members. And in cases where the vote is two against two, the chairman has the deciding vote." He looks around. His friend the organist looks pained and asks for the floor.

"Mr Chairman. In this case we need to think first and foremost about competence. On the western side we have Fridolf Söderström who has worked as a carpenter in America. He's just the man. As is Brynolf from Udden, who has built houses and fishing boats. Anyone who wants can go out to Udden and look at the house he built there last year."

"That's two," says Petter in his innocence.

"Mr Chairman!" says Adele Bergman. She looks the way she looks when she takes Holy Communion — someone has to. "Most of all we need a chairman for the building committee. Our excellent organist has been foreman for the construction of both the Co-op store and the Coast Guard station. I nominate him."

The organist looks pained. "I understand the viewpoint of the east side. Let us first hear their nominations. They have good candidates."

The pastor notes that the east villagers are not impressed by the organist's magnanimity. The word "tactic" is perhaps included in their muttered discussion. "Mr Chairman!" It is Lydia Manström, their designated spokesperson. "I nominate Gustaf Sörling and Håkan Ström. Sörling has been active in local government for many years and is very experienced. Ström is known as a good builder and shipper. We have here an excellent candidate for chairman and a committee member with a strong practical bent."

"Second," says the whole east block and the organist. The pastor looks at him furtively. "Are there other nominations? . . . No? . . . Yes? Please go ahead."

It is Gustaf Sörling himself. "I nominate Viking Holm. A relatively new force on the council who has already demonstrated his abilities."

The entire east side says "Second!" A certain unease is visible on the west side, which puts its heads together. The pastor has a sense of the situation. If the west side splits its votes among three candidates and gives too many votes to one of them without calculating in advance how many votes each candidate should get, the east side, with disciplined voting, has a chance of electing three candidates. Coup! A dilemma. The pastor proposes a recess and then a vote by secret ballot. Everyone agrees. The west side gathers quickly at one end of the schoolroom and the east side at the other while the pastor and Doctor Gyllen prepare the ballots at the speaker's podium.

They smile at one another. "You know what will happen?" Doctor Gyllen asks.

"Two–two," the pastor mutters. "In this case, the best solution. All the candidates are qualified."

"I hope. Was worse when they chose the site. Then was war."

The pastor sniffs. "The east side won, so that's where we'll build. The organist seems to think it best that the chairman of the building committee should come from there."

"He is right. We shall see. We're ready."

The pastor looks out across the gathering. Both camps still lively, but there is more structure on the east, where Gustaf Sörling looks to be giving directives. The pastor clears his throat, taps gently with the gavel. "Hello, everyone, we're ready to get started. Each person will get a blank ballot on which to write the name of your candidate. Then fold it and give it to Doctor Gyllen, who will put them in the basket. As you can see, it's empty."

Everything properly done. The names are written, placed in the basket, which the pastor then empties demonstrably, showing it to be empty. He and Doctor Gyllen put the ballots in two piles and count them. Eastern discipline is exemplary — of their fifteen votes, six are for Sörling, five for Ström, and four for Holm. The western ballots are less carefully thought out — seven for Fridolf, four for Brynolf, four for the organist. Sörling, Fridolf Söderström and Ström are elected. A second round of voting for Holm, Brynolf, and the organist. The easterners sense victory, since Holm will get fifteen votes and beat Brynolf and the organist, who will divide the votes on the western side. But the organist asks for a recess and whispers an urgent appeal to the westerners. There are visible protests, even anger, and the pastor's young ears pick up Adele Bergman threatening to turn in a blank ballot. But when the votes are counted, the east side is silenced. Fifteen for Brynolf, zero for the organist.

Now the chairman's vote will decide. The pastor would love to object that he is too young and no match for this clever gathering, but he does not dare to show the slightest uncertainty. Above all, he must not look at the organist to seek confirmation. If he does that, he'll have the east side against him forever. He smiles, sunnily he hopes. "Here I need the help of King Solomon. We have two good candidates with practical experience. If we view the thing positively, we get a good outcome however we decide. On the negative side, a good candidate will be eliminated whichever way we vote."

A whisper of goodwill is heard through the room, and Doctor Gyllen, who has been sitting straight and attentive, smiles a little. He goes on. "In this case, we should perhaps consider the balance between the villages, since both will provide labour." He smiles. "And Brynolf really did receive massive support in the second vote. So I will award the chairman's vote in favour of Brynolf Udd. Let me congratulate the elected members of the Health Care Centre's building committee — Gustaf Sörling, Fridolf Söderström, Håkan Ström, and Brynolf Udd. They may now choose their own chairman among themselves."

The assembly erupts into life and clamour. If there is anything they love it's strategic voting. Even though the committee is going to select their own chairman, everyone gets involved body and soul in speculation. The organist, who arranged to get no votes for himself, is now heard speaking out for Sörling, which upsets several people on the west side. "Fridolf possesses enormous practical knowledge that he ought to be allowed to use," the organist explains. "Sörling is a politician. Let him struggle with the paperwork. A world of accounts and disbursements that Fridolf won't have to deal with. Sörling likes being chairman. And the east villages win a prestige victory, which we can turn to our credit at some later date."

The pastor and Doctor Gyllen listen discreetly and exchange a quick glance. The pastor waits until he can catch the organist's eye and nods imperceptibly. If it is possible for Doctor Gyllen to have roses in her cheeks, they appear as tiny pink suggestions above her cheekbones. The pastor himself is noticeably amused and interested. He turns to Doctor Gyllen and says out of the corner of his mouth, "We'll vote for Sörling?" She nods. Done. Then they remember at the same time that the voting will be internal, limited to the newly elected building committee members, and they both burst out laughing. Quite suddenly they are as deeply engaged as the villagers, in a matter they have no say in. Still, everyone hopes that the members of the committee have listened to the arguments on both sides.

"Now then," the pastor says. "Has the building committee reached a decision about a chairman?"

"Yes. Sörling has had three votes, Fridolf one. Sörling is elected." There is a buzz in the gathering. Before heading out into the night and the darkness, Fridolf feels compelled to make a statement. "Sörling knows this stuff," he begins generously, but it's too painful, and he continues: "And if he's occupied with his papers at least I can work in peace!" Everyone laughs, even Sörling chooses to laugh. Fridolf glances around triumphantly.

"Excellent," the pastor says. "My friends, I think we've done good work today. We've studied the plans and been inspired by them. And we've elected a competent and effective building committee. At Doctor Gyllen's suggestion, I propose that the steering committee should meet in the near future with the building committee and Mrs Bergman and make some decisions about the next steps to take. According to the bylaws, special meetings of the entire membership can be called when necessary, which I will bear in mind. So I herewith declare the business portion of this meeting concluded."

In cities, everyone rushes for the doors when a meeting is over, but on the Örlands, people stay and talk. And today there is plenty to talk about — their own Health Care Centre and their own share of the construction work. Even Adele Bergman, who otherwise always winds up at the pastor's side, has other things to think about, and for a while Petter and Doctor Gyllen stand by themselves at the speaker's stand, gathering up their papers. Sörling is to have the plans, but for the moment they lie on the table like a bond between them. Over the course of the evening, they have developed an understanding, and now they both look at the plans and smile.

"Another experience richer," the pastor says. "It all went rather well, don't you think? I have to admit that even though

I try to be neutral, I got really caught up. One of these days I'll stand here conspiring with all the other politicians."

"Yes," says Doctor Gyllen. "It pleases me greatly to see freedom of speech used so well." She speaks more fluently now. "And their tactics work well. They chose good people, and a good chairman. Sörling needs to be chairman, otherwise he's difficult. As chairman, good."

"You've come to know them well."

"Yes. And I think they know us better than we think."

The pastor gives an appreciative laugh. "Well put. I'm glad we've had a chance to talk. I know you're very busy with work and studying, but we'll be seeing each other quite often, I think. My wife will be coming to see you soon. We're expecting an addition." He looks a little embarrassed.

"Congratulations," says Doctor Gyllen, neutral but not unfriendly. "I will be happy to see Mrs Kummel your wife."

"Thank you," the pastor says. "She's convinced that it will all go well. I worry more."

The doctor nods. "Many times it is the man who more needs the doctor's help. It is reassuring that Mrs Kummel is not worried. She is young. The second child is easy."

They both look down at the plans. "Just think if the Centre was already built!" the pastor says. "With a delivery room and everything. Now it will be at the parsonage, and that's a long way for you to come."

"I'm sure I'll have ample warning," the doctor says. But she too looks longingly at the plans. "It is difficult in many homes. Small spaces. Hygiene. But healthy surroundings, strong people. I believe you like them very much?"

"Yes," says the pastor, drawing a deep breath to continue, but then Sörling walks up and he switches gears and sticks out his hand. "Congratulations. They made a good choice."

Sörling is in good spirits. "Thank you, thank you. I think we can make this thing work." He too looks down at the plans and smiles.

"We stand here staring at these drawings and can't drag ourselves away," the pastor says. "I'm looking forward to the next meeting when we take the first steps towards concrete action. Mrs Bergman can hardly control herself she's so eager to start ordering. We're all enthusiastic."

"And getting such a big donation! But he knows us and wants us to do the work ourselves so we'll feel the Health Care Centre is really ours."

"He" is the Örlands' famous son, chief physician and professor, member of the Nobel-committee-otherwise-he-would-have-won-the-prize-himself for his epoch-making work on heparin, which is used to treat blood clots and has saved innumerable lives. "Even for a man in his position, that's a very large gift," the pastor says. "I doubt there are many people who remember their native places in such a grand manner."

"He had help," Sörling says, a little barb in his voice. "The teacher took him under her wing, went to Åbo and arranged for a scholarship to the lyceum. Then a scholarship to the University and medical school. He had help the whole way. Others have to make do without."

One of the others is apparently Gustaf Sörling. The pastor chimes in. "Yes, my guess is that there's more talent here than most places. And it's true that all too few get the help they need. Maybe he feels the same way and wants to show his gratitude."

Fridolf has heard the end of this conversation and walks over. "We're from the same family by way of my mother's father's father," he says. "I can tell you from the time he was a little kid you could see he was a different calibre. So there aren't so many of us here who could have done what he's done." His wears his family tree well, and he gives Sörling a kindly look. "We've done well this evening. You can put on a suit and go to Mariehamn and talk to builders. You're good at talking."

"And let's hope you're good at building," Sörling says. "Seeing you've been in America and built things for Rockefeller."

"Yes indeed," says Fridolf. "There have been no complaints about those buildings."

The pastor and Doctor Gyllen gather up their papers and walk towards the western group, where Adele Bergman's voice rings out more sonorously than the pastor has ever heard it, and where the organist can be heard in the background, still under pressure, explaining why he didn't want to be elected. "These are new times, and at some point we have to start thinking more about the individuals than about the relative balance of power between the villages. As it is, we've got the most qualified people, and I've been spared yet another job."

"Well said," the pastor says as he joins the group. "And isn't it fun to spend other people's money for a change. This evening really warmed my heart."

Politely, they turn to him and Doctor Gyllen, who remains a little in the background. No one really wants to go home, not even the pastor, who has the farthest to go. He had to ride his bicycle around the whole island in the pitch dark. Longingly he looks out the window. "If I had my own motorboat it would save me a lot of time."

"Wait till it freezes over," Sörling says. "You'll see what a short trip you have. If it's clear ice, you can skate. Otherwise a kicksled."

"But I don't have time to wait for that now. Brr, it's really cold tonight. Now what did I do with my scarf?" He says good night to those around him and out to the whole room in general, wraps himself up as best he can and goes outside. It is November fifteenth, cloudy, only a couple of degrees above freezing, so dark that he has to stand still for a moment before he can see his bicycle where he leaned it against the corner of the building. The Petromax lamp shines brightly inside the school, but he can't see a thing outdoors. He has to walk his bike through the gate so he won't ride into it. Out on the road, he swings up and starts to pedal, and then the dynamo whirs into life, a scraping sound like a locust. Now he can see enough to stay on the road at least, and thank God everyone has taken in their cattle, so the gates are open and he doesn't have to worry about riding into a cow lying in the road. When he picks up speed and pedals down the east village hills, his own dynamo also kicks in. It spreads warmth and builds a fire under his bass voice so that it starts to sing. He is a vehicle with a motor, central heating, and the radio's evening concert. So equipped, he travels through the night, pleased to be alone, pleased at the thought of arriving home soon to warmth and light.

Chapter Eleven

FATHER LEONARD HAS A HARD TIME tearing himself away,
stubborn as a child at bedtime, but now he's coming. Brings
his bicycle on the boat along with two big suitcases and a
certain method behind the contents, which consist of a great
deal of dirty laundry. Innocently he pours the entire load out
on the floor. Petter is angry but Mona is triumphant—just what
I expected! There is something about Leonard that dissolves
a person in smiles. Mona and her father-in-law are absolute
opposites, but she puts up with him, and he admires her, so it
could be worse. At their very first meal, Petter feels transported
back to the home he believed he had left behind him for all
time. His father talks a blue streak, speaks with authority of
things he knows nothing about and with astonishment about
things that ought to be well-known to him. Meanwhile he eats
methodically, and then comes the formulaic "This was good,
Mother, I must say." Then they all stand up, and father offers
his help by fetching water, taking out the slop bucket, and
carrying in wood. Mona thanks him kindly and says it was nice
of him, because this way Petter can concentrate on his pastoral
dissertation. And it's true that the house seems homier when he
sits in his study and can hear Papa in the distance commenting

on the newspapers while Mona carries on with her work. Maybe it really will work out. He sincerely hopes so.

Leonard spends the night in the preacher's guest room, where he will live until some actual travelling preacher appears. He feels better when he's among other people. When he's alone, his sighs echo through the room and his body tosses and turns on the groaning springs of his bed. Even if he's out of sight, no one can forget that he is a martyr to the rheumatism that makes his jaws creak, and to a bad stomach and to pain between his shoulder blades. That first evening he walks from window to window and notes that you can't see a single light from the parsonage, only the lighthouse, which blinks but bears witness to the presence of no living being.

That makes him think of America and the snowstorms on the prairie. He suggests that they rig a line from the parsonage to the cow barn so that Mona doesn't get lost in a blizzard where a person can lose her sense of direction and location in no time flat. Many people have missed the corner of the house by a metre or so and frozen to death on the prairie, helplessly, only a hundred metres from home. Mona laughs heartily. She thinks it's hilarious to imagine stepping from the parsonage on the Örlands straight out onto the North American prairie. Petter looks at them and thinks that maybe Mama once looked at Leonard the way Mona does now, disarmed and amused against her will. In an absence of filial love that he can't help, Petter sighs much the way Mama did when she was older. But at least he offers him a roof over his head!

He must see to it that his father enlarges his circle of acquaintance quickly, for the little parsonage family is not big enough for his social needs. Petter lets it be known that his father, a schoolteacher, will be happy to jump in if any teacher needs a substitute, and the young people's organizations are tipped off to the presence of a willing lecturer. He goes himself to visit Örlanders with connections to America. It is an effort to visit people here on the islands, but without complaint he rows across the sound with his bicycle in the boat, struggling along against a headwind. Then he sits at farms and talks about America, places and events that mean something only to those who've been there, who've frozen and starved and spoken English.

Winter sweeps in across the Örlands, piles up drifts but sweeps them away again before there's time to shovel. The wind howls around the house, and rugs and curtains flutter. Sanna is dressed in several layers of wool and scratches her legs through her stockings and complains and cries. When she's to sit on the potty, she says she's wearing so many clothes she can't find her bottom. There's a fire in the kitchen stove all day long, and fires are lit in the tile stoves morning and evening. Sanna's clothes are warmed on them before they can dress her. Keeping the house warm is an all-day job and they have father Leonard to thank for it. He's good with fires. The firewood is one of the pastor's payments in kind and has arrived on a cargo vessel. Many of his parishioners are not so fortunate and search the shores for driftwood all year long. The shortage of firewood is a big problem, and most of the farms heat only the main room and maybe one other. The parlour in the parsonage is between the dining room and the bedroom and has to be kept warm for the meetings and functions held there. The study must also be heated, and the guest room.

When the dampers are closed and the tile stoves are warm, the air in the house is fresh and clean and tempers are calm. They have to teach Sanna to stay away from the hot metal parts, but she can sit with her back to the stove and enjoy the warmth, along with the cat. At least once a day, Sanna and

Grandpa wrap themselves up in all their warmest clothes and take a walk on Church Isle. Grandpa talks about the ice freezing and his thoughts rush forward to the spring, when the ice will break up. "A first-class spectacle!" he assures Sanna. "Mother Nature demonstrating her grandeur and power." He doesn't think she understands what he's saying, but how could she fail to understand talk about greatness and might!

She is not allowed to sit on Papa's lap when he's studying or when he's instructing confirmation candidates. The latter turns out to be a great annual delight. The young people of the Örlands have a radiance that no shyness can disguise. They are just entering the most attractive period of their lives, but they are completely unaware of it. They feel ugly and hopeless as they sit there blazing with beauty, glowing with life. They're embarrassed because they're not polished and smooth but can't disguise their charm as they beam and blush. They think everything they say is silly and stupid, although they've already demonstrated their inborn way with words — a dominant gene out here, thinks the pastor, who has read about Mendel and his peas.

Now he's studying the catechism with them, and as he talks and instructs, the girls look at him to show that they're paying attention. But otherwise they look down, for at least half of them are in love with him and will nearly perish of shyness if he speaks to them either before or after the class. Of course they like the pastor's wife, who is nice and gives them hot tea when it's cold out, and the little girl who opens the door a bit and stares at them though the crack is sweet, but imagine if the pastor was single! Imagine if he lived in a cold, untidy parsonage and dreamed of someone who could be his beloved and take care of him and love him for the rest of his life!

Then he might see their blushes for what they are, a sign of ardent devotion. Then he would see the happiness offered him, the boundless love! Now he stands there with his lovely hair and his wonderful eyes and his melting smile, blind as a statue, and comments on the tenth commandment. Thou shalt not covet they neighbour's wife nor his asses or camels, and so on. But not a word about not coveting thy neighbour's husband. Ha! And how dumb does he think they are when he asks, "What is it we mean by 'covet'?"

"That you want something," says one of the boys helpfully.

"Absolutely right. Sometimes it can also mean that a person wants something that he has no right to. Here the commandment helps us to draw boundaries. We should not covet anything that belongs to someone else. In this way, the tenth commandment is a follow-up to the seventh commandment, which tells us that we must not steal. The tenth commandment deals with more difficult and less unambiguous problems. The thief who steals knows that he shouldn't. Legally, theft is a crime. If the thief is caught, he goes to jail. Coveting is not quite so simple. Today, for example, we do not consider a wife in a marriage to be her husband's property, which people did in Moses's day and even later. In modern times, adultery is not punishable by law, unless it leads to violence. Looking at your neighbour's wife with desire is no crime. So why do you think the commandment is still valid?"

Now he's captured their interest. Several of them have something to say, and he waits for a moment. As usual, it's a farm boy who speaks up first, the fisherman boys later, if at all. The girls only if he calls on them. First Ollas's Kalle. "Because it's hard to see where it will lead."

Good. And Grannas's Markus pursues the thought. "If there's a child, you don't know for sure whose it is. Though you can guess." There is murmuring and rustling in the room, as if everyone except the pastor knew of a particular case.

"Yes," he says. "In that case we're talking about adultery that goes badly for those involved and has consequences for others as well. But why does the commandment warn us even against desire?"

He sees that one of the girls gestures as if she wanted to say something. "Yes?" he encourages her. She blushes and looks out the window at snow blowing by in streaks and ribbons. "So that it won't go that far," she says.

"Absolutely right!" the pastor says. "Gretel has hit the nail on the head. We're getting right to the heart of it. The commandments aren't just a long list of prohibitions and don'ts and thou shalt nots that we've heard about no end since we were babies. Most of all, the commandments are about consideration and kindness. If we read on, we see how the Bible continues: 'Ye shall walk in all the ways which the Lord your God hath commanded you, that ye may live, and that it may be well with you and that ye may prolong your days.' On the surface, the commandments are about rules and prohibitions, but deep down they speak of the Divine benevolence that shines on God's children."

Although they're not supposed to, they whisper and talk a little whenever he looks in the other direction. Nothing interests young people as much as the relations between the sexes. Their eyes are wide open, and they feel their way forward. Everything else is unimportant by comparison, old and boring and tedious, a lot of talk, whereas everything about their roles as women and men is a matter of life and death. The catechism speaks as if the only thing that matters is learning to know our saviour Jesus Christ, while the teachers and unwilling students know perfectly well that a good future love life is the only thing that matters. When older people sing "thy eternal bliss", the youngsters sing "thy eternal kiss". They perk up their ears if you say "love" but lose interest if what you're talking about is God's love. It's a paradox that there are Bible classes for people at an age when their thoughts are full of sex, but at the same time you can see the sense in choosing an age when youngsters are most open and unguarded. People experiencing the bottomless despair of youth are prepared unconditionally to throw themselves weeping at the feet of Jesus.

Petter knows that he has priestly colleagues who exploit the depth of emotion and vulnerability of confirmation candidates to extort confessions and decisions that belong in the private sphere, a thing people learn to appreciate with increasing age and experience. In certain quarters, priests go so far as to coax forth statements that they find erotically stimulating. The pastor on the Örlands is on guard against any such impulse. He means to maintain a respectful attitude towards the feelings that run so high in young people.

He thinks about such things as he stands before his clutch of candidates. But most of all he thinks how, after his death, he is going to stand at the pearly gate and argue and plead until they have been let through, every last one!

The pastor's wife wears a sunny smile and is friendly, and none of the girls who curtsey to her dream that she is keeping an eye both on them and on Petter. She looks at the beautiful Örlander boys with their smiles and smooth glances the way she might look at objects in a museum, so little desire she feels for anyone except her husband. It's different for him. He has a tendency to confuse physical desire and spiritual passion. Maybe because they *are* related? But she pushes that thought away quickly. She is attentive to the transition from religiosity to eroticism, whereas Sanna, little as she is, is tempted by the atmosphere in the room and stands stock still, staring through the crack in the door as if waiting for the day when she will belong inside.

Before it got too cold to be in the church, they practised their singing with the organist. The pastor tells them about the hymnal's different sections and their use during the ecclesiastical year. He also lends support to their voices whenever the boys, whose voices are changing, have trouble. This sends a shiver through the girls. His voice is sure and warm and deep and comes from a breast that they would like to lean on. The church smells of cold and damp and naphthalene from the previous Sunday's silk shawls, plucked from bureau drawers. The girls feel lonely and left out during choir practise. The boys disappear up into the loft and take turns pumping the organ while the organist plays. Like all adult work, it is harder than they imagined, and although it looks mechanical it requires concentration. The organist plays as softly as possible and gives them their notes. The girls sing beautifully, the boys drone, and the pastor starts the hymn with his strong voice, "As gleaming pearls of dew . . ."

And so they head home. They say their thank-yous and goodbyes, and in a cluster they wander out to the gate and through it. A few more steps and the boys start to run. Run and compete, punch each other, shout. The girls walk on properly and modestly past the parsonage, then they too run down to the church dock. Some of the boys have been allowed to take boats, space enough for everyone. They arrange themselves by destination, jump into the boats so lightly that they bounce, flywheels turn, the Wickström motors start with a clatter, their exhaust shooting out like white flames. Laughter and shouts as they jostle their way out through the harbour entrance, last man out's a monkey, and at breakneck speed they crowd out into open water and separate, east villagers to the east, west villagers to the west.

The pastor and the organist stand there smiling and watch them go. "Just think if we'd been that free when we were that age," says the pastor longingly. "What would it be like if human life was organized so that we could hold on to youth's passion and boldness even after we'd gained experience and self-control." He turns to the organist. "Were you like that as well, a generation earlier?"

"As far as I remember," the organist says. "But boys didn't get to take the boat, we had to walk and wade and take rowing boats across the sound. It was a real trek. But still fun when we went in a group. On our way to church we were free from our chores and had a legal right to hang out together. We were often glad it was so far. But the pleasures of youth are not shared out equally. It was a heavy trip for those who had to walk alone." Then he adds, as an afterthought, "And what you say about their being so free, we didn't see it that way. And I'll wager they don't, either."

"No," the pastor says. "There's a lot we don't understand until we've lost it. Heavens, I sound like Ibsen." He looks embarrassed, but suddenly the parsonage door opens and Grandpa Leonard and Sanna come down the steps, wrapped up well against the cold. Leonard starts calling and talking from a distance, can't stop the words from tumbling out as soon as he has someone in sight. He talks about the candidates, pleasant youngsters, nice to see young people in good spirits getting along together. "I'm sure these boat trips lay the foundations for any number of marriages," he predicts. "And so they should. What better way to meet than in youth, at Bible study, which is the gateway to life as an adult?"

He appropriates the organist and wanders off with him, the pastor following with Sanna's hand in his. He has devoted himself to teaching confirmation candidates, and they have no idea what they have taught him — to be happy, and quick, warm in body and full of desire. It would be ingratitude without compare not to affirm the freedom in the life he now lives. To experience all this after his sullen, inhibited youth is the very epitome of grace.

PART TWO

Chapter Twelve

When the ice sets, you need to keep your ears open and your eyes on stalks. How the ice freezes, where there are dangerous currents. Which way the wind is blowing. Black streaks for weak ice, green for glass smooth, milky blue like a blind eye for the thin layer above an invisible hole – you need to know how to watch for such things. Obvious things. Always have an ice pike and a knife in your belt. Listen to the way the ice creaks. Don't be timid, because then you'll get nowhere. Don't be foolhardy, because then the ice will swallow you. The water is cold, you know, and deep.

In addition, there is another way of seeing and hearing that can't be explained. It's like seeing and hearing alongside others who have been out there from time immemorial and know everything about the weather and the ice, although they exist in a sphere from which they cannot reach out a hand and call "Beware!" It is you yourself who must listen and see and grasp what they mean. They are there, and their messages and warnings are laid out before you, if only you will see them.

I don't know how it began. When I noticed them. When they noticed me. As I grew up, we were many children and I was almost never alone. But I was only a little thing when I knew they were there. When I went outside, they stood as close around me as my brothers and sisters did indoors. Not unnatural, not supernatural. Just the world as I heard and saw it. They were part of it, nothing more.

When you are a suckling babe, mama's teat is the first thing you know about. The second is the weather. They talk about it all around you all the time. About the outlook, about how long it will last. When it will change. The way the sun goes down in clouds or how, still shining, it sinks straight into the sea and sputters like a fireball. The look of the cloudbanks. How currents of cold air move in. The way heat can stand like a wall, while a storm butts its head against the other side. The way the building groans, which is a sign, and you need to know what they mean by it.

A toddler stands on the steps and holds on, which is all he can do to keep from tumbling over. But he has already learned that what there is outside is the weather. That it's full of messages and warnings. That there are voices and eyes and mouths which you don't see but which you can hear and see within yourself. I don't remember when I became aware of it, it's a thing that was there in me before my memory began to flicker into life. Then I remembered that it had always been so for me.

I was like every other pup of a boy and thought that when people talked about the weather they all meant the same thing I meant. That the weather was the world, and that they were as tight in the world as a hazel thicket whenever there was danger afoot. I remember one time when I was out on the ice as a little boy. I knew suddenly that I needed to get to land as quickly as I could, for they were about to pull the ice out from under my feet. And believe me, the ice broke up behind me as I scurried towards land. But my shoes were dry when I climbed the cliff, and there they knocked me down and smacked me against the rock so hard my whole shank was black and blue. They taught me a lesson that day. You must make your ears hear what they say, although it's not like ordinary talk or the radio or a voice on the telephone.

It is something outside me that speaks to something inside me. And shows me the look of things, though it's not like in a theatre or a movie. Then I know where to go, and the mare that pulls the mail from the ship channel at Mellom knows she can count on me even when the ice is creaking. And when I leave her to walk in to a house on one of the outer islands, she stands quietly on the ice and waits, because even though she's smart and gentle, she doesn't see what I see, and she knows it. They crowd around her and she feels that they're there, but she doesn't know what they mean, and they don't know much about horses. I've learned that from experience.

The thing with them and me is that we have something in common. Although they're no longer like real human beings, nevertheless they once were, and therefore it's possible to understand the signs and warnings they set out. So you can move securely when you use your common sense and watch out for the things they're constantly showing you, in pictures, sort of, or inarticulate sounds. They wake you up, make you lift your chin from where it was buried in your fur collar, and look. They've opened a passage somewhere and send you an echo to prick up your ears. You can make your way through great dangers with the help of such signs.

If you're not receptive to them, you have to cross the ice all alone in the world. Many make it a long way, because the world is not malicious, just heedless. For the world, you're nothing, but human intelligence can bring us safely through great trials. Horses that are taken out onto the seal ice and tear themselves loose, they often manage to make it home as well, though they show their teeth and lay back their ears in pure terror when the ice creaks under them and they set out across green ice. So I say only that it's a help to know about those who surround you when you trot along like a dot on the ice and who keep an eye on you when you stop to rest on a skerry. If you leave bread and butter for them they may even shift the wind behind you. That has happened to me many times.

* * *

When the ice has set, it lies like a floor between the islands. The incessant wind sweeps away the snow, and skates and kicksleds come to life in the boathouses. The pastor too digs out a rusty sledge, replaces a couple of dowels on the chair and screws on the handlebars. With a whetstone he removes the worst of the rust from the runners. The rig is adequate, and soon enough he's kicking his way like a comet across the water world. He gets to the villages so easily and completes his errands so quickly that Mona hardly has time to notice that he's gone before he's already back. The kicksled also serves as a family vehicle. Now all three of them can go to meetings and gatherings. The pastor figures that Mona will sit with Sanna in her lap while he kicks the sledge along, but Mona is very eager to drive the sledge herself. It's hard to get started, but once it's going the sledge sails along in splendid form. Sanna shrieks with delight because of the speed and because she gets to sit in Papa's lap with his arms tight around her. Then they switch, for when they're visible from the village windows, it looks better if he's pushing. On the way home, he kicks more gently while Mona sits with the sleeping Sanna on her lap. The ice is bright from the moon and stars, the islands dark as rain clouds in the rippling light.

The ice is seldom this good, and many are out to try their luck. There is a lot of visiting between villages and there are barn dances on Saturday nights. Everyone is out and about, and darkness doesn't slow them down. There is a party at the parsonage, too. They've had friends on the Örlands since their first day here, there are many to thank for help and advice in word and deed, and it is always a pleasure to see their happy, friendly faces. The organist and Francine, the verger and Signe, Adele Bergman and Elis, and Lydia and Arthur Manström. They always have much to talk about, and with father Leonard in the house, there is competition for the floor. The pastor notes with a certain satisfaction that here he has found, if not his superiors, at least his equals. The talk is as lively as he could possibly wish, and the faces are happy and full of goodwill and interest.

With the extra leaf added, the table has space for all of them. The tea water is singing in the kettle, the china service is for twelve, and Mona's bread, butter, and rolls are worth travelling many miles for. The oil lamp swings gently in the air above their heads, the tile stove spreads warmth. There is a cold draught around their legs, but everyone has had the sense to dress warmly. The door to the bedroom stands ajar, and before Sanna falls asleep she hears Papa's happy, dark voice, Mama's bright laughter, Grandpa's amazement, and the Örlanders' happiest party voices.

They talk about the ice, the winter weather, the newspapers that now come only once a week, if that, and about those who believe they're isolated out here whereas in fact they've seldom had such a merry time. The Örlands might well be called the Society Islands in this blessed condition. Oops. They can't help themselves, they all look at the pastor's wife, who stares into her teacup, the pastor smiles a little, and for a moment, no one says anything. Then they talk about the way consumer goods are becoming more available and actually beginning to show signs of a peacetime economy, about the situation down in Europe and the terrible poverty and want in the German ports that seamen from the Örlands have reported. About the enormous need for aid everywhere, about the Americans who are starting to get their aid shipments organized, although Finland isn't allowed to receive anything by order of the Soviet Control Commission in Helsingfors—may it soon return to its Communist paradise! In any case, all this applies only to official aid, because private efforts and family initiatives are getting America packages all the way out to the Örlands.

"Although it makes you wonder who they think we are," says Adele Bergman. "It's nice to get good soap, but I don't understand why they send those funny little toys that toddlers stick up their noses and the older kids trample to pieces. And those terribly tight-fitting little skirts and blouses—who could possibly wear such things at work? Of course the girls grab them and make themselves look a perfect fright and think they're so modern, but is that what they call aid? We have our own flour and grain and sugar, and anyway it's better for the national economy to buy those things in a store!"

The pastor has an almost irresistible desire to say "Amen" when Adele Bergman has finished. Everything she says is true and right. She is an uncommonly competent woman who ought to be in the government and help build up what the war has pulled down. But hard-boiled as she is when it comes to the economy, she also has a tender heart and a thirst for what she calls a genuine faith. It is for her sake he says grace before Mona serves the tea, and he knows that she is passionately interested in the parochial issues they will unfailingly get into before the evening is over. Arthur Manström is always uncharacteristically quiet during those conversations, and the pastor suspects he is a free-thinker but likes coming to the parsonage for the sake of the intellectual stimulation. Lydia and Adele on the other hand are members of the vestry, as is the organist, and the verger has a fund of practical experience and incontestable knowledge of the customs of the parish. And he if anyone knows how terribly capricious, not to say malicious, the church's boiler can be. How many nights he has come plodding through the snow to keep it going. The congregation comes tramping in to warmth and light the next morning as if it were the simplest thing in the world, not suspecting that it has all been touch and go.

Yes, truly, life out here is full of drama, and now Arthur Manström sees a golden opportunity and grabs it. Hypnotized, everyone but Lydia listens to his stories from the First World War when he had a radio hidden in the attic of the east village school and maintained contact with the Swedish Free Corps, on its way across the ice to Åland. The Russians showed up again and again, and Lydia thought more than once that they'd been found out, especially the last time when they went up into the attic with some kind of device that could pinpoint the source of radio waves. But the wise and well-behaved little radio held its breath while Lydia played "Quake Not in Terror, Little Band" on the harmonium in the schoolroom below and led her pupils in loud and measured song. The Russians came back down the stairs, apologized for the disturbance, the officer saluted, and they marched away. Chaos up in the attic, but the receiver was untouched behind a panel in the wall.

Others chime in with additional examples of the way political events in the wider world have had a direct effect on the Örlands—the time the Germans blew up the lighthouse in their fishing grounds during World War I, the Russian submarines that sailed with perfect confidence past the Örlands in the final phases of this last war, when neither the Finns nor the Germans were a threat. What a close thing it had been. How securely the Russians sat in the saddle. How certain it seemed that they would take all of Finland and swallow it up in one bite. Exciting. Terrible. The Coast Guard stood there and looked at them through their binoculars, and sometimes there was a flash of reflected sunlight when the submarine captain had them in his sights.

And when all was lost in the Baltic States, boats started coming from Estonia. They were overloaded, unseaworthy, badly off course. Many of them thought they were already in Sweden. They had no food or fresh water, none of them, just a handful of worthless money to pay their way. Poor souls. Drowned bodies pulled from the sea—everyone remembers the handsome officer with his little black book filled with the addresses of Estonian girls. On the other hand, no one involved says a word about the handguns left behind as thanks for provisions and fuel and sea charts. "Because of course we helped them. The Russian Control Commission was already sitting in Helsingfors, we were required to report refugees to the authorities. But the police was our own Julius, and he didn't get in our way. 'It could be our turn next,' he said."

"Civil courage," says father Leonard with sincere admiration. "Julius, you say? From the east villages? I think I've seen him."

Not hard to figure out where Leonard means to take his sledge some day soon. But the verger has weighty things to say about the Estonians. "Two of them are buried here," he says, "as 'Unknown Estonian Refugees'. They had no papers on them. We showed them to some others that came ashore, but they turned their heads away and said they didn't know them. 'It might have been me,' said one of them who spoke Swedish. Since the Estonian government had been dissolved and there was no one to take responsibility, we buried them at parish expense. We made a wooden cross, too. Mona, you could plant something on their grave in the spring if you're willing."

174

Of course she is willing, and she contributes to the discussion by saying what a close call it was for everyone in Finland. If the Finns hadn't had their modern German antiaircraft guns, which forced the Russians to drop their bomb loads in the sea and in the woods, it could have been really bad for Helsingfors. She'd stood out on the granite outside her parents' house and watched — smoke and flames and searchlights and the drama when one of the bombers got caught in a cone of light and was hit and somersaulted out of the firmament. How the cheers echoed on the Helléns' hillside!

She sounds so bloodthirsty that Petter wants to tone things down a little. "Yes, weather like today's was the worst of all. Perfect flying weather, good visibility, you could count on spending the night in the shelter. In those days we could only relax when it was cloudy and raining hard. What a joy that we can now be happy about the lovely weather without a qualm. It's unbelievable. Every day since the war ended I've thanked God for peace. Every day it seems to me a miracle that we live in peace and freedom and that we're not dead or banished to Siberia. I hope the day will come when we can take it all for granted.

The organist thinks of his sons and the Bible school youngsters and joins in. "Yes, indeed. The young take it for granted already. They don't look at time the way we do. For them, the war is already the distant past."

"And may it always be so," the pastor says. He looks out the window at the moon reflected in the ice, the stars like glittering inlays. "More tea?" Mona says, but Adele takes a different tack for all of them and says that tomorrow is another day and now they need to go home. But first the verger wants them to sing "Shall We Gather at the River", which the people of the Örlands are accustomed to singing when they part and head home across dark waters.

Sanna wakes up as they sing "That flows by the throne of God" so heartily and warmly that it sounds as if the tiles, stoves and the kitchen range were singing along. "Baa, baa," Sanna sings too, in her warm cocoon. Now she hears them rise from their chairs, their joints creaking after sitting for so long. Chair legs scrape on the floor and the door to the hallway is opened—Oh, so cold! Mama says, "I'll bring your things into the kitchen to warm them up a bit. Come on in here to put your coats on!" The hanging lamp in the kitchen is lit, and one after another, the guests put their storm lanterns on the stove and light them. They stand there in their great boots, the women winding long shawls around their heads, all of them pulling on wool or fur coats, unfolding lap rugs. The pastor and his wife can't stand to see them go, so they too wrap themselves up warmly and accompany their guests down to the shore.

The kicksleds wait eagerly, drawn up on land, and now they are shoved happily out onto the ice, the women take their seats and the men push off, slowly at first, like the first revolution of a flywheel, but then off and away. They call to the pastor and his wife, whose strong voices fade backwards and grow thinner as the kicksleds pick up speed. Maybe they're not competing, not directly, not grown men, but they certainly give that impression as they strike out across Church Bay in a tight pack held together by their calls. The verger and Signe holler good night and swing round the island in towards their house while the Manströms, the Bergmans, and the organist and his wife head full speed out onto the long bays that separate the parish into two equally large, competing parts. They stay together for a long way until the Manströms head off towards the east villages and the others continue on together towards the deep inner waterways of the west. They are almost home before they part company, the organist and his wife heading a bit farther south at a good clip, the Bergmans swinging off to the west where the hills rise black before falling into the sea, which lies frozen far beyond the territorial limits.

"We can go all the way to Estonia if we like," the organist shouts recklessly, but he slows down anyway in the narrower passages between the islands and into their own shallow bay. He crosses it brilliantly and, just as he does in his boat, he knows exactly when to slow down enough to land smoothly at his dock.

Kicksleds are faster than boats. When the ice has set, you grasp clearly what the resistance of the water means for a body moving through it. Arthur Manström is silent as he kicks, otherwise he could undoubtedly deliver a lecture on the laws of physics. Beneath the moon and the stars, gliding over the moon and the stars, Lydia is absorbed, utterly and completely happy. No present obligations, no future to worry about, everything is now. As a child, she'd scream with joy when she went sledging. It is not much different from what Arthur Manström thinks he hears beneath his own breathing, in his thoughts. Deeply embedded in his fur hat and wolfskin collar, he is already formulating a description of the majesty of ice as it covers the waterways, sweeping away the wakes of skiffs, dinghies and fishing boats, sealing the fishermen's pastures and the yachtsmen's gentle billows.

The pastor and his wife stand shivering on the shore for a while after their guests have sledged away, listening to their shouts far out on the ice. Then these too die away, and they can hear the indescribable silence that comes when the ice has set. Otherwise you hear the sea incessantly out here. It is never so calm that the swells don't rustle and sigh, and the calm itself is carried by a voice that underlies the lazy days of blazing sunshine. Then the wind freshens and the surge grows stronger. When the wind begins to whistle it is time to take care, but even deep among the islands and indoors, the roar presses in and remains, like a delayed echo after the storm has passed.

Now it could not be more silent, or closer to the moon. The pastor and his wife shiver and put their arms around each other. Their steps squeak in the snow that lies here and there on the ground. The lamp burns in the parsonage window. The sheep in their pen, the cows in their stalls, Sanna in her bed. Peace at last on earth.

Chapter Thirteen

THE HEALTH CARE CENTRE is a gift to the Örlands, but most of all to Irina Gyllen. It is like a lesson in how long-range planning can produce results. How quick the Örlanders are to cite the old maxim, "Rome wasn't built in a day," and how easily it comes to Irina Gyllen's lips when she's talking to the district doctor. As the plans begin to take more concrete form, so Irina's hopes grow that the series of quiet inquiries she has made will help her get in touch with her son and eventually bring him to Finland. You need patience while the stones are carried to Rome and the inquiries go unanswered. But the fact that they've been made means that a growing number of people are aware of the case, and among them there must necessarily be a few who know the boy's fate. They do not yet act, but a foundation is being laid, and their knowledge shortens the path to action. Even in the Soviet Union, material conditions have improved since the war, so the boy's physical situation is less a source of concern that it was earlier.

Especially during the meetings, surrounded by shrewd, self-confident Örlanders, she is able to take courage. She can also let herself take pleasure and amusement in the touching form of democracy they practise. The constant voting and the straightforward distrust of the opposing side is like a lesson in democracy. Oh, if the wretched Politburo could be dragged in, bound hand and foot, and learn how it's supposed to work! The result is not guaranteed to be good, but the process is honourable, and the project creeps forwards. At times it takes great leaps: when the provincial authorities approve the site and the blueprints, when the first order for materials is called in by the magnificent Adele Bergman, when the first boatload of cement and lumber arrives.

When it comes to her own private project, she can't help being gripped by anticipation even as she's seized by panic and impatience. This bitterly cold winter, she sometimes wraps her fur coat around her shoulders and stands on the steps and listens. As long as there is open water, there is the comfort of knowing you can always get away by boat. Now, in this absolute silence, it feels more as if an unseen enemy could attack. Anyone at all could approach silently and invisibly across the ice. Idiocy! Fear of shadows! For shame! Here there is no need to flee, no danger threatens, all is well. Calm. Patience. A cup of tea, a sleeping pill, to bed. She locks her door from the inside, telling herself that the Ministry of Health requires that all drugs be kept under lock and key. Not untrue.

* * *

Uninvited, the cold comes straight into the Manströms' farmhouse, its walls full of wormholes. But Lydia feels younger when she can travel on the ice. Freer, more agile. She takes the kicksled to school, arrives in the morning from the sea and disappears in the afternoon out towards the sound. Like a sea sprite, like who she is. Arthur Manström's head is full of stories about mermaids and sea sprites, but he doesn't know he himself is married to one. The sea sprite adapts and lives among people as one of them, but when her boundaries are overstepped, she makes for the sea. That knowledge gives her the peace of mind she needs to stay. Now she steers the sledge into the Manströms' home bay and goes ashore and in. No one at home except Tilda, who has the coffee ready. Despite being told repeatedly, she always makes it too early and lets it stand and simmer on the stove, God only knows how long. It is hot, at least, and she peels off her plush outer coat, leaving everything else on and pulling on fingerless gloves before sitting down to drink it. A sugar cube between her teeth, coffee in the saucer, the saucer raised in a lovely hand, sipping elegantly. Butters a piece of bread, discusses the temperature outside and in. Seventeen degrees by the stove, six by the window, thirteen in the parlour, minus twelve outdoors. Cold, but refreshing. "The ice is wonderful," she says to Tilda. Tilda tells her of the traffic she's seen from the kitchen window. Horses have been out hauling hay from the island hay barns and boys have been out doing what boys do – ducking their work and skating off and ice fishing. But soon the ice will be so thick they'll get tired of boring holes.

When it's this cold and brisk, it's easier to get up and go into the bedroom with her bag of schoolbooks, change quickly from blouse and jacket and school skirt to everyday clothes. Wool all over and finally a big wool shawl, a wool scarf on her head and fishing mittens on her hands. Ought to get started on supper, but sits down instead and starts a "Letter from the Skerries", a regular feature in the *Åbo Reporter*:

"How are things out there?" people ask, sympathetically. "Fine, thank you," we answer. We're not being brave, it's the gospel truth. Now that the ice has set, our boundaries have increased a hundredfold, and we've got elbow room and polished floors as far as the eye can see. If you care to venture out here, you will see a jolly dance—old and young finding the shortest distance between two errands, giving us traffic like that in New York City but on skates, sleighs, and sledges. A pile of hay glides by over here, a load of sand over there, farther out in the bay comes an Örland grandfather in a go-a-courtin' sleigh loaded down with goods from the store and Brunte between the traces, as sure of foot as when he was a colt. Boys skate by so fast they are mere streaks, and the smaller children make glassy sliding tracks closer to shore.

"Cold?" you ask. Yes indeed, bitterly cold, but no colder here than in the city where you live. But lonely? Absolutely not!

But she has to stop. There are too many other things to do. Even those are a pleasure, for now that the fire in the stove must be kept going pretty much all the time, she can make baked dishes in the oven that always come out right and that everyone likes. Nestled down into their hay bales, the hens are puffed up like rabbit-fur muffs in the cold, but they are still laying. There is whole milk warming in a spouted bowl. She breaks a couple of eggs into the milk, whisks it a few times, and pours it over sliced potatoes, onion, and salt herring in a baking dish. A few pats of butter on top and into the oven, several sticks of wood onto the fire, and so, an hour later, a splendid, steaming, golden-yellow dinner. Fresh baked bread and home-churned butter to go with it. She will write about that in her next letter when she has time.

❆ ❆ ❆

By the time Lydia has put her herring dish in the oven, Adele Bergman has closed the store and gone home to the attic apartment. Elis is at home—where else would he be?—and has the coffee ready and warm. She has brought a length of coffee cake that she purchased at the store, which they eat with their coffee. And three hundred grammes of forcemeat that she will fry for supper.

"Lots of people at the store today," says Elis, "now it's so easy for them to get here. It's funny to see them coming on sledges when you're used to seeing them in boats."

"Yes," she says. "There's almost a party atmosphere. And nearly everyone buys a little something extra. The organist's boys were here and bought tobacco. They waited until Birgit was alone at the counter, but I saw them from the office. Except this time I didn't go rushing out and give them a lecture. I let them buy it, but I wonder if I should tell the organist. Sometimes I think we ought to take a vow of secrecy at the store. There's no other place to shop, someplace where no one knows you, and where are those boys going to get tobacco if they can't buy it here?"

"It was their lucky day, I see," Elis says, happy to hear she's in a good mood. And it will get better, because the post has come, and there are the daily papers, weekly magazines, letters and cards! "Look!" he says. "I shouldn't have shown them to you until we'd eaten!" They laugh. There are crosswords in the dailies, serials in the weeklies, news and greetings in the letters. Plus *The Humanitarian*, the organ of the Lutheran Evangelical Society, which has two subscribers on the Örlands—the pastor and Adele. The verger can't afford it, and the organist doesn't have time to read it after all his other duties. And the members of the vestry, who ought to subscribe, don't, out of laziness and lack of conviction. It's sad. Still, the day has had its pleasures, and thanks to the post, these will now stretch late into the evening.

There is a great deal resting on Adele's shoulders. She is well equipped to manage her temporal obligations. She needs

ne spiritual. This is why it is so important that the
ne Örlands should be a kindred spirit. Someone who
u.   nds why she worries about the thoughtless Örlanders
with their slumbering piety, someone who sees the importance of religious revival, a renewal of faith. Someone who
can inspire and lead. Someone like this very young priest
who preaches a pure and unaffected word of God and by his
very example has won the friendship and the respect of his
congregation. God grant that he is the instrument the Lord has
sent to preach salvation to the whole community!

✳ ✳ ✳

The parsonage too is observing a devout newspaper silence. The
post is collected at the steamboat channel where the icebreaker
Murtaja passes Mellom on its toilsome way to Mariehamn, then
carried on to the Örlands by Post-Anton and his mare. Much
of the mail goes to the parsonage, so Anton stops there and
does an initial sorting, since he passes that way in any case.
The mare is hitched in the lea of the sauna and given some oats;
Anton gets coffee in the house. The two of them are now on
their way home, and the pastor and his wife and the pastor's
eager father throw themselves on the mail — several issues of
Hufvudstadsbladet and *Ålandstidningen*, plus *The Churchgoer* and
The Humanitarian. It's the pile of letters they rake through most
eagerly. Official communications are set aside to be opened
later, but they grab the private letters at once, slit them open
with anything sharp that comes to hand. Three from Mama, a
greeting from the Helléns, a letter from one of Mona's friends
at the seminary and one of Petter's colleagues, a letter in unfamiliar handwriting on thick, luxurious paper with a Swedish
stamp that turns out to come from an elderly gentleman who

wants to know how best to lend support to the people of the island world which once, in his distant youth — oh, so long ago — gave him indelible, unforgotten revelations of God's magnificent creation. Definitely a letter worthy of a hearty reply. But now it's time to read the newspapers! Even at the parsonage, *The Humanitarian* is set aside till later and winds up in the study in an accusatory half-read pile while the three adults trade issues of *Hufvudstadsbladet* and *Ålandstidningen* among themselves. Sanna has to make do with *The Humanitarian*. She turns the pages attentively, rustling the paper and exclaiming, "My word!" and "I've never heard the like" and "Good ice, it says here."

The advertisements are also worth reading. The Co-operative Central on Åland announces receipt of a shipment of oranges — they hope Adele has her hand in. Maybe there were some boxes in Anton's sledge already, although he didn't say anything. It's worth asking, and getting there early when the store opens in the morning.

Domestic politics, murder, auto accidents, sports and international news, a sprightly column by one of the many Hellén cousins, the film listings in Helsingfors for the preceding week, book reviews, a new play at the Swedish Theatre, engagements, births and deaths, comic strips at the back of the Saturday edition — a world they don't miss but love to read about. The voice of home. And even though they've been happy to shake off their attachment to home, it's where they have family, old friends, culture, everything!

* * *

At the verger's house, the verger reads aloud to Signe from *Ålandstidningen*. Many astonishing occurrences in the province, plus some reflections by one of its priests that calls forth a comparison: "Neither life nor spirit. Ours does it better." It warms his soul. And there is more to read. He has in any case made a good start, whereas the organist for his part has not yet had time to collect his mail. His sons are nowhere to be found. How can such conspicuous boys be so invisible? And what's the point of their growing up when they spend their time out on the ice, all the way out to the lighthouses, looking for seals, without doing a blasted thing that might be of use here on land. There's a cow in the barn with strangles, there's wood needs chopping, hay to bring home from the island barn now that the ice is in perfect condition, drift nets to be mended so you don't stand there amazed at the end of July wondering where all the holes came from. Inside the house there are petitions and writs to be prepared, bills of sale to be drawn up, wills and estate inventories to be witnessed, the Co-op's accounts to be examined and audited, the township council's minutes to be completed and posted on the notice board at the store, an agenda to be proposed for the coming vestry meeting. No limits or end to it all. Not to mention the need to keep his fingers limber and hymns practised now that they finally have a priest who understands church music.

The organist is the eldest child of an able mother and believed when he married, deeply in love, that all women were the same. Capable and energetic, skilful and enterprising. Like Mona Kummel, he thinks admiringly, not like Francine. For Francine, a great many things are overwhelming. The household, for example. Childbearing and child care are exhausting. Animal husbandry, difficult. The organist is the first man on the Örlands to have been seen going into the cow barn with his wife at milking time. Francine is with him, but it's he who ties up a refractory wretch of a cow so it can't kick, and it's he who carries the pails and scrubs them. Indoors at the organist's, it's his mother who runs the household. Francine isn't lazy. She mends clothes and does a little of everything, but she rarely finishes. Without Mama, they couldn't manage, but he understands that it's because of Mama that Francine is less enterprising and always ready to give up too quickly, because Mama will always step in and finish a job when she's half done.

Maybe this is why Francine has bouts of despair and lies in bed and says she wants to die if she has any more children. No one understands that she doesn't have the strength. There's no one who can help her. His mother says she's small and weak. Is a woman supposed to have the strength of a man? Round and round, a circle of despair.

He chose her against his mother's express wish. He was calm and bold and certain, he who otherwise is so often nervous and full of doubts. People believe that they make correct decisions when they are calm, but calmness can be a form of self-deception. And what is in fact a correct decision? A prudent decision? Or a decision in line with an individual's deepest hopes and desires? That was the case when he proposed, and because he has had to defend that act to himself again and again, he has also defended his love and bolstered it on all sides so that he is the only man on the Örlands who openly sees to his wife's comfort, although everyone knows the way things are.

Adele should have had such a husband — masculine, good-looking, richly gifted, intelligent, responsible. Competent, effective. His only weakness Francine, who would actually have suited Elis better. Elis is a nice person, good-hearted, friendly, interested in much, but without the organist's industry and drive. In a different world, they might have made a quiet trade, but in this world that's not possible. You're married to the person you married, and that way, Adele thinks, you never have to worry that maybe he doesn't want you. No growing disaffection, no disappointment need ever intrude upon her relationship with the organist. Best that way, but oh! Nevertheless, he goes home to Francine when he's tired and worn out from work. He comes to the store before the day has sucked the life out of him, looks into the office on some errand having to do with the upcoming Co-op board meeting. Followed by discussions about the final clean copy of the minutes and the never-ending need for further meetings. His hand has held the paper and pen, his dear writing covers the page like his voice, and when he has gone, it lies open on her desk like a bright light all through the busy day.

Francine, on the other hand, after all these years, still feels as if she were living in a strange house, and sometimes she sneaks into her childhood home, desolate now that everyone is dead. So cold she can see her breath, the stove rusty, the beds empty. No one comes here, unless she stays too long and they start looking. She is expecting another child and knows it won't go well. She's too old, and she's embarrassed to say anything. She doesn't know what she thinks, it's as if she lay floating under the ice, her hair adrift, her memory adrift. What she's supposed to think and believe adrift.

He has such good words, he touches her so well. She thought at the time that with him she could live a good, protected life. As she grew up, she could never stand to watch the cow calve, and when her own time approached it was no better. And there was nowhere to hide. She's heard her mother-in-law say that Francine's deliveries haven't been especially difficult. What does she know about it? And then baby after baby, she who wanted to remain a child herself. But once the misfortune has occurred, she can let him come to her without anxiety, for now things are the way they are.

The organist tells her that the pastor's wife is presumably in the family way as well, though the pastor has only hinted. This news is supposed to be encouraging, but the pastor's wife is young and healthy and strong and spirited. For her, bearing a child is a dance she'll do quickly and well, the way she does everything. What does she know about what it will be like for Francine? Just one good push and the baby lies there, that's all there is to it.

Francine is not entirely mistaken, for the pastor's wife rarely thinks about being pregnant, and she's not really worried about the delivery. The former pastor's wife went to Åbo and sat there for weeks, waiting, but Mona Kummel hasn't the time for that. Moreover, the midwife on the Örlands has a degree in gynaecology, although her qualifications are formulated in Russian, and there is a homecare sister on the Örlands who can be engaged for the first week. In other words, all the arrangements are made and the pastor's wife has other things to think about. The household, for one thing, and being constantly prepared for unexpected guests, and the cow barn, where the first-class hay has kept the cows in fine form, their milk as good as it was in the autumn. Mending and darning, writing letters, the church choir created and led by the organist, where the pastor's wife sings first soprano and the pastor bass. Thanks to the incomparable ice this winter, it's easy for everyone to get to church. The two halves of the community have an equal journey. The choir members practise their parts as they kick their sledges, and when they get to the church, they and their voices are already warm. They sing a few verses to hear how they sound in the fine acoustics of the church, but then they all move to the parsonage, where they rehearse in the parlour.

The whole hall is full of their coats and furs, and the parlour is full of song.

Then Sanna bursts into tears, and Papa senses that what she's feeling amidst this sea of coats and the choir's mighty singing is a deep loneliness, which can affect anyone who stands outside of it all—ice, church, song. He picks her up and tells her not to feel bad, and then he whispers a secret—this summer she's going to get a little brother or sister and won't that be fun!

The church choir sledging its way home across the ice has figured out the truth. In fact, it's hardly news, for the rumour began spreading through the villages even before she was pregnant, but now it is confirmed—her breasts, the barely discernible swell of her belly beneath her skirt, her whole demeanor a bit more serene, as if smiling to herself just ever so slightly.

The evening light lingers a bit longer now, and during the day the sun eats at the ice, which softens towards afternoon, making runners sink deeper and sledges move more slowly. During the night it freezes hard, and in the morning the kick-sleds run normally. But the sun gains a bit every day, and there is unease in the air. Far out in the sea there is open water, and you can come across seals behind piles of ice. Several hunting parties are on their way out with specially built rowboats on skids. In among the islands, especially where there's a current, the ice has begun to bulge and turn blue. It's only a matter of days before small children are forbidden to go out on it. Older, more sensible people go nowhere without an ice pike and a knife in their belt. It is hardest for Lydia Manström to say farewell to the ice, because she must be a role model for the schoolchildren, even though the ice could support her for several more days. Several weeks if the weather turns cold again. But maybe not. Now both the sun and the villagers are bending every effort to hasten the breakup of the ice. People put their shoulders to it and shove, and the ice shows wet patches and dark areas of rot. It is soft and treacherous, and beyond the lighthouses the seal hunters can hear the roar of the open sea. Rifts and fissures open up right under them, and those who aren't light on their feet and can dance like a crane may easily fall in. That's as it should be, and the man who takes sensible risks can collect a pile of bloodily slaughtered seals at the edge of the ice. The state pays a bounty for the jaw, the boatyards buy the oil, and you can cure the skins yourself and sell them in Åbo. You can make blood pudding and cook the meat. Those who've tasted it say that the meat of seal pups is a delicacy.

For several months, the pastor had his congregation together and available. Now the people he's looking for are often away, unclear when they'll be back. The boathouses are seething with activity although the smaller bays are still covered with ice. Tracks from the skids on rowboats lead out and back. For all that was going on in their winter world, it seems like a long sleep compared with the activity now. Everyone has woken up and stretched, and the pastor must learn that Easter is no big holiday on the Örlands. People are in too much of a hurry. The pastor's wife has forced a crocus in a pot that stands blooming on the altar, the verger has changed the liturgical colours as prescribed, and the pastor stands almost alone in the church draped in mourning on Good Friday and not much less alone at High Mass on Easter Sunday as he proclaims the risen Christ. Christendom's holiest observance and most joyful festival, he declares into the emptiness, to Mona and Sanna and Papa and Adele and Elis, the verger in his pew and the organist and the pumper in their loft. No less true for that, but it echoes balefully in the empty space.

At home they've made the traditional twigs-and-feathers, and Sanna has searched for and found her first Easter egg. It can be opened and is full of small candies. Seeing it is a reminder that the war is really over. Sanna learns to go around and offer candy to everyone else before taking any herself. She's had a birthday and is now two years old, mature and verbal for her age, with an insatiable hunger for conversation and being read to. When Grandpa leaves in the spring and they themselves are fully occupied with their springtime labours, they plan to hire one of the confirmation-class girls to keep Sanna company.

Grandpa himself is into the starting blocks and listens constantly for signs of the ice breaking up. When there is open water, he can travel home and take care of himself for a good month before Mama arrives with all her possessions. The sun is right, the wind is right, he tells Sanna. Everything that gets the ice moving is good. And once it starts moving, it goes fast. Movement is good. Relocation. Life!

Chapter Fourteen

This is the time when the ice neither bears nor breaks. My mare has had a good rest for a week while I labour with the sledge. I set off very early in the morning when the ice is hardest, and there's not much mail in my bag, thank goodness. If I keep up a good pace, I'll get to Mellom before I start sinking into the ice too far.

You have to move fast so you don't fall through in the worst places, but not so fast that you rush ahead like an angry bull without seeing where you're headed. You have to pay constant attention to the look of the ice ahead so you don't go steaming into an area that you can't get out of. The interesting thing about such ice is that even though you've made it far into a field of that kind, the ice won't hold if you try to go back the same way.

You can't ever turn and go back. That's why it's so important to have a clear picture of where you're headed. Across Örland Sound I try to take a straight course, though it's a strain if the wind pulls me to one side. Once you've come across and have the large islands in sight, you've covered the longest stretch, and then I usually go into the outermost farms where there are warm stoves and a cup of coffee and maybe a letter to put in my bag.

When you're in a boat on open water, you're over the worst once you get in among the islands, in the lea of the wind. But when you're sledging bad ice, you have every reason to be careful. Because that's where the currents run, and that's where cracks open up in unexpected places. You don't always see them, because the water flows and floods under a thin layer of ice, and if the sun is in your eyes you can't always see the difference between those patches and bearing ice. At this time of the year, I always wear sealskin shoes, because I can feel through the soles how far under the surface the water is moving, so I know when to take care.

You need to prick up your ears so you can hear how the water murmurs and moves. And so you can hear how the ice is alive beneath your runners. Also when your speed slackens on wet ice you should listen to the way it sounds in front of you and be on your guard for when the ice starts to pull apart beneath your feet. You must continue forward no matter how heavy the going and not even think of turning back. Your whole body must be an instrument to register the consistency of the ice. You hold your breath sometimes, and fear can make heat blossom like a rose beneath your furs, and then you kick forward as fast as you possibly can. Your whole body is a gauge, making constant judgments as you move.

And then of course I know that I'm not making my way across the ice alone. Before I leave, I see how the journey will be, and I'm forewarned the whole way. There is nothing odd about that, but neither is it a thing that I can describe in common words. I don't know what they look like, and even though I often joke with them and tell them to get off the sledge and lighten the load, I don't believe they have weight in the sense that we do. They exist in the world in a different way, although they once were like us. That's why they help me and lead me forward. If they had never been like us, they would not understand the kind of guidance I need.

So for the moment I have made it to the Mellom pier and into the waiting room, where I usually boil myself some coffee and have a sandwich and sleep under some furs for an hour or so until it starts to be time to expect the steamer. The Mellom postman and I take turns going up on the hill to watch for it. When it comes, that's when we have our best chance of getting wet, the postman and I, when we collect the mailbags out at the channel. The boat brings necessities to Mellom and a few passengers, so the ship stops its engines and glides into the edge of the ice and throws out its gangway. The mailbags come tumbling across, and I take mine and head in towards land off the quaking ice. Maybe for the last time this year, or so it begins to feel.

Yes, it has happened that I've come with a sledge and had to get myself home by boat. One of the closest calls I ever had was when all of Örland Sound broke up behind me with a great crash and roar just as I came in among the large islands. I knew that day that I had to hurry and I sledged along for all my life was worth while the ice thundered under my feet and floes shot up across one another behind my back. I made it dry-shod to the outermost farms and had to borrow a boat to get home.

The outlook has never been so bad that I didn't dare go. Julanda has told me many times that I'm not right in the head, going out in all sorts of weather and ice conditions, but I have to say that the salary I'm paid makes it my duty. The ones out there understand that it's not just about me. The mailbags must also get through. Through all these years, I've never lost a mailbag, so I know that they worry about my burden, not just about me, as I travel the ice where they've staked out the way.

※ ※ ※

When the ice is at its worst, the two island priests talk to each other on the telephone. The experienced Fredrik Berg has warned Petter Kummel that they can't speak freely from the heart, because the operators listen. Petter suggests that they speak Finnish when discussing sensitive matters, but when he spoke to Central about another matter, Edit tactfully let him know that she understands Finnish quite well after her years as a housemaid in Åbo. So they have to watch their words although there is much to discuss. Work first, but then . . .

"So how are things otherwise?" Petter asks. "Out here we're completely isolated until the ice has gone. The seal hunters are out, and Anton goes to Mellom once a week with his sledge. We're stuck where we are. I don't know how Anton does it. He doesn't come back until night when the ice has frozen hard, because by then his sledge is weighed down with all the newspapers he brings out, mostly ours, I'm afraid. I'm ashamed every time I open them. Anton risks his life for them over and over again. 'The mail must go through, whether it bears or it breaks,' he says, proudly."

"Yes, it's a deed worthy of Finland's White Rose. Did you know he'd won it? The postmen out here usually do—if they survive. It's easier here, what with the steamboat channel going right past us. If you need to, you can leave Mellom twice a week. But you need to have a good reason. It's a job getting out to the channel and a job to get on board. Nothing anyone does for the fun of it."

"No, we're very happy just to be able to stay at home. People wonder how we're going to get through the winters here, but we don't get cabin fever or even get restless. We're completely content that our world has shrunk. What's remarkable is that it's big enough. All the human types in the world at large exist right here on the Örlands. And every kind of conflict and problem. How is everything there?"

Petter has noticed a happy, triumphant note in Fredrik's voice, as if he were biding his time. "Yes, indeed," he says. "I hardly dare say it out loud for fear it will vaporize like dust, but yesterday we passed a proposal for a new parsonage. Not just a confirmation of the decision that already exists but a decision about implementation: labour allocations among the villages, appropriation of money from the Central Fund. When the motion passed, we stared at each other as though it couldn't be true. Good heavens the coffee we drank when it was over!"

"Congratulations," Petter says. "Do you think that's the end of the delaying tactics?"

"If only it were. Technically, we've come significantly closer to the goal, which will make it harder to delay the process. I feel quite certain on that point. But you can bet your life that they'll be in very fragile health when it's time to start building."

"That's excellent news, in any case. How did it come about?"

"In January we had a vestry meeting in the parsonage during the worst cold snap all winter. I made sure it was freezing; we lit the fires in the tile stoves just before they got there. We didn't even need the wind for them to get the hint. The cold came in through the walls and the floor right on cue. The lamps blew out, the curtains fluttered. The coffee was cold before you could get it to your mouth. An icy chill crept up your legs if you sat still for half a minute. The children had colds and coughed and cried so you could hear them through these thin board walls. It was perfect."

Petter laughs. "Out here, everyone knows that when you come to the parsonage you leave everything on except the outermost layer. Sometimes even then someone will go back for their coat. We've had fur hats at the table, and lots of wool scarves. They take those for granted. That's what it's like here in winter. In any case we have wood, which is more than I can say for some of the others out here."

"Maybe it's time to ask for a new parsonage yourselves."

"I think I'll wait until I've got my pastoral degree and then see if I can get posted to this parish. Now I'm afraid someone will snatch it out from under my nose. I should have kept quiet about how much I like this place."

"You seem quite certain."

"I am. How's it going with your own degree?"

"Fine thanks. My dissertation is almost finished. I'm thinking of going up for the exam this spring. Then we'll start building, and in my free time I'll keep an eye out for available parishes. The parsonage will be done in two years, and our furniture will be on its way to the mainland. And you?"

Petter's sigh makes the curtains flutter in his study. "Oh my. I had hoped to make a lot more progress than I have. I go absolutely cold when I think that it will soon be spring. We have a thousand plans for the garden and the farm. And then we'll have all the guests and the preachers. It's hopeless."

"Plus I've heard you're going to add to your family."

"How in the world do you know that?"

"I've got my spies. Seriously, you need to know you can't keep anything secret out here. When will it be?"

"In July. I'm stunned."

Fredrik has a good laugh into the phone. "We heard about it well before Christmas. But Margit will be happy to have it confirmed. We've got nothing on the way, but if that should happen, I'm sure you'll hear about it before we know it ourselves."

"Did they say if it will be a boy or a girl?"

"You've already got a girl, so of course they think it will be a boy. They call him Little Petter. The priest's boy. Etcetera."

"Well, well. Like I've said, the people out here are interested in people. I wonder if they know when I'll be ready for the pastoral exams. It has to be this autumn at the latest. I've made up my mind."

❋ ❋ ❋

And they go on talking. "Dear Brother" is the way the clergy address one another in letters, and that is precisely what Petter feels towards Fredrik, the older brother he never had. As they fulfil their obligations in their respective parishes, matters often arise that they need to discuss. If one of them doesn't call, the other one does. One day Fredrik hears an odd rumbling and a chair scraping as if Petter were leaping to his feet. Fredrik interrupts himself. "What's happening?"

"It must be the ice breaking up!" Petter cries. "I have to go out and watch. Forgive me, we'll have to talk later." He hangs up and rings off and hears his father pulling on his boots in the hall. "I'm coming," he hollers. "Mona, what are you doing? You have to see this!"

It doesn't matter that the dough has finished rising and needs to go into the oven. He lifts the trough out into the hall, where it's cold and the yeast will stop working, and helps her get her boots on. He sweeps a quilt around Sanna and rushes out onto the steps. Father Leonard is already on his way to the bell tower and starts climbing. He throws open the shutters with a bang. "Come!" he cries. Mona takes Sanna from him. "Go on up," she says. "We can see fine from down here."

And it's true, they can see and hear the ice breaking up from where they stand on the bell-tower hill. But from up in the tower, there is a view of the whole sea. All the way from the horizon in the west to the cliffs, knobs, skerries, and bedrock of the island world to the north and northeast. The entire landscape holds on tight as great shelves of ice climb across each other and heave themselves onto granite slopes. Suddenly the bays are open and the water surges and leaps and throws itself over the moving ice floes, which crash into each other with a great banging and cracking. The shores are lined with a border of growlers piled up so tightly that they butt and bellow among themselves. They push right across the smaller skerries and scrape them clean the way the glaciers once did, stuff themselves up onto larger islands and build huge jousting, shoving logjams. Out towards the open sea there are streaks of black and green and violet that combine and expand while the ice cover moves in waves, creaking and complaining, breaking and bawling. Farther out they can hear the thunder of the open sea as it tears itself free. There is a golden streak at the horizon from the sunshine of the day, but the deepening twilight brings darkness to the land. Silvery and white, the ice towers up against the blackness. Father Leonard has tears in his eyes. Petter stands in awe.

Down below, Mona is on her way home with Sanna. She is struggling to get free, and although he can hear nothing because of the rush and the roar, he knows that she is squealing and calling and wants to come up to him and that Mona is repeating impatiently that they've already seen the ice breaking up and there won't be anything more. No point in standing out here freezing and catching cold for nothing! Once again, Petter feels that he has failed his daughter. Of course he could have carried her up the steep stairs and kept her warm so she could see. For Sanna, the important thing is to be with him, and all too often he leaves her behind.

He and his father look at to each other again and again and say, "To think that we got to see this!" But the wind that pulls apart the ice is terribly cold once the sun has set, and soon they have to close the shutters and feel their way back down the steps. Tottering and dizzy. What a display! What power! In his head, Petter is already composing his Pentecost sermon about breaking the ice in the world of the spirit, when all the dams of doubt and scepticism will burst. He has now felt rapture in a concrete form and can transfer it directly to the Divinely gifted rapture that loosens our chains and lets us look straight into the world of bliss.

✻ ✻ ✻

Once the ice has broken up, everything moves quickly. So quickly that you lose your breath and wish you were back in the life-giving isolation of winter, which allowed you to think through your thoughts and plan for the day ahead. Now spring runs away with everyone and drives its own agenda. The seal hunters had their boats at the edge of the ice but got sufficient warning and made it home, squinting and sun-burned, without any losses and with seals in a row on the floor. Now the hunt for seabirds will begin, eiders and old squaws, which fly along the edges of the bays and land in their tradi-tional places, and there the men sit in their hunting coverts and blast away. Hardly a man in church, consequently, and only a few womenfolk because of the lack of available boats. In the barns, the floorboards are visible. The cows are dry and people can only hope that they'll make it through these lean weeks until things start turning green in earnest. It is not the case that summer breaks out as soon as the ice has gone. On the contrary, it can be cold and raw for weeks, and that's when things get tough.

At the parsonage, the peace of winter has been driven away. Papa paces about, stressed and incoherent, and Petter recog-nizes the symptoms. Now that the ice is gone he's going home to tar his boat, put it in the water, and talk Granboda village to death before Mother arrives with all their worldly goods sometime in June. Now Mona has to fit him out, see to it that his clothes are clean and mended and that he has bread and butter to go with the fat spring perch he's going to pull up from his favourite perch hole. At the parsonage, too, they are happy that net fishing can begin, but it is one more time-consuming chore that steals time from pastoral studies. Once again, he stands and wonders how he'll have time for all the work that's falling on him like a house.

Chapter Fifteen

As LONG AS THE ICE REMAINED, it seemed a long time until Mona's confinement but now her pregnancy too is progressing with frightening speed. No one knows better than Mona how much they need to get done before she can start thinking about having a baby. They have to finish the haymaking, and before they start on that, there's a great deal to do in the garden that they didn't have time for last spring. The kitchen garden needs to be fertilized and enlarged, a new drainage ditch must be dug, they have to sow and plant, and just imagine if they'd had time to break up part of the meadow and sow feed grain! Not to mention that they need to look after the everlasting fences, take the sheep out to the islands, groom the cows so they don't have to be ashamed of them. They must be plump and shiny for the congregation to admire. It would all be so much simpler if they had a horse! When Petter has passed his pastoral exams and been made permanent vicar, their finances will get a bit better, but the loans, the loans! Should they borrow more and buy a motorboat and a horse, or should they wait a year? Why not break in Darling, Goody's heifer calf from last year? Then they could plough up another piece of land. Worth a try!

Time rushes by. They get a lot done, as they notice when they look around, but a great deal goes undone as well. When they make lists of all their work, they notice that Sanna is never mentioned once, and their consciences bother them. They're neglecting their child for all the other important things they have to do, although she's a little more than two years old, full of curiosity, and loves to talk and philosophize. Most of all, she likes to be read to, but whichever one of them takes the time to read her a good-night story can barely stay awake once there's a moment to sit down. Time to do something about it, and that's how Cecilia comes to the house, one of the confirmation candidates who is good with children and reads well. It will be her job to spend time outdoors with Sanna and read her fairy tales all spring and summer. Now, Sanna, you'll have company and a real pal!

In years and size, Cecilia is the missing link between Sanna and the adult world. She is smaller than Mona, and at fourteen, she is halfway between them in age. She is child enough to be able to play and enjoy the story books as much as Sanna, and old enough to have a sense of order and responsibility. She appears at the parsonage like a young lady, knocks before entering and curtseys, but all with the fluttering heart of a little girl. The pastor's wife has a reputation for speed and resolve that could frighten anyone, but in reality she is kindness itself and says they are happy she could come. Cecilia gets her own room in the attic — something she has never had before. The pastor's wife has put some grape hyacinths and narcissus in a glass on the chair meant to serve as a bedside table. It is all lovely beyond description, with a wonderful view across the water. Sanna follows her up the steep stairs on all fours, with careful concentration, and looks at Cecilia rapturously. "Are we going to read?" she asks, eyes sparkling.

"Yes, indeed," says Cecilia. "As often as we can! And play!"

Sanna is prepared to begin at once, and so is Cecilia, but Mama tells Sanna that first they're going to let Cecilia unpack, and then she'll come downstairs and they'll all have coffee and get to know each other. She takes Sanna with her, and Cecilia hears them talking on the stairs: "Is she going to live here?" "Yes, this summer. Then she'll go to school." "I'm going to go to school too, with Cecilia." "Well, not quite yet. Do you like her?" "Oh, yes." "Good . . ." and then they go into the kitchen and Cecilia stands in her room and pretends she's a grown woman, the children's nurse at the parsonage. The best view in the house and a bureau where she can keep her clothes. Not many of them, but you don't need many in summer. It takes two minutes to put everything into the drawers, but grownups generally take such things seriously, so she stands at the window for a while and gets used to the room, and then she goes down the stairs. There is a smell of coffee from the kitchen and the door is open so she doesn't need to knock. Sanna comes towards her and takes her hand. "Come and have coffee!" she says. "I get to sit next to you."

The priest has come in. She curtseys and he takes her hand. Sanna curtseys too and takes Papa's hand, and the pastor says Welcome! And how nice that she could come. "Just look how happy Sanna is." Both the priest and his wife hope she'll feel at home, and she says that she already does. She blushes each time she has to speak and hasn't the courage to look at anyone but Sanna, who looks back open-heartedly and smiles. "Drink coffee now!" she says impatiently. They can all see that she's eager to start having fun, but the pastor's wife tells Cecilia not to be too nice and let herself be ordered around by the little princess, who's been given too much leeway. "Just tell me if she gets too unruly and headstrong! You're a sensible girl, and you have younger brothers and sisters, and I'm sure you know it's a mistake to be too indulgent."

Cecilia wants to ask if the pastor's wife also had little brothers and sisters, but it's the pastor who answers, almost as if he'd read her thoughts. "Both Mona and I have younger siblings, so we have no illusions. You have to keep after them or they'll take over the whole house." But he says it lovingly and is so sweet to Sanna, who looks at him starry-eyed, that anyone can see that his parenting principles allow for many exceptions. And anyway, who would want to be strict and curb this little girl's eager expectations!

The pastor and his wife have had great piles of children's books sent from their childhood homes, and Sanna has received several new books for her birthday. "Don't read any more than you want to yourself!" says the pastor's wife, who doesn't want Sanna to become a tyrant, but Cecilia says she thinks it will be fun. Suddenly she utters several sentences in a row: "I didn't get to read much when I was little, because no one did. The first stories I read were in my first reader. Once I had learned to read, I read the whole reader in a few days. And I got scolded because I wasn't helping."

They give her a kindly look and nod. They sit peacefully at their coffee, take one more piece of buttered bread before the plate of sweet rolls goes around. After only a few days at the parsonage, Cecilia has learned that the pastor and his wife take mealtimes seriously. They sit down to eat no matter how great a rush they're in, and meals last long enough that everyone leaves the table refreshed. "It will be a broadening experience for Cecilia, who is clearly intelligent," she heard the pastor tell her parents when he came to ask if she'd like to come and help with Sanna during her summer vacation, and now she sees how that works. When you get to see the way clever, educated people live, you develop thoughts and plans for your own life that broaden you!

As she reads aloud to Sanna and takes her out for walks and answers her thousands of questions—the pastor and his wife have taught her to take them seriously and answer them as best she can—June gallops away. Guests arrive from every direction and are stuffed into the house so that Cecilia must occasionally sleep in the sauna. That comes to an end when an amorous visitor from one of the sailboats forces his way in. Cecilia flees to the parsonage in tears, and the pastor and his wife abandon their guests in the parlour and talk to her in the kitchen.

"He said I was sweet," she sobs. "He wanted a kiss." She shudders and cries. The pastor's wife says she was absolutely right to run away. No one on a sailboat has any business in the sauna, least of all late at night, so of course she was scared. Tonight Cecilia can sleep in the kitchen, and early tomorrow morning the priest will go talk to the sailboat people. The pastor's wife wants to go herself, and she wants to go now and say what she has in her heart, but the pastor thinks they should sleep on it. He says maybe the man didn't really mean any harm, but it's asking too much for a fourteen-year-old girl to know how to deal with a big man who comes barging in at ten o'clock at night. Cecilia is still crying and telling them she's so sorry for everything, and both the pastor and his wife are kind and tell her not to forget that it wasn't she who forced herself on someone. She has done nothing wrong and doesn't need to apologize. "On the contrary, we're the ones who ought to apologize," says the pastor's wife, "for all Petter's countless relatives who pushed you out to the sauna. It never crossed my mind that you wouldn't be safe, not even here on Church Isle!"

She gets more and more worked up, and Cecilia stops crying and is frightened in a different way — well maybe it wasn't as bad as all that! Oh my! And the pastor, soothing and concerned, says that all's well that ends well. "Now we need to think about the sleeping arrangements, and tomorrow we'll come up with a solution of some kind." The pastor's wife says indignantly that they no longer have any extra bedlinen at all — not a thing! — because of all the people they have in the house. It's not a home any more, it's a kolkhoz! In the end the pastor himself, who's a man, has to trudge down to the sauna and carry up Cecilia's bedclothes, which she can spread out on the kitchen floor. "So now *we'll* sleep in the sauna," says the pastor's wife angrily, "and your parents can move into the bedroom." Her tone of voice is such that for a moment Cecilia feels sorry for the sailboat tourists, who will now really have to watch their step.

In the morning, when they've slept on it, the pastor attends to the matter with diplomacy and tact. There is no inquisition, he just installs himself and his wife on the shelf in the sauna, speaks calmly with the summer sailors and explains that they have so many people in the house that they themselves were forced out. Cecilia was frightened by something the night before and shouldn't have to sleep in the sauna by herself. They spend an uncomfortable night in the sauna, and it occurs to Mona that she is in the final stages of pregnancy and at least has the right to demand a decent mattress to sleep on, not just a collection of winter clothing as if they were hobos in a barn, where at least they'd have hay to sleep on. Here the barn has been scraped clean and there are people everywhere! Having a baby now would be very much like giving birth in a certain stable! This is a joke, but the pastor gets very anxious and questions her in detail about pains and premonitions. How is she feeling? Should he go up to the office and call Doctor Gyllen just to be on the safe side?

"Oh come on! Don't I have the right to complain just this one time? Other people make a big deal of their pregnancies while I get chased out of my own home. I'm not going to sleep here one night more!"

No, of course not, and in the morning Cecilia herself solves the problem. Blushing and curtseying, she says that they've told her several times that she could happily take a few days off and go home if she wanted, but she herself has wanted to stay. Now she wonders if she might go home over midsummer. She'd be happy to take Sanna with her if that would help.

"Good heavens, no!" says the pastor's wife. "If you take her along it won't be time off. Petter's sister should be able to do something! You just go on home, and have a nice holiday!"

The next morning, one of the sailboats sails away, end of story. All the boats and the great crowds of guests at the parsonage are there to celebrate midsummer in the outer islands, and when it's over, the guests need to understand that it's time for them to leave so that peace can return to the house. As soon as the holidays are out of the way, they're going to make hay, and only when it's been taken in can the pastor's wife take things a little easier, as befits her condition.

Midsummer is the year's biggest holiday on the Örlands. Midsummer Eve is a part of their pre-Christian heritage, and Midsummer Day, the Nativity of Saint John the Baptist, is a great church festival. They have no difficulty combining their two religions, and the delicious herbal scents of Midsummer Eve, which cause hymens to break and put new life into old people, has no argument with the chaste smell of birch in the embowered church. The church is full to overflowing, and everyone turns a friendly face to the priest and sings the summer hymns, which the organist plays with newfound feeling. It is not perhaps Saint John the Baptist that appeals to people so much as the lovely summer and all the summery, slim-waisted, broad-skirted dresses, blooming with sprays and garlands, visible proof of the rich herring fishing last summer, which filled many pockets with cash.

Sanna too has a new dress, sent to her by the Helléns, beautifully sewn with puff sleeves, a round collar and a wide skirt. To go with it, she has white socks and light summer shoes with a strap. No sweeter child has ever been seen, and the pastor looks at her as if he were in love, and she prances about and flounces her skirt until Mama tells Papa he should stop making so much of Sanna's dress. The last thing they want is for her to grow vain and insufferable! "Excuse me," he says, "but it's just so much fun having such a fresh and darling little girl!"

"Two girls," he corrects himself quickly, but she just snorts. "Oh, stop being silly. The way I look!"

He's moved to see that Cecilia, too, has come to church with her family, even though she's on vacation. Sanna greets her with a cry of joy and holds her hand in the churchyard. And without any of Mona's mixed feelings, Cecilia says, "How pretty you look in your new dress." Both he and Mona tell the parents how pleased they are with her and how pleasant it is to have her in the house.

The air is warm, no one is shivering and no one is in a hurry. In small groups, a large part of Örland parish stands gathered by their family graves, pulling weeds and watering occasional flowers, but mostly talking among themselves. Several young people wander down to the church dock and sit there talking and looking at the summer sailors, who feel suddenly very crowded and realize that they're taking space meant for the churchgoers' own boats, which swing at anchor anywhere they can find space in the little bay. But none of the Örlanders complains; they all call out cheerful greetings when they see people in the sailboats. The girls sit as if they were posing for a magazine, their skirts arranged prettily around them, their elegant legs in high-heeled shoes draped gracefully along the edge of the dock. Like young dandies, the island boys stand talking casually beside them. The naked eye can see no sign of uncertainty or artificiality, even though the entire arrangement is based on aesthetic calculation and close attention to detail. The weekend sailors are pale. Some of them have drunk too much the night before and are not well. They all feel shabby and unkempt, so one by one they disappear into their cabins and come out again dressed up in their yacht-club blazers, but they are second-rate sales clerks compared with the archipelago gallants, and they would never dare set sail within sight of these sovereign experts!

* * *

After midsummer, scruples sweep through the guests at the parsonage, and a few days later all of them are gone. The pastor and the verger cut the grass, and Cecilia curtseys and asks if she can rake. She can keep an eye on Sanna at the same time. She stands with her eyes on the floor and avoids looking at the older woman's belly beneath her apron, but it escapes no one that she, young as she is, is thoughtful enough to think that the pastor's wife, in her condition, shouldn't spend hour after hour in the hay meadow. It takes longer for Signe and Cecilia to rake up the hay now that they're working at Örland speed. Last summer, Signe had to hurry to barely keep up; the pastor's wife worked like a whirlwind. It rains in the middle of the process and the hay has to be turned yet again. If the pastor's wife weren't so impatient she might learn a lesson from how calmly and imperturbably Signe and Cecilia go about their work. The hay must be turned yet one more time, and the pastor's wife can smell and see with her naked eye how the quality declines, but Signe and Cecilia move placidly along the windrows — two goddesses of fate who weave and weave. The pastor's wife suffers and snorts, but then comes a period of high pressure that lasts, and the hay that the Holmens and the pastor cart into the barn, with raking help from Signe and Cecilia, retains nevertheless a decent nutritive value. The pastor's wife provides the meals and is still so quick that anyone deciding to help hardly has time to rise from the table before she's already up and running.

Once the hay is in, there is a period of relative calm at the parsonage. Cecilia and Sanna play outdoors in the fine weather, and Sanna asks lots of questions and shows what she can do: climb and run and count to four and, as it happens, five and six as well, and sing "Baa, Baa, Little Lamb". After supper they sit and read and read until Mama comes in from milking and reads the evening prayer and says good night. Despite the beauty of the summer, Papa spends the quiet days in his study, preparing for his pastoral exams. "I can't deny that it's terribly boring," he confesses to Cecilia, "but it's a thing I have to do if I'm to become the vicar here. Next year I'll be happy I did it, although it's not so much fun right now."

The pastor's wife still goes out and milks the cows, but whenever he's home, the pastor goes with her and carries the milk pails and washes them. It's hard for her to bend over, and when she sits down to do the milking, she has a hard time reaching the udders and getting to her feet again. But there will be no mawkishness on that score, it's all perfectly natural, and he ought to know that other women have had a much harder time and have still done what they had to do! On 13 July, she stands in the choir loft and sings "Where the Birches Whisper" at a wedding. The whole church whispers as they turn around, but her stomach is hidden behind the loft railing, which they should have known it would be. She has declined an invitation to the wedding feast. The pastor is there but says his thank-yous early and bicycles home. Those who see him report that he rides like the wind.

On the morning of the fourteenth, the pastor's wife goes out to the cows as usual. They don't answer when she calls, so the pastor has to go find them. They're not as familiar with him, and it takes time for him to drive them back to the meadow gate. She is sitting on a milk pail looking thoughtful. When she starts to milk, it goes slower than usual, and she stops now and again as if listening.

"How are you?" he asks timidly.

"Fine," she says. "But it may be today."

Nervously he says, "Shall I call?" Doctor Gyllen, he means, and she snorts.

"No! We'll wait and see."

They walk slowly to the well with the strainer and the pails. Petter hauls up water in the pail and washes it out, then he lowers the milk containers so they stand on the bottom. The water is only a few centimetres deep. In a matter of days the well will be completely dry. "With our hay already in, it would be nice to get some rain," he says. "But for the rest of the Örlanders it needs to hold off another week or so."

For once, she doesn't say that the Örlanders have only themselves to blame for waiting too long to make their hay. She walks a little as if she were wading, and climbs the steps slowly. They come into the kitchen, and Mona shows him where she put the big pot with the fish soup she made the evening before, in case anything should happen. Everything is ready, the sheets have been changed, and clean sheets are waiting in the cupboard. He wanders around stricken with tenderness but feeling a little like a young bull following a heifer uninterested in mating. She dismisses him irritably and says, "Stop fussing! What good does it do?"

Nevertheless, she suggests that they eat earlier today, and by eleven o'clock they've already got the soup steaming on the table along with good fresh bread and butter. "Goody," says Sanna. She's in a frisky mood, and Petter notes that she doesn't seem to have the least idea that something is afoot. Cecilia looks both worried and uncertain. In her imagination she can see the boat with the doctor sinking so that she herself will have to act as midwife. What is she supposed to do? She hasn't the least idea! And how will she dare?

The pastor's wife herself stands up before they've eaten their rhubarb pudding. "For supper, there's soured milk in the cellar, and you can fry eggs and put them on bread," she instructs them. "Maybe Cecilia would be kind enough to wash the dishes." It is almost noon. She goes into the bedroom and the pastor follows. When he comes back out, he goes to the telephone and calls Doctor Gyllen.

While the operator spreads the news across the Örlands, Cecilia stands in the kitchen washing dishes. Sanna stands beside her, talking happily and handing her one dish at a time. The pastor comes in and says that maybe Sanna can take her nap in the sauna today, since it's so warm in the house. Then they can take a walk out to Hästskär and see if they can find any wild strawberries. Sanna is excited at the prospect and again unaware that the pastor has a frog in his throat and is talking oddly. Through the kitchen window they see there's a boat on its way into the little bay. "It's the

Hindrikses' hired man coming with Doctor Gyllen," Cecilia identifies them.

"Thanks be to God," the pastor says. He hurries back to the bedroom with the news, much more relieved than his wife, who knows that nothing is going to happen right away. Cecilia gets ready, taking Sanna and grabbing a hat and rubber boots and a blanket for Sanna. On their way to the sauna they meet Doctor Gyllen on her way up from the dock. She walks at her usual brisk pace and carries her black doctor's bag, which the youngsters in the village believe to contain babies. When she's rummaged around a bit, she finds an appropriate infant to leave behind when she leaves the house. Cecilia's not allowed to tell that story to Sanna, because the pastor's wife has told her not to repeat old wives' tales but to tell things the way they are so that Sanna doesn't get all confused by a lot of nonsense.

"Good day." Cecilia curtseys and looks at the ground; Sanna hides on her safe side. "Good day, good day!" says Doctor Gyllen. "So you girls are going out to walk. Good idea." She walks on, but not as if she were running. Cecilia and Sanna go to the sauna, and of course Sanna can't even think of sleeping in a new place. She twists and turns on her blanket on the shelf and then sits up, her eyes full of life. Cecilia sings all the songs she knows along with several hymns, and Sanna sings along. Normally, she quiets down after a while, but not today. Cecilia sings several lullabies, but no child was ever more wide awake than Sanna. There are mosquitoes in the sauna, and Cecilia has to agree that it's not a good place for a nap. But at least they've managed to kill almost an hour. Cecilia takes the large dipper from the sauna to hold their wild strawberries, and in boots and sunhats, they head off.

First they must pass the parsonage. The pastor is sitting on the steps, his face grey, and Cecilia is afraid that Sanna will rush up to him, but she is full of the promised expedition and just calls out, "We're going to pick wild strawberries!" and hurries along the path as if she were afraid of being captured and stuffed into bed. They stride along in their boots, past the churchyard and out into the wilds of Hästskär, where the world loses sight of them in dense thickets and in deep ravines under high granite walls. Where the cows have grazed, it is open and fine, and, just as Cecilia promised, there are wild strawberries. Masses of wild strawberries. A colossal abundance of wild strawberries. They have ripened large and sweet this lovely, dry summer. There are so many that they have to watch where they step so they don't crush too many with their boots. Sanna picks them one at a time, smells them and looks at them and puts them in the dipper. Cecilia adds hers and tells Sanna that she can eat some if she likes, but Sanna is focused on the picking and is proud of the pile building in the dipper. Time passes quickly. For the first time, Sanna is far away from Mama and Papa and she feels big and full of her task — picking wild strawberries for dessert!

Cecilia is not used to small children with such perseverance, but Sanna is enchanted by her berry picking. "Look Cecilia!" she says every time. Cecilia is picking too, and the dipper fills. Too soon? she wonders uneasily. She suggests that they rest for a while, and Sanna leans against her and falls asleep as if on cue. They sit there in the afternoon sun for almost an hour. Far away, Cecilia hears terrible screams. If she didn't know that the pastor's wife was giving birth, she would have concluded that some cow had got its horns caught in a tree. Cecilia shivers and imagines it is she herself. It's awful. But Sanna sleeps calmly and deeply. Then it grows quiet and peaceful, all she can hear is a seabird crying, and then Sanna wakes up. A little groggy, she sits up. "Good morning!" Cecilia says. "Shall we start home with all our wild strawberries?"

Sanna says she's terribly hungry, and Cecilia says they've been gone longer than she expected and they should have brought some sandwiches and something to drink. "But we've got food right here! Let's eat some strawberries to give us the strength to get home!" They have been sitting in a sort of tiny magic garden, a natural little pasture surrounded by juniper bushes, granite slabs and warm stone cliffs. "Like in a room of our own," Cecilia says. "And look, here's our very own privy!" And sure enough, between a big stone and an overgrown juniper bush there's a little space where they can piddle in complete privacy!

They wander home hand in hand, in complete agreement that it has been a wonderful afternoon. All the rocks are facing in the wrong direction on the way back, and it's harder to walk, though Sanna marches along energetically. Like the cat with the seven-league boots that they read about, Cecilia says. She can see by the sun that it must be four-thirty by the time they arrive at the parsonage. She reconnoitres carefully but all seems quiet and calm. The door opens and the pastor comes out, beaming. "Come in, come in," he begins, but Sanna cries out, "Papa, Papa! Look! We've been picking wild strawberries! Thousands of strawberries!"

"Well, look at that!" Papa says. "You've come at just the right moment, my little strawberry girls. There's wonderful news. Come in and see."

The doors to the house stand open, and Doctor Gyllen is sitting in the dining room with her helper, Sister Hanna, calmly drinking coffee. Papa's cup is half full at the head of the table. Sanna rushes in and shows them the wild strawberries in the sauna dipper. "Let's put them in a nice dish before we take them in to Mama," Cecilia suggests. Papa goes to the kitchen with them. Cecilia takes out the good soup tureen and pours the berries into it. Nothing could be prettier, and while Sanna hops up and down with delight and impatience, the pastor says, "Thank you so much, Cecilia. This was perfect. It's a girl, and now I'll take Sanna in and show her. Come, Sanna."

He carries the wild strawberries like the chalice in church and they walk into the bedroom. The window is ajar and the room smells good. Sanna toddles in, "Look Mama, wild strawberries!" Papa holds out the tureen in all its glory and Mama admires it. "What a splendid dessert for this evening! What a good girl!" She's lying in bed looking happy and satisfied, and there is a tray of coffee on the chair beside the bed. "Coffee in bed is only for birthdays!" Sanna knows to say, and then Papa says she's right, because today *is* a birthday. "You've got a little sister today, and it's her birthday. Do you want to see?"

Now she sees that there's a little packet beside Mama, wrapped in the little baby blanket that once was Sanna's. Papa lifts it up as carefully as if it were lamp glass, loosens the blanket a bit, and there inside is a tiny little baby. A squashed, vivid reddish-purple face, with black hair pasted along its scalp. You can see from far off that it has no teeth and no eyes.

"Ooh," Sanna says.

"Not exactly a beauty," Papa says, "but she'll get prettier in just a few days. This is your little sister, and you're the only sister she has in the whole world."

Sanna says nothing. Of course Papa has talked about a sister or brother, but she thought it would be someone like herself, not this thing. When it's someone's birthday, you're supposed to be happy and sing Happy Birthday, but suddenly she just wants to cry, and cry she does, big tears and a loud wail. Papa puts the strawberry tureen down on the bureau, right under

Jesus on the cross, and lifts up Sanna. "There, there, Sanna! You've been having lots of fun all day and now you're really tired." He rocks her and talks to her and then he says they'll go and see if they can't find some supper, and then he's going to call Grandma and Grandpa and Gram and Gramps and tell them about the wild strawberries and Sanna's sister!

He would have left the strawberries behind if Sanna hadn't reminded him. He puts her down and takes the bowl and they walk through the parlour to the dining room, where they see that Sanna has been crying. "It was a shock for her to see her little sister. But she'll get to be more and more fun every day, I promise."

Doctor Gyllen has stood up and asks him to call for the Hindrikses' hired man, but the pastor says that he hopes she can stay and have supper with them. He can hear they're already working in the kitchen — nothing very special, soured milk and buttered bread and wild strawberries, but they'd be happy if she'd help herself. They have enough soured milk for everyone. Mona clearly had her suspicions when she made it the day before. And at just that moment Cecilia comes up from the cellar with the bowls of soured milk balanced on a tray, and Sister Hanna comes in from the kitchen with small plates and a basket of bread.

"Khleb!" says Doctor Gyllen and sits down, because the only thing she misses from Russia is the bread, the loaves of dark bread that keep that afflicted people on its feet. On Åland, loaves are not a part of the culture, but it does belong to the pastor's mainland heritage, and here it is, thick slices of splendid bread along with home-churned butter piled on a plate, something the suffering Russian people have had to live without for years. "Ah! Kvass!" she says when the small beer is carried in, suddenly realizing that she has missed that, too.

ICE by ULLA-LENA LUNDBERG

While Cecilia and Sister Hanna lay out the food, the pastor makes his calls. Sanna stands beside him, and he begins by saying that he has two important pieces of news: Sanna and Cecilia have filled the big sauna dipper with wild strawberries and, meanwhile, Mona gave birth to a daughter. Yes, a fine healthy little girl, although at the moment she looks like a boxer who's stayed in the ring a few rounds too long, or like Dopey in *Snow White and the Seven Dwarfs*. And yes, everything went well, Mona is healthy and happy and sends her love. The homecare sister is in place and ready to do the milking, all is well.

At the table, Doctor Gyllen has to withdraw her outstretched hand, for the pastor is saying grace. "Bless us, Oh Lord, and these thy gifts, which we are about to receive from thy bounty, through Christ, Our Lord. Amen."

"And the wild strawberries," Sanna reminds him.

"Yes, of course," says Papa. "Bless especially the wild strawberries. Thou hast created them, but Sanna and Cecilia have picked them."

They can choose how to eat them, either heaped up on the soured milk or by themselves, with sugar and milk, after eating the soured milk with sugar and cinnamon and scraping the bowl clean. Papa and Sister Hanna choose to eat them with the soured milk, but Doctor Gyllen says she's like a child when it comes to wild strawberries — she means to follow Sanna's and Cecilia's lead and eat them separately. "Just with sugar, no milk. Heavenly!" For the first time, Sanna dares to look at Doctor Gyllen, who always looks the same but looks almost happy at the moment.

No matter how hurried you may be when you arrive, and no matter what your eating habits are at home, at the parsonage you will spend a long time at the table. Until finally Doctor Gyllen says they must call the Hindrikses' hired man so they can have some peace in the house and Sister Hanna can go to the cows. The pastor will go with her and instruct her, but first he calls the Hindrikses and thanks Doctor Gyllen for her services, and she suddenly hears herself say, "My dear Pyotr Leonardovich, you have a good home here and your wife does you honour. I am happy that I was able to help her a little, but on the whole she did it all herself."

He too is a bit surprised to hear his name in Russian, but mostly he feels honoured. Presumably it means that he and the doctor are now on very good terms, and that with him she can open a chink in her harshness and abruptness and surprise herself. Now she goes in to say goodbye to the pastor's wife and comes out smiling to say that Mona is now hungry. "Everything looks very good, but if anything should occur, you have only to call, day or night."

Sister Hanna sends Cecilia in with a tray so that she too can see the new baby, and Sanna goes with her. Cecilia curtseys, blood red in the face, the china rattling on the tray. "Congratulations!" she whispers. "Thank you," says the pastor's wife in her normal, energetic voice. "Oh, I've been longing for a little something to eat. Bread and butter, soured milk and wild strawberries. You can put the tray right here and then have a look at our little addition!"

Sanna is suddenly an old hand with her sister, and when Mama turns down the blanket, she encourages Cecilia. "Don't be afraid. It will look better tomorrow." Then the baby moves, waves its little fists a bit and opens its eyes a crack, enough that they can see a tiny flash of brightness. She opens her mouth and says waaah waaah. "Ooh," says Sanna. "Does it want a strawberry?" "No," says Mama. "The first few months she can only drink milk. But I'm going to eat some of your wonderful wild strawberries. It was so nice of you to save so many of them for me." It's hard to talk because the baby screams waaah waaah the whole time. "Quiet!" says Sanna, but the baby isn't listening, and Mama just lets her cry.

"We should go," Cecilia says, but then Mama says she has something she wants to ask both of them. "What would you say to letting Sanna sleep in Cecilia's room tonight, what with the baby crying and fussing. If Cecilia agrees, of course."

"Oh!" Sanna says. "Oh yes!" And Cecilia says, "Yes, of course, if you'll promise not to chatter all night." "Good," says Mama. "Then I'll ask Papa to carry your bed upstairs when he gets back from the cows. And you need to be nice to Sister Hanna and do what she tells you, because she's going to be here and help us out for a week. She's a nice woman and likes children and cows and wild strawberries."

When they leave the bedroom, Papa and Sister Hanna have gone out to the cow barn. The Hindrikses' hired man is on his way into the church inlet, and Doctor Gyllen is on her way to the church dock. She's in amazingly good spirits and wonders if that means bad news is on its way. It seems to be a part of human mentality that people lull themselves into a state of well-being and security just before some fatal blow befalls them. No doubt a characteristic favoured by evolution, since it gives people a small buffer — lower blood pressure, lower pulse, peace of mind — when the blow arrives.

As soon as he's killed the motor, the hired man yells, "It's a girl, I heard." Doctor Gyllen has stopped marvelling. She accepts the fact that in some mysterious way (in which the telephone operator can be presumed to play a not insignificant role), every person on the Örlands, every horse, cow and sheep, knows that the pastor and his wife have had a girl, even though the entire congregation has wished them a son.

Chapter Sixteen

IT'S NICE HAVING THE HOUSE FULL OF WOMEN—Sister Hanna in the guest preacher's room, Cecilia in the attic, Mona and the two girls in the bedroom. In the parish, people are saying, "Better luck next time," because out here people want boys who can work and drive boats. Girls are fine after you've had two boys. "We've still got time," says the pastor confidently, and it becomes proverbial: "'We've still got time,' said the pastor." "If you have girls, you'll get boys," is another saying he's picked up on the Örlands. But for the moment, things are quiet. Like a little island of calm in the midst of all the summer's activities, where the pastor's family can be by itself with the help of friendly Sister Hanna and dear Cecilia, who keeps Sanna from feeling neglected.

Papa calls her Lillus, and after a few days, Sanna stops calling her "it". When she turns out to have eyes, and then when she grips Sanna's fingers hard, Sanna begins to think she'll be able to have her around even though it's sad how little she knows and can do. Mama insists that Sanna herself was just as little once, but Sanna finds that hard to believe. They must all help her, Papa says, so she'll grow up and get to be as smart as Sanna. But it will take a long time, he says, realistically. Both Mama and Papa say she'll surely turn out all right, although she'll need a lot of help and looking after on the way.

Sister Hanna is a nice woman and talks to Cecilia and therefore to Sanna. It's so pleasant to work in the parsonage, she says. Everything is well arranged, and everything was ready when she arrived. They understand her and appreciate her, and she feels like a princess in the guest room. She's very fond of the pastor's wife, and the pastor is too good for this world. He takes such good care of his wife! He's an example for everyone, if only people knew enough to follow his example. This priest's whole life is like a sermon. You have to admire such a young man who already knows so much about how life should be lived.

She stays for two weeks, but then she has to move on to a house in mourning, she explains, and Sanna cries. "A house in mourning here too, when you go," says Papa. Mama thanks her heartily, and Papa makes a little speech. "You have been like a good angel in our house," he says, and all except Lillus walk with her to the boat that has come to get her. Papa goes straight home and writes a letter to the local council about what a blessing this homecare aide has been to his family. He sends his warm thanks to the elected officials who so wisely decided to create this position in spite of strained finances.

Thanks to Sister Hanna, he has also been able to spend hours in his study, and there are times when he begins to foresee the end of his efforts and to believe he's got a handle on his dissertation. Fredrik has of course passed his exams with flying colours and has sent Petter his questions, not a bunch of hopeless theological hairsplitting but problems that, with rigorous study and thoughtful consideration, he ought to be able to tackle.

Here on the Örlands, it's a contest between the pastor and Doctor Gyllen as to which of them will finish first. They each ask about the other's progress when they see one another at the meetings of the Public Health Association. Their conversations these days have an open, friendly tone. They can even tease each other a bit. If only they could do an exchange? So the pastor could get the doctor's professional experience and the doctor could acquire the pastor's ability to write Swedish! He has to learn the names of various potentates in the history of the church and she the names of a number of distinguished figures in Finnish medicine and memorize their specialities. She knows clinical medicine from A to Z, but "Ach, Pyotr Leonardovich, the cultural! Medicine is same all over Europe, but each country has its authorities! Titles and designations! God have mercy!" She stops herself, for she doesn't like to refer to God in the pastor's presence. He notices her embarrassment.

"Perhaps he will," he comforts her. "After all, the emphasis must be on your medical, clinical qualifications. And in Latin rather than in Swedish. Which by the way you speak much better than you think. Of course they're going to pass you. We all think you should have the right to practise medicine even without the Finnish medical exam."

"Thank you," Doctor Gyllen says. "And I think I know that the entire parish, I too, think you ought to be permanent vicar even without extra theological examination."

"Thank you," he says in turn. Seeing them from a distance, the organist thinks they look like a couple of thieves at a market, and the kindly Hindrikses, who can read their doctor better than she suspects, hope that in the pastor, who is well educated like herself, she will find a person she can talk to about the things that weigh on her mind. The Hindrikses, and the Örlanders in general, don't need to spend years at a university studying psychology to see that people need to talk to each other to ease their burdens.

Sometimes this thought occurs to Doctor Gyllen herself, who, in moments of weakness, is strongly tempted to speak to this friendly young priest. She would surely be disappointed, as he has so obviously been spared the pain that torments her, but the temptation to expose herself to this disappointment remains distressingly strong. Two things hold her back — the fear that her self-control will collapse and she will go to pieces entirely and sit there sobbing, swaying, unravelling; and the danger that she will calm herself with a pill and then have no need to speak to him, although she has set the time and place.

For the third year she has her parents as summer guests. Petter has met them at the store and at church, where once each summer they attend a service as a kind of social obligation, despite that fact that the general's wife is Greek Orthodox. Now the pastor gets the idea to invite them to Lillus's christening, which will take place in the church, with coffee after at the parsonage. The pastor's own parents will come, along with one of his wife's sisters and her fiancé, plus friends from the area. It would be an honour if . . . They owe Doctor Gyllen their thanks and would be delighted if . . . He is a little embarrassed and almost expects them to thank him and decline, but very cordially they say yes.

The front pews in the church are occupied by Petter and Mona's relatives and the first friends they made on the Örlands — the organist and the verger and their wives, Adele Bergman and Elis, Brage Söderberg and Astrid, along with Cecilia and Hanna, who've been such a great help to them. Everyone in a festive, benevolent mood. Then the general and his wife with Doctor Gyllen, all three of them inscrutable. A warm-hearted christening, Lillus gurgling and delighted by the water on her head, by Papa's voice, by everything so big. She is frightened when they all start singing, but she gets over it quickly, and after the baptism the pastor once again invites everyone present to the parsonage.

The general knows better than to sit and stare, and his wife learned early how to conduct herself. Doctor Gyllen has trained herself to look a firing squad in the eye without blinking, and no one can see what any of them are thinking. She doesn't usually attend christenings. Pulling out new babies is not a problem, it's a job, but freshly scrubbed infants dressed in white as the centre of attention can stir up feelings. Which are held in check with the help of half a pill, which doesn't leave her muddled but allows her to function normally in social situations. Still, it's a relief when it's over and she can stand up, shake hands, congratulate the parents, and take a professional look at the baby, which looks very good! Remembers to greet Sanna as well. The organist, who understands children, says, "Congratulations on becoming a big sister," to her as she stands earnestly beside her mother, and others follow his example.

Cecilia has run to the parsonage and got the fire going in the stove, and Mona and Sanna hurry after her with Lillus, who has filled her nappy and can be smelled from a great distance. Lillus! The others follow along at an easy pace. The pastor brings up the rear, walking quickly, and falls into step with the Gyllens, honoured guests who nevertheless draw attention to the fact that they are not members of the inner circle of friends. "A beautiful christening," says the general's wife, and the general adds, "Beautiful weather too. I allow myself to hope it is a good omen."

"Thank you," the pastor says. All sorts of things stumble on his tongue until he says, "A day to remember for us. I'm happy you wanted to be here."

Doctor Gyllen is walking beside him, full of something she wants to say. She stops and takes off one shoe and shakes it. Nothing comes out. Her parents walk quietly on, arm in arm. The pastor waits politely. Doctor Gyllen straightens up, as tall as he. She talks the way she did when she didn't want people to see that she was talking, without looking at him. "I too have a child. I am in such distress."

The pastor pauses long enough to keep himself from blurting out some empty phrase. No religious talk, as he knows what she thinks of that. "Is he still in Russia?" he asks, a neutral question.

"You know that it's a he?"

"People have mentioned it. Not gossip. With all respect. But still that you had to leave your son behind. The way things are in the Soviet Union, everyone understands."

"I abandoned him. How can I live with that?"

"My dear friend, when it happened you couldn't know you'd be separated for such a long time. I understand your sorrow and pain. I admire your strength and composure."

"You don't know what it was like. You never knew when you saw people if it would be for the last time. Colleagues. Friends. Your husband. Your child. If I had stayed, KGB would have separated me from my son. But that's no excuse. I can never forgive myself."

"In many situations, we're our own strictest judges. I don't want to force my beliefs on you, but as a priest I can offer you one comfort. There is one who offers mercy and forgiveness when we can't offer them to ourselves. He understands your choices. He sees your anguish. He forgives you."

228

She has not looked at him, but now she looks away even more, if that's possible. "The important thing is not how I feel. The important thing is my son. No contact possible. Letters have been sent. Official. Private. Red Cross. Nothing. Not even my father. Russia is like another planet."

"I know. I don't know if it would help you if we went through what can be done. I'm certain that you and your father know all the possibilities and have tried every channel. But sometimes it can help to discuss matters with an outsider who is sworn to silence. Nothing we speak of will go further. Maybe by pure chance we'll come up with something new. In my line of work there are also examples of miracles."

He smiles, understands perfectly well that she sees things differently, but he nevertheless enjoys shocking her with his naiveté. She almost smiles back, digs in her purse and shakes a pill into the palm of her hand and swallows it without water, throws her head back so it will slide down. "Yes," she says. "Thank you. And forgive me for detaining you. Now we must go to the parsonage. Christening coffee cannot begin before Papa and Pastor arrive."

They go in. The doors are open between the dining room and the parlour, there is a great buzz, and all the chairs are in use. The idea is that Mona should sit with the baptized baby in her arms while others serve, but it's hard for her to see how slowly it's all going, and she hates having her mother-in-law in the kitchen. Soon enough, Lillus is put to bed and Mona takes over. With help from Cecilia, who is willing and biddable, everything goes smoothly. And when the guests who are not staying on – in every corner of the parsonage – get up to to, the pastor says to Doctor Gyllen, "I'm planning to come to the village tomorrow. We need to talk about the roof-beam celebration for the Health Care Centre. Would it be all right if I look in during the afternoon?"

"That will be fine," says Doctor Gyllen. "But I don't expect any miracles."

* * *

And here he is, where everyone can see, his briefcase in hand, knocking on Doctor Gyllen's door. A long meeting, there is clearly much to discuss concerning the Health Care Centre. Her parents are out rowing in the nice weather. The general's wife has a parasol raised against the sun, the general has a handkerchief on his head with knots tied at the corners, his braces over his undershirt, his trouser legs rolled up, and his lily-white feet on the duckboards. They row to an island in the bay and have coffee on the granite slope.

The pastor greets her with a smile, the doctor thanks him for yesterday's reception. "It was all very pleasant." As for the roof-beam party, maybe better to return to it when Sörling is ready to suggest a date. In any case, they need to discuss the refreshments with Adele Bergman. So:

The pastor has to start, he's used to that. "All of this must feel like small potatoes compared with your own struggle."

"Don't misunderstand me. I don't think what happens here is unimportant. This is the right way to live, normally. Precious."

"Yes, I feel the same way, ever since the end of the war. It's good that we understand each other on that point. Moreover, I realize that here in Finland there's a great deal we don't understand about Rus —, about the Soviet Union. This Iron Curtain they talk about makes it hard for information to get through. Propaganda on their side, propaganda on ours. What are things really like over there?"

"A little better, I hope, now that the war is over. Materially. Maybe not the same hunger. But otherwise my information is quite old. Years have gone. No channels which function. Total isolation. We know nothing. We do not hear even rumours."

"Before the war there were lots of rumours. People disappearing. No one knew anything for sure."

"People who have never lived there don't understand. No one knows what it was like."

"No. Did you know other Finns in Leningrad? My father was in contact with Finns he met in America who moved to the Soviet Union, but then there were no more letters."

"Many are dead. Others in camps. Yes, I knew Finns. In happier times, in their youth, my father knew Edvard Gylling. He looked me up in Leningrad. You will think it comic, but we always spoke Swedish together. Except last few times. We didn't dare. We spoke only Russian, only the most common phrases. 'I am happy to see you, dear Edvard Gylling.' 'And I to see you, dear little Irina Gyllen.' 'How is your dear family?' 'Fine, thank you, in good health. Fanny especially sends greetings.' That was his last visit to Leningrad. Then arrested. Fanny taken away. Grown children, no contact."

"Terrible."

"He was a good person. An idealist. A socialist. Ach, if he had only stepped back when the civil war in Finland could no longer be prevented."

"Like our own great donor, who knew enough to flee to Sweden. He had relatives here who helped him move on."

"Gylling could have done the same. But he could not betray his ideals. What he saw as the cause. He could not betray his comrades."

"He made the wrong decision for the right reasons. While things are happening, we have no access to the final accounting."

"If he could have persuaded Fanny to stay in Sweden with the children or go to Finland when it was still possible!

We were such good friends. Our names so similar. We had nicknames for each other. We always spoke Swedish. About our youth. Although I had more Russian than he and had lived longer in Russia. I was admitted to medical school before the Revolution."

"You lived through all of it."

"Yes. I knew how poor, ignorant, dirty, helpless the people were. We were many who thought the Revolution must happen to change these evils. How could we? So stupid."

"You believed in reforms, ideals. That's not stupid."

"Years went by before we understood, and then we didn't want to believe. I could pursue my studies, I took examinations, specialized. Got married. My husband like me. Those years, when we could have emigrated to Finland. The Finnish immigrants also."

"People act on the information and the hopes they have. No one can demand that you should have known then what you know now."

"Yes, but later. People start to disappear. Arrests. Everyone afraid. People afraid to talk. Afraid to telephone. Suspect each other. It takes astonishingly long time, my dear Pyotr Leonardovich, before you realize you are not paranoid to suspect your friends of being informers. You do everything from fear — wrong things, immoral things, ugly things. You've never had to see what you can be driven to do."

"No."

"And the worst of all, you let time pass until you can no longer save yourself. Contacts with Finland broken. No more invitations to consulate. Russian police at the gate, always asking for invitation, name, papers. The best doctors gone, new doctors and commissars, surveillance. My husband and I told ourselves for long time the regime needs doctors. They can't manage without us. We're safe. If we just work, not talk, not attract attention. Then we had our son, born in 'thirty-two. For him we do everything."

"Yes."

"There is so much envy. Everyone has something that someone else wants. Your job at the hospital. Your apartment. Something so unimportant you can't even imagine. We discuss all the time, my husband and I, what is best for the child. If one of us is arrested, the other gets divorce. Disclaim the other, we forgive each other in advance. Live quietly with child. Hope for better times."

"I sympathize completely with everything you say."

"Yes. But then just betrayal. He is arrested, for what? Enemy of the people, saboteur. Divorce as we planned, but not right, immoral. And no use. If he, Russian, blameless, is arrested, why then not me? You cannot imagine such terror. I thought only of saving us. Me and my son. Then I got chance—I cannot tell you how or through whom . . ."

"Of course not!"

". . . but I got chance, without my son. And I was so terrified, I deserted him. I thought: in Finland we can arrange exit visa for him, legally, with help of legation. Selfish, wrong! Then came the war, all diplomatic relations broken. Five years! I can never forgive myself."

"For pity's sake! If you had stayed you would have been arrested yourself. You'd have disappeared like so many others. Your son would have lost his mother anyway. Now at least you have a chance of getting back in touch."

"Thank you. Yes, that is rational thinking. But think of the child. Abandoned by his mother, completely alone in the world. He doesn't think like you. He has simply been abandoned."

"Do you know anything about the people you left him with? Your husband's relatives?"

"No. Strangers at that address, no contact. Unable to trace father's parents either. Maybe also arrested."

"The Finnish Consulate?"

"Yes, father has certain contacts. A brave person rang the bell of the apartment where I left him. Other people there. No information about earlier residents. Nor about father's parents at their address. But otherwise Finnish legation in Moscow very cautious. We must not provoke great powerful Soviet Union that swallows us in next war."

"I suppose you've tried to contact orphanages in the Leningrad area."

"Yes, but you understand — evacuations. And I'm glad for that. Otherwise the boy would not have survived the siege. But it meant chaos in documentation."

"He's a teenager now. Maybe he's tried to find you? He knows that you came from Finland. He knows your maiden name, maybe even remembers the name of his grandfather. If he contacts the Finnish legation . . . Or no, he doesn't know you fled, and it can't be easy for an adolescent in the Soviet Union to contact a foreign legation."

"His parents are enemies of the people, Finland an enemy in the war. How could he, a fifteen-year-old boy?"

"No, that was silly of me, too optimistic. What I mean is later, in the future. But it's now you need to make contact."

"I don't even know if he's alive. If he is alive — a boy at the worst age. If we saw each other now, it might not be a happy meeting. Accusations, hate towards me. Hate towards Finland."

"You can grieve about that later. What's important now is to find out if he's alive and how he's getting along. Everything else follows from that. My dear Doctor Gyllen, I will keep all of this in my mind and in my heart. You may well believe that there is nothing to be done, and for the moment perhaps you're right. You've thought of everything, you have contacts that I can't even imagine. But believe me, it helps to talk about things, the person you talk to can keep his eyes and ears open and perhaps stumble across something that proves to be useful. Things happen all the time that no one ever expected."

"Miracles?"

"Forgive me. I know you don't believe in them. Neither do I, but I hope for them. Allow me to do so for your sake. Please don't take it the wrong way, Doctor Gyllen, but I'm going to pray for you. For your reunion. Privately, of course," he adds quickly.

"Yes of course, naturally. What can I say? Thank you."

They both smile. The pastor is not going to embarrass her by saying a prayer at the table. She is not going to depress him by telling him how she feels about religion. She is happy that she's been able to maintain her self-control. No tears, no turgid self-accusations. On his side, he has not been unnecessarily pious. He gets ready to stand up and smiles apologetically. "Remember you can always talk to me. My vow of silence is absolute and includes even murder. You have your own medical confidentiality. Oh my, it's only two months now until we both face our respective examinations. Thank you for talking to me, but now we have to study."

"Thank you for coming," she says, finding it absolutely impossible to say anything more.

"Don't mention it. My wife and I owe you a huge debt of gratitude, you know that."

She stands in the window and watches him as he cycles homewards. Before he's out of sight, he stops at some bushes and eats raspberries. Only then does she realize how totally absorbed she was by her own problems when he was talking to her. Örlanders never let anyone leave without offering food or drink. Even when food is scarce, Russians never forget the rules of hospitality. She should have given him coffee! She should have bought a coffee cake at the store now that such things are available again. He tried to give her hope, and she sent him away hungry!

The pastor has added Doctor Gyllen's son to the list of things he prays for, and he prays a first prayer as he rides. He thinks of Doctor Gyllen, unnaturally self-controlled or perhaps petrified and frozen to the core after all she's been through. And he thinks about what it would be like to have to leave Sanna and Lillus, to suddenly not come home one day. If it was a matter of saving their lives, certainly, but if it was a question of saving his own? A terrible choice, and slim comfort he came up with for Doctor Gyllen: that under present circumstances she would have been separated from him in any event. But which sounds better to an adolescent? My parents were liquidated, or, My mother abandoned me and fled to Finland? Doctor Gyllen lives with this every day. Dear God, let her be reunited with her son.

Chapter Seventeen

A YEAR AND A HALF AFTER HIS ARRIVAL on the Örlands, Pastor Petter Kummel is about to make his first trip to the mainland. It is the end of September, beautiful Indian-summer weather. Bareheaded, because his handsome head of hair lifts his hat off his head, light topcoat not used since his arrival, cassock in his suitcase. His dissertation sent on ahead, notes about it in his briefcase. Since the trip is a long one — boat to Mellom, steamboat to Åbo, train to Helsingfors, bus to Borgå — there is reason to believe he'll have time to rehearse a number of fine points in church law and theology and polish his prepared sermon, so his briefcase is stuffed with abstracts and other papers of every kind. The heart inside the shirt is relatively calm. In his free moments, he has actually managed to read a great deal and has real faith in his ability to elucidate a variety of topics. And it would be presumptuous to believe his dissertation the worst ever written!

The postal boat leaves in the evening to meet the night boat from Mariehamn at Mellom. All three of his girls are down at the church dock to wish him a good journey. Lillus is asleep in her carriage and, like so many times before, it is Sanna who clings and kisses and Mona who says brightly, "Now don't worry! You're going to do beautifully. But watch out for the traffic. You haven't been on a city street since May 1946 and cars aren't like cows. And give our love to the Helléns and tell them we'll all come to visit next summer."

The verger rows him over to the steamboat pier, and when he turns his head in the rowing boat, he sees them smile and wave and then turn and go back to the parsonage, for the evening air is chilly and it's time for Sanna to go to bed. He holds out hope nevertheless and, sure enough, when half an hour later Post-Anton passes Church Isle, Mona and Sanna are standing up on steeple hill like dark silhouettes against the light sky, waving. He can almost hear them calling, "Have a good trip! Good luck!" Everyone on the boat smiles, because people don't do this on the Örlands. Here you're gone when you step into the boat and at home when you step ashore.

Post-Anton, like all other two- and four-legged creatures on the Örlands, knows what this is about—the pastoral examination, which means that the pastor could obtain the post of incumbent vicar of Örland parish. Cecilia and Hanna, the organist and the verger, have all seen how he sits and reads and reads and writes and writes. For once the entire population of the Örlands is in agreement. It is senseless that such a good priest should have to be grilled by the high priests in Borgå before he can apply for a post he is clearly cut out for. There are not many passengers, and he manages to exchange a few words with Post-Anton before they reach the Mellom islands.

They speak of the lovely weather and how long it may last and about his travel plans. Anton is familiar with Åbo and Helsingfors, but Borgå is an exotic place where the bishop resides and where the diocese's well-being is decided for better or for worse. Anton knows there is an ancient cathedral there, like a shell around the bishop's exalted person, and the pastor tells him about the chapterhouse, which is from the Swedish time. His thoughts are fully transparent, and finally he cannot restrain himself from asking, "How do you think it will go?"

* * *

He laughs as if it were a game of some sort, and I smile as well, and I say, "I'm sure you'll do fine on your examination!" But I have my own interest in the matter, for I am used to seeing seaways in my mind but think very little about the way things are on land. I saw him stand there waving to his wife and daughter as if he already longed to be home, so I don't know why I also saw another woman, of a kind he should not meet. For heaven's sake, I cannot tell the pastor to "Watch out for fallen women" like a fortune teller in a tent. No, God forbid. But there's someone there who's a real stone in his path. What can I say?

"But there will be headaches," I say. "You must be prepared for that. I don't have such powers of divination that I can tell you what's going to happen, but this much I can tell you from experience, that there are things which do not go as planned. There are stones on a person's path. If you are prepared for that and can avoid them, you'll be fine."

It is painful to see how uneasy he becomes. I should have said nothing. "I am as well prepared as I can be," he objects. "I have train and bus timetables and I've booked lodgings in Borgå. Brought my alarm clock so I'm sure to wake up. What could go wrong? Even if the boat should have engine trouble, I have so much leeway that I should get there with time to spare."

"Yes, yes," I say. "All of that will be just fine. Pay no attention to what I think, but when things get difficult, it's generally about people. For women, men; for men, women. You know a lot of people in Finland and who knows who you'll run into?"

"I've arranged things so I won't see anyone until after the exam," he says. "But then it will be a real circus. I'm prepared for that."

"Good," I say. "Then everything's as it should be and everything will be all right."

It's late when we get to Mellom and dark as pitch, but who should be standing on the pier to meet us but the Mellom priest. It's nice of him, and our priest is really, really happy to see him.

"Well I'll be! What are you doing here?" he shouts. "In the middle of the night!"

"Of course I had to be here to wish you luck!" the Mellom priest says. "It's not every day the island deanery gets to send one of its own to the Inquisition!"

That's the last I hear, but I can see that they stand there chatting and then the pastor asks me if I think he's got time to run up to the parsonage for a few minutes before the steamboat arrives. "Yes indeed," I say. "It would be a major miracle if it sticks to the timetable now that they've got the fore hold full of animals on their way to the slaughterhouse. You can safely take it easy for an hour. If it does come I'll send Kalle up to warn you." He leaves his suitcase in the waiting room but takes his briefcase with him, though it's equally heavy.

❄ ❄ ❄

The priest from the Örlands sits at the Mellom parsonage surrounded by goodwill, drinking tea and eating a cheese sandwich. He has his own sandwiches with him, but the pastor's wife at Mellom says he should save them. "Oh, the days we've spent on those boats in our time!" she exclaims. "And what an awfully long time it takes! And we're only going between Mellom and Åbo, whereas you're coming from the Örlands and going all the way to Borgå. You'll be happy to have those sandwiches tomorrow morning."

So there he sits keeping them up in the middle of the night, drinking tea and being grilled in a very friendly way by Fredrik, who is an expert on the pastoral exams, which he passed with the highest marks. He thinks Petter sounds collected and sensible and is convinced that the exam can only go well. Of course he's nervous, and it's understandable that he takes his leave relatively soon and says he feels easiest down at the pier where he can hail the boat himself. Now he's feeling on top of the world and thanks them for their hospitality and good luck wishes.

When he's gone, Fredrik stands at the window looking out, although his wife has gone to bed and repeats that it's late, middle of the night, soon the wee hours. Yes, yes, and finally the steamship arrives, seriously delayed. He can see Petter in his mind's eye, frozen, shivering, sick of waiting, nervous. And he was so happy that I came down to meet his boat!

No one can see a ship approach in the darkness, its side lanterns glowing, its bridge lit up, without feeling yearning and sadness and, at the same time, strong, unalloyed excitement and expectation. Change, in short, although even as a child he had learned to be suspicious of the change that was the very breath of life for his inconstant, unstable father. Now he's on his way, be it to sink or swim, and after the cathedral there will be a whole series of stimulating get-togethers and a visit he's been looking forward to in particular — to Mona's home and the Helléns, where he can talk to his heart's content about all Mona's wonderful achievements and about Sanna and Lillus.

As the ship thumps across Delet Bay, he manages to get an hour's sleep on a sofa in the smoking saloon, but then it's time for all the landings in the Åbo archipelago. The moment he falls asleep, he hears the change in the engines as the ship nears land, the footsteps of heavily burdened crewmen, shouts between the ship and land, bumps and blows as the ship hits the pier.

Then loading and stowing, shouts and orders, new passengers who come in talking loudly and slamming doors. He has to sit upright on the sofa in case it gets crowded. On and on, a long series of repetitions through the far-flung archipelago.

He can smell Åbo from as far away as Erstan, and when they approach the river, the fumes they encounter are suffocating to a man who has lived undefiled in the fresh sea air of the Örlands. Åbo reeks to high heaven, but at the same time he has to go out on deck and look at the city, which is large and mighty and clamorous. The shipyards work around the clock building ships to pay the war reparations to the Russians. The vessels in the docks will all go east. Farther up the river in the mechanical workshops, men are welding, grinding, and scraping. Slowly, skilfully, with dignity, the *Åland II* approaches its berth. Above the trees, he can see the tower of the cathedral where the clock strikes nine as the giddy, sleepless passengers stagger ashore. The calves and other young animals in the open hold look around with eyes that are used to seeing greenery and twitch ears that are accustomed to a gentler kind of noise, not knowing what awaits them as the slaughterhouse truck backs up to the edge of the quay.

By now the pastor is already moving briskly towards the railway terminal, a trim figure between a suitcase and a briefcase, walking with the bustle of the city in his step. He has already missed one train and needn't rush to catch the next, but hurries anyway because others do. Much to look at, he stares like the country bumpkin he's become, puts down his baggage on the floor of the terminal with relief. Buys his ticket, clatters away through a familiar landscape. Nothing has changed, as if he'd left it all astern when, liberated, he sailed away to the Örlands. No one he knows boards the train at stations where he has acquaintances, no one knows that he sits on this particular train, and, incognito, he sweeps past his old school station and what was for many years his home. Free from all of it!

Then Helsingfors, where he went to university, marked by the war when he left, marked by the war still. But the same restless activity as in Åbo, building and repairing. He will see many people here on his way home. Now he crosses Mannerheim Road to the bus station, finds the Borgå platform, sits down in the sun and waits for the next bus. He takes out his notes and tries to read, but with so much activity around him he finds it hard to concentrate, and his eyes are as curious as a child's — there's so much going on, cars and trams, the ice-cream stand that has sprung up after all the years of war. As an adult, he is happy that everything has returned to normal, while his childish eye hunts for everything new — automobile models, clothing, the new design of the street lights. Of course he hasn't missed traffic and crowds! Of course he loves seeing them again! If only he were free of his exhaustion, his aching unease. That's why he's travelling directly to Borgå, so he can rest and read his most important notes one more time and then sleep one long, quiet night. Wake up rested and clear-headed.

When he arrives in Borgå late that afternoon, still in possession of his suitcase and briefcase, he leaves his things at the small hotel and asks about an inexpensive restaurant. He's been travelling all night and plans an early evening. The desk clerk gives him a meaningful look and tells him a person has been there asking for him — a woman.

The pastor is amazed. "I don't know anyone here. Did she say who she was? Did she leave any kind of message? Are you sure it was me she was looking for?"

No and no and yes indeed, she asked for him by name.

ICE by ULLA-LENA LUNDBERG

"My goodness. Well, since I wasn't expecting anyone and don't know who she is, I'll get something to eat and go for a little walk. I ought to be back in an hour or so."

Why this intense unease? Mostly, of course, because he desperately needs to be alone this evening and collect himself for tomorrow. But also because the clerk called her "a person — a woman" in a certain tone of voice, not "lady" or "young lady". If it had been someone from the cathedral chapter, she would have left a message. But also, and most of all, because he can in fact recall a certain female person from this area. No no no.

Mona has admonished him to eat a good meal once he gets there, despite the expense, because he'll need his strength the next day. If she knows her husband, he'll be way too nervous in the morning to eat anything but bread and butter. Obediently, he orders meatballs served with boiled potatoes and gravy and lingonberry jam. It smells good, but it nauseates him. It's all the rocking and bouncing taking its toll, he tells himself. He's also nervous and, he can't deny it, scared. He picks at the food without the sensual pleasure he had anticipated. Finally he orders a cup of tea and an apple pastry, an unnecessary expense the way he feels. When he's finished, he goes for a walk, watches the traffic in the river and has a look at the houses and streets of the old city, the cathedral looming overhead. Such pleasure he's had from that walk in the past, and so little he has now. He must return to the hotel because that's where he has his things, even though the weather is so nice that he could sleep under a bush or in a boathouse by the river.

Pastor Kummel enters the hotel the same way the animals on the *Åland II* were herded into the slaughterhouse trucks on the quay. And sure enough, a female person sits in one of the

244

chairs by the window. She stands up at once. "Petter! Do you remember me? It's me, Hilda."

He extends his hand. "Of course I remember you, Hilda! How are you! And how in the world did you know I would be in Borgå?"

"Your mother wrote to tell me. It made me so happy in my adversity. You come as if sent by Providence."

"Has something happened?" he asks sympathetically, while thinking of his mother. It's kind of her to stay in touch with her former housemaids. And typical of her to spread far and wide the news of her children's plans and intentions. Including, apparently, times and places. Mama! You think you're an adult and live your own life, but in the background, always and eternally, is Mama.

Hilda bursts into actual tears. "My husband is dead and I don't know what to do. I must talk to you."

"Hilda, dear Hilda, this comes so suddenly. Didn't Mama tell you that I have a big examination at the cathedral chapter early tomorrow morning? It's very important, and I need to spend the evening preparing."

She weeps. "When a person's in distress, she has the right to speak to a priest."

She has clearly boxed him in, and clearly he has to do as she asks. But it is not what the desk clerk expected as he stands there following every word and gesture. The pastor has registered as Pastor Petter Kummel, and this woman appears to want comfort from this man of the church. If only he knew how complicated it was. If he had the slightest idea, the clock on the wall would stop and the ivy wither. Petter points to the chair she sat in. "Shall we sit down? Tell me what's happened."

She rolls her eyes towards the desk clerk. "Please, Petter, in private. You must have a room?"

Petter is in despair, and it's good if the staring desk clerk sees it. This is nothing he has arranged. But, as a priest and a human being, what is he to do? Petter turns to the clerk apologetically. "I understand perfectly well that there is a rule against entertaining guests in the rooms. But this lady is a former servant in my parents' home, and as a priest I cannot turn her away in her need. Could you permit us to talk in my room?"

"Well, all right, then," the man says. "As an exception, this once." He hands Petter the key.

"Thank you," he says. "Please, follow me," he says to her and walks ahead down the corridor, unlocks the door and holds it open. One chair, which is for her, and the bed, where he is forced to sit. As inappropriate as it could possibly be under the circumstances, for Hilda and a bed figured in a nighttime episode that gives him considerable anguish.

The same pressure in the bladder then as now. Hilda slept in the kitchen, and it was through the kitchen he had to pass in order to get to the outhouse. He was sixteen years old, obsessed with the stories told him by the men in the hospital ward where he was taken for his tuberculosis. He thought constantly about women and sex, masturbated, begged God for forgiveness and the strength to resist. Never thought of the women in the house in that way, was only afraid of disturbing them when, quiet as a mouse, he closed the kitchen door before tiptoeing up the stairs to the boys' bedroom.

She, awake, "Is that you Petter?"

"Sorry, Hilda, did I wake you? I didn't mean to."

"Don't be sorry. Come and sit here."

"I think I'd better get back to bed. It's the middle of the night. I apologize again."

"Don't be silly. You're a big boy and can do as you like. Come over here and sit down like I'm telling you."

And he, obedient, sits down. She: "Like that. Only a little closer." She laughs quietly, deep in her throat, and presses up against him. He leans away, tries to stand up, she pulls him down. "Now, now. Don't you know what to do? Such a big boy."

It's as if he'd been clubbed. No will of his own. Only half conscious. Knows only that he must be quiet so he doesn't wake up the whole house. She throws off the covers, and there it is, the smell those awful, obscene men talked about, the smell of sex that makes it stand up straight! She reaches her hand down to the crotch of his pyjamas. "Yes, you *are* a man." Contented sigh. She takes his hand and puts it on her body. Her nightgown has ridden up. "What do you think of this?"

It is hairy and wet. Warm, alive. She takes one of his fingers and puts it into what he realizes is her vagina. "Do you want to try? So you're not so shy next time?" She sighs again and wriggles a bit and moans. "Don't make me beg. Come on."

She is amazingly strong, or maybe she needs no strength, his body is willing and lets itself be pulled onto her and presses eagerly when she leads it to the right place. Suddenly and irreversibly engaged in what the encyclopedia describes as coitus, when the male organ is introduced into the woman's vagina. Conception occurs when, on ejaculation, sperm cells swim to the fertile egg in the woman's uterus. Oh dear God.

This is what he thinks only seconds after his orgasm. That she could be with child. That he can become a father at the age of seventeen and have to live in a forced marriage for the rest of his life. Was it for this he was saved? His promises to God? Come to this? Terrified, he tears himself free, grabs his pyjama trousers, almost sobbing. "Well, where are you going in such a hurry?" she asks from where she's lying. "Wasn't it good?"

"I didn't mean to," he blurts out. In any case he can still move, to the attic stairs, up. His brothers sleep and snore. He can't moan out loud, he can't hang himself without waking them when he kicks away the chair. Powerless, he lies down on his bed, sticky and smelly. He has a math test at school in the morning and should be rested and alert, but what does that matter now, whether or not he succeeds at school, since he'll have to leave when it becomes clear that she's with child.

How did he survive the night? How did he get through the following year, when he came down to the kitchen as late as possible, snatched a slice of bread and grabbed a gulp of coffee without sitting down before rushing off to the station. Came home and ate with the others, left the table as soon as possible and studied, skipped evening tea so that he would never ever have to go to the outhouse at night. Peeked at her out of the corner of his eye to ascertain whether she'd grown heavier, an expert at avoiding her gaze. She, hurt and angry. Mama: "How have you managed to get on Hilda's bad side?" Total terror for eight months. Meanwhile, he has started thinking that the possible child isn't even necessarily his, that she had planned it in order to frame him instead of the actual father, who had taken to his heels. Then exhaustion mixed with relief when he realized that she wasn't pregnant, that no one knew anything. At the same time, disgust and fear at the thought of how easily it happens, almost before you know it. Without the love he'd imagined was the basis of everything.

❋ ❋ ❋

Now an exact parallel. The same merciless pressure in his bladder. He never should have drunk that big cup of tea. Where she's sitting blocks the way to the WC in the corridor.

He unhinged from discomfort and fear. She in tears. "I don't know what to do."

"Tell me what's the matter."

"I don't know where to start. I'm so unhappy I just want to die."

"Hilda, you said that your husband died. Was it recently?"

"Not exactly died. Ran off. I'm completely alone."

"Do you have any children?"

"No. Or rather a girl who's with my mother. I have to work."

"What work do you do?"

"I clean for families in town. I can't hardly manage."

"I understand it must be hard. And badly paid. And when you're depressed . . . Do you have friends you can talk to?"

"Who'd take the trouble?"

"Don't say that. I remember that Hilda had a lot of friends. You were a whole group of girls who went out together on your free afternoons." If his bladder bursts, he'll be an invalid forever. He has to get up. "Excuse me. I just have to . . ." He sidles to the door, leaving it ajar. An endless distance to the end of the corridor, but at least the WC is free. Ah! The flush can be heard in the whole house, you might as well stand on the roof and shout what you've been doing.

He left the door ajar so she wouldn't start going through his things, and maybe she hasn't, either, but of course she's searched the room with her eyes. He smiles benevolently, as relieved as that night he came into the kitchen from the outhouse. More relaxed, he sits back down on the bed. She has had time to think about the conversation they've had and doesn't like his interrogation.

"I didn't come here to talk about how I live and work. Everyone who works has the same life — drudgery and bad pay. What I need to talk about is where I'm to get the strength to bear it."

"Yes."

"When I had a man, I thought I had something to live for. He was no great shakes, but all the same he was a kind of protection or what should I call it. I had someone to wait for. It's more fun to cook when there's two of you. More clothes to wash, of course, big heavy men's clothes, but it's still better. Do you understand what I'm saying? That I don't know how I'm going to live all alone. It's dreadful. Nowadays there aren't any live-in housemaids any more, like at your place. Back then I thought it was horrible, you didn't have any life of your own. But it's awful being alone. Do you know what I mean?"

"I'm trying. At least I think I understand. You miss your husband. So it's lucky he's not dead, just gone. Do you know where he is? Because then maybe you can repair the damage. Maybe you had a fight when he left. Maybe he doesn't know that you feel the way you do. Tell him! The same way you've told me."

"Well of course he's got someone else. Younger than me. And now they've got a kid together. I had my girl with another fellow. What would he want to come back to me for?"

"I see." Suddenly he can't repress a colossal yawn. "Excuse me. I got no sleep last night on the way to Åbo. My head is spinning."

"I'll be going," she says, giving him hope. "But first I have to ask if as a priest you can't give me some comfort. What would Jesus say?"

He knows very well what Jesus would say. "Come unto me, all ye that labour and are heavy laden, and I will give you rest." But he can never, ever say to her, "Come unto me." He smiles crookedly, feeling almost drunk. "Jesus says, 'Follow me.' He means that if we live as true Christians in prayer and faith, we can experience a different sort of joy and meaning in our lives. One way of approaching that kind of life is to go to church. There is a genuine fellowship in a congregation. There you're not alone."

He can hear how empty it sounds, and she objects, quite rightly, "That's all very well. But I wonder. Just look at me. You can see I'm working class and not the kind of person who moves in refined circles. They don't accept people like me at the drop of a hat."

"Don't think that far ahead. Just try to develop a spiritual life. Don't forget to pray. We can bring everything that oppresses us to Jesus. Go to church. Sing the hymns. Listen to the priest. It may seem dry and irrelevant, but by and by it will all open up. The stories from Jesus's life turn out to be about our own lives. The lessons and parables give us counsel and instruction if we're open to them. We think not only about what we want ourselves but about what may be God's will for our lives. In prayer, our thinking grows clearer and we can find solutions to problems that seemed insurmountable before."

"You can certainly talk. Just like your father."

"I take your question about Jesus seriously."

"It's hard to think about Jesus in heaven when what you need is a man here on earth."

Slow steps in the corridor that almost stop outside the door. Someone is listening. Petter, self-controlled: "If we read the New Testament we see that Jesus was not so otherworldly. He was a carpenter, a worker. He knew what it meant to be poor. He sympathized with the sorrows of his fellow men not by pitying them but by showing them new paths to follow." The steps move on. "When he saved the adulteress from being stoned, he showed that we are not put here to judge one another. But he also showed her how to change her life. 'Go and sin no more.'"

"Do you think I'm an adulteress? Then what are you?"

"That's easy to answer. A great sinner. No one is free of sin. That's why Jesus came into the world, to save us from our sins."

"I came here to get help and comfort, and you just talk about Jesus."

"Hilda, you came here because I'm a priest. But if we leave that aside, what is it you want to talk about?"

"That life shouldn't be so boring! That you ought to get to have some fun! That someone should like you. That you shouldn't have to get old. That work shouldn't be so hard. That you ought to get paid better. That you shouldn't always have to skimp and save and borrow money. That you ought to be healthy and not have to go to the hospital. That you should have a husband who likes you. That people shouldn't be so mean. That you shouldn't ever have to cry."

Against his will, he is touched, and he answers with warmth. "There are a lot of us who could subscribe to that. There's much that every one of us has to do without."

"No, I really don't think you can compare yourself with me. Your mother writes about eminent postings and rectories and a fine wife and darling sweetie-pie kids. Money in your wallet and folks that bow and treat you to coffee. What do you know about it?"

There are many things he could reply to that, among them that there is truth in what she says. He counts himself fortunate at having come out of darkness into light. It means he owes everything to other people. He can't show her the door because that would be the most comfortable thing to do, indeed the only sensible thing to do given tomorrow morning's examination. His peace of mind is already deeply shaken, time is passing, and nothing can be repaired. By virtue of his ordination, he is put in a position to be the servant of his fellow men. She is unhappy and bitter and cries genuine tears. If his calling means anything, he must find the strength to sacrifice his convenience even in situations where his own future career is at risk. He can hear Mona's furious objections, even the amused forbearance of the cathedral chapter, but here he sits. Nevertheless, he makes an effort.

"Not so much, I admit. But I'm trying to understand. But Hilda, it's very late. Goodness, it's eleven o'clock. And here we still sit. What are people going to think?"

She gives him an ugly smile. "Tomorrow you'll leave. What difference does it make?"

"I'm also thinking of my examination tomorrow."

"You'll come through with flying colours. You're so smart."

"I've never said I was. It's Mama who brags. It embarrasses me to think of it. The truth is, I haven't had time to prepare the way I should have."

"I'll go. But I also came here in order to see you. I hope you haven't become so sanctimonious that you've forgotten how I slept in the kitchen."

"No, Hilda, you'll have to forgive me. That was twelve, thirteen years ago. A half-grown boy isn't really responsible for his actions."

She snorts. "Grown up enough when it came right down to it."

"Please, Hilda. We did wrong, both of us. But we never did again. Nothing further happened. Now let's change the subject." He is sweating under his shirt and exhausted. In his bag he has his cassock and collar, which he can never again wear with honour.

She snorts again. Her behaviour is equal parts genuine despair and a desire to wound and torment. She is not only spiteful.

It's rather that cruelty and envy are parts of her misery — people grow malicious when everything goes against them. "Easy for you to say, with a wife and children, nothing wrong with your married life. But I have nothing. Utterly alone."

"Yes," he says. "I know." And thinks that if he is silent and lets her talk, she will eventually get it all out. Then he can go with her to the front door and say goodbye in the presence of the desk clerk and wish her good luck.

But he's not to get off so easy. She has a great deal to say, and she has to say it several times because he doesn't react in the wonderfully comforting way she wants. He sits there like a block of wood, nods occasionally, is cross-eyed with exhaustion, bleats, "I'm trying to understand. It must be hard." She weeps, almost shouts, and he hushes her. "Think of the other guests, who've already gone to bed. Please, Hilda, it's late." Sometimes he sneaks a look at the clock. It's twelve. It's twelve-thirty. Thinks of Mona, who wouldn't be as angry with Hilda as with him. "How can you be such a milksop! There's no one on earth let's himself be used the way you do. You should be in an institution!" And then finally he stands up, three hours too late.

"I know it's hard. But it's when we've come through such despair that we reach clarity and can leave some of the pain behind. Then the worst is soon over. But now I have to say good night. I'll see you out."

She leaves, indignant and disappointed. He remains, devastated. No point in even thinking about his notes, the important thing now is to get a few hours sleep so he'll know his own name in the morning at least. He takes out his pyjamas and is suddenly freezing, lies shivering uncontrollably, his teeth chattering, beneath the thin blanket and the flimsy bedspread. A tremendous headache hovers behind his brow. A little sleep is all he needs, but at four o'clock he is still awake and remembers that he hasn't set his alarm clock. Gets out of bed and sets it. Thinks that now he dares to fall asleep and still has time to get three hours. But he's as wakeful as if he were paralysed and taken for dead, full of horror, unable to move, unable to do anything to keep the coffin lid from being nailed into place.

He is still awake at five, five-thirty, thinks he might just as well get up and try to read a little, but falls asleep as he thinks the thought. Flies out of bed when the alarm goes off, stumbles to the floor with a violent headache, doesn't think he can stand up if he tries. Remembers that Mona has packed a tube of aspirin just in case. Climbs arduously to his feet and, moaning, swallows three. Forces himself to get moving, washes in the sink, shaves laboriously and naturally cuts himself and has to stop the bleeding with a piece of newspaper. Takes out clean underclothes, a clean shirt, his cassock that Mona has folded so carefully that it looks fine even without being hung on a hanger all night, fastens his collar at his neck with difficulty. Good morning, Pastor Kummel, slept well? Well prepared, to all appearances.

Rakes everything else into his suitcase. Makes an ineffective sweep of the room to see if he's forgotten anything. Shame-facedly checks that his wallet is still in the inside pocket of his coat—yes, his money is safe. Checks his watch, checks his watch, checks his watch, the face of which is blurred and the numbers drifting. His headache has entrenched itself in his left temple and feels as if it were pushing out his eye. Its tentacles have a grip on his skull and are squeezing. He doesn't know how he's going to deal with the desk clerk but takes his things and locks the door and goes down, heavy steps like an old man. "Good morning."

"Well, good morning, good morning. Yes?"

"I'd like to pay for my room, but I'm hoping I can leave my suitcase here until I'm finished at the cathedral chapter sometime this afternoon."

"That will be fine. Yes, of course. You had a late night."

"I must apologize if we disturbed anyone. It turned into quite a lengthy pastoral session. One of the drawbacks to my calling, to put it crassly."

"Pastoral session?"

"Yes. When someone seeking help speaks to a priest."

The desk clerk laughs right in his face. "That's good. First time I've heard that one."

The pastor sees this as the first station in today's Via Dolorosa. Receives the ignominy graciously, lays his bills on the desk, thanks the man, and goes.

Straight out into the autumn morning's stinging sunshine. His eyes ache and throb. Half blind, he walks to the restaurant and orders coffee, a glass of milk, and a cinnamon roll, in hopes that the sugar will give him a little energy. Compares his watch with the clock on the wall. "Is your clock right?"

"A little fast, but not much. If you're starting at nine, you ought to make it."

"Thank you." But the chicory coffee tastes awful, the milk is tepid, and the roll expands in his mouth and catches in his teeth. He runs his tongue around his mouth, no chance to brush now. Leaves most of the food behind, takes his briefcase and leaves. He was ordained in this cathedral, received his appointment from this cathedral chapter. Neither the place nor the people are unfamiliar. He has met them all before — the dean, the priest assessor, the bishop himself, who personally congratulated Fredrik on his exam. He himself is a known face and name for them too, that's what's so awful. Once called promising, now about to be exposed as an utter mediocrity. He who'd thought to walk in with the stout heart and openness given him by the people of the Örlands, a priceless gift.

He has an open and unaffected face that he cannot hide. The secretary at the front desk greets him with an encouraging, comforting smile. "Pastor Kummel? Welcome. You've had a long journey from the Örlands. Has everything gone well?"

"Yes, thank you," the pastor says.

She smiles maternally. "How nice. The dean is a little late, but he'll be here, he always comes. Maybe you'd like to sit down and wait for a moment."

He sits down in a chair with his briefcase like a baby in his arms. The nice secretary brings him a cup of coffee. "We have some real coffee from Sweden," she says. "Have some, you'll feel better." There are two cubes of sugar on the saucer. He stirs them in and drinks the coffee leaning forward, afraid of dripping on his collar. His hand is shaking. The dean doesn't come and then does come, noisily, through the door and up the steps. "Good morning, good morning," to the secretary, "not terribly late am I? And this is Pastor Kummel? Hello, how are you. Yes, I remember you. I've found your dissertation very edifying. Come in, come in, we have a great deal to talk about."

The priest assessor sits on his bench as if carved in wood, but he stands up and shakes hands. Both men are cordial, prepared for all to go well. They begin gently with some small talk about Örlands parish to put him more at ease. They ask him how he likes it there, and he answers honestly, "I love my congregation. I loved the work right from the start and have been hugely well received."

At least he gets the words out of his mouth without slurring them and can form whole sentences. If he's had a brain haemorrhage, it must be very small. The priest assessor asks him what aspects of parish life he would classify as particularly important.

"My first thought is High Mass, which is well attended on the Örlands, but there are also the other offices, paper work, and my work on committees and boards, where I have good people to work with. Then there's the instruction of confirmation candidates, Bible readings and study in the villages, which brings us to the unofficial part of my work, in other words, a priest's unscheduled activities in day-to-day encounters with members of the congregation. But if I'm to prioritize, then it's Divine service that I consider most important. You gentlemen have certainly heard that Örland is a singing congregation, and consequently the liturgy is dear to their hearts. Sermons are no simple matter and require a lot of work, but they are gratifying because the congregation actually listens, and if I say anything they think is cockeyed, they let me know."

They nod appreciatively, thinking that now they've got the pastor warmed up and the rest will be merely a formality. They have no reason to suspect that his energy has reached its limit, and that his answers in the discussion of his dissertation on the Sixty-eighth Psalm will grow steadily more and more fragmentary and incoherent. When they switch to an examination of his command of church law, they find troubling gaps in his knowledge and an uncertainty about terminology that they had honestly not expected. As regards the works of theology and church history he was required to master, they would have preferred a more comprehensive grasp of the material and a more coherent analysis of the passages under discussion. They don't know exactly how much sweat is running down his back, pasting his shirt to his body, but experience does perhaps tell them that an abundance of sweat is his reason for sitting so stiffly and holding his arms at his side, knowing as he does that every careless gesture releases a cloud of body odour.

The session drags on and on because they are so eager to give him a chance to redeem himself. Both of them wonder silently if he is ill — he raises one hand and presses his thumb and forefinger to his eyes, as if to keep them from falling out. His face is rigid, and his mouth moves reluctantly. Very painful for all parties. Of course they can pass him, but he has simply not risen to the high marks that his dissertation seemed to promise. A real shame, since high marks are required for the more qualified postings.

The dean clears his throat. "The dissertation was excellent. On the other hand, the discussion regarding it was less rewarding. When it comes to knowledge of the literature, there are a surprising number of gaps. On the basis of the dissertation, I recommend 'approved', but without honours. What does my colleague think about his understanding of church law?"

The priest assessor clears his throat. "Somewhat sketchy, I have to admit. The terminology is insufficient. But there was good understanding of practical application. Commitment to the life of worship a plus. I too recommend approval without honours."

"Then we're agreed to give Pastor Kummel a grade of 'approved' on his pastoral examination?"

"Yes."

"Thank you," the pastor says. "Almost better than I deserved."

A short pause. The dean: "Now that we're finished and your answer cannot affect our judgment, may I ask you, Pastor Kummel, if you're not feeling well?"

A pause and a sucking in of breath, a suppressed sigh. He focuses with difficulty. "I don't mean to make excuses, but I have a headache that's killing me."

"We thought there must be something. It might have been better for you to have claimed illness and come back in the spring. But done is done."

"Yes," the pastor says.

"Hrmm," says the priest assessor. "The bishop said he would like to, hrmm, congratulate the pastor on his examination. I'll go and see if he has time to see you."

This takes some time, and the pastor is not wrong to suppose that the bishop gets a description of the exam. Then he's told to go in, and there stands the bishop, smiling benignly, so full of health and well-being that Petter's eyes swim. "Good day, good day," he says and takes Petter's hand, gripping it so hard that he can feel it in his head. "You're a long way from home! How are things on the Örlands?"

"Fine, thank you. I'm grateful for the appointment. I think I've found my place."

"I'm so pleased. Hmm. On the other hand, I was sorry to hear about the result of your examination, which was something of a disappointment. I understand you're indisposed."

"Yes, you might say. A tremendous headache. But I'm not trying to excuse myself. The way things went, I'm happy to have passed."

"That's one way of looking at it, of course. But your ambitions were rather greater."

"I'm happy with 'approved'. It means I can now apply for the incumbency as vicar. When the position of incumbent vicar of Örland is posted as vacant, you will find my name among the applicants."

The bishop chuckles. "I don't think we need to use the plural in this case. I don't know when was the last time the Örlands had an incumbent vicar. Interesting! Pastor Kummel, have you considered the possibility that your talents might be put to better use in an urban parish where young people and workers face greater challenges?"

Petter smiles self-consciously. "I have marks indicating that my talents are meagre. And my calling is to the Örlands." Which sounds false, though it's true.

"In that case," says the bishop, still genial, "then I'll simply have to plan on a pastoral installation off the edge of the map. Try to arrange it for the summer so we'll have nice weather and the priest assessor won't get seasick. But now I'll let you go so you can start to do something about that headache. Where will you be staying?"

"At my wife's family farm outside Helsingfors. Tomorrow I'm going to officiate at the wedding of one of her sisters."

"Well, how nice. Yes, then I'll wish you a pleasant journey back to the Örlands and ask you to give my regards to your young wife."

"Thank you," Petter says. They shake hands. His briefcase waits loyally in the chair outside. The secretary hands him his freshly typed certificate of completed pastoral examination, discreetly enclosed in a brown envelope. He pays the stamp fee, thanks her, and reaches for his coat. "I'm very sorry about your headache," she says behind him. "Be sure and get some real rest."

So out into the fresh air, the sun cruelly blinding. Walks by way of the hotel, thanks the desk clerk humbly for watching his suitcase, whereupon the man triumphantly produces his alarm clock, which he'd left in the room. "Other things on your mind?" he supposes. Petter thanks him again, avoids stumbling on the doorsill, has to put down his bag to open the door, two murderous steps down to the sidewalk. He's sweating terribly in the sunshine, wades like a drowning man to the bus station, where of course the bus to Helsingfors has just left. He sees a park bench under a tree and sits and waits and waits. When he's finally on his way, he falls asleep with his briefcase in his arms and is lost to the world for almost an hour. In Helsingfors, people are starting to leave work and head home, there is a lot of traffic at the bus station and it's a wonder he doesn't run straight into the arms of someone he knows. He tries to avoid looking at people, and no one expects to see him, and they don't.

One more bus ride and he finally arrives at the Helléns'. Most of the people in the house are at the clubhouse getting things ready for the wedding, but Mrs Hellén has been waiting for him and is happy to see him. "Well, now we can have a wedding, now that the priest is here," she says. "I was starting to worry." She smiles and then turns serious. "Come in and sit down. How are you? Didn't it go well?"

"Yes, it was all right. I passed. Just barely. I haven't slept for two nights and I have an unbelievable headache."

"It shows. Now you need something to eat, and it's important to get a lot to drink. We've got the house full of people and they all need to eat, so I've made a big pot of meat soup, and you can have bread and butter with it. Now, tell me all about it."

Mona often says of her mother that she's like a wall. A clam that never opens. Impossible to have an intimate conversation with. She never gives a personal answer to a question that can be a matter of life and death. Always the same—courteous, tactful. All the things that Petter likes her for. Most of all, he loves her discretion. Mona sees it as lack of interest, but to him it's like a miracle compared with his own mother's loose talk and constant gossip.

"Yes, I will," he says. "Just between the two of us. I've had some really bad luck. I thought I was pretty well prepared and I'd arranged things so I'd have a quiet night in Borgå. So I reach the hotel in good spirits, only to be confronted by a housemaid we had years ago, Hilda, maybe you remember her? Unfortunately, Mama had told her I was going to be in Borgå, and there she sat, red-eyed from weeping. She'd lost her husband. What could I do? People have the right to turn to a priest. I'm to comfort them and give them courage. How could I have lived with myself if I'd turned her away on account of my exam? It turned into an awkward situation. She wanted to come up to my room, and then she wouldn't leave. She talked and cried, and I was so tired I couldn't get her to stop. It was past twelve-thirty when she left. And by then I was so shaken I couldn't sleep. I got up with a burning headache and made a pretty poor show of it at the chapter house. I didn't deserve any better than the miserable passing grade I got. I should be happy it didn't go worse. I'm ashamed of myself. And now I have to call Mona, who's waiting to hear how it went."

"She's already called. She thought you'd come on the three o'clock bus, but I told her you'd probably come with the five. I was right. Go and call her right away, then you'll have that out of the way before the others come home."

The telephone is on the wall beside Hellén's desk. Petter sits down and orders the call. Fru Hellén doesn't leave the room, and he's grateful. She sits there as if she understood that he needed a protector and can't be left alone. The call comes through almost immediately. He can picture the operator on the Örlands at full alert. She's very businesslike about reporting long-distance calls.

Mona: "Hello!"

He decides to begin with the news that all of the Örlands is waiting for. "Mona!" he shouts. "I'm sorry you had to wait.

263

But everything took so much time! Anyway, I passed, that's the main thing. So how are you and the girls?"

"Fine. But how are *you*? You sound funny."

"I've got a terrible headache. I have to admit it didn't go exactly the way I'd planned. I'll tell you all about it when I get home."

"But anyway you passed?"

"Yes. But . . . Mona, I'll see you in a few days, and then we can talk more. I just need a good night's sleep and I'll be human again. It will be absolutely wonderful to get home."

He leaves her with all her suspicions aroused. She doesn't sound good when he ends the call. He turns to his mother-in-law apologetically. "You can't start explaining things on the phone. In any case, I'll soon be home."

"Absolutely," she says. "I'm thinking about how we can get you to bed as quickly as possible. I've put a bed in the weaving room, and I'll tell everyone not to disturb you. But there's going to be a lot of activity in the house all the same, so I'm going to give you a bromide to sleep on. Now don't look so horrified, I take them myself when I need one, and I'll be taking one tonight. Tomorrow you'll wake up clear-headed and you'll be in fine form for the wedding. If you want to wash, there's warm water in the sauna, and I suggest you go out before the others come back. You'll all have time to talk in the morning."

He wonders if she's noticed how bad he smells. And his cassock! He can't possibly stand before the bridal couple smelling like a pigsty. She sees that he's deeply embarrassed about something and leans her head to one side.

"I know how much you must have to do," he begins, "but the truth is that I've been sweating like a pig all day and you can smell my cassock a long way off. If you know any means of getting out the odour, I'd be more than grateful."

A tiny sigh escapes her. The sweat pads have to be unstitched, washed, ironed, and basted back in. But she tells him he can leave his cassock — and his shirt too — in the sauna. And in the morning she'll deliver it to him in better shape, along with his washed, ironed shirt. "Thank you so much! I'm like a child, and you're never rid of us!"

And indeed he does feel significantly better the next day. Yesterday feels pleasantly distant, surrounded as he is by friendly faces and lots of questions. The wedding goes well; of course it goes well when you follow the prayer book and the bride and groom say yes! The next day he visits relatives in Helsingfors and theological friends in the evening, and in between he shops for the clothes and necessities on Mona's list. He also makes a private visit to a goldsmith and buys a piece of silver jewellery for her — in memory of his pastoral exam was his idea — now a memento of a somewhat different kind. He had thought all this would be diverting and fun, but what he feels most of all is a consuming homesickness. Of course he'd imagined how nice it would be to climb aboard the Åbo train and happily return to the Örlands, but not that it would feel as if he'd escaped with his life by the skin of his teeth.

How willingly he puts up with the dreadfully uncomfortable journey just for the joy of going ashore at Mellom quay. In September, the night sky is dark, but he knows that Post-Anton is there with the connecting boat and that it's only a matter of hours. It is also a quite unexpected pleasure to see Fredrik, in the middle of the night, standing on the quay as he steps ashore with his suitcase and briefcase and an extra box.

"Well, welcome back! May I offer my congratulations?"

"Is it really you? Giving up a night's sleep? I don't know what to say. I passed, but not with honours. I'd like to tell you the whole story, but there isn't time. And the telephone . . . I'll write you a letter."

Fredrik has stood there beaming benevolently, ready to pound him on the back and congratulate him. Now his happy anticipation is visibly replaced by a worried question—what has happened? Simultaneously, for one fleeting moment, his concern is overshadowed by an almost parenthetical realization that he is not altogether displeased by Petter's not having passed with honours. But the moment passes, and the concern remains. "Now I'm really curious! If you need pastoral counselling, I'm at your service."

❋ ❋ ❋

Cargo is quickly transferred. We don't stand here dawdling, for everyone has come a long way, and those on their way to the Örlands have a good distance yet to go. The pastor and the Mellom priest shake hands warmly, promise to write, hope to see each other soon. "Thanks for coming. Sorry the news wasn't better. Best to Margit. Best to Mona," they say. He's put his things on board, his person as well, the whole priest and his effects on their way home.

Kalle and I have our hands full navigating our way out through the tight passage in the dark of night, but once we're out in more open water, he comes into the wheelhouse and says hello. "You were right about the headache," he says. "I barely managed to get through the day. How in God's . . . how in the world could you know that?"

"Not so hard. I had a headache myself when I went to meet the Governor of Åland."

"You mean bigwigs give us a headache? Well of course. But you were right about stones on my path, too. There was a real boulder."

"In human form, I'll wager."

"Yes indeed. The case falls within my vow of silence, but how could you know?"

"I couldn't know. Only imagine."

"Like when you're out on the ice. You can see how it's going to be."

"You shouldn't take me so seriously. I just talk the way we do when we get older and know that things seldom work out the way we'd expected. If you're prepared for that, you somehow get through it. And you did. You passed."

"Yes, thank heaven. Now I can apply for the incumbency here and settle down in earnest. Oh my goodness, how good it will be to get home after this ordeal."

It is autumn and so still dark when we get across the bay, and in darkness we tie up at the steamship pier. The church is still there, and the parsonage, and the pastor's rowing boat is pulled up on the granite. The verger has rowed it over for him, and now the pastor transfers his things to it and pushes off. He vanishes in the darkness and all you can hear of him are his oars creaking in the oarlocks and the oar blades dipping into the water. His wife has been lying awake and heard us pass, for I see a lantern moving swiftly down to the church dock. The water in the church inlet is bright, and I see him gliding in towards the lantern like a black shadow drawn to the light.

* * *

"Welcome home!" she calls and he calls back "Thank you" and "How I've been waiting." Quickly he hands his luggage ashore and steps ashore himself, pulling the boat up after him with one hand, the other already embracing Mona. It feels almost the way he had imagined this homecoming before he left, with his pastoral exam completed and much to tell. His distress is nearly gone, maybe he can get through this as well!

They don't know where to start, if they should go in the house or sit down here on the dock and talk. "The wedding," Mona says. "How did it go?" "Like clockwork!" he says. "I bring greetings from absolutely everyone. They all asked about you and the girls! And they all wanted to see the pictures! They're excellent and went from hand to hand."

While they're talking, they've started walking as well, since she imagines he'd like some breakfast after his long trip. She carries his briefcase — "Like a stone! How can you walk around with this thing?" — and he his suitcase and the box full of the things he bought in Helsingfors. "I think I got everything," he brags. "Wait till you see!" He's looking forward to showing and telling. About Hilda, too, but not yet, and it's a deliverance that there's so much else to talk about — the wedding, her relatives, his purchases, the trip, all sort of things, while they reacquaint themselves and recapture each other's trust.

Once inside the parsonage, Sanna wakes up and is joyous, more than Mona, who is suspicious and on edge, and while they're eating, Lillus wakes up, and eventually Mama has to go out to the cows, who have picked up his scent and know that he's home. As long as Sanna is around, it's enough to talk about the wedding and give the silver brooch to Mona, who thinks it an extravagance, and the little things he's bought for Sanna and that the Helléns have sent to her, but when Sanna quietly takes her nap and they sit down together in the kitchen, he can no longer put it off.

"Now tell me what happened in Borgå. I've been really anxious. You did pass didn't you, after all your studying?"

"Oh yes. Approved, but not with honours. It's really embarrassing that I did so poorly even when it came to questions where I was on home ground, what should have been like mother's milk to me." When he says 'mother's', he gives a little grimace of pain, which she picks up at once.

"Don't tell me your mother has anything to do with this!"

"You read my mind. Yes. I don't know where to start. You remember Hilda?"

Dear God, of course she remembers Hilda. Their marriage was preceded by detailed confessions. No sin was left untouched. Hilda was the greatest. Hilda was also the sin he'd wanted to confess to everyone in the perfervid atmosphere of a Moral Re-Armament meeting. Hilda is the person Mona hates most in the world. Her pulse quickens. She gets red spots on her neck and the tip of her nose turns white. She would like to scratch the woman's eyes out. "What does Hilda have to do with your pastoral exam?"

"Mama had written to tell her I was going to be in Borgå. She came to the hotel. Completely hysterical. Her husband had left her and she had to talk to someone. I reminded her of my examination but there was no stopping her. It was like I'd been drugged. You can imagine what I was feeling. As a priest, it was my duty to listen. No priest can refuse a human being in spiritual need. You can imagine the horrible conflict I felt. Privately, I was in despair. Time was passing. As she talked, I developed a terrible headache. Then I couldn't get to sleep."

"She was in your room?" He nods. "Dear God."

"Yes, it was awkward. It was ghastly."

"What time did she leave?"

"Twelve-thirty."

"Twelve–thirty! What's wrong with you? You know what a slut she is, and you let her destroy your peace of mind and your future career? It's one thing to talk to her for an hour and send her on her way, it's another thing altogether to let her sit there — what was it? Over four hours! — and let her sabotage your prospects. And what do you think people thought!"

"She was desperate."

"And what about you?"

"In such a situation, a priest isn't supposed to think about himself."

"You really believe she came to you for spiritual counselling? From *you*?"

"It's not an either or. It's a matter of both and. She came because it was me. That doesn't mean she wasn't also miserable and desperate. That's what I had to keep telling myself."

"And comfort her? Are you out of your senses? I can just imagine the kind of comfort she had in mind. You must have known that yourself."

"When you put it that way, yes. But I was so intensely uncomfortable that I couldn't imagine that she . . . Ugh!"

"Did she try?"

"In words maybe. I changed the subject to Jesus." He gives her a crooked smile. She doesn't smile back.

"The fact is that you allowed her to destroy your examination. What kind of Jesus complex do you suffer from? Although not even Jesus . . . There are lots of examples of him going out into the desert because he couldn't deal with people any more. Sometimes I don't understand you at all."

She stands up vehemently and begins pacing back and forth. Mona at her most unreasonable. Mona when she is most like her temperamental father, who can pace about in a rage for several hours amidst a torrent of words. The whole household cowers and keeps its mouth shut, and now Petter stays silent and draws his head down between his shoulders. It's not his fault that Hilda appeared at the hotel. Even if he had shown her the door, she would have ruined his night's sleep. There is no possible defence, because Petter owed it to his wife to throw out the baggage that has caused so much unhappiness!

Quite right, but he was so flustered, he was virtually paralysed.

Rubbish! For a year and a half, she's walked on eggshells because of his pastoral exam, and then he throws it away in a single evening, one night, with a trollop who had led him astray once already. Doesn't he ever learn? Is he a complete idiot? A total milksop?

While she rants, she starts working in the kitchen, refusing to let her indignation interfere with the efficient performance of her duties. Food is scrubbed, peeled, sliced, shredded, and mashed while she scolds him. He just sits there, unproductive in his stupidity and lack of enterprise, a sheep rather than the shepherd he had meant to become.

An oppressive afternoon, which he spends as a refugee in his study, with his letters and newspapers. At some point, he must also concoct a sermon for Sunday, which under the present circumstances he needs to manage discreetly and without complaint. Now that he's free of his studies, he has also promised to spend more time with Sanna. She stands looking at him from the door. "Come," he says. "I've been so sad without you."

At the supper table, she puts his plate down hard. "I was mad because I missed you so. I could hardly wait for you to come home. And then all this. As if you hadn't learned a thing. It's almost enough to make me lose my mind. And of course I'm maddest of all because it was so unpleasant for you. I should have gone with you, but how would that have looked, with a two-month-old baby? Then it would have been my fault that you couldn't sleep! And anyway at your age you ought to be able to take care of yourself!"

She's well on her way to starting again, and Sanna sits in her chair stiff with fear. But she stops talking, sits down, and bursts into tears, and Petter is no longer a failed clergyman but a husband, who finally knows how to use the beautiful voice he's been given, the unshaven cheek that he can press against hers. A warm breast and good, knowing hands.

Chapter Eighteen

A TERRIBLE STORM ON CHRISTMAS EVE. If it keeps up, there won't be a soul at the early service Christmas morning. It's not a problem of thin ice, because the ice hasn't set yet, only made small attempts in the bays, where snow and ice trim the beaches while the open sea rolls free. Now full storm, squealing, wailing wind, and dark as a coal cellar by three in the afternoon. It rains as if the sea lay not only around the Örlands but also above it, pouring its water over them in great cascades. In the worst gusts, the beacon light is invisible, and the whole world is drowned by the merciless waves.

"For those in peril on the sea," the pastor prays. "And keep the parsonage afloat, too," he adds, more or less as a joke. For the rain forces its way in where the window frames are in poor condition, and the foam from the wave tops is thrown against the glass like snow. The wind howls through the house and drives the smoke down the chimney. Open doors slam shut, the boards creak in the walls, the rag rugs meander across the floor. It's impossible to get the Christmas prayer on the radio, which just crackles and stutters in Russian and Finnish.

The pastor understands better than he did last year why Christmas prayers are not held on the Örlands. At this time of year, it's enough that the congregation comes to the Christmas morning service. Earlier, when the weather was nice, he thought they might hold private Christmas prayers in the church, just the four of them, but now he's lost the desire. It's bad enough that Mona has to go out to the cow barn in this storm. They don't really know how much of a fire they dare have in the tile stoves, and the kitchen range spits out smoke and sparks through the burner rings in the worst gusts of wind, so someone, he, must be both babysitter and fire warden. He lights the hurricane lamp, checks that it's filled with lamp oil. Mona bundles up, they joke about her getting lost on the prairie. "Aim for the light in the window!" he calls farewell as the door closes.

The cow barn is more protected than the parsonage, lower and sheltered by hillocks. It's still cold inside, and even though Apple and Goody stand there like a couple of stoves their breath is visible. The calves are freezing in their pen, pressed up against each other. The sheep are in their winter coats and doing fine. All of them turn to look at the hurricane lantern and greet her the way they always do, bleating, bellowing, tossing their heads.

Mona is completely at ease in the cow barn. Completely natural. She enjoys herself here in a different way from up at the house with the children whining, Petter on the phone, a thousand tasks waiting to be done, everything she hasn't had time for like a noose around her neck, keeping her from breathing freely. Here things are simple — mucking out, providing hay and water, washing and lubricating udders, milking, straining, hooking the milk cans to the yoke — Merry Christmas and good night. Those who bleat and bellow never say too much, hurt no one's feelings, avoid irony, do not philosophize, never quibble. No hidden meanings, no complications. There's heat and cold, hunger and satisfied hunger, waiting and arrival, peaceful darkness until dawn. It is her repose, although many think the work is hard. She is happy to spend time here, and now that it's Christmas she talks a bit more, pats and scratches a little longer, is a little more generous with the hay, pours out some oats from the sack special-ordered from the Co-op. The milk is warm and frothy, creamy and nutritious. Peace.

In the cow barn it seems like the wind has died down a little, but when she steps outside, it tears at her hard. If the milk pails weren't so heavy, she'd fall down. The rain pounds on her like surf, she loses her breath, thinks that out here on the Örlands you can drown on dry land. Makes her way up the steps, which are shiny in the light of her lantern. Pulls open the swollen door, Petter comes to her at once. "How did it go? I was afraid you'd blow away!" He takes the milk cans, the sieve, helps her out of her outdoor clothes. In this weather, they wash the milk cans in the kitchen. No problem cooling the milk today.

They are all bundled up to the teeth, Lillus in her sleeping bag with a cap on her head, Sanna in wool from head to toe, parents wearing all the wool clothes they own, Papa with earmuffs on his sensitive ears, Mama with a large woollen scarf around her head, everyone with layers of warm socks on their feet, the whole family a hymn of praise to the native Finnish sheep. Brrr! And the temperature hasn't yet fallen below freezing!

But this is Christmas Eve, and now the Christmas supper is put on the table—lutfisk with white sauce, potatoes, a Christmas ham straight from the oven, stewed peas and carrots, Christmas cakes and coffee for dessert. The Christmas candles flutter and drop wax on the Christmas runner. Sanna is exhausted from waiting, and whines and complains. Lillus is screaming in sympathy. It's enough to take the joy out of being parents, but they make an effort and group themselves around the tile stove in the parlour, very carefully light the candles on their Christmas juniper but have to put them out again, to Sanna's intense disappointment, because otherwise the draughts will ignite the whole tree.

In the terrible storm, they can't hear if Santa has come, but Papa goes out to the back hall to have a look. The verger has explained to them that the Örland Santa is a little shy and doesn't like to come into the house but leaves the presents just inside the door instead. Sanna is afraid he won't come because it's blowing so hard, but Papa has heard that he came with Post-Anton two days before Christmas, so it can't hurt to have a look. And, glory be, it turns out he has snuck in and left a whole pile of Christmas presents in the firewood box!

Oh. But first we need to think about why we get Christmas presents this evening. Well, it's because the baby Jesus was born this very evening. It's in memory of his birthday that we receive our own presents. And that's why the Christmas gospel is read in every home in Christendom this night. So Papa opens the Bible and reads a long story, and even though Sanna loves stories, she gets bored. She twists and slides back and forth in her chair and scratches her itchy wool socks and, finally, bursts into tears. Not exactly the way her parents had pictured this Christmas Eve, which had less squealing and commotion and lacked the nervousness they're all feeling because of the storm and the danger of fire on a night like this. But they must celebrate Christmas, so Papa closes the Bible and takes Sanna on his lap, and Mama carries in the basket of presents. Red sealing wax and string, it's a shame to unwrap such pretty packages! First of all, there are books, mostly for Papa but also for Mama and three story books for Sanna! In addition, socks and mittens and a Santa for Sanna and a Christmas angel for Lillus, who immediately stuffs it in her mouth like a cannibal. And still more — marzipan pigs and a box of homemade toffee for everyone. In a bowl on the table are all the Christmas cards Post-Anton brought, along with Christmas magazines to read over the holidays. It's overwhelming, and Sanna gets sick to her stomach and throws up on the rug before she's even had a piece of toffee. Sanna! My goodness, as if all the Christmas cleaning wasn't enough to deal with, now this! Don't cry, Sanna, Papa knows you've got a delicate stomach and you didn't throw up on purpose.

Whew! When they've finally got the girls into bed and might have a little quiet time, just the two of them, there is no peace. They make their rounds and check the tile stoves and the kitchen range, where they now let the fire go out, and Petter says that if he had a slightly more active imagination, he could easily believe he heard calls for help from a shipwreck among all the sound effects produced by the storm. He wanders from window to window and laughs at himself a little. "Soon I'll be just like Papa in a storm, nervous and confused. For that matter, I'll bet they haven't gone to bed yet. Shall I call and thank them for the Christmas presents and get that out of the way?"

His poor mother is celebrating her first Christmas on Åland, resigned and teary-eyed when she thinks about earlier Christmases on the mainland, surrounded by her children and happily anticipating the many Christmas parties given by her relatives and friends. Never been a storm like the one raging across even the large island of Åland this night. Papa will be no comfort, running around the house groaning like a wraith. The least Petter can do is call and talk to her cheerfully and supportively, but when he cranks the phone, with an apology already on his lips for interrupting the operator's own Christmas celebration, there is no response. He cranks and cranks and waits and tries again, but realizes at last that the storm has blown down the lines somewhere and that they won't be able to call out until after New Year's. Poor Mama, who has undoubtedly been counting on a chat.

There isn't much more they can do except make another circuit to check for fire and see that the girls are firmly anchored under their quilts but have their noses free. The door to the parlour is closed, and the tile stove keeps it warm into the wee hours, but it's still cold! At last they lie in their own beds, talk a little about the weather and how the excitement was too much for Sanna and wonder if a living soul will come to Christmas morning service. "The one day of the year when the sermon comes easily!" Petter says, disappointed in advance. They doze off but sleep lightly and wake up again. Remarkable, the pastor thinks, how uneasy you can be in a storm even though you're safe and secure on land with your whole family gathered around you. What must it have been like for the holy family without a roof over their heads that fateful night?

There is a lot of nasty creaking and crackling in the house, and at two o'clock he's up again with his flashlight in hand, checking the stoves and opening the door to the icy attic stairs, listening and sniffing, but there is nothing to suggest that the stove chimney has cracked or that sparks are smouldering in the insulation. There is still some warmth on the ground floor and all is well. Remarkable that he can nevertheless feel such disquiet, anguish almost. It has stopped raining, and the beacon blinks reassuringly, the storm gusts are not as strong as they were earlier. The storm is putting itself to bed, so you can too! he scolds himself. He finds his way back to his bed where there is still a little nest of warmth.

"What's wrong?" Mona mumbles.

"Nothing," he answers. "Everything's fine. Sorry I woke you." He sleeps again a little, and when he finally sleeps deeply, the alarm clock goes off. He jumps up as if it were an air raid warning, but sinks back down when he realizes where he is. Still pitch-black, but he smells Mona's good scent as she gets out of bed. He hears the rasp of the match on the matchbox and then she lights the lamp. They listen — complete quiet. When she gets to the kitchen, Mona suddenly screams and Petter rushes out to her with his trousers at half-mast. It's nothing. For an instant she thought that the church was in flames, but there is a light in the sacristy window simply because the verger is there to build a fire in the boiler, which is one of his duties.

At least someone believes there will be a Christmas morning service. They've thought about how they'll do this. The simplest would be for Mona to stay at home and fire up the stoves and make breakfast, but Christmas morning is one of the high points of the church year. It's not a long service, so they'll have time to build fires and have breakfast at almost the normal time when they get back. Now they have just a cup of last night's coffee from the Thermos and a quick sandwich. Then Petter goes off to the church while Mona dresses Sanna and Lillus and follows after.

The verger meets him at the church door, expecting praise and getting it, profusely. The bulging radiators in the church are banging away, and the church is getting warm. With every minute that passes, the air is a little less raw. "My dear fellow," says the pastor, "what time did you get here?" "Four o'clock," says the verger proudly. This is his big night of the year, when he overcomes his fear of the dark and can calmly proclaim that the dead do not celebrate Christmas Mass at midnight, at least not in Örland church. The pastor reports that he himself was up at two o'clock and the storm was still raging. Then it calmed quickly. "But my goodness the size of those seas!" "Yes, it takes a time for the surf to settle." They talk quietly as they prepare the church. They had the candles ready back at the beginning of Advent, and two potted tulips stand on the altar. The verger has posted the first hymns on the number board. Now they light all the candles, on the chandeliers, on the altar, on the pulpit. The church is to shine like a lantern as the congregation approaches. While they're at it, the organist comes running in and takes the pastor by the arm.

"Come! You've got to see this!"

The Örland congregation is coming towards them across the hills. The seas are too high for anyone to want to come by boat in the dark. So they've started early from all the villages and now they can be seen in a long row of blinking, swinging lanterns descending the last slope. The verger runs to the steeple, for the bells must ring as they approach, the big bell and the small one tolling for all they're worth.

The organist warms his hands on a radiator, and the pastor hurries to the sacristy. The first to come in fill the church with footsteps and noise, rustling and shuffling. "Merry Christmas!" they wish one another in their strong, Örland voices. The long walk with swinging lanterns, watching their step on the slippery rocks, has made them bright and talkative. But then the voices change and grow rapid and frightened, and soon the organist comes into the sacristy. "You need to hear this before we start."

It seems one of the last to arrive is a ship's pilot from the west villages who has heard on the pilots' radio that a large American freighter has gone aground and sunk off the island of Utö. The pilots on Utö have rescued many of the crew, but a number of them are missing. "Many of us had a bad feeling last night," he adds, understandably enough.

"Thank you," the pastor says. "I'm glad you told me. I'll say a prayer for them." He looks at the clock and sees that it's past time. Mona is sitting in the church wondering why they don't start. The verger stopped ringing the bells some time ago. But now the organist hurries to the loft, the organ pumper starts to work, and the organist begins playing the opening bars of "When Christmas Morn is Dawning" — a little too fast.

The whole church is glowing in its Egyptian darkness and the talking dies down reluctantly. When the organist indicates that the hymn is now beginning, they are ready. It is one of their favourite hymns, which they've waited all year to sing, but now they're distracted, the dissonances are unexpectedly great, the bellowing more distinct, the differences of tempo more audible. The pastor is at the altar, singing as he always does, but not happy, horrified, as is everyone who's already heard the news. "The Lord be with you," he sings, as usual, and Lillus answers happily a little ahead of everyone else. Anyone would be inspired in these wonderful acoustics, and the pastor takes them through the liturgical embroidery and through the lesson. When they sing "Starlight on Sea and Sand", there are people talking out loud in the back rows, and many in the front pews turn around. In the loft, where the younger boys have gathered, they talk and run around without restraint.

No calm, no collective expectation when the pastor climbs into the pulpit. "Dear friends, brothers and sisters in Jesus Christ," he begins as usual. "Let us pray." The older people obediently bow their heads and then everyone listens, for now the pastor will give them the information that led to all the hubbub. "This night, on Christmas night itself, the whole crew of a freighter has been fighting for their lives in the storm off Utö. We thank you for the pilots on Utö, who put their own lives in danger to rescue many. We pray for those who have lost their lives at sea. God, be merciful to them and receive them into your fatherly embrace. Let the light eternal shine for them. Amen."

After this, it's easy to return to the subject of light, the church lit up for celebration, for the feast of our Saviour's birth, but also to the light in the bell tower that faithfully and steadily blinked all through the storm-lashed night. And on to the Star of Bethlehem that wandered through the night and led shepherds and wise men to the stable and the manger. We ourselves surrounded by deep darkness, but in the centre a light that guides us from age to age. The light is Christian hope, personified in the body of Christ, which is a lantern to guide our steps and light up our path. In the silence that follows, everyone can clearly hear a foot colliding gently with a storm lantern on the floor, a little clinking that jingles through the church. The candle flames flutter in a draught, no one misses the parallel with their own trek with swinging lanterns through the deep darkness towards the shining church.

They sing "Lo, How a Rose E'er Blooming from Tender Stem Hath Sprung!" while the pastor changes his robe and returns to the altar. In his closing prayer he prays especially for all those struggling at sea, then the Our Father and the blessing. Finally, Topelius's "I Seek No Gold or Majesty, No Pearl or Shining Gem". The organist is about to begin his postlude, his showpiece, but the organ pumper is facing the other way, talking to someone, and people are already standing up in their pews and talking loudly. When the organist finally starts playing, they just talk louder. The pastor takes off his vestments quickly and the verger is back in the church before the postlude is over. As soon as he's finished, the organist leaves his music on the organ and comes down to the others.

In the middle is Anders Stark, the pilot who heard the news on his radio. He's in a hurry to get home to hear more news, but repeats what he knows once again: The freighter is called *Park Victory*, a big devil, oh, beg pardon, and he himself was her pilot once. From the American South, lots of Negroes and such people. A crew of at least twenty-five. The pilots on Utö have rescued at least half, they think. The ones still out there haven't got a chance. The Coast Guard has been out all night but has no hope of finding anyone else alive.

Then the pastor notices that no one from the Coast Guard is at church today. It's starting to get light outside, and a couple of boys who've been up on a hill having a look around come back to tell them that both Coast Guard boats are gone, obviously to take part in the rescue mission along with the military from the base on Utö. They must have been called out during the night, over the radio. "Good Lord, you've got to have guts to go out in a small boat in this weather," someone says. Brage's parents and wife are in the church but didn't know he'd gone out. He was on duty at the station and celebrated Christmas there. "First Christmas pike at home and then Christmas ham at the station, because Björklund's from the mainland and pike won't do," Astrid explains. She doesn't seem particularly worried. It's another thing the pastor admires in his parishioners — their fatalism. What happens is what's meant to happen.

Definitely light outside now, grey on grey, black where the sides of the hills are whipped with rain. Icy cold. Mona can guess that there will be a lot of visitors during the day and hurries home with the girls. They have to sit in the kitchen while she gets a fire burning in the range and puts pots of water on the rings. Then she quickly builds fires in the tile stoves and manages to measure out the coffee and slice the bread before the first of them arrive. First they have to count the collection and make certain every candle is out. The verger goes down to the boiler room two extra times to make sure that no coals are smouldering and that the insulation is not smoking anywhere. The radiators have started to go cold, but you never know, and the pastor promises to check again at dinner time.

No one really wants to go home, except Anders, who left in a rush, and by and by the pastor, the organist, the verger, Elis and Adele, and several men from the west villages, who are hoping the pastor's phone is less dead than other people's, head for the parsonage. There's a lovely warmth coming from the tile stoves and the open oven door, and they all crowd around the kitchen table and pass around chicory coffee and bread and butter and slices of Christmas ham. "Such luxury!" Adele says about the ham, and the pastor's wife thinks the same thought as, mournfully, she watches the disappearance of the ham, which would have lasted them three more days. But she comes from a farm herself, and she knows there's nothing worse than having a reputation for stinginess and lack of hospitality.

Several of them crank the telephone energetically and fiddle with the radio, and in the midst of the static and the hissing they suddenly hear a clear voice from Finnish Radio talking about the Christmas Eve tragedy, the American freighter *Park Victory*, that sank off Utö. The U.S. Embassy conveys its gratitude to the pilots on Utö for their heroic rescue efforts. The Embassy has arranged for the survivors to be taken to Helsingfors, where they will be housed until they can travel home. The pilots have rescued fourteen men. Eight bodies have been recovered and two are missing and presumed dead.

The men look out the window. "With this wind, they'll be coming here," they predict, and it takes half a second for the pastor to grasp that they mean the two missing crew members, whose bodies will be driven towards the Örlands by the wind and the currents. That's why they figure the Coast Guard from the Örlands is still out. They're moving slowly, with the wind, and searching the whole way. Nevertheless, they come home empty-handed, and it's Post-Anton who finds one of the bodies shortly after New Year's.

❈ ❈ ❈

Much can happen to a body that winds up in the water in a storm. You can figure the direction roughly, but you also have to reckon with currents which, in places, can move in the opposite direction to the wind and carry you on great detours. Then, when you start to approach a coastline, you have to deal not only with the current among the islands but also with reefs and rocks that you rub against and have to work your way around before you can move on. In amongst the skerries, the wind trundles around any way it likes, and if you're a corpse at its mercy, you can end up in odd places.

I thought it was a seal, I did. But when it didn't move, even though I came so close that it should have caught my scent, since I was upwind, I realized it was a man who'd washed up on the rocks like a big bull seal. A lifebelt and dark clothes, there's no big difference between seamen and old bull seals.

It was a Negro. Not as black as I'd thought they were but more grey, maybe they lose some of their colour when they die. Otherwise just like a human being. A cap with earflaps so I couldn't tell if he had woolly hair like they say Negroes have. Oilskins and good shoes on his feet. I wondered if I should try to pull him into the boat, but he was heavy as hell, and postal boats are supposed to carry the mail, not dead seamen. So I just pulled him up a little more so he wouldn't drift away, and then I stopped by the Coast Guard and told them where he was, and then home with the mail.

"How did you happen to find him?" they asked, of course. "Those rocks aren't on your usual route."

"Well, no," I said. "But I saw which way I should steer."

Brage knows what I mean. But Björklund was irritated. "What do you mean, you knew which way to steer?" he said. "If you can tell us where the other one is too, then we can stop searching."

"No," I said. "If he's caught on something and is on the bottom, or inside the wreck, for example, then I can't see anything. Any fool knows that."

This is the darkest time of the year, and there's a lot of movement in the water, storms and currents. These are hard trips for me, even though I go only twice a week. That Christmas night I slept like a dead man. All the light was knocked out of me, I didn't know a thing. Not a dream, not a sound could have woken me. In my sleep there was only the storm thundering away, while I lay deep down in my furs, dry and out of danger.

If I had been awake and able to hear and see, what could I have done, even with a thousand signs? There were a lot of people who did have them. The pastor himself said he was up wandering around the house and heard all sorts of things. The one who should have heard and seen was the captain of the Park Victory. They were waiting for a pilot, and the bridge was fully manned. Their radio was on, calling and crackling, which makes it hard to hear anything else, hard to figure out why there's such an urgent unease in the pit of your stomach and where your fears are coming from. Do they carry a message, or are you just suffering fearful premonitions in the terrible storm? The pilots said that they tried to call on the radio and tell them to move farther offshore, but others who were out that night said they could hardly hear anything, mostly just occasional words, many of them Russian, so chopped to pieces they were impossible to understand. The engines pound and roar and the props thrash and whip. In that kind of hell, it's not easy to grasp *that there are spirits out there who are trying to get you to see how you can save yourself.*

I have the greatest admiration for the pilots. When they are dead and gone, they'll be out there too, that I know, and anyone with ears and senses will be safe. They were ready to sacrifice their lives, it says in the newspapers, but let me tell you that they knew exactly what to do to save themselves and still rescue as many as possible. You need one man to manage the engine and the rudder, and he needs a voice that can be heard and eyes that can see. And then you need men who know precisely to the tenth of a second when to fend off and which wave to turn on. That they managed to rescue so many in two little pilot boats, I respect them for that. More boats came out later from the military on Utö, but without the pilots they would have pulled out maybe three or four still alive. They all had lifebelts, but there's a horrific power in the waves, and it was indescribably cold. Those who drifted in towards land were dashed to death on the rocks.

The pilots, yes. As they worked out there, they had others toiling beside them in harmony, I know that. It must have been so, for I've had the experience myself, many times.

Chapter Nineteen

PEOPLE MIGHT WALK ON THEIR OWN LEGS right up to their death. But that's the end of it. From then on they are a weight to be moved, lifted and carried. Be spoken of and talked about in their very presence, important decisions made. Doctors will examine the body and determine the cause of death — drowning and hypothermia. The authorities grant Doctor Gyllen, no, Midwife Irina Gyllen a dispensation to perform this duty, which eliminates a good deal of trouble and expense. The local policeman, Julius Friman, is present as witness and recording secretary. An easy procedure at the present temperature. The seaman still looks newly drowned, washed clean by the sea and odour free.

On the Örlands, the bodies of those newly dead are kept in a shed at their home farm until the burial. Traditionally, dead seamen are kept in the pastor's boathouse. The Coast Guard brings the body, and it turns out there are trestles and planks stowed away in a corner for this very purpose. Pure good luck that the pastor never sawed them up for firewood. Österberg, the carpenter in the east villages, brings a smoothly planed coffin in his boat. The pastor's wife lines it with white paper curtains from the war years that she's found in the attic, and she contributes a pillowcase and pillow. The pastor and the verger heave the seaman into the coffin, staggering under his unexpected weight. They cover him with a paper shroud and the pastor reads The Lord's Blessing. Together, he and the verger sing, "Now the labourer's task is o'er; now the battle day is past; now upon the farther shore, lands the voyager at last."

Then he lies there and waits for Sunday, because the pastor knows that many people are interested in this burial service and Sunday will give them a respectable reason to be present. It seems right, too, that this man who died alone in a howling gale should thus be embraced by a large parish community.

While they wait, the verger struggles to dig a grave in the cold, rocky soil. He gets help from the church crofter, for pay, and from the pastor when he has time between phone calls. There is much to be discussed and organized. The man's wallet is sent to the U.S. Embassy, and he is identified as Eric Alexander Cain, from Brooklyn. A Swedish-speaking official at the Embassy calls and there is a vigorous discussion of the arrangements. The dead man was a Baptist, but the Baptists and the Lutherans are close, and a traditional Örland burial will not be a problem. Whirr, he rings off, and then in the afternoon he calls again. He has spoken to the Baptist Church in Helsingfors, but it's a long way for the Baptist minister to come, so he has no objection to Pastor Kummel, assuming the pastor is willing? "Yes," Petter promises for the second time, and whirr, they ring off. The next day the fellow calls again to talk about the expenses, and the pastor answers that the parish itself pays the very modest expenses for the burial of a stranger. He reports that the man is already in his coffin and what the coffin cost, and the official says that of course the Embassy will pay for all costs verified by an invoice. Petter thanks him, and, whirr, they ring off. Ring ring, he calls back to discuss a possible floral tribute. Petter explains that flowers have to be sent out from Åbo and won't survive the long trip from Mellom to the Örlands in an open boat. What they can do, and his wife has already started, is to make wreaths of juniper greens. There are frozen, dark blue juniper berries in the greens, and to give the wreaths some colour, she picks sprigs of red rosehips and uses them as decoration. "Beautiful and dignified," Petter assures the Embassy functionary, and the man sounds impressed but also distant, as if he were talking to an Eskimo. "That will be excellent," he says, and promises to arrange for a spruce wreath with a ribbon from the Embassy to be sent out on Thursday's boat from Åbo. "Thank you," Petter says. Whirr.

And on Friday morning, Post-Anton arrives weighed down by an enormous wreath of spruce and red paper flowers, plus a ribbon with gold lettering, a little American flag, and a large rosette in red, white, and blue adorned with an American bald eagle. Mona's wreaths from Örland parish are smaller, but together they make an attractive arrangement on the coffin and later on the grave. The men of the vestry carry the casket up from the boathouse and set it down on the coffin stone outside the churchyard gate, as tradition dictates. The bells ring, and the congregation sings the departed to his grave. The pastor performs the burial service. In the biting wind, freezing temperatures and icing in the bays, he says a few words about the seaman from the vast land of America who met his death in the cold north. Alone, a stranger, but now reunited with the worldwide community of Christians. His body sinks into the cold earth, but his spirit rests by the heart of Jesus.

And that's the end of Eric Alexander Cain and his story, or so they think. But a month later there arrives a pretty blue airmail letter from the U.S. Embassy addressed to the Rev. Peter

Kummel. When he opens the envelope, twenty-five dollars fall out. The pastor can see that the letter was written by a Mrs Inez Cain, the mother of Eric Alexander, but he has never studied English, just Finnish and German and a little French and Latin, plus Ancient Greek and Hebrew, and he has to ask his father for help with the translation. Papa is in his glory, and the translation comes back at once. The letter is well-written and expressive. Mrs Cain thanks Pastor Kummel for giving her son a Christian burial. It would give her comfort in her great grief if he could tell her something about the funeral and the grave itself. She is enclosing twenty-five dollars for its beautification, which she hopes he can use for that purpose.

The pastor is ashamed. Dreadfully ashamed, for two reasons. First, because he did not himself write a short letter to tell her about her son's funeral and the churchyard where he lies. And second, even more shameful, because he unconsciously assumed that the seaman came from a background where his people slaved on cotton plantations and could neither read nor write. How could he be so thoughtless, so prejudiced? What reason does this woman with the lovely handwriting and the friendly message have to believe that he will put her cash gift to proper use?

Now the letter goes quickly back to father Leonard, who is given detailed instructions about what to write. 1) A warm thank you for her kind letter. 2) The deepest sympathy for her son's tragic and untimely death. 3) A description of the funeral and burial. 4) An assurance that the pastor's wife herself will see that flowers are planted on the grave the following spring, together with their thanks for the monetary contribution, which will be used for a cross with engraved nameplate. 5) A final word about Jesus's promises, which conquer death.

If he believes for a moment that Papa will follow his instructions, he is quickly disabused of his error. Petter has at least had the foresight to have the letter returned to him for his signature, which has kept his father from immediately mailing it off to America, beaming. What his father returns to him is a terribly long, tightly written letter. Even without knowing English, it is easy to see that Petter's instructions have not been followed. Papa begins by writing four pages about Negro slavery, which he opposes. Then he writes three pages about his own difficult years as an immigrant in America. Next, he writes about the weather in this part of the world, which has given him rheumatism, destroyed his nerves, and brought the life of Mrs Cain's son to an end. On the last page, when he has tired of writing, he has scraped together a few lines about the funeral, the plantings, and Christian hope.

Papa! Why does it have to be this way? Every time Petter begins to develop slightly friendlier feelings towards him, it turns out to be misguided. How is a man to honour such a notoriously foolish father? Who rushes off half-cocked, who lacks balance and all sense of proportion? As usual, Petter is left feeling bitterly disappointed at the end of an unnecessary detour by way of a father who can't even help him with a simple letter in English, a language he is so proud of knowing. There is no one else on the Örlands who can help him. A couple of older men have been in America as carpenters, but their English is spoken and practical, and he doesn't want to embarrass them by giving them a task they won't be able to handle. He himself is childishly unwilling to admit that he doesn't know English, and he lets several weeks go by while he goes around feeling ashamed of himself for various reasons before he does what he should have done in the first place — writes an appropriate letter and sends it to his contact at the U.S. Embassy and asks him to translate it.

By then he has much else to think about. Mona, whom he's always considered to be healthier and to have a stronger constitution than he himself, has come down with rheumatoid arthritis and has been ordered to take medication, stay in bed, and, the worst part for her, have complete rest for four weeks. Again they have reason to be extremely grateful to Doctor Gyllen, who made the diagnosis, and to the local council, whose newly established homecare service makes it possible to get help with the milking and the two little girls.

Doctor Gyllen frightens Mona into realizing that unless they can drive her illness into remission, she will wind up a cripple. Mona has seen cases in her own village that make her listen, and she now lies wrapped up in bed, as protected from draughts as it is possible to be in the draughty parsonage, with woollen arm warmers drawn up over her elbows and wool on top of a flannel nightgown covering her body. Her joints are swollen and painful at this acute stage of the illness, but total rest will help the body to fight it.

Petter feels terrible guilt for having dragged his wife out to this icy lair, this abode of wind and weather, and possibly having destroyed her health for the rest of her life. Is it the cold that's to blame? he wonders contritely.

Not necessarily, Doctor Gyllen thinks. It is hard to explain why a particular disease affects only some of the people in a population living under identical circumstances. It seems to be the case that there is more than one reason why disease breaks out. She is only speculating here, but in the course of her quite comprehensive practice in Leningrad she noticed that when women Mona's age came down with acute rheumatoid arthritis it often happened some time after a completed pregnancy. Almost as if the body's adjustment made it more susceptible to this kind of illness.

And, she adds, before he's had time to ask, "A large percentage of this category regained full health under conditions I have prescribed for this patient."

This is of the greatest interest to Mona, because she has seen her rheumatoid arthritis as an indictment of her failure to wear enough warm clothes. In fact, she has dressed warmly, and the doctor's words are a considerable comfort. She means to follow doctor's orders to the letter even though complete inaction is going to make her crazy. She is not allowed to do handwork or even strain her wrists for any extended time by holding a book or a newspaper.

Four weeks! It's hard to imagine how she'll be able to hold out for such a long time when there's so much to do. They can't hope to keep Sister Hanna for four weeks, and in any case she wants to take care of her cows and her children and her house herself—separate and churn butter, knit stockings, write letters, and go to the outhouse. Now she has to answer the call of nature in a potty chair in the bedroom, which others then have to carry out.

She listens to the radio for as long as she can stand the static. As often as he can, Petter comes in and tells her what he's busy with, and when the mail comes she can read the papers if she's careful turning the pages. The pastor is busy as a bee, for, in addition to all the duties of his office, many of the practical chores fall to him as well. Mona was so efficient that they were hardly noticeable before, but now he's got more than he can handle. Sister Hanna has her hands full too, and he tries to help her as much as he can—fetches wood and water, builds fires in the tile stoves, and often goes with her to the cow barn to help with the mucking out and the feeding. In the evenings, they lie in the dark and talk. These conversations are her greatest comfort and the bridge that leads from one day to the next. His voice, his hand holding hers, his thumb massaging the inside of her wrist, the hope in his words.

Of course Sanna often sits on the edge of the bed or moves about the room and talks sensibly. She has started liking her little sister now that she knows her mother can't devote herself to her. Sister Hanna places her at her mother's breast when she's hungry, but Mama can't lift her or change her. It's so cold on the floor that she mostly has to sit in her crib, where she would live like an animal in a cage if Sanna didn't keep her company. As soon as she walks into the bedroom, Lillus gives a happy shout, and when she's in the right mood she thinks everything Sanna comes up with is fun.

Sanna also talks to Sister Hanna, who goes quietly about her work in the kitchen. When she has time, she comes and talks to the pastor's wife. About her duties, about what she's to do and how, about where some things can be found and where others may be hiding. But also about many other things, about terrible diseases that have struck people on the Örlands, whole clusters of children left motherless, a helpless father left alone with his entire brood, his animals in the cow barn and no way to deal with it all. The need for help is inexhaustible, and still it was overwhelmingly difficult to get the local council to pass the proposal to create a home aide. Sister Hanna looks sad and bitter at the memory, and Sanna listens. "It's awful when the people who have our fate in their hands have no feeling for the troubles of their fellow creatures."

Mama and Sanna are all ears as Sister Hanna tells the story. Votes were taken again and again, and she names all those who voted no. She emphasizes that it was only when the organist became the new chairman that he managed to persuade his cohort to vote for the resolution and then cast the deciding vote himself. Mama and Sanna heave a sigh of relief and cheer, for the organist is their idol, and they can both bear witness to how badly Sister Hanna's services are needed. The bedroom becomes a zone of warmth and mutual respect. Mona, who has always had difficulty accepting help, finds it a little easier when Sister Hanna tells her again and again how comfortable she is in the guest bedroom.

If only no wife and mother becomes acutely ill and dies! For the moment, everything is working nicely at the parsonage, but how will it be in future? Was he selfish and thoughtless, Petter wonders, when he applied for the post of pastor on the Örlands? If Mona can't stand the climate and the cold, draughty parsonage, that puts his decision in a whole new light. Is it fair of him to insist on staying on if doing so puts his beloved wife's health at risk? When he was in Borgå, the bishop was very friendly and understanding and implied that a priest of Petter's calibre could make an important contribution in a significantly larger parish. At the time, of course, he said that his calling was to the Örlands, but if that calling means that he must sacrifice his wife's health, then it's time to reconsider.

He says, in the darkness of the bedroom. In just a couple of weeks, a good deal of Mona's pain and swelling has abated, and she is in good spirits. "Oh, now don't go rushing off again half-cocked," she says. "Let's wait and see how things look a month from now. Appointments won't be announced until the spring, so we can wait. Doctor Gyllen said it wasn't necessarily due to the cold. If I get well, I want to stay where you feel at home, it's as simple as that. No point in wasting energy on a lot of unnecessary speculation!"

"Don't say that just for my sake," he tells her.

"For my sake too, you dimwit. You've become much nicer since we came here. And where else do you think I could have my own cows? Don't forget I feel at home here too."

For even though the islanders are in many ways her rivals for Petter's time, attention, and favour, there's no denying that they have a great attraction for Mona as well. She hasn't come to know as many of them as Petter has, but the ones she's met she likes, and she is much more particular than he. She had thought she would have to spend much of her enforced confinement with the radio and Sanna's chatter as her only company, but it turns out that many of those who have business on Church Isle come in to say hello. Without the least embarrassment, they sit down and talk for a while and it is as naturally as an eighteenth-century queen receiving visitors while lying in her bed. Then they have coffee in the warm parlour and discuss their errand with the pastor. Best of all, of course, is when the organist stops by, gallant and handsome, with a warming smile. "And how is the patient today? Just fine? And the young ladies?" He looks at Sanna, who stands on the threshold admiring him, and at Lillus in her crib.

"Sit down for a moment if you've got time and tell me what's going on out in the world," says Mona. Insightful as he is, he talks about the conditions in his cow barn where he has five cows and various younger animals, a horse in his stable, and nine ewes and a ram in his sheepfold, always of interest to the pastor's wife. Then he tells her of the latest schism in the local council about the allocation of funds to the school library in the east villages that is open a few hours a week. The opposition — short-sighted, narrow-minded, uncultured — cannot see that reading is an important educational benefit for the public good. Then about the winter communications, functioning relatively well this year although Anton has his work cut out for him. Finally, less willingly, and only when she asks, about Francine.

Yes, the boy was born severely retarded. Doctor Gyllen said so and the hospital in Åbo has confirmed it. In addition, a congenital heart defect. Blue, due to poor oxygenation. Best, frankly, if he were to die. Poor child, poor Francine. Exhausted and unhappy, of course, thank heaven they have Mama in the house. What would they do without her? So the housework is getting done, but Francine is miserable. It's a shame about their daughter. He's trying to be both a mother and a father to her, which isn't easy when he has to be away so much. Which reminds him that, however pleasant it is to sit and talk, he has to go find the priest and discuss the coming vestry meeting and then get home. So thanks, and see you again. Hope you'll be feeling better soon.

Yes, for however singular and beautiful the Örlands are in themselves, nevertheless the people are their main reason for wanting to stay. Mona doesn't want to mention it for fear of tempting fate, but she feels that she's getting well and wants desperately to get started on all the springtime work. It will be their third spring on the Örlands, and they've already accomplished much. Conditions in the cow barn are good, they've added to their farmland, their crops will be a joy to behold when the time comes, the fences are repaired, and they've put money aside towards a horse and a motorboat. It will take a catastrophe to get them to leave all this.

Chapter Twenty

WHEN THE PASTOR'S WIFE starts getting dressed for the installation of the new vicar, she finds she can no longer get her arms into the little black wool dress that witnessed Petter's ordination. It's not that she's grown fat, just that hard work on the Örlands has developed her muscles and joints. Her girlhood is behind her, and she can only laugh. "Look there!" she says to Petter. "No seam to let out, and anyway I really don't have time to let out seams." She sounds surprisingly cheery, he notes, and the fact is that his wife is not a bit unwilling to revolt against the unwritten law that dictates black, black, black as the festival colour for women of the church. Black wool is not recommended for the pastor's wife as she leaps like a doe among her many duties. Instead, she has no choice but to wear her new summer dress, recently arrived in an American package, which fits beautifully and has a pretty collar, bloused sleeves, and a wide skirt. It has a pretty pattern in blue and fuchsia and is cool as a dream compared with the black wool. The first time such a creation has appeared in the front pew at the installation of a vicar! Petter's engagement necklace around her neck, her hair rolled and combed, cleared for action!

"You're so pretty today," says the pastor, although he knows she'll answer, "Oh, go on!" The vicar-to-be can still get into his cassock. Perhaps it has grown with him, since he has worn it every Sunday since his ordination. To be sure, it sits as tightly as a suit of armour, but the seams hold. He will simply have to see to it that he grows no more substantial than he is right now. It's as warm as burning Gehenna on a day like this, but they have decided never to complain about the heat on the few warm days they are granted on these wind-tortured islands. And it is truly a good thing to have such fine weather on this day, when Church Isle will be covered with people all day long.

What would they have done had it rained? After the service, they will serve coffee to at least four hundred people, and after the open-air programme of speeches and songs, the guests who have come a great distance will be served dinner—potatoes, fried pike with horseradish sauce and several square metres of lettuce that the pastor's wife has raised in her kitchen garden, tender and delicious, which she'll serve with a dressing of eggs and cream mixed with a little sugar, salt, and vinegar. The famous local breads—black and homemade white, her own butter, her milk, and her well-brewed small beer. For dessert, prune whip with whipped cream, an Åland speciality. Help in the kitchen, of course, but under her own watchful eye. Plates, coffee cups, bowls, and silverware borrowed in big baskets from the Martha Society and the youth centre. All this food and activity spreads out across the kitchen and the dining room, but the parlour is a protected zone. Here the visiting dignitaries are served a substantial breakfast of porridge, cheese sandwiches, and coffee or tea, to hold them through the long installation service.

It's like a royal visit. First the bishop, the bishop's wife, and the assessor will arrive from the east on one of Åbo's fast Coast Guard cutters. Many of the Örlanders have already arrived and stand on the bell-tower hill keeping a lookout. When the foaming prow of the boat is seen in the distance, a message is sent to the parsonage at once, and the vicar-to-be and his wife stroll down to the church dock to receive their visitors with a smile. Welcome, welcome! And thank you, thank you! The Coast Guard crewmen, like aides-de-camp, ready with discreet hands as the bishop — in his doctor's hat, cassock, and bishop's cross — steps ashore with his wife. Handshakes and great delight on all sides about the weather, about seeing one another again, about the Day and all it will mean for the life of the faith in the outer islands. "And it's so beautiful here. So indescribably lovely!" The gentlemen walk slightly ahead, scrutinized by Apple and Goody, who then focus their attention on Mona, who does not stop and pat them but informs the bishop's wife, "Yes, they're ours, I tend them myself. Without cows of our own, we'd have a hard time feeding ourselves out here."

When the dignitaries from the east have been settled in the parlour, word arrives of the boat arriving from the west. "A big devil of a boat, oh, excuse me, the biggest Coast Guard ship on Åland. From the station at Storkubb, a real destroyer. Does thirteen knots. Going like hell out there on the sound, oh, beg your pardon."

The priest would like very much to be up on the hill watching the party from Mariehamn come flying across the water — the Åland governor and the dean with their wives, reporters, plus the priest from Föglö and Fredrik Berg and his wife, picked up in Mellom — but his role today is too dignified for that, so he makes his excuses to the group in the parlour and he and his wife receive their guests on the dock. The newcomers are effusive and hearty. The governor is charmed by the pastor's young wife, while the dean gets his first impression of his new ecclesiastical colleague, truly a pleasant meeting! Apple and Goody stand nearby in a cloud of flies and watch and, out on the bay, the clatter of motorboats steadily increases. The congregation is on its way to church early in order to get a good seat. Cecilia is watching Sanna and Lillus, at a comfortable distance but still close enough to see all the people. Sanna is deeply offended at not being allowed to attend the installation even though she has promised to be quiet and good. She could sit with Grandma and Grandpa and Lillus could stay outside with Cecilia. Like all of Sanna's arguments, it is sensible and well thought out, but Mama has decided otherwise, so that's all there is to that.

Consequently, Sanna does not get to see her father standing before the altar surrounded by the dean and the priests from Mellom and Föglö, who read the words of the Bible and lay their hands on Papa's head as he kneels before the altar. The bishop says, "God hath given thee all them that sail with thee." That means that the parish of Örland is his, and he is theirs. Nor does she get to hear the organist sing his showpiece "A Precious Thing to Thank the Lord" while accompanying himself on the organ with one hand, but when they all leave the church, it's more fun. Cecilia and Sanna and Lillus go up to the attic, and when Cecilia opens the window they have a good view and can hear what people say.

It must have gone well in there, for everyone is happy and talking cheerfully. The congregation pours out first and then they stand and wait, dividing themselves into two groups so that Papa can guide the bishop to the coffee table outside the parsonage. Behind them come the dignitaries and the guests and Grandma and Grandpa and Mama. When she gets there, she makes a sharp survey of the coffee table and then hurries quickly and, she hopes, unnoticed, to the kitchen. Several well-briefed coffee ladies stand at the ready. Gaily and graciously, they pour coffee for the bishop and his wife and wish them bon appetit. There are great heaps of sandwiches, and more are brought out on trays, and when the bishop, his wife, the assessor, and the governor have seated themselves, the congregation can help themselves. There are planks laid on sawhorses where older people can sit, the younger sit on rocky outcroppings or on the grass. It's like when the children of Israel made camp in the wilderness, Cecilia tells Sanna, and manna came from heaven. "Coffee and sandwiches," Sanna translates, and Cecilia runs down to the kitchen and brings some sandwiches and juice up to the attic. Fortunately, Lillus has fallen asleep, and Cecilia and Sanna stand by the window and drink their juice and eat sandwiches while the children of Israel laugh and talk below them.

When they are finished eating, the church choir performs. They have to wait a moment for the priest and his wife, who come running, and then they sing with all their might. They begin with "Bright Clouds Sailing", and anyone concerned that the wind will carry away their voices can stop worrying. They sing "Great is God's Mercy" and "Imagine When the Mists Have Vanished", and when they are done, the bishop stands at the top of the steps so his voice will carry. The Örlanders are experts at public speaking, so they appreciate the fact that he makes himself heard, although to tell the truth, the content is a little too general and sounds like any other sermon, all about Christian upbringing and the importance of piety at every level, whereas the congregation longs to hear what he thinks of the Örlands and the lovely weather and whether he didn't feel a little giddy when the Coast Guard cutter really opened up.

The lean assessor follows his bishop and he too delivers a discourse on how impossible it is to hide from the living God. All too true, and everyone present can also agree that the majority of human beings wander a path of affliction, captured in the iron grip of sin, but would it have been out of place to say a few words about the Örlands and about how people here wander the path of salvation, at least today? The vicar himself lightens the atmosphere after the final choir performance by signalling that now the celebration is over. He thanks the congregation for making the day festive and unforgettable with their singing and by their very presence. "Now we part for today, but I hope we shall see one another again every Sunday. Getting to Church Isle can be difficult, but the church awaits you with open arms."

That means they should be off, for only the guests are invited to dinner. Among them are the Örland church council and vestry, but the rest of the lay people start moving towards the church dock, where their boats are tied up in multiple rows. It goes quickly after all the sitting, and soon the bay echoes with the clatter and sharp detonations of motors cranked to life. Cecilia and the little girls go down to the dock with all the others, and as they're coming back they run into Fredrik Berg, the priest from Mellom, who understands that these must be the parsonage children. Cecilia knows that normally Sanna hides and Lillus cries when any stranger comes too close, but there's something about Fredrik Berg — maybe the fact that at home he is often mentioned as Papa's good friend — which makes them stare up at him with delight. As they approach the parsonage, Mama and Papa see with astonishment that Lillus is sitting on Fredrik's arm and beaming, while Sanna holds his hand, talking for all she's worth.

"Quite the ladies' man," says Papa, and Mrs Berg, who appears for once at a party instead of just toiling in the kitchen, in black (although she has now learned something from Mona), adds, "Yes, that's the way he likes it. One around his neck, one holding his hand, one in reserve."

They're all in good spirits, relieved perhaps that the heavy programme is over and that an easier socializing lies before them, among friends and colleagues. Food will be welcome as well, to tell the truth. The long dinner table has been set on the grass below the stairs. The sun is shining, there is still no wind, an uncommonly lovely afternoon. There is a buzz of conversation, the new vicar and his wife are beaming with happiness, nearly everything has gone off without a hitch. The food is on the table.

And now the event takes off! When they've all found their seats and tucked in and rejoiced in the day and the company, there breaks out a feast of speechifying that will live in memory. Cecilia has taken the girls' food up to the attic, and while Lillus gobbles down her mashed potatoes and gravy and adorns her whole person with the prune whip dessert, Cecilia and Sanna stand at the window and listen.

Papa speaks first, welcoming everyone and thanking them for making the day so festive. He extends especially warm thanks to the bishop and his wife, to the governor and his wife, to his visiting fellow priests and their wives, and to his parents. Above all, he speaks of his love for Örland Church and its parishioners, who have won his heart and boundless respect. "We will grow old here," he promises. He speaks beautifully, and everyone looks appreciative and pleased. Sanna applauds enthusiastically. Cecilia thinks Sanna should have been allowed to sit at table, smart and sensible as she is.

Papa's speech opens the floodgates, and the fireworks begin. The bishop responds by saying how delighted he is that the Örlands have their first permanent vicar since time immemorial, a young, hearty pastor, passionate in spirit and faithful to the Lord, and at his side a wife to stand with him through all of life's vicissitudes. The congregation could not have chosen a better way to manifest its support for this young couple than with its song and its presence here today. It is a sad fact that Örland parish often winds up beyond the edge of narrowly drawn maps, but today's celebration has, at one stroke, established it as a central and valued member of the diocese. He pauses for a moment and then, with a slight bow to the governor, he expresses his gratitude to the representative of civil authority for showing such a kindly interest in the affairs of the church.

This is sufficient to bring the governor to his feet. He assures those present that it was a great honour for himself and his wife to be invited. It has been an unforgettable occasion. He has met old friends and made new acquaintances. It is a dear sight to see the people of the outer islands dressed for a celebration. Surrounded by such goodwill, the vicar of Örland can count himself truly fortunate. It is a pleasure for him to take this opportunity, on behalf of all the guests, to thank the host and hostess and the elected representatives of the parish for this perfectly wonderful day.

Then Uncle Isidor speaks. His voice quavering, he begins by conveying greetings from the entire family and the members of his former parish. "Dear nephew," he says. But he has become emotional in his old age, and his voice breaks. He starts over. "Dear nephew. To see such a young man find his calling and win his place in the world — it fills us all with inspiration and gives us hope for the future."

The assessor, who is the next to speak, reveals his earlier prejudice against the fishermen and fisherman-farmers of Örland when he says that this day has given him an entirely different picture of the Örland Islands and its laity. This is a smiling countryside with gifted and affectionate people. The hymns were memorable, and what collections! This poor parish actually leads the collection statistics for Åland. And what can one deduce from this? That the vicar is to be congratulated for such a congregation, and that the congregation is to be congratulated for having received a vicar who can bring out their best qualities.

Still amazed, he sits down, and then Sanna's idol rises, Fredrik Berg, in sparkling good humour. For him, this has been a splendid day. All these people have had an intoxicating effect on him. He has spoken to the bishop and the dean and has met the governor and had long conversations with the organist and Adele Bergman and chatted about shared concerns with the priest from Föglö. Now he knocks them all out with his wit. Out here in the outermost archipelago, he begins, conditions are so special that people have to come up with their own solutions to problems and make their own independent decisions. Against this background, the distinguished gentlemen present may perhaps see fit to look with indulgence on the creation, on their own initiative, of an island deanery, where clerical concerns can be aired and mutual decisions reached by means of telephone conferences. As dean of this illegal deanery, it is the speaker's particular joy to be able to take part in the consecration of his esteemed fellow clergyman as vicar. "My dear fellow priest!" he concludes. "Your name, Petrus, puts you under obligation. On the rocky cliffs of the Örland Islands you shall build your church, and here you shall carry the keys to the kingdom of heaven."

The whole table applauds enthusiastically, and Sanna up in the window claps and claps and wishes that Uncle Berg would look up just once, but he doesn't. He looks quickly at the people at the table and then down at the tablecloth and tries not to smile. His wife appears to like him better than she did earlier in the day when he ignored her completely and seemed not to care that she knew hardly a soul.

Priests are good at talking, and there is no one with a clerical collar under his chin who doesn't feel called upon to say a few words. The bishop and the dean of Åland rise at the same moment, but the dean must yield to the bishop, who takes the words from his mouth. "The Archipelago Deanery comes as a complete surprise to me," he says in an authoritative tone, but smiling, so everyone will see that he is mocking the gravity of his office. "But after due consideration I am prepared to give it my blessing. Everything that contributes to harmony is a benefit to the diocese."

The priest from Föglö wants to know how to join, but Fredrik Berg is strict and says that he must first give up his bus connection to the Åland main island. The Föglö priest won't do that, but he very much wants to belong to the archipelago group. This gives the dean of all Åland's parishes his chance, and he extends a chivalrous invitation to the new group to attend all future meetings of the Åland deanery. He salutes the new vicar on behalf of all his fellow Åland clergymen.

Now all the priests have had their say, and it is admirable that father Leonard has been able to restrain himself all this time. Of course Petter has known all along that Papa will have to open his mouth at some point, and now he smiles from fear and looks down at his plate. Papa! No nonsense now, he wants to say, but Leonard has already started, as usual without the slightest idea of what he will say but with complete confidence that it will be excellent. "My dear son!" he begins. "If I, young and undecided, like a reed in the wind, sailing along between the Scylla and Charybdis of temptations, if I had been told then that my eldest son would become a priest and vicar, maybe a dean one fine day, I would have laughed out loud. Me, a free-thinker, with a son who's a priest! I can truthfully say that God guides our steps in mysterious ways. Spiritual breezes blew my vessel past hidden rocks and into the bay where your mother waited. I give all the honour and credit for your becoming what you've become to her, not to myself." And so on, mostly about himself, his own inconstancy and restlessness, whereas even as a child, his son showed himself to be calm, responsible, a rock. "Which, by the way, another speaker today has already referred to, quite rightly. Consequently it is perhaps forgivable that on a day like this, an old father can feel like a youth, who still has much to learn, compared with such a son. Or like an old ram in a herd of which the shepherd is his son. Perhaps it is meant to be so, as generation follows generation. Humble and chastened, my wife and I this day thank God for our son, who has given us such joy."

Here he actually stops. Petter gives him a friendly nod and mouths thank you, and the whole table applauds. "Original, fantastic," they say to one another. Meanwhile, the organist is collecting himself for the speech he's to give on behalf of the Örlanders. He is nervous and begins in a thin, strained voice and gets a frog in his throat. It is hard for him, usually so humorous, to find the light-hearted tone that prevails around the table. It feels like some kind of upper-class mannerism and it makes him more serious than he'd meant to be. Adele looks at him, knows how nervous he can get, even though he manages everything so well.

"Dear Petter, dear Mona," he says, now in a normal voice. "Young and lively and irresistible, you stepped straight into our hearts. In the beginning, we didn't dare to believe you'd stay. Today, we dare to express the hope that we won't have to change priests for a long time to come. We've been given a spiritual guide who understands us, a man who is not only educated but who also possesses great practical competence. In this poor little parish, he can make a real contribution, God willing, a life's work. For example, we're working to build a bridge to Church Isle. The foundation has been laid, thanks to the help of a generous Swede, and our vicar himself heads the volunteer effort that began last winter. But more money is needed. Perhaps there is someone at this table who can help us move ahead. This kind of work is one of the chief activities of a priest out here, while at the same time he must preach the word and administer the sacraments. Two tasks of great importance, and we hope that you, Petter, will remain our vicar for years to come, and you, Mona, his tireless helpmate."

He sits down, and the former verger, retired but in service again on a day like this, rises, beaming as only an old man can, and insists that in the course of his long life he has seen the local priest change so many times that he's lost count. "Now our only wish, Petter, is that you remain with us."

It is now so late that the little girls must go to bed. Sanna is very, very tired after her intense participation in the drawn-out events of the day. Lillus, who has taken several naps in the course of the afternoon, is wider awake but still willing. While the speeches continue outdoors, they come down the attic stairs. There are people working in the kitchen, and Cecilia takes the potty into the bedroom along with a bucket of water so they can wash their hands and faces at the washstand. Then they sit in their beds while Cecilia says their evening prayers with them, adding on her own initiative a thank-you for the beautiful weather, which made the day so lovely. Sanna falls asleep almost at once, while Lillus sings and speaks. Cecilia wonders how much she's understood of what has happened and what she thinks about it. She herself feels a bit superfluous.

In the kitchen, they're preparing coffee and cakes that the pastor's . . . the vicar's wife has made in baking pans. Wild strawberries mashed with sugar with a layer of whipped cream between the layers, topped off with sweetened whipped cream. When the cakes are carried out, there may be some left on the baking sheets, and anyway they'll need help with the dishes, so she leaves the door ajar and heads for the kitchen.

She stops for a moment in the hall and listens — such a merry babble, and such happy, loud voices. The whole crowd draws its breath when the cakes are put on the table. Delighted cries. Is there no end to his hospitality? Is there no limit to what can be stuffed into a dean's belly? The bishop helps himself first. With all his authority, he urges the others to be cautious — the cakes are so tall that no matter how thin a piece you cut, your plate will overflow.

Cecilia can see the vicar's wife in her mind's eye, smiling and saying, Oh, it's nothing. They have eaten and eaten all evening long, and now they're still eating, as if they were trying to make up for the shortage of food all through the long war. Adele sits lost in thought, trying to figure out how much food she would have to order if this whole bunch lived on the Örlands.

The temporal side of the event has also been a great success, and out in the kitchen by the dishpans, the Marthas are in high spirits. When the vicar's wife comes scurrying in to ask if they don't need to take a break, sit down, have a cup of coffee and taste the cake, they say yes indeed but they'll soon be done and then the coffee will taste extra good. "It went really well," says Lydia Manström, who is working in the kitchen as a Martha even though she has every right to sit at the table like a Mary, that is to say, as a member of the vestry. Quietly she wonders if they're never going to leave, and the vicar's wife laughs and says she thinks they've started to discuss it. The long-distance guests have their transportation all arranged – the Coast Guard cutter is waiting patiently. Mona is exhilarated and happy even though she's so tired she's reeling. But now she must go back out again, because she can hear that people are starting to stand up, singing their thanks before they leave the table, and Petter is already on the steps asking for her. And so they stand arm and arm and say farewell to their guests, although they'll be going down to the dock to say farewell again, so hard it is for all of them to part.

The vestry and the council also head off in the wake of the surging Coast Guard cutters, but for them a quick reunion awaits. The very next day, all the Örlanders who helped or contributed to the celebration are invited back for coffee, which will give them a chance to relive the events of the day in relative peace and quiet and allow the priest and his wife to thank everyone properly, as they deserve, with great warmth, communal song, and the love and respect of their new vicar.

But now, finally, they stand there stupefied – Petter and Mona, Grandma and Grandpa. Thanks to the Coast Guard, the house is not full of overnight guests. Grandma and Grandpa are to sleep in the guest room, Cecilia in the attic. It is utterly quiet, a slight chill in the air, and they shiver as they stand on the steps. Petter, who has been standing as if bewitched, shakes himself loose. "Now let's go in. Wouldn't it be nice if we all caught cold on the warmest day of the year? We'll have a cup of tea, and then everyone to bed."

Mona looks out across the desolate party site. A couple of her finely woven tablecloths overlapping on the long table are covered with ugly sauce and coffee stains, but it's a small price to pay. Before they went home, the Marthas did a huge job – all the serving dishes, platters, and bowls have been cleared, washed, and sorted according to where they came from. There is warm water on the stove, and before long it's boiling and everyone gets a cup of tea. Not even father Leonard has more to say. The lively conversations, speeches, and babble of the day echo in everyone's head, along with the music from the organ and the breasts of the Örlanders. Cecilia has said goodnight and gone up, the others say goodnight and pour wash water into pitchers and go to bed. The vicar and his wife long to lie flat on their backs and say a few words, entire sentences if they have the strength, before they sleep.

But Mona has a hard time relaxing. It's midnight, but she worries that there aren't enough pastries left over for the locals. She set aside a considerable quantity of sweet rolls in the cellar, but at some point during the day she grew nervous and pinched some of the reserve and put them on the table. In the middle of the night, she stands in the cellar with a flashlight in her hand and counts sweet rolls and counts Örlanders and counts the people who may wander in uninvited. If no one takes two, there may be enough.

It is not true that you can lay your troubles before the Lord and lay your head calmly to rest, trusting in Him, because the church of Christ is heavily dependent on its ground crew. Ask and you shall receive—well, yes you shall, if someone has done the baking and set the table. Everyone has thanked God for this fine day, and Mona can go so far as to thank Him for her health and strength, which, thanks to Doctor Gyllen, allows her once again to work like a dog. But if the dog didn't work, they'd all sit there twiddling their thumbs while their stomachs rumbled. Miracles are thin on the ground; work is everywhere waiting to be done!

Chapter Twenty-One

IN THEORY AT LEAST, the vicar and his wife can take it a little easier now that his pastoral exam and installation are behind them. For Petter, it means that he allows himself to enjoy the beautiful days that August still has up its sleeve. The congregation is busy with its fishing, and he has no pressing duties except Sunday's sermon and occasional functions. He makes his pastoral visits to the elderly and deals with the recurrent paperwork in his office, but he does have a little time to himself, so he sometimes goes out for a walk with Sanna. It is a great concern to him that a good clergyman must neglect his family. A shepherd who devotes most of his time to his family must necessarily neglect his parish.

It breaks his heart to look at them, Sanna and Lillus, the way they love him and forgive him everything, no, do not even see that there is anything to forgive. Adoring and happy, they cling to him and love him however much he is away, however little time he has for them, however much he forbids them to stick their noses into his office, however often he goes off and leaves them. They stand and wave for as long as he's in sight, and when he comes back after what must seem an eternity to a child, he can hear their joy even before he opens the door. There are a lot of sentimental verses written about a mother's love, but as far as he knows, very little has been written about children's love, which is like God's, unconditional and boundless.

However much Sanna watches over Lillus and however hard she finds it to believe that Lillus could survive without her big sister, she abandons her nevertheless when she and Papa go out for a walk. They wander around Church Isle and look at plants and birds and Sanna learns all their names. They climb hills and jump on rocks and splash in the water, and as they walk Papa talks about things that he knows all too well what Mona would think of. Like this business of studying. "It's remarkable," he says to Sanna, "but after all the trouble I had studying for my pastoral exam, which was sometimes terribly boring, I still have a desire to study. Not theology but something else. Botany, for example. Someone could make a terrifically interesting study of the flora in a well-grazed landscape like this one. You could have ungrazed areas as test sections for comparison. My suspicion is that an intensively grazed landscape will have a greater diversity of plants, whereas in the ungrazed area just a few dominant species will take over. It would be fascinating to study the way plants adapt to intensive grazing. The ones that manage to bloom have to grow low and fast, maybe creep along the ground. Where the soil is shallow, the way it is here, it dries out quickly, so the species that survive have to be better than average at tolerating dry conditions. It's questions like that that interest me! Would you like to be my assistant? That means my helper. What do you think?"

"Yes!" says Sanna, where Mona says, "Don't you think you have enough to do? When you were finally done with your pastoral exam I thought we'd get a little rest on that front." True, true, but Sanna says, "Yes!" Willing, full of love, her hand lies in his. All right then! Botanical assistant it shall be.

But then he goes on thinking out loud. "But even more, I think I'd like to get into ethnology. What an unbelievable field of study the Örlands could be! In fact, I have a unique opportunity to get to know people here and to understand how they think. What other job lets you go into people's houses and get to know people the way I can do as a priest? You know what? I think I'll study ethnology as an academic discipline and have botany as a side interest, just for the fun of it."

"Yes!" says Sanna.

"Thanks," says Papa. "As soon as we've got a motorboat and a horse and the bridge is finished and everything gets much easier, then we can start. I've got lots of ideas about what I could write my dissertation on. People's ideas about signs and omens, for example. The old skin-clad men who warn of dangers, dreams that carry messages. Those kinds of things. The closest word is folklore, but I could also write about information-sharing in a rural community. Communications are difficult and everything is far away, and yet when something happens, word spreads like wildfire. Of course the telephone has a lot to do with that, but what's interesting is that it was probably the same way before the Örlands had telephones. If people call each other in a certain pattern then I'd guess that same pattern was the basis of information-sharing even before the telephone. Family relationships are decisive here, and my hypothesis is that newcomers without family ties remain far outside the well-established information networks. But I have to test the theory and be able to prove it. There are an incredible number of interesting dissertation possibilities just here on the Örlands. It's a small, defined area, in the winter it's even isolated. It's fantastic that all this is here just waiting for me!"

"Yes!" says Sanna. She looks at him earnestly and understands that he's talking about important things and she'll be allowed to be part of it as his assistant. His hand is warm, his voice deep, but then he sighs.

"But where will I find the time? Mama and I have way too much to do, and we never get enough sleep. We can't go on like this indefinitely. And yet I'd still like to find a new subject to study, now that I'm finished. Do you think I'm out of my mind?"

Sanna stops and laughs, and Papa starts laughing too. "Oh well," he says. "You've got to have plans for the future, even when you don't know how you're going to make them happen. Come on, let's go get those perch from the live box and clean them like Mama asked us to."

＊ ＊ ＊

As if to prove his hypothesis about the way information travels on the islands, a large quantity of smuggled liquor arrives on the Örlands, and the parsonage is the last place to hear about it.

If the priest hadn't come cycling to the store on a perfectly ordinary Wednesday afternoon, they would never have had to know that a large cargo had been dumped in the outer archipelago and taken in hand by local Örlanders, this news having made a detour around the Coast Guard, the parsonage, and the police. The scene was utterly peaceful as he approached on his bike. For some reason, the phrase "pastoral idyll" crossed his mind — peacefully grazing cows, no visible activity anywhere, woolly clouds in the sky, a benevolent sun shining down on all of it. Like life on earth before the Fall, he thought, smiling, and the faces he began to see as he pedalled into the largest of the west villages beamed with goodwill and bonhomie. Down by the village harbour they were remarkably stationary, sat where they sat, waved slowly and royally in answer to his greeting. Like a quiet Sunday in the middle of a weekday.

What was it they put down in the grass when he came? They were clearly on some kind of break, half sitting or half lying down, and they made no effort to rise or get busy with something when he came. One of them started to sing and the others hushed him but burst out laughing. Their good spirits were perfectly normal. Their particularly good spirits were not.

"May I sit down?" the vicar asked. "Please do," they said, as they always did. But they laughed and wouldn't look at him.

"Would I be wrong if I guessed that something amusing has happened?" he said.

They glanced at each other furtively and their bellies bounced with mirth. One young smart aleck said, "Yesterday's catch was a little better than usual." They lay back on their elbows and guffawed. The phrase "drunk with laughter" occurred to the vicar, and then simply the word "drunk". Quite simply, plastered. Drunk as lords, or maybe not — able to talk but clearly unsteady on their legs.

A tough situation for the priest, who was seen as a kind of authority figure and who might be expected to report them. He found himself in a situation where he didn't belong and wasn't welcome but where the level of inebriation led to his being cordially received. He couldn't just get up and leave, so he said, breezily, "Fish with corks and labels, sounds like. Fish that sort of gurgle."

They laughed till they cried. And of course one of them, in accordance with the rules of hospitality, asked if he wanted a taste. They looked at him expectantly. His answer would show what calibre of priest they had. Whether they could feel respect for him. They wanted him to have a drink with them, but on the other hand, if word got around that he sat tippling with the men that time the load of liquor came in, he would never be able to regain their respect for his office. "Thanks for the offer," he said. "But I catch my own fish."

There was no great reaction to this statement, and he started to walk to his bicycle. "Have a pleasant day," he said in farewell. "And congratulations on your catch."

For the first time, he felt like a total outsider. Who should have had the sense to stay away. He did his shopping at the Co-op without seeing Adele and biked straight home. Both Coast Guard cutters lay at their dock, he noticed, neither out on patrol. He heard later that both Brage and the police had been at home and invisible, seized with a sudden strong yearning for the home fires and old newspapers that needed to be read from cover to cover.

There was a great deal that he heard afterwards, and his already multifaceted congregation gained one further dimension—they appeared to possess intimate knowledge of the various types of distilled spirits, knew the names of the most exotic brands, and seemed to have considerable insight into the prices they would bring on the black market and in restaurants. He himself was like a newborn baby in that area and full of conflicting emotions. On the one hand, he should strongly disapprove and condemn what had occurred. On the other hand, it was a manifestation of the anarchic and pragmatic attitude towards land-based law that he found so exhilarating and admirable in his sovereign Örlanders. On the third hand, he saw more clearly than ever before that he was excluded from certain aspects of their lives, no matter how much he had convinced himself otherwise.

* * *

Chastened and torn, he turns inward instead towards his neglected children. During all the preparations for his installation as vicar, Lillus has her first birthday. At breakfast, Papa puts a rose on her plate. Quick as a wink, she stuffs it in her mouth. Mama leans forward and digs it out amidst Lillus's injured screams. "On her plate!" she scolds her husband. "You know she puts everything in her mouth, and you put it on her plate! We've been trying to teach her to eat only what's on her plate!"

Papa looks abashed. Thoughtless. As foolish as father Leonard himself. But was it really so dangerous? Anything Lillus doesn't like, she immediately spits out. She investigates things by stuffing them in her craw, and there an automatic sorting process takes place. Stones, bits of wood and birchbark from the woodpile, candle wax, soap, napkins, pen wipers, erasers, buttons are all rejected. As far as they can tell, she rarely swallows things she shouldn't, and when she does, they presumably come out the natural way. She chews larger things experimentally. The parsonage contains nothing at Lillus's height that she hasn't nibbled on. Towels, curtains, tablecloths that hang over the edge — all have damp hems, and she chews on the hem of her dress and on her collar, and she tastes boots and wool socks in the hall. Her father notes that she goes about it calmly, almost scientifically. Mama rushes over and stops her, but when Papa sees her gnawing on the leg of a chair in the parlour, he laughs and knows what he'll say next time some sailboat visitor asks why the Örlands are so barren. It's because of Lillus, he'll say. The Örlands were once covered with pine forest, but then Lillus came into the world and started to nibble. Eventually the forest was chewed down, and then she started on the broad-leaf trees and the bushes. But mostly she munches on the furniture and accessories in the parsonage. Miss Woodworm, he calls her, the scourge of the Örlands.

She's beginning to be so much fun, he thinks. She's started to walk, and soon she'll start to talk. He can already communicate with her. They play while Mama milks the cows. "What does the cow say?" "Moo!" "What does the ewe say?" "Baa!" "What does the pig say?" "Oink!" "What does the kitty say?" "Meow!" On an impulse, he says, "What does Papa say?" Lillus is in ecstasy, laughs so her eyes disappear. "Moo!" "Does Papa say Moo?" he asks, and she shouts, "Moo!" and throws herself on the floor with hilarity. Then he says, "What does Mama say?" She stops for a moment as if weighing his ability to get a joke. "Usch! Pugh!" she says, looking at him out of the corner of her eye, which sparkles with merriment. He is so surprised that he whoops with laughter, and then she laughs too. When Mama and Sanna come in from the milking, they are lying in a heap on the floor shouting, "Moo!" and "Usch pugh!" and "Baa!" and "Moo!" and "Usch pugh!"

"What are you doing?" Mama wants to know. "Don't get her all excited just before her bedtime!"

"Sorry," he says. "Do you think a person can have a sense of humour even at this early age?"

"Maybe," says Mama. She has already dragged Lillus off the floor and Papa stands up shamefaced. She examines Lillus, who has accumulated new stains and wrinkles since she saw her last. Her hair is like Kivi's *Seven Brothers*, the whole child like an unmade bed. "Sanna was always much tidier," Mama says. "Lillus looks like she lived in a sty, and yet I run myself ragged trying to keep her clean."

Lillus screams and cries. Left to herself and Sanna and Papa, she is sunny and content, but Mama, who does the actual parenting, finds altogether too much in Lillus's character that must be driven out and replaced with regular habits and sound morals. In principle, Papa agrees with all of this and bows to his wife's methods because she's the one who takes the day-to-day responsibility. But he understands why big tears run down Lillus's cheeks. Lillus doesn't like regular habits. Left to herself, she happily takes a couple of naps in the course of the day, rolled up under the cupboard or next to the tile stove, but when Mama discovers her, she hauls her out and forces her into bed, and then she can't sleep. One of Mama's tasks is to teach Lillus that you take naps in bed, and that you don't eat when you're hungry but at fixed times. When she wakes up at night and cries, Mama lifts her crib into the study and closes the door so she'll learn not to expect to be picked up in the middle of the night and coddled. At night, you're to sleep, and in the morning, you're to wake up bright and cheery!

Regular habits and sound morals are well and good, but it's a little sad for children raised with such consistency. Sanna, who is Lillus's other influential mentor, makes no such demands but is more sensitive to Lillus's nature. When she has fallen asleep somewhere, Sanna doesn't report the fact, although she answers when Mama asks, and when the sisters work on something together, there are no screams or tears. But there are when Mama gets involved and gives Lillus instructions. Poor Mona, Petter thinks. Someone has to do the essential parenting and so be the least popular person in the house. It's not fair. Easy for him to be popular, he who only appears in their lives sporadically and gets all the love.

The question now is whether he has witnessed a newly awakened sense of humour in his fifteen-month-old daughter. There are many reasons to think so, and there is a great deal going on in her present phase of development. In the kitchen they have a newly arrived household piglet in a box by the stove. There he squats, shivering and unhappy, bereft and fearful. Here the priest sees the awakening of compassion in Lillus, the realization that other creatures are like us. She sees how frightened he is, and how utterly alone. His skin, which is like her own, trembles over his whole body, his eyes blink in terror, he drools a little the way she does and whimpers. "Oink, oink," says the piglet, and then Lillus goes to him in his distress. Glowing with compassion, like the angels who came to Swedenborg in his deepest adversity, she sits down by the box and pats his head, the way Sanna often pats hers. She talks to him in a friendly tone of voice, and the piglet listens and understands. He takes small hops with his legs and leans across the edge of the box and nudges her with his head, and she nudges back. He has stopped trembling and found courage and hope, secure in the knowledge that there is another creature like himself in this world.

The telephone rings in the study, and Papa has to answer it. It's a long call and, when he comes back to see what's become of Lillus, she's lying in the box beside the piglet. Both of them are asleep, lightly, silently. In his sleep, the piglet is sucking on the hem of her dress, and she has a potato skin in her hand that she has shared with him. It is hardly a sanitary arrangement and ought to be stopped, but Petter finds it difficult to tear her away. It's as if he were looking into another world where there is no distinction between species. Carefully he retreats to the dining room and sits down with a newspaper so he can keep an eye on Lillus but can pretend that he didn't see her climb into the box with the piglet.

Soon Mama and Sanna come back from the cow barn and Mama gives a shout. "Come and look!" she cries and grabs Lillus out of the box. The piglet collapses, trembling, when the dress is torn from his mouth, and Lillus screams in terror at being so abruptly awaked from her animal sleep. "Usch!" says Mama. "Pugh! You stink of pig! Look at this mess! She's been lying right in the pig filth! You were supposed to be watching her!"

This last to Petter, who is ashamed of his disloyalty. It's not as if he didn't know what Mona thinks of Lillus's piglet life. It's hard, because he's so impressed by the humanity he has seen awakening in Lillus, even if it's directed towards a pig. He mumbles that he'd begun to read and was apparently blind to space and time. While he's excusing himself, she gets the clothes off the screaming child and mixes bathwater in the big washbasin. The dress, which was washed and ironed, must now be washed and ironed, and the child, too, needs washing, not gently, while she screams and squirms.

Sanna looks at the pig with interest, and at Lillus, and when order has been restored, Swedenborg banished to a partition in the cow barn, and Lillus scrubbed and stuffed into her nightgown, Sanna suggests that Lillus behaves the way she does because she doesn't know she's a person.

Papa is awestruck. What a daughter he has! Yes, how could Lillus know that she's a person? She's at an age when she could just as well live with the cows in the barn or the sheep in the sheepfold. She would see it as perfectly natural, even though her prospects for the future wouldn't be good. Compared with calves and lambs, she is little and defenceless. Sharp hooves would step on her and large bodies crush her to death. It's not clear that she would understand how to suckle a cow, and nevertheless she would not know enough to wish for any other life.

Sanna obviously has a scientific bent, and she immediately tests her hypothesis. Lillus is sitting in her crib and is wide awake, as she usually is when it's time to sleep. Sanna hangs over the edge and gets her sister's undivided attention. "Lillus, are you a pig?"

Lillus is in a good humour and ready to go along with whatever Sanna suggests. "Oink, oink," she yelps and laughs.

"Are you a cow?"

"Moo!" Lillus shouts and laughs at the top of her lungs. This reply can be considered a yes, and Sanna continues. "Are you a sheep?"

"Baa," comes the answer, strong and persuasive.

"Are you a kitty?"

Papa notes with surprise that Lillus is thinking it over. She does not continue the game with the animal noises but is clearly considering her relationship with the cat and looks uncertain and unhappy. She looks at a big scratch she got on her underarm when she tried to eat from the cat's bowl and the cat struck out with claws bared. Her mouth trembles at the memory, Mama chasing out the cat and scolding Lillus for not knowing better than to steal its food. No, Lillus is no cat, and Sanna continues.

"Are you a dog?" Sanna looks at her disapprovingly, angrily, and shakes her head, and Lillus shakes her head and looks appalled, for Sanna hates and fears dogs and does not want a sister who is a dog. "No! No!" Lillus assures her, and Sanna summarizes. "Lillus thinks she's a pig and a cow and a sheep. But not a cat or a dog." "Right," says Papa, and Sanna goes on.

"Are you a person?"

This is hard. Sanna gives her no hint. How is Lillus to know if she's a person? She looks at Papa for help, and he smiles and nods just slightly. Aha, but she hesitates when she looks at Sanna, the great authority, who says only, "Answer. Are you a person?"

Lillus vacillates. Papa seems to think that she is, but she has no strong feelings one way or the other, not like pig or cow or sheep. Uncertain, she looks at Sanna. "Yes?" she tries.

Sanna is pleased. "She doesn't know. You heard it yourself!" she says to Papa.

"But she's inclined to think she is," he says. "Good, Lillus! Sanna is a person and Mama is a person and Papa is a person and you're a person. We're all people. The organist and the verger and the whole congregation!"

That's a large group, and Lillus looks overwhelmed but rather pleased since both Sanna and Papa are included. Mama comes in and puts Lillus on the potty. Sanna reports that she has taught her she's a person, not a pig.

"Good!" says Mama. "A big improvement. Now I want my two human children in their beds and I'll read you a story."

Papa stays and listens to *Children of the Forest*, although Mama signals that he can go. Sanna is completely absorbed. She knows the story by heart and moves her lips as it's read. Lillus lies in her own world, a worm in the mould. What she reacts to is direct address, touch, smells, tastes in her mouth, things that move — a story read aloud still has no meaning for her. He has no memory of when they noticed that it was time to start reading to Sanna. How could he be so unobservant about his own child? Now he has a second chance with Lillus, and he means to be there when Lillus responds to her first story.

PART THREE

Chapter Twenty-Two

As WINTER DRAWS CLOSER, his third on the Örlands, it seems
to Petter that he has come far. He has just as much work as
before but is calmer and more at ease with his duties. The
sermons have begun to come easier, at last. The text and the
length provide the framework, and as his own experience of
life on the Örlands has grown, he is able to find more and more
natural associations between the biblical texts and the life of
his congregation. The points of contact are no longer limited
to the Sea of Galilee and the desert as a metaphor for the sea,
but now include all the human strengths and weaknesses that
unite people in the distant past with today's Örlanders. They
resemble Zacchaeus and Caiaphas and Naomi and Ruth and
the wise and the foolish virgins.

It is easier, now, to make it clear that Jesus is talking about
them. The Örlands have become a biblical landscape that he
makes use of in his sermons. When Jesus went up on Storböte
and saw the glory of the archipelago, the devil appeared and
said all these things will I give thee. He has to add that it would
have been a great temptation for the priest himself. But we need
not own what we love. If we're at peace with God, if we've
retained an unaffected soul, we can read God's presence in all

of creation. A presence is not something we can own, we can only gratefully receive the blessed moments when it is revealed to us. It is then we glimpse the face of God, like an intimation, in the constant subtle changes in nature's countenance.

When he roams through the biblical stories, the scenes change and well-known figures vanish from sight and wander on unseen. The same thing happens on the Örlands, where so many people leave. People on the islands talk a great deal about the problems that arise from seeing more and more young people move to Sweden. They come back during their summer vacations, and those who suffer most from homesickness or who know that they're needed for the fishing take the whole summer off and find new jobs in the autumn. There is a great deal of coming and going, and Post-Anton carries all of them, the cocky and the frightened, the heedless and those who already know that nothing is easy.

Others travel quietly and with self-restraint. The hardest to part with is Doctor Gyllen. Both Mona and Petter still have trouble expressing their friendship for her, stiff and guarded as she still is, but on a deeper level, they feel a love and a gratitude that fill their hearts. Once they've reconciled themselves to the fact that much of this must remain unspoken, it begins to be easier to behave naturally around her. Everyone knew that she would move as soon as she'd passed her licensing exam, but when it happens, they feel deprived, as if they will now find it difficult to live their lives.

Yes, Doctor Gyllen has passed her Finnish medical exam, grilled by a professor with an aversion to her Russian accent who hunts for a weak spot that will bring her down. Little does he realize that he is a trifling amateur beside the tyrants she has had to deal with. One little Russophobe? Ha! A pinprick. Somewhat foreign in her oral presentation, but an admirable

grasp of the clinical questions, impossible to shake her professional expertise in that area, and superb when it comes to
her speciality, gynaecology and obstetrics. Harrumph, but
unquestionably approved with honours.

Helsingfors no longer frightening, unnatural, but unsus-
pecting, safe. Nice to stay with Mama and Papa, comfortable.
Opera in the evening after the exam, shopping the next
day — hard to imagine what to wear. Mama buys appropriate
presents for the Hindrikses and suggests that she herself buy
a suit, walking shoes, winter boots, rubber boots, blouses, a
new skirt, undergarments. A jacket, a winter coat, maybe ski
pants and a windbreaker for night calls in winter. Oh, she
could buy a house for all the money spent, some of it Papa's.
She also sees to the Örlands' medicinal needs, and her own,
and discusses some purchases for the Health Care Centre with
the National Board of Health. They apologize for all the forms
and papers and, her guard down for one moment, she laughs.
"For a person coming from Russia . . ."

And then a thing that she will touch on briefly when the
priest asks about it: a visit to Papa's diplomatic friends, to the
foreign office, to the President's chancellery, to the Red Cross
and the Salvation Army, to contacts within emigrant circles,
to the Mannerheim League for Child Welfare. Even a letter
of appeal to the Soviet Union's newly expanded legation in
Helsingfors. Nothing.

Back to the Örlands, warm congratulations, great sadness. Of
course the Örlands haven't a chance of keeping their own doctor. Doctor Gyllen's four years become a happy interlude when,
thanks to strict Finnish regulations, they had a doctor and a
midwife of their own, four years when all the babies born can
be identified by their deep, well-hidden Russian navels. Now
Doctor Gyllen is looking for a job somewhere else. She has a

hard time with Finnish and wants to stay on Åland, and there's a position open in a clinic in the northern archipelago, which of course she gets. The Health Care Centre on the Örlands isn't finished yet, and she won't have a chance to enjoy any of its benefits. That's just the way it is, she says, you leave places you've loved and learn to appreciate other places. Soon, the Örlands will get a registered nurse instead, and then it will be good to have a brand-new building to go with the job.

Sadness and activity. Money is collected from every farm for a handsome cash gift to be presented at the farewell coffee. Lydia Manström letters the inscription. "To Doctor Irina Gyllen, with gratitude from the people of the Örland Islands. Years of labour for the doctor, years of good fortune for the Örlands." Since Doctor Gyllen was located physically in the west villages, the balance is restored somewhat by organizing the coffee at the school in the east villages, where Lydia heads the entertainment committee. The eastern side will also have the Health Care Centre, in whose creation the doctor was so involved, and so it is right and proper that the party take place nearby. A damned shame, say a hundred voices, that she never got to see it in use.

In memory of the doctor's arrival one early spring, they sing "Winter's Rage is Over".

Most of all, they love the line about "the purple waves of summer", at which point the whole room joins in, and Petter wonders if he might not be able to express his feelings more adequately by singing his thanks. Fortunately, council chairman Sörling speaks first, and Lydia presents the cash gift. Doctor Gyllen, impassive in her new brown suit, thanks everyone by bowing slightly to right, left, and centre, thinking that the poorer people are, the more generously they give. No Bohemian crystal vase with a silver foot for them, thank heaven. And then the vicar, with a warm smile, and his red-cheeked wife by his side.

"My heart is full to overflowing as I attempt to convey the gratitude, loss, and emptiness we all feel," he begins. "There is probably no home on the Örlands where people have not waited eagerly for the doctor and felt their pain and worry lessen when they heard her footsteps in the hall. It seems to me that my wife and I owe her a greater debt of gratitude than anyone else, but I know several others who feel precisely the same way about themselves and their families. We can't rank gratitude, no more than we can rank love or sorrow. We can only unite in extending our deeply felt thanks for the years that have passed and for the help we've received. We offer our congratulations on your Finnish medical examination and on your new medical post and ask for God's blessing on your future career."

The doctor bows and thanks him, and then Bergström is on his feet to thank Doctor Gyllen on behalf of the provincial council for her tireless work for public health, for her unsparing toil and dedication. We shall never forget our doctor, he promises, and many Örlanders have tears on their cheeks.

Then Doctor Gyllen herself must speak before they can all have coffee. She has calculated her dosage carefully. One and a half tablets in the evening gave her a good night, half a tablet that morning keeps her stable. A little distance to what's going on, a measured emotional delay.

"Esteemed Örlanders," she begins. She has rehearsed. "It is with regret that I shall now leave the Örlands. You are good people, and I have had a good life among you. But human life consists of movement and change. I leave the Örlands to return to my true mission in life, which is that of physician. Perhaps we shall see one another, for one day I hope to open my own practice in Mariehamn, and then I can serve you there. How happy I will be when some good friend from the Örlands comes through the door. So dear people, I say only 'Till we meet again.'"

The good Hindrikses weep openly, the mother and the daughters, but the sprightly Marthas start singing "I Love My Native Soil" and then go off to get the coffee. Big-bellied copper pots and modern ones of enamel, all of them full and steaming, the first cup to Doctor Gyllen. The platters they bring in are overflowing with sandwiches, rolls, and cakes. Doctor Gyllen recognizes Mona's sweet rolls and the Hindrikses' bread, which she saw them baking the day before. Who baked the cakes is less certain, but the butter has to come from farms with milking cows, and the farmer cheese could be from the parsonage. Adele has probably bought the sausage, maybe the ham as well. A big party, drowned in the rising buzz of conversation. She sits between Sörling and the vicar, both of them remarkably tongue-tied.

"That was tremendous," Doctor Gyllen begins, to the surprise of both Sörling and the vicar.

"Yes," the vicar says. "But only the tip of the iceberg. All the things we can't manage to express are thirty times greater."

"Fifty times," Sörling overbids chivalrously. "But you were here while the war was raging, Doctor, and you shared everything with us, and you know we didn't have a lot."

Doctor Gyllen smiles. "The war didn't rage much here. I came to peace when I came to the Örlands. The Finnish army to protect me, and no bombardment. At first I could not believe that people could live this way. Always fish, potatoes, bread. Often butter. Good for people's health."

"Yes!" says the vicar enthusiastically. "People think this is a poor place, but the diet is ideal. All thanks to Baltic herring and the other fish. There was much more hunger in the cities."

They continue to talk of such things, which is good, because if they tried to say what they're really feeling, they would deeply embarrass the guest of honour. In Doctor Gyllen's company, you really understand the importance of keeping things superficial. Goodwill is expressed in a different form: several pairs of eyes keep watch on the doctor's cup and plate, and as soon as her supply begins to ebb someone immediately rushes up with the pot and the platter. When all the plates start to look empty, the vicar and his wife stand up. They have been asked to contribute to the entertainment with some songs. They sing folk songs they grew up with along with some humorous duets, and then they tell the crowd that in June they're going to make a little tour of their home province with these songs, plus several songs from Åland. They're going to show off their children, and Petter will be marrying relatives on a virtual assembly line, but the singing will be to raise money for the Health Care Centre. Everyone applauds, and Doctor Gyllen catches their eye and thanks them with a little smile and a little bow.

The half-pill has worn off, and for the first time, she's forgotten to bring the box. And the worst is still to come, the part she fears, when they gather and sing "Shall We Gather at the River" as a farewell. Although they know she's not a churchgoer and probably doesn't believe in God, nothing can stop them. Then the party breaks up. She hardens herself as they come forward one by one and thank her and say goodbye. Younger women whose babies she's delivered curtsey, somewhat older ones assure her that they will have no more children now that she's leaving. Patients of all kinds display healed wounds, show broken arms without a sign that anything was ever wrong, assure her that their headaches have lessened and the ringing in their ears subsided.

Thank you, thank you," she says to all of them. "Goodbye, goodbye." Many cry. They want to see her cry as well, but that's not possible. She has trained herself never to show any emotion that might betray her. Finally she walks to the school dock with the Hindrikses. She won't have to say goodbye to them until tomorrow, and now they surround her as usual, chatting amiably, for the last time. With dismay, a result of the medicine's having worn off, she wonders what it will be like to live by herself in the clinic in the northern archipelago, without the Hindrikses. Do they understand how much she has loved them, indirectly, in the gaps between pills? Erika Hindriks hasn't changed since she arrived, but the girls have grown and become young women. She says to them, "Take care of yourselves when you head out into the big wide world."

Do they realize how painful it would have been for her to involve herself closely in their lives as they were growing up? In them, she has seen the time pass. In the face of their hopefulness, she has watched her own fade. Thank goodness they're girls. It would have been worse with boys, who would have grown into great louts while she was there, hardly recognizable from the eight-year-olds they once were.

A great many random thoughts go through her head during the boat trip home. Her only defence is silence, never say too much, never reveal yourself. Very impolite, ungrateful, after such a party, but the Hindrikses forgive this too. They'd probably be frightened if she were suddenly to change. If she were to disturb the picture of her they'll come to preserve. Accept her, ask nothing more of her than what she lets them see.

* * *

"How will we manage?" is a question people ask in every house. Five years is long enough to forget what it was like to do without. On the other hand, people have a wealth of terrible stories about people who died of peritonitis, intestinal obstructions, blood clots, gangrene, blood poisoning, because they didn't get to the hospital in time. "You people from the Örlands always arrive when it's too late," is a remark that can be cited in every house. During Doctor Gyllen's time things have been different. Whatever she couldn't deal with herself she sent in before it had progressed too far, using the Coast Guard as emergency transport. Now they're being abandoned. How are they supposed to know, how can they make such judgments? They can't expect much from a newly graduated nurse, and it will take a long time for her to learn.

"How did we manage before?" is the obvious question. The answer is equally obvious: "Worse." This is said in every house, but perhaps least of all at the organist's, where Francine has had a hard time with Doctor Gyllen's matter-of-fact tone and firm methods. She is aware that the doctor's praise for brave, capable women having babies does not apply to herself. Francine doesn't want any part of it, doesn't want to be present, resists. "No," she says. "It's not happening. I can't do it." The doctor mentions her four strong, healthy, beautiful children. "They were also born somehow," she says impatiently. "We try again. We push again." As if she were the one having the baby. And the boy, of course, damaged, retarded. Hole in his heart. Now dead. For the best, but never again. Didn't dare ask Doctor Gyllen about birth control, just wanted to disappear, never see her again.

Lydia Manström is now more alone than ever. Not that she and the doctor were close, rather that she took comfort from that fact that they could be. If the opportunity arose, if the circumstances were right. She has something she'd like to discuss. Is it the doctor's impression, too, that boys and young men force themselves on many of the girls in the period when young people are experimenting and forming relationships?

That it's almost a given that the man, the boy, violates the girl he's decided will be his? Or that a girl, in the worst of cases, can circulate among several of them? And suffer a merciless contempt, not to put too fine a point on it.

The problem is hard to define. Obviously there are different degrees of willingness and different degrees of resistance. Certainly there are girls who expect it, prepare for it, provoke, entice. That's the best case. But those who don't want to. Those who haven't decided. That can be hard. On the other hand, maybe it's these very girls who need some kind of physical persuasion. So the question is, doctor, do you see this as a problem? Or is it just life? She herself has brought heifers to a bull and seen how frightened they are, and how eager.

In short, what's the definition of rape? Lydia has pondered this question for years. And now she'll never be able to bring it up. Maybe just as glad she never did. She would only have got tangled, implied something that she would have been ashamed of later. Maybe it's not a problem for other people, not even for the ones who are its victims when they're young. Maybe in fact that's the way it is for most of them, and everyone accepts it as the way it has to be. A part of becoming a woman, an introduction to womanhood?

What could the doctor have said about that? The doctor, who is so reserved and strict? For four years, she has imagined that they might talk, quietly and without a lot of fuss, these two who can both keep secrets, and no one who saw them would suspect. There is of course a chance that the doctor would have looked at her with complete incomprehension — a woman with a professional education, a salaried position, the mistress of a farm, chairman of the Martha Society, active in the parish and in public health. And the problem? Well, excuse me, it was really nothing.

Ill at ease, she stands up, takes a swing through the kitchen and into the parlour. There are school papers waiting to be corrected, but nevertheless she takes out stationery, unscrews the ink bottle, dips her pen, and writes.

"Tomorrow we'll start saying 'In the doctor's days,' for tomorrow she leaves. Never again will the Örlands have a doctor of our own. It was edifying to witness the touching expressions of gratitude that these fisherfolk extended to her today. There was not a dry eye in the assembly when the chairman of the local council and the local priest expressed everyone's thanks for her admirable contributions to public health. Now we feel nothing but emptiness when we think of our future without our doctor."

※ ※ ※

In the performance of her important duties, Adele Bergman has the support of an iron constitution. Elis, on the other hand, often feels there is something wrong with his heart. So Doctor Gyllen has listened, tapped him on the back, taken his pulse, looked into his eyes, and remarked how nice it is to see a healthy man for once. Now they're wondering what will happen. As long as Doctor Gyllen was on the Örlands, she held sickness and death in check. Those who died while she was there were the victims either of old age or accidents. A few sad cases of cancer, but otherwise "state of health — good", as she herself said over the telephone to the provincial health director and which the operator passed along for the edification of all the islanders.

Adele was one of the doctor's most faithful supporters, and she feels her absence deeply. Nevertheless, she is not entirely unhappy that the Örlands' most prominent free-thinker has now moved away. It has been a thorn in her side that the doctor, however unintentionally, has given easily influenced young people reason to believe that it is modern and even admirable to turn their backs on church and religion. The priest doesn't seem to take it that seriously, and when she brings up the doctor's liberal views, he looks embarrassed and mumbles something about how hard it is to see into the human heart. Even though Doctor Gyllen doesn't know God, God knows Doctor Gyllen and uses her skills for the benefit of many.

An evasion that doesn't entirely please Adele Bergman. Hard-boiled in business, burning with Christian zeal, she aspires to complete surrender, a deeper insight into the need for salvation. It is not enough to seek it for your own sake, all Christians should also take responsibility for their brothers and sisters and open their eyes to the Divine light.

Thanks to the new priest, spiritual life on the Örlands is on the upswing. Many now go to church quite often, prayer meetings in the villages are well attended. That's good. But Adele sees many habitual Christians among the participants, and for them religion is form without content. Where is the heartfelt, personal faith that permeates and transforms the entire life of the true believer?

The priest, from whom she hopes so much, won't look her in the eye. "I'm wary of the term 'habitual Christian'," he says a bit apologetically. "When people come to church, we mustn't push them away by calling them that. Isn't habit itself a source of firmness and fortitude in the life of faith? Maybe habit is precisely the thing that sustains people's personal faith. Where we hold our devotions, the door is open. God is present. We must believe that."

"But what about personal commitment?" Adele insists. "People are so dreadfully lukewarm. It's enough for them to go to church once in a while as if they were buying an indulgence.

Then it's back to normal. Egoism, personal advantage, cold calculation. How are we supposed to open their hearts?"

If Adele didn't know what a good Christian he was, she could swear he was embarrassed. "I ask myself that same question when I write my sermons. What do we know about the hearts of our neighbours? Open to scripture but at the same time open to temptation and pressure and even to direct exploitation. We see that in many sects."

"Your fear of sectarianism is really very High Church! I'm talking about the need for revival, the spiritual winds that should not blow only at Pentecost!"

"You are so right. But I'm uncertain. Revival divides a community. Most of all, I just don't think I'm up to leading a revival. How do you do it?" He smiles disarmingly, but of course he could if he wanted to! His reluctance is a barrier, as is the way he takes refuge in all his administrative duties and the work on his farm. He is getting to be more and more like other Evangelical Lutheran priests, who divide their duties into segments — preaching, parish work, administrative duties, farming. Forgetting that their entire lives must be a lesson from scripture. The smallest activity must be a sermon about God's goodness to those who give themselves without reservation! That's what priests should be, like medieval monks whose only duty was to love God and their fellow men.

Petter's ideal is absolute truthfulness, yet there is something about Adele that makes him less communicative, makes him weigh his words. It seems to him suddenly that there's no point in saying certain important things. For example, that when he looks into the beloved faces of the Örlanders, what he most wishes for them is not revival's constant self-examination. He's more inclined to wish them the freedom of a Christian soul. The freedom to be unharassed, untormented, untroubled.

Happy, if that is possible more than momentarily. Life is full of worry and want and sickness and sorrow; he would so very much like to spare them eternal damnation.

If God is love, he loves the Örlanders, with their foxy ways, their wolfish grins and their cloven hooves, their sheep's clothing and their borrowed feathers, their rabbit paws and tiger hearts. Rapid shifts and dodges, all of God's spirited creation embodied in them in sparks and flashes. Snouts and paws, fur and scales, whistles and calls. An auk, an eider duck, a wagtail, a snipe. A wing brushing the brow, the round head of a seal breaking the surface. A smile spreading over all of it, quickly gone, rapidly returning. Beyond categorizing and moralizing, the priest sometimes thinks.

The priest struggles with a strong sense of sin and is diligent about self-examination. Is this actually something he wishes on others? He doesn't want a return to church discipline and refuses to be a religious policeman, with God on his tongue as he condemns. No killjoy, which he has been for himself often enough. But rather a guide towards true joy in Christ, not deflated by anxiety and fear of discovery, derision, and punishment. A road you travel in daylight, with a burden no greater than you can bear.

The Örlanders are as social as herring and combine in different, shifting communities, most eagerly in their families and villages. Instigating a religious revival that bursts those bonds is not for Petter. "No," he has to say to Adele, spelling it out. "I'm not the man to lead a revival. As best I can, I will preach the Word, which redeems and liberates. Guide, not compel. Example rather than decree."

"If only it were that easy!" says Adele. "People are simply too stiff-necked. Contrary and hardened. They wear smooth, happy faces, but oh my."

"Yes," Petter says. Simply. For of course she's right. Deadly sins cut a wide swath through the villages, virtues are shadowy figures of derision. But they are rampant among people who also have a capacity for sympathy and compassion, trust and goodwill. They can't live without other people, and therefore they are attentive to society's rules, which mustn't be violated. A light side and a dark side, open as a book, full of secrets. Smiling, turning away. Benevolent, malicious. Never only the one or the other.

When you get right down to it, he thinks, the Örlanders have opened the path to Christian fellowship for him much more effectively than he could have done it for himself. The Örlanders have freed him from constant introspection, which is a form of egocentricity — as if everyone kept a constant eye on him. Maybe that's what people do on the Örlands, but in that case it's a happy and indulgent eye, more forgiving than the devastating gaze he used to fix on himself. He speaks better when he's not looking at himself so grimly, and he thrives on the fellowship that the congregation so generously offers him.

On the Örlands, it seems natural to avoid a petty focus on people's shortcomings, seductively easy at times to be indulgent towards wickedness that can't be ignored. The free-spoken Örlanders open the box a bit and out slips something about tyrannical husbands, swindlers, and adulterers, and, secondhand and only as a rumour, and in whispers, a hint about rape and bestiality. He can talk seriously with a sinner who seeks him out, he can try to help a victim, but the public condemnation that Adele expects of him is beyond his capacity. "Let him who is without sin cast the first stone" is a fine exhortation even today, but it is hardly an adequate answer when considering the plight of those who've been subjected to an outrage. So what kind of priest is he to be? An attentive friend, always ready to talk and listen. But is he to render himself half blind and deaf in the process? Maybe so. And the alternative? The path to salvation is not as straightforward as Adele wants him to paint it.

Chapter Twenty-Three

THEIR THIRD WINTER. Petter has lived through every kind of weather out here on the Örlands and moves easily on land and water across his parish. The darkness is not completely dark. Because the islands are not covered with forest, the land lies open to the sky. Starlight and moonlight can reach it, or the gliding streak of light between sky and sea. "Out here we're always in touch with heaven!" he says to people who ask if he's not afraid of getting lost in the dark. He feels strongly that just because the church lies at one edge of the parish, its priest must not use that fact as an excuse for withdrawing during the winter months. As pastor, he must live with his congregation, and when do they show a greater openness to the church's message than during the dreary winter months, when the wind whines among the scattered houses, and the meagre flames of the oil lamps flicker?

Mona is happy that this is the last winter he'll have to go out on the ice or in a boat in full storm. The work on the bridge has progressed, if not far enough then at least satisfactorily. All the work is being done by volunteers, so they can't insist on regular hours, just be grateful when some fellow appears with a horse and sledge. Petter has put in countless days of labour, hauling, pulling, carrying, hammering and nailing, and, most of all, keeping everyone in in good spirits. When he gets home, he's frozen stiff and exhausted, for his cheer-spreading and bridge-building require a kind of mental energy that takes its toll.

It's cold, wet work, exposed to the weather, and no one likes it. That it gets done at all is proof, according to Adele, of the priest's unusual ability to lead and inspire. If anyone complains, she snorts loudly and points out that the bridge is not being built for the benefit of the pastor's family but in order to make it easier for the whole congregation to get to church! But it will soon be done, and with the bridge in place, next winter will be a piece of cake, and in the spring he's going to do something about that motorboat as well.

He is happy and full of faith in the future, and Mona, who never stops working, has stopped worrying and listening for him as much as she used to do in previous winters when he came home late. You can't blame a wife for having confidence in her husband and for accepting the fact that he lets people stand and talk to him for far too long so he's never on time. She simply has to believe that he'll finally get home. Sometimes so late that she has to fight to stay awake. She doesn't want to miss having tea with him and talking over the events of the evening before they collapse into bed.

It has been a winter without dependable ice. The post comes rarely, and then only on the *Aranda*, a ship that can break thin ice. Post-Anton has overexerted himself and torn open an old hernia. He's had an operation in Godby, where he's in hospital for a second week. Without the *Aranda*, there would have been no post at all. Now in early February there's been a real cold snap, and there is hope that the ice will finally freeze hard. And then just as the weather changes, there are suddenly northern lights.

They're the first northern lights Petter has ever seen. The family is long since in bed. He blows out the lamp in his office, hardly able to keep his eyes open. But he notices that there is something odd about the light outside, which flames up such that he thinks for a moment something is on fire. But it's too green, and when he looks out, he sees that the whole sky is billowing. Enormous swatches of greenish light are whirling around in the sky. The northern lights — the actual aurora borealis here on the Örlands! He rushes into the bedroom. Mona is asleep, the girls are asleep. The room is dark, but the northern lights are streaming on the window shades. "Mona!" he says. "Wake up! You have to see this."

She wakes up with a start and sits bolt upright in bed. "What is it?"

"The northern lights. It's unbelievable. Get dressed and we'll go out on the steps and look."

"Can't we see just as well through the window?"

"Yes. But it's completely different when you're outdoors."

"The window will be fine for me. Don't stay out too long and get cold."

They rarely share each other's experiences, and now that they can, she doesn't want to. He wakes Sanna instead, lifts her up in her quilt although Mona hisses indignantly, "For goodness' sake, let the girls sleep! What do the northern lights mean to them? Nothing."

But Sanna has awakened in his arms. "Papa!" she says, and knows immediately where she is. "Do you want to come outside and look at the northern lights with me?" he asks. "It's a fantastic phenomenon in the sky that most people never get to see. Come, sweetheart." He wraps her quilt around her and carries her like a child, his big girl. "We'll let Lillus sleep," he says. "She's too little to understand what she's seeing."

Despite Mama's protests in the background, they go out, closing the door behind them so as not to let out the heat, and stand silently on the steps. The whole world is aflame in green and white. "It's a kind of optical phenomenon that has to do with temperature, moisture in the air, reflected light, stuff like that," he says. "I can't explain it exactly, I have to find out, but the important thing is that we're seeing it and will always remember how it looked. It's one of the wonders of nature."

"Yes," Sanna says. If she wasn't sitting on Papa's arm, she'd be afraid. The light tumbling above them doesn't reach the ground, which is pitch-black. It doesn't light up anything on earth, it's only the sky that flames and seethes, a huge, cold, burning radiance. But more important than the view is Papa. The warmth in his enthusiastic body, which vibrates when he talks, the feeling of being huddled up so close. The cold air on her back, his warm chest in front, her cheek against his. That they're out on their own, without Mama and Lillus. Just her, his confidante and assistant in his study of the northern lights.

He himself feels Sanna's involvement intensely, the firm body under the quilt, the wakeful intelligence in this attentive and concentrated little figure. He feels the grace and joy of this living child especially strongly today, against the background of the sorrow afflicting the Örlands at the moment. The little eight-year-old who was sent to Åbo with a burst appendix several days ago has died of peritonitis. Now once again everyone notes how defenceless life has become since Doctor Gyllen's departure. He will conduct her burial service once they've brought her home and then speak to her memory at a prayer meeting he intends to hold in the west villages. His thoughts are already occupied with what he will say, and Sanna, alive in his arms, makes him think of how he would not be able to bear her loss, while the parents of the little eight-year-old have no choice but to bear their own.

* * *

There are a great many people in church the following Sunday. The ice has begun to look more dependable, and people have come on foot, carefully, leaving space between them, without mishaps. A relief after this unusually troublesome winter. Many people, almost everyone from the east villages, attend the burial, the parent's grief heart-rending to see, the priest powerfully involved because of Sanna.

The evening is dark, cloudy, perhaps it will snow. So far there has been almost no snow on the Örlands, and in order to make it easier to travel on the village roads, he takes his bicycle and rides it across the ice to the west villages. With the help of the headlight he can follow the path the congregation took, and if he maintains an adequate speed he'll go straight and true and run no risk of skidding and falling on the slippery ice. On the carrier he has his briefcase with the incessant tracts sent out by the Seamen's and Heathen's Mission and the Evangelical Society, which he feels bound to distribute. Quickly and safely he makes it across. It's not far to the farm, and he arrives just half an hour after leaving the parsonage. He's early, so he has a chance to chat before they begin. Mostly they talk about the ice, how much easier everything is now that it's finally freezing hard. The men sit contentedly talking while the women change clothes after the evening milking before joining them.

The temperature rises once the women arrive. They talk about the dead girl and they talk about her mother, how she's doing, and the pastor says he's been thinking a lot about his own little girls, how it would feel to lose them. There is no one at the meeting who has not suffered some loss. At such times, the comforts offered by the church can feel meagre and God's word seem pale.

"But then," he says, rising to his feet, and they all understand that the meeting has begun. "But then we fail to consider that the words and the promises work in the longer term. They don't fall unheard to the earth and die, but lie there and sprout in secret, like seeds, and bide their time. Sorrow grows slowly into hope and trust. The words that appear to fall to the ground are not wasted, no more than a life cut short before its time is wasted. Our little Anni rests securely near the heart of Jesus. Down here, she still lives in memory as the songbird of our Sunday school and as the beloved child she was in her home. We grieve with her parents and sister, and we miss her everywhere we're accustomed to seeing her, holding her mother's hand, safely beside her father on a pew in church. Her death can seem cruel to us, and God, who permitted it, can seem a heartless God.

"I wish you could see her walk across the bridge of light that leads from our world to the heavenly world. Free from earthly bonds, as we sing in the hymn, with buoyant steps on her way to her heavenly father. We can entrust her to his embrace, free from fear and pain. As a reminder that there is 'a joy beyond the grave and a future full of song', as we sing in another hymn, I suggest that we sing hymn 222, 'In Heaven, in Heaven'."

That they are all in tears is not a source of pride to him. As they sing, their voices break in the middle of a line and words are swallowed. He himself holds the melody steady, and he knows the words by heart. His voice carries. Their fellowship is strong and warm by the time the meeting is over and coffee, bread and butter appear on the table, the real bread and wine of the outer skerries. Their faces are ruddy, but their tears dry up, and people begin to chat. This is the way people make their way in the world, with talk, with a thousand ways of expressing interest, pleasure, horror, sadness. They are all in very good humour when it comes time to sing "Shall We Gather at the River".

Most of them leave on foot. Petter is left standing alone with his bicycle beside the house. He has a hard time handing out books and tracts that he doesn't think his sturdy, lively parishioners will have much use for, and his briefcase is as heavy as it was when he arrived. He ties it firmly to the carrier and walks his bicycle out through the gate.

"Be sure to watch out for that spot near Kläppar where the current's made a hole in the ice," his host calls after him.

"Not to worry," says the pastor confidently. "I'll just follow the path you all took this morning."

The clouds have thickened since he arrived, and it takes a while for his eyes to get used to the dark. He pedals hard to get the dynamo going, but can't see much beyond the little cone of flickering light produced by his headlamp. The surroundings are gone, the path barely distinguishable from the well-grazed slope around it. Then he comes out onto the gravel road where the wheel tracks glisten with ice. In the middle, his tyres grip well. Soon he's down by the dock and wheels his bike out onto the ice. Concentrating on his balance and pedalling hard, he keeps himself upright.

It is very dark. He can see neither the moon nor the stars, but the shiny ice gleams in the bicycle headlamp, and when he comes around the point he can see the light in the parsonage window. On evenings when he's away, Mona puts a lamp in the window towards the bay so it will shine like a guiding star and welcome him home. Now that the ice is in, all he has to do is head for the light and ride until he's into Church Bay.

He's moving well, singing "Shall We Gather at the River" as he pedals. He isn't thinking much about where the congregation walked, because suddenly, when he's already into the bay, the ice breaks under him, a crashing of glass and a hole that swallows him and his bicycle. They go straight to the bottom, and he kicks his way upward and breaks the surface and swims.

At first he feels only intense embarrassment. Goes hot with shame in the ice-cold water. He's muddled, half his head is throbbing where he hit it on the edge of the ice or on the handlebars. He wants to laugh at himself — it's actually the first time he's gone through the ice. It's in the summer when the water is pleasantly warm that he likes to capsize his sailboat, and even then only occasionally. He can hear Mona lecturing him, relieved that it wasn't worse, telling him he should have walked his bicycle and felt his way forward instead of zipping along as if he were on a road. The last thing the verger said as he left was that the ice wasn't safe. Yes, yes, but this isn't so bad.

His body is warm and he's a strong swimmer and he knows what to do. As he treads water he twists his way out of his coat and gets his boots off, first one and then the other, and heaves them up on the ice. The effort required is unexpectedly great. Until you're in the water, you don't realize how low you are, and suddenly he's tired, as if his strength had run out all at once. With a jolt in his aching head he remembers his briefcase tied to the carrier, full of tracts, a Bible, a hymnal, and a copy of The Songs of Zion. If he can get them out of the water quickly, perhaps they won't be completely soaked and can be saved. It's a question of money, quite a bit, which he will feel obliged to replace. He makes the quick dive that he likes so much — swivels like a seal and kicks his way downward. Searches a little along the bottom; yes, there's the bike. On its side, handlebars sticking up, and then the carrier, his briefcase firmly in place.

He has to come up for air, dives again and comes straight down to the bicycle, starts working on the twine, remembers how he tied it. It seems to him that his hands are warm and supple, but they are oddly stiff. It feels hopelessly difficult, but you mustn't lose courage over a little setback, and he swims up again to get a breath and then back down. He picks at the knot without result, pulls and the whole bike moves, lets go and swims up for air. He's winded and exhausted, though he figures he's been in the water fifteen minutes at the most. Dives again. Doesn't try to pick at the knot again but puts his foot on the saddle and drags and pulls on the briefcase. This doesn't seem to work either, but then something gives, the briefcase jerks free and comes up with him. He's been down too long and taken a mouthful of water, and he flaps his arms wildly when he gets to the surface and snorts and almost vomits. The briefcase weighs him down like an anchor, but with a great effort he gets it up on his shoulder and heaves it onto the edge of the ice. The movement strains his shoulder, and his arm feels unusable, harder now to pull himself up.

Funny that you can get so tired. He's really looking forward to getting up on land, can see himself running up the hill so he doesn't freeze solid. Then through the door. Whew! Mona's horror, the warm tile stove. How nice it is to peel off the heavy wet clothes and get help towelling himself dry. Warm pyjamas, wool socks and wool sweater, fire in the kitchen range, the heat streaming straight out, boiling water in a pot. Hot tea. "Let me catch my breath first and I'll tell you all about it."

Now all he needs to do is find an edge of the ice that will bear his weight. Then he just has to heave himself up, pull himself forward, roll until he dares stand up and walk. But he finds that it is more difficult in practice than in theory. It ought to be a simple matter, he thinks, to break the ice until he comes to an edge that bears, but it goes slowly and his movements are strangely languid and his limbs are heavy. Again and again he has to rest with his arms on the ice. And when he's come far enough that he dares to lift himself up, he can't, and because of his sore shoulder, he lacks the strength to pull himself forward.

The important thing now is not to panic. Rest for a while, then try again. Don't rest too long, however, for then he risks freezing to death. Try again. No. Recalls that the Örlanders always say that the first thing to remember when you're going out on the ice is to have something sharp, an ice pike, a knife in your belt. Why doesn't he have anything sharp with him? He admires the Örlanders for all they know and can do, but he's learned nothing from them. If he dives back down and breaks a mudguard from his bicycle, he's got a chance. But he knows he no longer has the strength for such an extended effort under water.

Only then does it occur to him to call for help. It's embarrassing, it's humiliating, he who's the eldest and an example for others. He should not put himself into such situations, he's behaved like a complete idiot, and the fewer who know it the better. Nevertheless, he now hollers "Help!" and hears for himself how feeble it sounds. The parsonage is near, but of course the windows are closed and sealed. Unless Mona goes out on the steps and listens, she'll hear nothing. He needs to make a bigger noise. It's hard to get his voice to carry from down so close to the water, but it's absolutely necessary. If he yells and moves around, maybe he can stay warm a little better. If he's to get out of this ice hole, someone has to hear him.

"Help!" he shouts, louder now. For heaven's sake, his big booming bass must carry far enough for *someone* to hear it. Anyone! Mona going out to listen for him, the verger on the other side of point with something to do outdoors and stopping to listen to the wind. Someone he hasn't thought of, out on the ice on some late errand.

And above our earthly troubles, God in his heaven who sees to us in his mercy and feels our plight. Between his calls for help—which carry better if he doesn't try to form consonants but just brays, aaaaah aaaaah—he prays. To God who lets no sparrow fall to earth, to the God of compassion, the God of mercy. Send me your angels, send Mona on swift feet, feather-light across the ice, the verger out to test his sledge. Maybe the wind will carry his voice to the east villages. Maybe someone will hear. Dear God.

The pain boring into his head no longer feels quite as strong. It's as if his shouts were deadening all pain. He shouts steadily, repeatedly now, like a foghorn, with brief intervals to catch his breath. Everything is going black, he slides down and gets a mouth full of water, which wakes him up and he coughs and shouts. Have mercy upon us. Deliver us from evil. It occurs to him that he is dying.

* * *

In the parsonage, Lillus has a cold, she's snivelling and fussing and can't sleep. Mona has her hands full—warm honey water, turpentine on her chest, a scarf and a knit cap. Blow! In between, she wanders around and scolds herself for being so uneasy. Petter should have come by now, his endless evening meetings

ICE by ULLA-LENA LUNDBERG

can drive a person crazy. But it really is terribly dark. What if he's lost, what if he's ridden up on some rock and knocked himself unconscious! If he's not here in fifteen minutes, she's going to call central and ask if they've heard anything. She goes out on the steps and listens but hears nothing. Not his whining dynamo, not the creaking and squeaking of his bicycle, nothing. She goes back in and is mad at herself for being so scared. She tries to sit down but can't get anything done. The minute hand on the clock doesn't move.

In the east villages, a man has heard odd sounds across the ice, but as far as he can tell they're coming from the west villages, and if someone there has fallen through the ice, they can pull him out themselves. He's on his way back in but takes a swing around the boathouses, and there's another man standing and listening. "Could that be someone in the steam-boat channel?" Both are struck by the same awful thought: the *Aranda* passed by yesterday, and the thin ice that's frozen in its wake could be a death trap for anyone who didn't know it was there. Now there are three of them gathering ice pikes and ropes, but the voice is coming less often now and sounds hardly human. Maybe an animal, but what animal sounds like that? In the houses, people have started calling around, and the central switchboard operator sends the message onward. Is there anyone who hasn't come home this evening? Has anyone ventured out near the steamboat channel? Is there anyone out on any kind of errand who hasn't yet come home?

It takes a while for this message to get out. It's late, many have gone to bed, and there are many to call. There is discus-sion and speculation in every household. Could it be . . ? But tonight? No, I don't think so. The operator calls the villagers, relatives. The parsonage isn't on the unofficial list, but then, finally, the host of the prayer meeting remembers. "My God, the priest was here! No! He must have got home a long time ago! Do we dare call the parsonage and disturb them?"

The operator arms herself with her most official voice when she gets the pastor's wife on the line, whose voice sounds unusually timid. "This is the operator. We apologize for calling so late. But a question has come up. Is the vicar at home?"

The west villages have later habits than the east, and there are several men ready to go out with sledges and ice pikes and ropes. Quickly, in single file, the lightest first, they move towards the steamboat channel. Stop often and listen. Quiet now. Was it all in their imagination? A fox howling on one of the islands? Dark as the inside of a sack, you can hardly see where the channel goes, notice it only when their ice pikes hit slush. Then they all back up. They make sweeps across the channel with their flashlights, turn them off in between. Easy to miss a hole if no one calls. But something has made everyone uneasy. Everyone out there on the ice has known someone who fell through and drowned.

* * *

Petter is shouting less now, what explodes from his mouth every time he surfaces is mostly water. He no longer has the strength to hold onto the edge of the ice and soon he'll no longer have the strength to cough the water from his lungs. He can feel his body only occasionally and then only as burning fire. His arms won't obey, his legs don't kick any more like the good swimmer he once was, like a seal, like a dolphin. But his head is clear, despite the pain that chases through it. His ears can hear — the splashing that reveals how terribly slowly he's moving, the chunks of ice banging into each other and into the edge, the rustle around him of water being splashed up onto the ice and slowly freezing. The wind that blows like deep sighs, which then rush across the ice like a train, carrying the voice from the parsonage out over the emptiness of ice and cold.

His eyes can see—different degrees of darkness, the coal-black depths of water, the greyer black of the ice, the murmuring, expanding blackness of the sky, with neither moon nor stars. Yea, though I walk through the valley of the shadow of death, he thinks. Darkness shall be as light. Have mercy upon us. Have mercy upon us. He is pushed under the surface and comes back up, has now lost arms and hands, legs, the lower half of his body. A terrible pain in his breast, almost like a wound. His eyes fixed on what has been a bright and living sky. Life that is so hard to relinquish.

All the things he often says. About the dead who have fought their fight and now rest by the heart of Jesus. About the embrace of the Father. About the ways of the Lord which we do not comprehend but later shall understand. About our earthly vision which is like looking into a dark mirror that only imperfectly reflects the light of heaven. The heavenly light that now, in his dying moments, he sees no trace of. Just phrases. Jesus's heart is nothing to Mona's, the embrace of the Father cold and dismissive. His own embrace as a father, which should not be denied to Sanna and Lillus and the other children they've thought of having.

His shouts like bleats across the ice. The effort makes him lose his grip and sink into the water again, his mouth still open. Water in his lungs, an ineffective snorting when he comes back up, a slow hand and underarm laid on the ice like a block of wood. Have mercy upon us. Have mercy upon us. Before he died, Jesus too felt he'd been utterly abandoned. My God, my God, why hast thou forsaken me? Left me on the cross, in a hole in the ice, and forced me to be present at my own death in complete darkness and annihilating cold.

To terribly ill, dying people he often says that perhaps sickness and suffering exist so that we can reconcile ourselves to death and put ourselves confidently in the hands of Our Saviour. When we are no longer capable of anything ourselves. Then we must die. We must let go, we must let go, we must let go. But even when there is no hope, we hope. That Mona will come across the ice with a lantern. Show us thy light.

To let go of everything. Which death requires. It's no act of will, it is done to us when we die. First he lets go of Lillus. She drops like a fallen mitten, still asleep. For a little while he fights to hold onto Sanna and Mona. Mona, his deeply beloved, strong and incorruptible and capable, who is the basis of his life and happiness. Left now to her loneliness, no less than his own. Cut off, behind a wall of ice. Sanna, his northern-lights girl, for one moment more on his arm, her cheek against his. Then gone, left in a world no easier than his.

No body now, just pain, no longer shaped in his image. But a mind that is still attentive and notes that the pain suddenly slides away and that his body returns in familiar form, warm in the sunshine on the granite by the parsonage, full of pleasure in his health, youth, and vigour. With his intellect, he understands that this is what you feel when death steps in, but even if that is so, he embraces the feeling and thinks that he will live.

Chapter Twenty-Four

"No," says the pastor's wife, her voice oddly thin. "He hasn't come home yet. Has something happened?"

The operator pauses for a moment. "Cries have been heard from the ice. We're trying to determine if anyone is missing."

"No," she says. "Not he. He was at a prayer meeting at Månsas farm. It probably ran late."

The operator doesn't say the meeting ended a long time ago. Her mouth dry, she says, stiffly, "A number of men are out looking. We'll send a message for them to search towards Church Bay. I'll call the organist."

A deep breath in, a disorganized beginning.

"Please, Mrs Kummel," the operator says. "Stay inside with the children. Keep the stove hot, boil water. We'll call as soon as we know anything. Now I have more calls to make."

She rings off and calls the Coast Guard to tell them it's the priest who's missing. Now they head out, one to tell the men at the steamboat channel that they're looking in the wrong place, one to search the entrance to Church Bay where there's a strong current. The men from the nearest villages have been summoned and are on their way. Hurry, hurry.

Then she calls the organist. He's a night owl, and she can hear that he's still up. He sounds frightened even before she tells him what it's about. It's never good news when you get a call this late, when telephone central is officially closed. "No," he says. "Not the priest. God in heaven, not the priest."

"I know you're a good friend of theirs. Could you possibly? It could be you'll be needed there tonight. Brage will rouse the verger as he goes by. When we know something, I'll call Sister Hanna."

Neither of them says it's probably a false alarm.

* * *

Mona opens the door outside, remembers she's not wearing a coat, puts one on, stocking feet, back in, cow-barn boots the closest to hand. Out, listens. Runs down towards the church dock, nothing. But wait—voices! It must be him coming home, with some companions, talking and talking. She mustn't let him see how scared she's been, she must have the tea ready and scold him just a little. She turns and runs back to the parsonage. Lillus is awake, crying and fussing. "Quiet!" says Mama. "Now go to sleep!" Her angry voice wakes up Sanna, too, and both she and Lillus lie quiet as mice, scared to death, and fall back to sleep from pure terror. Mona is busy in the kitchen, then out on the steps. Definitely voices!

It's the verger and Signe who show up. "Mona," the verger says, with his reassuring authority. "They've found his briefcase and coat on the ice. A hole. We mustn't believe the worst. They're dragging for all they're worth. If they find him, it doesn't have to be too late. We'll do our damnedest. We'll fight with everything we've got."

Mona stares at him, but only for a moment. Her teeth chatter when she talks, but she seems perfectly collected. "We learned first aid in home economics. And the Coast Guard can help. Are there many men out?"

"Five or six. Seven counting Brage. They started searching at the steamboat channel. That was the trouble."

"Then we have to make sure there's hot coffee for all of them. And light the lamps. Dear Signe, can you help me set out cups while I make the coffee?"

Neither of them finds it unnatural — she needs something to do or anxiety will kill her. While the two women are busy in the kitchen, the verger goes out on the steps. Voices in the air, then lamps and lights coming up the hill, the steps of people moving quickly and heavily, as if they were carrying a body.

* * *

Once they knew it was the priest they were looking for, it was easy to find his bicycle tracks and follow them across the ice and into Church Bay, too close to the rocks. And there was a hole. Dear God. Dark objects on the ice where water had washed over them and frozen them solid. Boots. Overcoat. Gloves. Briefcase. Good God. Not what we think. Surely he's pulled himself out and lies freezing somewhere on land. But there are no tracks. Brage is equipped with a coil of rope and two drags. But it's hard to get close enough without breaking the ice. They stand spread out around the hole and calculate. The water isn't deep, maybe eight or ten feet, but before they can talk it over, Brage has ripped off his outer clothing and his boots, tied a line around his waist and wrapped the other end around Julle's arm. He goes down, his body protecting him so well against the cold that he hardly notices, feels around with his feet, finds the bicycle almost at once. The others throw in a drag, he fastens it, and they pull up the bicycle empty. A black skeleton, stone dead, it clatters onto the ice. Brage goes down and searches on. Something on the bottom, soft. A body. He kicks his way up. "Here he is. I'll bring him up."

He grabs the wool sweater and pulls. The priest comes easily, limp, just a short way, and then Brage feels a tug on his own line as the men give a hand and get them both up quickly, Brage lively as a beaver and the priest dead, a white face in the dark, wet hair, a motionless body. Brage tows him to the edge of the ice and gives orders in rapid gasps—the sledge first, the lightest man behind it, the others behind him ready to pull back. Here. Take him. Back away all of you. Brage himself gets out with almost no help, crawls a ways behind the dragged body, tests the ice, stands up and slides forward, turns the priest on his stomach and tries to get the water out of his lungs.

Someone throws a coat over him, his boots come skittering. Julle shouts, "You need to get somewhere warm, both of you. Run Brage, you'll freeze to death!"

At the same moment, the organist approaches on his kick sledge, having risked his life at full speed all the way from the southern tip of the west villages, with his ice pike and his sheath knife ready to hand. "Is it him?" he shouts.

"Watch out!" Brage yells. "I'm not going to drag up anyone else today!" They all laugh, a short, voiceless guffaw which is more frightening than a call for help.

"We need to get him up to the parsonage," Julle says. "Lucky you're here, since you know his wife. Grab hold and let's go."

They leave the sledges, ropes, and drags by the church dock and then they walk quickly with the body between them and their flashlights twinkling, while Brage half runs up the hill, swinging his arms to beat his body. Knows as well as the priest knew how to keep warm if you've fallen in the water.

The verger comes to meet them. "No. We'll put him by the stove and do everything we can."

The priest's wife in the door. "Is it him? Thank you, all of you. Carry him into the kitchen, it's warm there."

It's now midnight. The priest lies in front of the stove as if he were sleeping. Soaked through, but they've seen him that way before. Brage rolls him onto his stomach and starts working on him. Water spurts from his mouth, there is hope. "Let me take over," the organist says. "You need to dry off and get something hot into you. Then we can take it in turns."

"Of course," the priest's wife says. "I didn't see. Change clothes by the tile stove in the dining room, it's warm. I'll get some of Petter's clothes, although he's wearing his warmest things." To the others she says, "Signe will give you coffee. Please sit down. You must be frozen stiff."

Signe shoos them out of the kitchen with the coffeepot in her hand, Mona runs to the bedroom and grabs trousers, underwear, a shirt and sweater and gives them to Brage. "Thank you," she says. "Without you, this could have ended badly."

They all look at each other, then into their coffee. Does she think . . . ? Or is she just trying to persuade herself. But she knows. You know, but you hope. When she's back in the kitchen, they go to the study, close the door and make phone calls. To the hospital — drowned and dead. Is there nevertheless something they can try? Brage comes in when he's dressed and talks. The hospital confirms what he already knows to do. However pointless. Must anyway try. They also talk to the operator and confirm that it was the priest and that he is dead and leave it to her to spread the news. Brage comes in again and asks them to call the homecare aide. "Tell her I'll

PART THREE | CHAPTER TWENTY-FOUR

come and get her in the morning, early. They'll have to find someone else for the Bergfolks, where she is now." They also call their families to tell them they've found the priest dead and will soon be home, there's nothing more they can do. Then they greedily drink more coffee, which Signe has kept hot. Those who feel superfluous start pulling on their coats, look in at the kitchen where the stove and the oven are spreading warmth. The priest on the floor, limp in Brage's hands, the last time they'll see him, they all think. "Goodbye then, and thank you for the coffee," they mumble to his wife.

"Goodbye and thank you," she says, smiling appreciatively the way people do when they say thank you. The organist has taken over from Brage and is working like a smith at his bellows. "Thank you for coming," she remembers to say. "Are you tired? Should I take over for a while? How do you think it's going?"

"We've got out a lot of water," the organist says. "That's good. Now we'll turn him over. I'm going to see if we can't get his heart going, that would be best of all. Forgive me, I have to press so hard his ribs will creak."

Mona tries to concentrate on finding a pulse. Nothing at his wrist. Not on his neck. His temples are still. Then she sees the terrible black-and-blue bruise on his forehead. "Oh my. He hit his head badly. But otherwise he doesn't look so bad. Not rigid from the cold."

The organist is working intently. He doesn't need to say that below the surface, where Petter lay, the temperature is above freezing. And then you don't go stiff. And it's too soon for rigor mortis.

When Mona searched for a pulse, she also looked at his wristwatch. Half past nine. That's when he went through the ice, and cries were still heard a little more than half an hour before he was found. He wasn't on the bottom for long, there's still hope. He's young and strong. "Are you tired?" she asks again.

He thinks maybe it would be good for her to work on him herself, to feel for herself that there's no life in his body. They got his airways open a long time ago, they've been fighting to get his heart going for more than an hour, but there hasn't been the tiniest response, not even a spasm to indicate that some nerve impulses are still functioning.

She knows her first aid, no question about that. She labours by the hot stove until the sweat is on her brow, she groans the way he would groan from her treatment of him if there was the least life left in his body. But he reacts to nothing they do. After all their efforts to bring him back to life, he now looks much more dead than he did when they carried him in. Brage has braced himself with a cup of coffee and a sandwich in the dining room, telephoned the hospital, and comes back into the kitchen. "Let me," he says.

Again she sits on the floor beside him, trying to find a pulse but then just sitting, holding his hand. His hand that has been so warm. Torn by the sharp edge of the ice and his struggle with the bicycle, but not a drop of blood. Nothing still alive in that body.

Brage is now working just for the sake of appearances. Mostly he looks at her, and she sits quite still, apparently calm. Looks at the organist, sitting at the kitchen table with his back turned, his shoulders heaving. The verger and Signe crying at the end of the table. He lets the body lie quietly on the floor. "I don't think there's anything more we can do."

"No," she says. "I know." The last time they will sit this way, united. Never again. "I'm going to sit here for a while. Forgive me. You must be very tired."

The whole kitchen is crying, all of them, except her. She is the only one of them who can express a complete sentence. "There's a great deal we have to deal with in the morning, but for now I'll just sit here." On the wet, crumpled rag rug by the stove. Beside him for the last time.

Signe remembers that they usually have tea in the evenings, and she pours a cup for the pastor's wife, who actually drinks it. "Thank you," she says. "I was thirsty." Signe fills her cup again, and she drinks it again. The body tells us what it needs to replace its losses. No groaning from her about how she wants to die. She knows perfectly well that she has to live, take care of her girls, provide them with a living, a home when they've left the parsonage. Work, work, work. For the last time now, quietly by his side. Time and the clock run on and on, except the one on his wrist, which has stopped.

In bits and pieces, the organist tells what they've arranged. "Brage is going to pick up the homecare sister early in the morning. I'll call the priest in Mellom, who will certainly phone here. We'll come back in the morning and carry him down. To the shed. What we're going to do about everything — we'll work that out tomorrow. But now you have to go to bed and get some sleep before your little girls wake up. The verger and Signe and I will stay here till Hanna comes."

"No," she protests. "Not at all! I'll manage all right. You should all go home now."

They look at each other. Brage stands up. "There's nothing more I can do here. But my God if only we could make this not have happened!" He gathers up his clothes, which lie in a wet pile in the dining room. In the hall, his overcoat is still soaked, the priest's sports jacket on a hanger looks pretty thin. He goes to the study and calls the Coast Guard, which can certainly come and pick him up in their light icebreaker after everything he's done this night.

The organist follows him to the study. "I'll ask the verger and Signe to sleep in here tonight. Someone needs to be here to answer the phone if people start calling first thing in the morning and Mona has managed to get to sleep."

In the kitchen, the pastor's wife doesn't want to go to bed, and both the verger and his wife understand that she wants to sit where she is for the last few hours she has with her husband. Signe tiptoes into the bedroom and gets a pillow and a quilt. As she gives them to her, she gets such an utterly dismissive look—an unspoken "Go away!" — that she recoils and retreats to the study. When the others are out of sight, Mona lies down on the floor beside him and pulls the quilt over her. Seems to be asleep, not a sound when Signe looks into the kitchen timidly, turns down the lamp on the table, quietly withdraws. The organist leaves, Signe and the verger try to make themselves comfortable on the bed in the study, ready to jump up if the least little wheeze is heard from the phone. When Brage and the organist have gone, the house is deathly silent—a ghastly phrase!

＊ ＊ ＊

Word goes out, in the morning by telegraph. The news has gone to the *Åland Courier* and to the correspondent for *Hufvud-stadsbladet* in the capital and to the national radio. Now it's a matter of getting word to everyone who needs to be told before the news goes public.

The priest in Mellom is speechless. He says. Although priests are talking machines and have something to say on every occasion, there is nothing he can say. He says. "Unbelievable, incomprehensible. It simply can't be true. That's all I can say. He was so young and strong, so full of life. Here today, gone tomorrow. As they say. No!"

"Yes," the organist says. "I know that you were friends. As was I, a friend. We must contact the cathedral chapter. There are a lot of things to take care of, Sunday service, confirmation classes. But first the funeral. I think I speak for the widow if I say that we hope that you, his colleague and friend, will conduct the funeral service. But it would be good if you spoke to her yourself. The sooner, the better."

"The widow," says the Mellom priest. "Mona. It's inconceivable. The little girls. Of course I'll call. Thanks for letting me know. We need to stay in touch. We're going to have to work together these next few weeks."

"When you call, it would be a good idea to ask Mona if she wants you to call and give the sad news to his parents. I'm not sure, but I believe she isn't on the best of terms with her mother-in-law."

"Thanks. I won't forget. But what will I say? What *can* you say?"

He is shaken. He is more shaken than he has been for a long time. Naturally he thinks of himself, of how suddenly things happen, of how the fact that you're young and healthy and strong is no safeguard against death. But mostly, of course, he thinks of Petter, who has become his true friend during the three years they've been colleagues in the archipelago. Maybe his only friend, in the sense of being able to open up to someone, let down his guard, set aside his elegant irony. Even now he wants to call him to talk about this dreadful thing that has happened and its repercussions on his own working agenda, but now that possibility is closed. Now it is with fear and displeasure that asks to be connected to Örland Islands twelve, a number that for three years he has asked for with a smile on his lips.

It isn't Mona who answers but the homecare aide. "Mrs Kummel is in the cow barn," she reports.

"In the cow barn?" he says. He can't believe his ears.

"Yes, she absolutely insisted. There's no stopping her. The verger went with her. I'm staying inside with the girls."

"I don't understand. It's incomprehensible."

"That's what we all think. Everyone is crying except Mrs Kummel. We're worried about her. It would be good if you talked to her. Call back in half an hour."

Behind Hanna's collected voice lies an hour of horror. Fetched by the Coast Guard at seven that morning, she climbed the steps to the parsonage with dread in her heart. The pastor's wife standing in the kitchen, the body lying by the stove, horribly dead. The verger and Signe in tears, Mona white around the nose, distant, but in some way still glad that Hanna has come. Hanna, who was with them through childbirth and illness, now also through a death. Mona tries to avoid her, but Hanna can't help embracing her and saying, "There, there, dear heart." She is utterly stiff and hard and struggles a little to get loose, takes a couple of steps backward — space, please. "Thank you for coming," she says. "Now I can go to the cow barn, now that I know that you can take charge here."

"But dear girl you can't go milk the cows! I'll go, or if you want me to stay here, Signe can go." She looks at Signe, who nods eagerly, yes, of course, but Mona tosses her head in irritation. "No, I'll go myself. Why shouldn't I?"

Then they hear Sanna coming through the dining room, so big now that she can reach the door handle if she stands on her toes, and so strong she can pull it down and open it. The verger and Hanna form a wall in front of the stove. Sanna amazed.

"Good morning, darling," says Mama. "Did you sleep well? Come, let's go back to the bedroom. There's something I have to tell you." And so they walk away, just the two of them. No one else is invited. The bedroom door closes.

It doesn't take long. No shriek is heard, or sobbing. What does she say? "Now, the bad news is that Papa is dead. He drowned last night. Fell through the ice. It's going to take us a while to grasp the fact that he's gone. Don't be afraid. I'm here, and Lillus, and Aunt Hanna." Maybe no more than that. And Sanna, curious and full of questions from dawn to dusk, does not make a sound. Asks no questions, for what do you ask? Just one question, "When is Papa coming home?" And the answer, that he's not coming home, that he's in heaven now, what can she say to that? It happens quietly and calmly, and then Mona is back in the kitchen.

"Hanna, maybe you could help Sanna get dressed and get Lillus up, while I see to the cows. And then we need to get some men who can carry . . ." Away the body, she means. They can't have him lying there dead, scaring people. The kitchen is the natural gathering place in the morning, and how could they keep Sanna out for any length of time? She gets a sheet and spreads it over him, and the verger notices that the Coast Guardsmen are still there, standing in the lea of the cow barn, smoking. Brage too has thought about the body and wonders if they need help, so he's in no hurry to leave. The verger asks them to fetch the sackcloth stretcher, which is rolled up in the sacristy in case someone should faint in the heat of the crowded church, and wait outside. There will have to be a shroud, but then it would be a big help if they could do the heavy lifting and carrying.

Sister Hanna is in a quandary, not knowing if she dares to ask, but asks anyway. "What shall we do about a shroud? Will that sheet be enough?"

Mona is banging around with the milk buckets in the hall and answers with little or no show of interest. "Make a shroud if it's supposed to be done some special way. Then get him out to the shed without letting the girls see." She goes into the bedroom and sees that Lillus is still asleep. Sanna has climbed into the crib beside her and sits there with an ugly, introverted expression on her face, staring straight ahead. Just looking at her makes her angry. "Wait till I come back," she says. "Then we'll have tea."

She takes the milk cans and goes, and the verger follows her although she says forcefully that she needs no help. When they're gone, Hanna and Signe work together to shroud the body, awkward and difficult down on the floor. The wartime sheet, with Mona's monogram, is barely long enough and they have to start over from the beginning with less of the sheet around his head and shoulders so it will reach all the way to his feet. When they're finished, Signe calls the Coast Guardsmen to come in. They carry in the stretcher and lift the shrouded body onto it. With a thought to the girls, in case they should look out the window, Brage grabs the blanket still there in the kitchen and throws it across the body so it will look like any ordinary load. They each take one end, Hanna opens the door, they go out and walk in step, at a respectful pace, down to the boat shed. They put down the stretcher while they arrange sawhorses and planks, then lift the body in its shroud and lay it out. Brage hesitates but then spreads the blanket over it in case someone should come in accidentally. Then they walk down to the Coast Guard cutter in the sludge of broken ice by the dock. When Hanna sees the boat nosing its way out of the bay, she knows they've finished.

* * *

Inside the cow barn, Mona plunges into the warmth of her animals, their faith in her ability to feed and meet their needs, to gently draw the milk from their udders. Apple and Goody mumble in a friendly way, but the sheep bray and bleat as if there were some danger she would forget them. The hens flap their wings, wanting and not wanting her to collect their eggs, praise them, and leave an empty hollow in the hay. It seems to Mona that she could endure it here. She takes the milking stool and sinks down by Goody's side, an outrageous case of *lèse majesté*, because the laws of the universe require that Apple should be milked first. She shuffles and shifts and bawls. "Pardon me," Mona says and almost laughs. She moves to Apple's stall, teat salve in hand, milk pail in place. And just sits there, her head resting against the indignant cow, who must now be slaughtered in the autumn.

"As if she were crying," the verger thinks as he busily gathers forkfuls of hay and wanders back and forth between the cows and over to the manger in the sheepfold. Yes, there by the cows, she's crying, wiping her eyes and nose on the sleeve of her milking coat, starts milking again, stops, shakes and sobs. Goody, the only creature on the earth she could live with, stops eating and looks over the edge of her stall, growls like a little bear deep in her stomach — don't cry. Then Mona starts to cry big tears that roll down onto the cement floor. "Good," the verger thinks, weeping openly as he takes the water buckets and draws water from the cowbarn well and goes back in and gives it to the cows and sheep. He glances at her as he mucks out and cleans the floor. Between attacks of sobbing, she milks evenly and energetically, moves to sit beside Goody, and Goody, better than any human being, lets her cry, all four of her stomachs bulging with sympathy.

The verger does all he can to help. Sees that she's finished milking and takes the two pails from her. The big milk basin in position, the cloth in the strainer, in with the first batch of milk.

"Thanks," Mona says. She stands up, takes her stool in one hand, pats Goody. "We have to go now. So much butter and milk and cream we're going to need these coming days!" She's already thinking about all the food that will have to be prepared for the funeral, about what she'll have to order from the shop, about where she's going to put all of Petter's unavoidable relatives. Who take a laden table and good beds for given.

She dries her nose a last time, and lifts her head, ready for battle. "Yes, dear Lord. I'm guessing the phone is going to start ringing off the hook."

Together, she and the verger walk back to the parsonage, talking about everyday things. She kicks off her boots in the hall and hangs up her milking coat, hesitates about whether to go into the parlour or the kitchen but goes resolutely into the kitchen. Lillus comes toddling gaily towards her. Her cold is much better and she's had a good long sleep. "Papa," she says, and it makes Mona furious that it's Papa Lillus thinks of when she sees her Mama! She thinks Papa has been in the cow barn with Mama, which he is sometimes, and how she'll sit on his lap and have her morning tea.

"Papa's not here!" she says, incensed. "Papa's dead!"

Lillus doesn't know what it is to be dead, but she can see that it makes Mama really angry. She looks scared and backs away. The tears come as if someone had pushed a button. "For shame! Be quiet, Lillus! Where is Sanna?"

The Curve

William Street,
Slough, SL1 1XY
Renew books by phone 0303 1230035

Self Payment 11/02/2020 17:56
XXXXXXXXXX8203

Amount Tendered : £4.70

Amount Paid : £4.65

Change Given: £0.05

Amount Outstanding : £0.00

Sanna comes at once, not a word, and takes Lillus by the hand and takes her to the table. Sister Hanna lifts her into her highchair. She and the verger and Signe feel helpless and uncertain. They expect her to pick up her children and hug them, but she keeps them, too, at a distance.

"Come, Mona," says Sister Hanna. "Hot tea and sandwiches. Eat while you can. The Mellom priest will be calling soon."

"He doesn't need to!" she says. But she sits down and eats, to everyone's surprise, but quite logically, for she has to keep up her strength. If she doesn't, who will? Now and then she glances at the floor by the stove. The rug, she saw, had been hung over the railing by the steps to dry. The wet spot on the floor is a good deal smaller. A person's traces are cleaned away at breakneck speed. No one can ever imagine what it was like to live beside him.

* * *

While Mona drinks her tea and eats her sandwich, and while Sanna sits silently and Lillus fusses, the priest in Mellom paces and suffers agonies. His own parishioners call, one after another, to ask if it's true. Which it is, although it's hard to grasp. But beg pardon, he can't talk now because he's promised to call Pastor Kummel's wife on the Örlands. Although to himself he wonders why, what can he say? His wife wonders too. Maybe she ought to offer to speak to Mona Kummel, but they've only met the one time, at Kummel's installation, and what can she say? "You talk to her," she tells her husband. "You know what to say." She wonders what it would be like if it had been Fredrik who'd drowned. Conflicted feelings, obviously. Grief, worry about the children, loss, regret for the loss of their routines. But also relief. Back to Grankulla. Back to a life of her own.

Mona Kummel answers in an amazingly energetic voice. It sounds as if she was just swallowing some food. "Yes, hello?"

"Fredrik Berg here. I heard the unbelievable news. My wife and I want to extend our deepest sympathies for your loss."

"Thank you," says Mona Kummel. There is silence.

"Where do you find the strength? How are you getting along?"

"Thank you. I don't have much choice."

"Do you have anyone there with you?"

"Yes. The homecare sister. The verger and his wife, all of them terribly helpful. The organist is a great support. We're not alone. In fact I don't know how I'm going to put up with all the people who will come rushing to the house these next few days."

She sounds more irritated than prostrated with grief. Pretending to understand, he goes on. "Maybe it's well that there is much to do and think about. It forces a person to keep going. You have the girls — a big responsibility. You can always count on me, under all circumstances. You know that Petter was not only my colleague but also my best friend. And now, presumably, I will have responsibility for the Örlands until . . . Well, they'll let us know. I've already spoken to the organist. I know that Petter valued him highly. It will be easy to work with him." He rambles on.

Now and then she says "Yes." And like a wind-up mouse that scurries around on the floor, he prattles on. "It's too soon to talk about the funeral, but of course I want to be there." He draws a breath to continue, but she breaks in.

"No, it's not too soon. We need to decide as soon as possible so that I can tell everyone who calls and we won't have to get in touch a second time. Here on the Örlands, funerals usually take place quickly. And I think that's right. What would you say to next Sunday, the thirteenth?" He can see her looking at the wall calendar in the study, pen in hand, ready to mark the day. With a cross? With a neatly written "Petter's funeral"?

"Of course," he says. "We'll make the arrangements."

"Good," she says. "Then it's decided. Those who can't come will simply have to miss it."

Is he hearing her right? A tone of triumph? But she continues. "I wonder if you would like to deliver the eulogy and conduct the burial service? I know that both Skog and Uncle Isidor will want to do it, but you're his good friend and colleague. You've had a lot in common out here these last few years. It feels right to ask you."

"Of course, it would be an honour. And unworthy. Of such a man. How in the world can I do justice in a single speech to his personality, the effect he had on everyone he met? The joy he brought to the congregation. And now the sorrow. It will be hard. But of course."

"Thank you," Mona says. "Then we've answered the essential questions, and you can feel free to report what we've decided to anyone who asks. And one more thing. I must call his parents, but I hate the thought. His mother. No, I'd really rather not."

"Of course I can make the call," says Fredrik Berg, amazed at the organist's psychological insight. He permits himself a crooked smile. "Priests are supposed to be experts at delivering bad news, although I haven't done so well this time."

"Not at all," says Mona Kummel. "I appreciate the fact that I can speak to you plainly."

"Good," says the priest in Mellom. "When I've spoken to his parents, I'll notify the deanery and the cathedral chapter. And remember, you can contact me for any reason. I'll try to do all I can." "Good," says Mona, too. "Thanks for calling. Give my best to Margit." She rings off. The operator stands with her mouth open, as does the Mellom priest. It's true, as he often says, that grief has many faces. As a spiritual guide, you must confront your own inadequacy more often than another human being. He pulls himself together, ignores Margit who asks how it went, just says dismissively, "I have to call his parents now. Time's passing, and it would be awful if they heard about it from someone who thought they already know."

Talking to Petter Kummel's mother, he does at last encounter something expected and predictable. Silence. Horror. Denial. "No, it can't be true. It must be someone else. A terrible misunderstanding. Petter is an excellent swimmer. Thoroughly familiar with waterways and ice conditions around the Örlands. It's unthinkable. No, my dear Mr Berg, please get your facts straight before you try to frighten us to death."

"I sincerely wish I was mistaken! But unfortunately it's true. I've spoken to the organist, who was present when they carried his lifeless body to the parsonage. They worked all night trying to revive him, but it was impossible, he'd been in the water too long. Had perhaps frozen to death before he went to the bottom. I have spoken with Mona. She asked me to call. She was there and knows that he's dead. She's keeping herself under such tight control that I'm afraid her heart may break."

"I don't understand."

"None of us do. It seems incomprehensible. It is so painful to have to break the news to you, his dear parents."

"I had three sons. Now two are already dead. What's the meaning of it all? How am I to bear such grief?" Now her voice breaks, and she gives the phone to her husband.

Petter's father, whom he remembers as peculiar, something of a dreamer, very unlike his son, sounds astonishingly calm.

"How is it possible? Petter, who is so much wiser than I! But he is dead, you say, and I must live."

"Yes," says the Mellom priest. "I know that you have a brother, Dean Isidor, who can talk to you much better than I can. I'll call him and ask him to get in touch."

"Yes, Isidor," says Leonard Kummel. "He has had much affliction on account of my children. First Göran. Now Petter."

Just as well to get it said at once. "I hope he can come to the funeral. But Mona has asked me to conduct the service, as Petter's friend and closest colleague."

A short pause. Fredrik begins to suspect that Mona has perhaps carried out a coup. Best not to let on, and in any case the elastic Leonard Kummel moves quickly on. "Yes, yes, I see. That sounds appropriate. You must forgive me . . . It's so hard to think clearly. My daughter, my son, they must be told. I'm crushed."

"I understand. There must be many you'll need to contact. I too have other calls to make. But don't hesitate for a second to call me if there's anything I can do. Anything at all. I'm so terribly sorry for your affliction."

As they're speaking, the morning's news goes out across Finland, and now all hell breaks loose. The operator on the Örlands sets her own priorities and puts through calls to the parsonage first. Others can wait, including even the Co-op. They're put through in the intervals and are interrupted when necessary. Calls wait in an endless queue, everyone needs to talk to everyone, exclaim, express their horror, pour out their feelings. Calls to the organist have the second highest priority, right after the parsonage, because official calls go through him, from the rural deanery, from the cathedral chapter. On Åland and the mainland, the coordination is not as good. There are unexpected and inexplicable traffic jams, some lines are completely blocked, on others there are unreasonable delays. Some people call a second time to find out what became of their first call, which doesn't make things better. "We're putting them through in the order they were placed, so please be patient," say operators all along the coast.

For every minute that passes, Petter Kummel has been dead one minute longer. Mona doesn't want to be distracted, she wants to concentrate, she wants to be alone, but the telephone rings. The only voice that could make her happy is his, but to her surprise, her mother's cheers her a bit when she calls. Mama, who never makes a big fuss. Mama, whom she can copy at a time like this — close up, button your soul, give nothing away!

"I thought I'd heard a ghost when I heard the news on the radio. Tell me it's all a mistake."

"No. Petter drowned last night."

"Dear heaven, how could God let such a thing happen?"

This from Mama, who hardly believes in God. Mona decides to answer as if she'd said, "How did it happen?" She describes the accident, the bicycle, the items on the ice, the search at the steamboat channel. Too late. "I didn't hear a thing, though I was out on the steps, listening. Lillus had a cold and was fussing and crying so I was in the bedroom with her. If I'd been alone in the kitchen, I might have heard something."

"Mona, sweetheart," Mama says, appalled but also fearful, afraid for her daughter and the powerful feelings that at some stage must come out. "How are you? Dear child, how are coping?" She remembers last summer's visit to the Örlands, Mona full of energy, radiant with well-being, Petter so obviously all she wanted in life. And now this.

"I'll just have to deal with it," says Mona angrily. It's her way of dealing with everything — with anger. "There's going to be a huge amount of work. The funeral is set for next Sunday. All Petter's relatives. It's enough to make you crazy. I don't think you need to come."

"Of course we'll come, Papa and I. Papa doesn't know yet. He was out in the stables, and now he's out ploughing. It snowed here last night. It's beautiful. We'll figure out some way of getting to Örland. Maybe the Coast Guard can help."

"Yes. I'll call when I know more."

"Thank you. But first and foremost, you've got to promise me not to work yourself to death. Get all the help you can find. Tell me if there's anything I can do. Anything we can bring. Anything at all. You understand, we want to help. And those poor little lambs! How are they doing?"

"Lillus doesn't understand a thing. Sanna gets it, more or less, but . . . oh, they're both so little that most of it goes right over their heads. The homecare sister is here, they're being well taken care of."

"Good," says Mama, who has learned not to ask follow-up questions. "Tell Sanna that Gram and Gramps will be coming for a visit soon. And now don't forget to tell me if there's anything I can do."

"Yes, yes," Mona says. Ever since she was a little girl, she has totally lacked confidence in her mother's ability to get things done. Of course she can get her to read stories to Sanna, but she, Mona, faster and more efficient, will have to do all the practical work herself!

In any case, phew, another phone call out of the way, and more to make. Brave, kind people along the coast, and of course her mother-in-law has to talk, although she should have realized that Mona asked Fredrik Berg to call because she didn't want to speak to them herself. But no one can avoid her fate, and Martha Kummel chatters and weeps while Mona grows more and more distant, never crying or sniffling so that Martha can tell the world that she's gone completely to pieces! "What can I say?" is all she says when Martha wants some kind of emotional response from her, wants her to sob and carry on and be grateful for Martha's platitudes about how we can't understand the ways of the Lord, how he lets no sparrow fall to earth (but he let Petter), how Petter will always be with them in their hearts. Mona knows that every word she utters is repeated and embroidered by the unctuous Martha, and therefore she says almost nothing. Let her report that Mona is dumb with grief! She only tells her about the funeral and insists that Petter would certainly have wanted his good friend and colleague to conduct the service.

Phew! She gets sweaty and worn out from all the phone calls, a constant harping about the same things. The whole time forced to say something other than what she would rather put like this: Petter is dead, and all joy and happiness are gone from my life. Nothing can compensate for such a loss. If only I could drive all of you away, if only I could chase you off with an axe, if only you'd all vanish from the face of the earth. It would not ease my grief, but it's what I'd prefer.

Chapter Twenty-Five

I know only what I've heard. That he drowned. You might also say that he drowned because he was a good swimmer. While he still had time, it never occurred to him that he couldn't pull himself out. He did everything he should have, got out of his boots and his overcoat, and thought it was a small thing, strong and athletic as he was, to heave himself onto the ice. Or you could say that he died of bad judgment. What was he thinking when he used up his strength rescuing his briefcase? A contributing cause of death was the good breeding that taught him you must take better care of other people's property than of your own. Would he have done that if he'd been thinking clearly? Another cause of death was perhaps the blow to his head that knocked so much sense out of him that he didn't know enough to start calling for help before it was too late. Carelessness was another cause of death. Here on the islands, no one goes out on the ice without a knife in their belt, whereas he pedalled away like some kind of Jesus who thinks he can walk on water. The Aranda also contributed to his death. If she hadn't passed that way, the men who heard him wouldn't have assumed that someone had fallen into the steamboat channel.

No, my friend, there isn't a single cause of a person's death, it's not that simple. People die from a number of different factors that work together to prevent a rescue.

Of course people ask me if I didn't have some foreboding. What sort of premonition do you think I could get in Godby, well inland, among strangers? That you have a weight on your chest and feel anxious and helpless is completely understandable. In retrospect you can see all that as some kind of warning, but what good does it do you to know that something dreadful is happening, when it could be anything at all and you know nothing and are fearful as a child? I can't say that I thought of the priest and felt he was in danger. I didn't think of anything in particular. It was just a general sense of uneasiness and depression, the kind of thing that can affect anyone who's completely in the dark.

If only the thing could be undone! There's such a small margin, so much that could have happened just a tiny bit differently, and the priest would stand today in the Co-op laughing about his cold bath. Much more likely than his being dead. It's that I wonder about – if those who were out there with him, curious and importunate, if they didn't understand that they only needed to lighten him a bit, just enough to let him get his chest up on the ice. Is it true, as I suspect, that they don't exist unless you sense their presence? The way the air gets thicker when they gather, how strongly you have to drive your thoughts for them to understand. They wish us no harm, I have many examples of that, but unless you yourself urge them on, they'll just hang around the hole in the ice and watch you die, as if they had forgotten even the fact that a person who is dying has the strongest desire to live.

* * *

The priest's wife has a few days' respite before the funeral. She has saved and separated milk, churned butter. The Co-op has delivered flour and she has baked and baked. She has cleaned and cleaned. She tends her animals in exemplary fashion. Some community representative is always nearby—Sister Hanna, the verger, the organist on a worried visit. "Please, Mona," they say. "Everything doesn't have to be perfect. You'll make yourself sick. At least let us help you. Sit down. Rest. This is terrible."

She doesn't tell them what she's feeling. She says very little. When she talks to Sister Hanna, it's only about practical matters. She is closed to the concerned helpers trying to keep an eye on her without being too obvious. When she walks down towards the church dock, they know she's going to the dead man in the shed. A coffin has been delivered, lined in white, but it has not yet been closed, and Mona goes there once a day to make certain he is actually dead.

The temperature is still below freezing. The body is frozen. It doesn't change in any objective way, but grows day by day more irreclaimable. Mona has examined every mark on the body, which is covered with traces of the accident and the rough attempts at resuscitation—the black mark on his forehead, the skin scraped from his hands, the pressure marks on his chest, the scratches and discolorations from the rescue operations. His nose slimmer than in life, his mouth white and narrow, as it might have become in old age. His eyes, the lids open a tiny slit, give hope, even now, for a glimmer of life. A man so loved, so dead. How could you?

According to the verger who watches over her, she cries in the shed. Wails, with open mouth, terrible to hear. But good that it comes out, they all agree on that. Maybe it will be better when her own relatives arrive, they tell each other, hopefully, thinking secretly that it will be a relief to hand off the responsibility.

For what happens at a funeral is that the survivor is thrust back into the family and clan that she believed she had escaped.

The priest's wife sees them approaching and surrounding her and cutting her off from the parish community she has been a part of, from the new friends who are not burdened by ties to the past or by double loyalties. From the settings in which she is a free and independent individual, freed from the troubles and failings of her youth. All this will be taken from her. The dear people of the Örlands will be shoved aside by the approaching relatives, who will return her triumphantly to the scenes of her deepest defeats, where she had constantly to assert her right to a life of her own, now spent.

If she could commit murder, she thinks. If she could close every unctuous mouth, cut off the empty phrases with a knife. If she could sweep them away, put the whole bunch of them on a desert island. If she could be an angel of vengeance and dispense punishments in accordance with what their sins deserve, if she could expunge them from the surface of the earth. Even then he would not come back to life. Even then she would not regain her life with him.

* * *

When the first funeral guests arrive, the deceased's parents and relatives from Åland, delivered by the Coast Guard in its light icebreaker, she takes the fish casserole steaming from the oven. Oven-warm bread on the table, freshly churned butter, the best china. The pastor's wife herself: "Welcome, welcome. You must be frozen and worn out. Hang up your coats, there's food on the table."

She has roses in her cheeks from the heat of the stove and her usual rush of activity. She successfully parries her mother-in-law's effort to embrace her. She notes the tears on Martha's cheeks with irritation—such an exhibition. They have also brought some huge, hideous wreaths, which clutter up the hallway, as if their coats and suitcases weren't clutter enough. "Come in, come in," she hurries them along. "Don't let the heat out. Come in and sit down."

She thumps down herself for a moment, but she can't stand to look at their long faces and their grimaces. "Where do you find the strength?" her mother-in-law chirps, and she answers, angrily, "Where would we be if I didn't?" A good question. Sister Hanna has left the parsonage because the guests need the guest room, so there's no one but Mona to keep everything going, a child can see that. Stupid questions, terrible hypocrisy. What could they possibly help her with, these people who are used to being waited on hand and foot at the Parsonage Hotel!

The little girls are silent as the grave, the guests have forgotten to greet them. Now they shower them with attention, since they don't know how they're supposed to deal with Mona. Sanna recognizes both her Papa's mother and father but looks anxiously at Mama when they ask her things. May she speak or will Mama get mad? Lillus stretches her arms out to Grandpa, but Mama shoves her back down into her highchair. "Sit still! You'll tip it over!" It's unnatural, the girls as quiet as mice, Mona unreachable in her efficiency, Petter dead.

Full of anxiety, they meet the next wave to appear. It is Mona's parents, Petter's siblings, and Uncle Isidor, who came from the east, got off the steamboat in Mellom, and were conveyed onwards by the Coast Guard. Mona is in the parsonage with the girls and her preparations, and in the icy cold on the church dock they fall weeping into each other's arms, groaning and grieving. The Åland phalanx, which arrived first, reports that they don't know what to do with Mona. It's impossible to reach her, she refuses to talk about anything but the practical arrangements and turns a deaf ear to every effort at solicitude or sympathy. We can't help her, we can't do anything, we can only sit there like a guest while she rushes around doing things. It's not natural. What are we to do?

"We can go inside before we freeze to death," says Mona's mother drily. They are startled, and the flood of emotions abruptly stops. Quiet, courteous Mrs Hellén sounds amazingly like her daughter. She starts walking up to the parsonage, followed by her husband. The others look at each other and eventually follow along in a loose cluster, fluttering and wobbling in their despair and horror, while the Helléns walk straight ahead into the parsonage.

No emotional scenes here. They take one another by the hand. "Sweetheart! My poor little bird," Mama says. "Stop," says Mona. "Here come the girls." Cautiously, Lillus hiding behind Sanna. Gram pleased, Gramps delighted. Give us a hug! Sanna remembers them, she is Gram's friend and intimate. Mona knows that Mama doesn't know how to deal with children until she can talk to them, but she looks at Lillus and, in a conversational tone, says "Peep." Lillus takes a little hop and says "Peep" back. Then she rises into the air on Gramps's arm and sits there as if cast in bronze. Quite pleasant. Mona wouldn't have believed this of the parents she criticizes so harshly. But just as she might have said something, they hear the inescapable troop from Åland murmuring hesitantly outside. The door opens and nothing happens.

"Come in, come in!" Mona shouts. "You're letting out all the warmth!" She greets the newcomers, tells them they can eat in the dining room and then they'll have coffee in the parlour. And no, thank you, of course she needs no help. She sets out the coffee things on the sideboard and slices bread in the pantry. Then this new group seats itself at the table and eats, for they wouldn't dare do otherwise. Ready to burst with sympathy, which now lies like a cold lump in their bellies. The floods of tears that flow so freely when they talk among themselves have ceased. Attempts at conversation get prompt, dismissive answers. What are they to do? How will it all end?

Coffee in the parlour as promised. A braided coffeecake, brushed with egg, sprinkled with pearl sugar. Please help yourselves! Deathly silence, all the more noticeable because it's normally impossible to get the Kummels to shut up. Only Mrs Hellén converses, and Hellén himself rumbles agreement in his bass. "Good coffee cake," Mrs Hellén says. "You can certainly bake — better than I." That almost makes Mona smile, because she's not wrong. In adversity, when there's no way out, Mrs Hellén escapes into diversionary remarks, just now about the food, the wind, the temperature. The Coast Guard, the boat trip, seasickness, the length of the trip, the relief of getting back onto dry land. She continues with friendly questions to the surviving Kummel siblings about their jobs and homes, their future plans and hopes. She gets a conversation going, although the young people shake their heads and signal each other that they can't believe their ears. All her life, Mona has found her mother's refusal to confront unpleasant situations annoying. Now she suddenly sees that it has some advantages, can even save her from a still more unpleasant situation, namely, that her self-control might run the risk of collapsing. If she has an ally in this assembly, it is, to her astonishment, her mother.

And when everyone has been assigned a place to sleep in the guest room, study, dining room, parlour, or attic, and when it's been decided who the pallbearers will be, and a number of other exhausting questions have been answered, Mrs Hellén says in friendly conversation that she doesn't suppose the Co-op will have a black veil. And therefore she has brought an old veil with her, which she can help Mona fasten to her hat. In fact, she is wrong — Adele Bergman promptly delivered a veil — but the thought was excellent and allows Mona and Mrs Hellén to withdraw to the bedroom while the others cluster at the other end of the house with their sighs and tears and their gestures of complete helplessness whenever Mona's situation is cautiously broached.

Mama has her own funeral hat with her in a carton and Mona brings out the pretty black felt hat she had to buy for Petter's ordination. The veil would fall better if the hat had a broader brim, but it will do. The veil her mother brought hangs nicer and smells better than the stiff, unused one from the Co-op, which has absorbed the stink of tobacco smoke and kerosene in the store. "Thanks," Mona says. She starts sewing it to the hat right away, while Mrs Hellén stitches on her own. Mona knows what she looks like in it, but Mama sees her eldest daughter in mourning for the first time. As soon as she's hidden behind it, her shoulders begin to tremble and there is a snuffling sound, as if she were sobbing. Quickly, she throws it back over her hat. "Oh, just because I'm wearing a veil, I think I have to start crying."

Mrs Hellén smiles evasively, the way she does, and says, "Yes, yes. It's hard. It's dreadful, having all of us here in the house. Tell me if you think there's anything I can do. I'd really like to help, even though I'm the way I am."

Mona gives her a quick evaluating look. "If you could keep your old friend Martha from interfering constantly, that would be a real boon. If you talk to her, she can't talk to me."

"True enough," Mama says. "And I can spend time with the girls. Read to them, for example."

"They're going to be hopelessly spoiled!" Mona says. "No routines and no rules. They're impossible if they get too much attention."

* * *

While the two women sit in the bedroom, the verger comes in through the kitchen right into the group of funeral guests, like living proof of the saying that no matter what you're doing, you'll be interrupted. Surprised, he excuses himself for his work clothes — he has come to help the widow with the evening milking. Whereupon they all start talking at once. For heaven's sake, Mona can't possibly go out to the cow barn under the circumstances! Can't someone else go? Is there no one who knows how to milk? No one to ask? This is terrible!

No one in the group knows how to milk a cow or else they would. With pleasure. Finally the verger himself raises his voice to say that it's Mona herself who insists on going. "She says she wants to go by herself, but I go with her anyway. And I must tell you", he adds with all the weight of his office, "that I don't know how we'd get through this without the cow barn, because in the cow barn she can weep."

That gives them something to think about. Mona too heard him come and emerges from the bedroom followed by Mrs Hellén. "You came this evening too!" she says. "You know I can manage by myself. But let's go. If Berg and Skog arrive while I'm out, make them some tea. I'll come and throw together some supper for everyone when I'm done. In the meantime, make yourselves at home." A general invitation, but the order to make tea is directed to Mrs Hellén and banishes the elder Mrs Kummel to the outer circle. Nothing more to be said, she closes the kitchen door, puts on her milking coat in the hall, pulls on her boots, and then off she goes with the verger in her wake.

Almost as if they'd been waiting around the corner of the house for a signal, Berg and Skog come in. When the Coast Guard unloaded the mourning relatives at the church dock, Berg and Skog continued to the west villages, where they prepared the next day's funeral service with the organist. They ate and talked and are now going to spend the night in one of the attic rooms at the parsonage.

Mrs Hellén thinks that Berg looks terribly down in the mouth, while Skog can hardly contain his desire to arrange and direct. As Petter's predecessor in this parish, he had, on his own initiative, decided and announced that he, who knows his Örlanders, would deliver the sermon. Until he was informed that Berg had been asked to conduct the funeral, he had simply assumed that the call would come to him. Hard to explain why they've chosen the colourless Berg from the neighbouring parish, who has had very little contact with the Örlands, while Skog himself, with the ability to play on the Örlanders' emotions like a keyboard, must content himself with a sermon. Well, he can say a lot in that sermon! In the course of the discussion at the organist's table, he has expressed his views on a great many subjects and was irritated by Berg's tenacious resistance. It seems that he and the widow have made all the decisions and that they have completely won over the organist to their point of view.

Well, what's done is done. But now they have to greet the relatives from the mainland all over again, having met them once already, on the boat, and make a much greater effort with those who came from Åland to the west — the grieving parents and the male representatives of Petter's father's home farm. Many think them empty phrases. Even Fredrik Berg thinks his words sound hollow, although he means it from the bottom of his heart when he says that he, who counted Petter as a friend and brother, knows better than most what they have lost. It is difficult to pull his thoughts together into something personal when the food seems to have a higher priority than the death. Mona's mother, Mrs Hellén insists on serving tea to the new arrivals, although they try to insist on waiting until Mona returns. "These are Mona's orders," Mrs Hellén says as she pours. "It seems to be a rule of the house that everyone must get something warm in their gizzard as soon as they come through the door. Drink this now, and then you can have a second cup with the rest of us."

With Skog on hand, there is at least no problem with the conversation. He quickly takes over the grieving parents and, at last, says all the things that a proper priest is supposed to say to the devastated parents of a beloved son who has died before his time, in the bloom of youth. They hang on his every word, and, trembling and weeping, they speak of the absolute incomprehensibility of what has happened. Berg sits silent, but it doesn't matter, for Skog leads the discussion with authority. Mrs Hellén tiptoes carefully to the kitchen. Ingrid, Frej's little seasick wife, is unobtrusively washing the dishes, and Mrs Hellén peeks into the pantry. Everything prepared — sliced bread, butter on small plates, farmer cheese. She chats a bit with Ingrid and has her suspicions confirmed. The seasickness is a result of a newly confirmed pregnancy. "So strange, just at the same time as Petter's death." "Yes, yes," says Mrs Hellén. "Such things happen. It's so nice of you to do the washing-up, Ingrid. Maybe Charlotte could dry. I'll start setting the table for evening tea in a few minutes."

Charlotte comes in, weeping, and Mrs Hellén looks around for the little girls, both of whom are anchored on Hellén's lap.

She has to admit that he has a fatherly touch with children. She goes around on sore feet and sets the table, conscious of the fact that Mona doesn't want her to, but it's a way of getting them all into bed a little earlier so her poor daughter can rest and gather her strength for an exhausting Sunday. "Where will we find the strength?" she wonders, as she's wondered for thirty years, padding about, all but invisible under Skog's ringing voice.

Almost everything is ready when Mona comes rushing in. The verger has gone on to the church. If he builds a fire in the boiler this evening, then all he'll have to do early in the morning is add wood. She looks around, displeased. "What in the world have you been up to? I was going to do all this when I came back! Go sit down, Mama! I'll do the rest." She greets Skog quickly and waves away his condolences, greets Berg, an ally, more heartily. And she keeps her emotions under control, under tight control as she puts the girls to bed and her mother reads them a story. Mona leads them quickly through their bedtime prayers ("God who holds all children dear") and then goes back out to the others, who are starting to gather their things and get ready for the night. The only sensible thing is to get to bed. The ones just arrived have a long, trying journey behind them, and the day to come will be heart-rending and difficult. Another reason not to sit up and talk half the night is that they're afraid of Mona and don't know how to behave. Darkness and silence may be preferable.

❈ ❈ ❈

Still, it's wrong to say that the house lies at peace. It is not necessary to express the thoughts of the people lying in bed, shivering, afraid they will never get to sleep. It's enough to take a look into the attic room under the northernmost gable. The energetic Skog has built a fire in the tile stove, but it's still cold. He and Berg sit opposite one another at the wobbly table that has stood here since long before Skog's time. Berg puts his briefcase on the table and opens it to take out his aspirin. Skog extends his hand. "May I see?"

Berg, timid, as if he were trying to hide something shameful, "What?"

"The eulogy. Surely that's what you were going to show me."

"No, not really."

"You have written it, I suppose?"

"Naturally."

"Well then, give it here. I'll tell you what I think. I know exactly what will work with these Örlanders."

Berg, feeling coerced, "I don't know that I want it improved. It's hard to explain. Imperfect as it is, it's what I want to say."

"What sort of nonsense is that? You want it to be good, don't you?"

"Of course. But I also want to speak to Petter's memory in my own words."

"I could really help you. I know how the Örlanders think."

"It's hard for me to compromise about this."

"I simply don't understand your attitude. Can't you take criticism?"

"Yes, I guess that's the problem. You didn't know Petter the way I did. I'm grieving. I have a hard time seeing the whole thing coldly and critically."

"All the more reason to listen to an experienced colleague."

"Perhaps. My arguments are weak. But I can't."

"Don't be such a little girl. We're colleagues. This is a professional consultation."

"Why is it so important to you to read my poor eulogy?"

"You seem so uncertain. As if you needed help."

"I get the feeling that you want to direct and control me."

"You've buried yourself out here for too long. There are fresh ideas in the city. We no longer speak of individual effort. Now it's all about teamwork, working together."

"I've read about that. But I've wrestled with this eulogy. I'm the one who's going to deliver it. It's not a matter of teamwork."

And so on. Skog, somewhat older, does not give up. Fredrik Berg can feel that his cheeks are red, his eyes moist. His forehead sweaty, his armpits damp, the cassock that must on no account smell bad tomorrow. He hasn't even the strength to get up and go to bed, just sits there like a sullen child and refuses. His gaze wavers, can't look this self-important man in the eye, this Skog, who thinks it's only a question of time until unreasonable Berg has been beaten into submission and his eulogy criticized to death.

Because that's what it's about. If Skog says a single dismissive word about the eulogy, Fredrik will never be able to deliver it. He'll be forced to flee with his tail between his legs while Skog pulls out the unctuous speech he has probably already written. Why must a person have good arguments against a conceited and contemptuous authority? There is nothing he can do but refuse.

"No. It's a principle of mine. I let no one read my speeches and sermons in advance."

"The vicar calls on principle?"

And so forth. Finally, Fredrik manages to get up, dizzy with exhaustion. "We're getting nowhere. We need to go to bed. We have a great deal to do tomorrow." The voice of reason. He starts getting ready. The oil lamp on the table leaves the rest of the room in merciful shadow, but he is as timid as a girl as he tries to avoid exposing himself as he undresses. He brushes his teeth at the washstand, anxious about spitting and making noise. In everything he does, he behaves like a toffee-nosed young lady, and, going grey with shame, he lies down finally in his bed, frozen to the marrow, afraid to move, afraid to make the slightest peep that would arouse Skog's contempt. He would like to take his briefcase into bed with him; on the grounds that his aspirin are in it, he has instead placed it as close to the headboard as possible.

Skog, on the other hand, takes his time going to bed. Without embarrassment he empties his bladder in the chamberpot, snorts and hawks, wipes his armpits, undresses and puts on his nightclothes, throws himself into bed, rolls over, lies still and prays a semi-audible evening prayer, which to tell the truth Fredrik Berg has not uttered, changes position several more times, then lies still and quickly falls asleep, deep breathing, with a little pup-pup-pup as he breathes out. Sacerdotal snoring. Dear God.

The sleep of the righteous. A good conscience the best pillow. All that hogwash that people say, whereas Fredrik, sleepless, desperate, ill, lies awake as if paralysed. The perpetrator sleeps like a pig, the victim lies awake in guilt and shame.

Downstairs, those who don't fall asleep hear the priests' discussion only as a distant murmur, as if they were exploring some profound theological question about the mystery of death prior to the great burial service on the following day. Mona is sleeping in the bedroom, making the best of a few poor hours of exhaustion before waking at four o'clock to an icy room. Petter's bed has been carried out to the dining room, where Uncle Richard is camping. The coffin in the shed has been closed and the cover nailed down. Now there is nothing left but duty.

* * *

In the doctor's apartment in the attic of the medical clinic in the northern archipelago, Doctor Gyllen spends the night before the funeral pacing. Even without drugs, her feelings are blocked. "Incomprehensible," she has said, like everyone else. "That dear, good man. And his wife and the little girls. How can such a thing happen?" But at the same time, an inexplicable feeling of guilt is eating at her heart despite her efforts to reject it.

She heard about the death days earlier, on the radio, like everyone else, and when her father called a short time later, she thought that was what he'd called to tell her. Together they would repeat the words. "Incomprehensible. Dear Petter Kummel who's become such a friend." And they did so. But Papa had another reason for calling.

"Irina. A letter came. Our Kolja is alive. We have an address."

Complete silence. Her self-control so practised that she can no longer show emotion even in an empty room. Not even a sigh. No tears.

"Irina, are you there?" Papa says. "Did you faint?" To Mama: "I'm afraid she fainted."

"No," Doctor Gyllen says. "Don't tell me such things. I no longer dare to hope."

"But it's true, Irina. Be happy! We've been waiting for this for nine years." He starts telling her who the letter came from—the child's aunt in Kazan—and how the letter made its way to Finland. They can't make contact directly because of the regime, but they have a go-between, a good person, whose name can't be mentioned over the phone, with contacts in the legation. "Irina, you can write. They can write."

"Thank you," Doctor Gyllen says. "There's nothing I can say. My heart too full. I'll write to you later this evening. To him. Yes? Oh God. What can I say?"

Now Mama comes on. "How wonderful that I've lived long enough to see this happen!" She talks on, while Doctor Gyllen stares out the window. A light wind, a little snow. The first patient already arriving, sweeping the snow off his boots on the steps. The medical assistant pottering about downstairs, wondering why she doesn't come down. They usually do a little run-through before the day starts.

"I have to go to work," Doctor Gyllen says. "We'll talk later, we'll write. It's like Pastor Kummel's death, but the opposite. It's incomprehensible."

She rings off and is about to go downstairs, but instead she makes another call, to her dear friends the Hindrikses on the Örlands. Greta answers, and when she hears that it's Doctor Gyllen, she says, "We do nothing but cry. We just can't believe it's true. If only the doctor had been here, we keep saying. If the doctor had been here, maybe he could have been saved. But they say he was in the water too long. They worked on him all night, but not a sign of life. How could it happen?"

It could be that Doctor Gyllen called to tell them about her son, but she sees that on the Örlands there is no space for anything but the priest. That's as it should be, and she's glad she said nothing, for in the course of the day's work and later, at home, having her evening tea, Doctor Gyllen works through a lot of thoughts — religious superstitions she never imagined she was capable of. It's about a simple coincidence, one of many in the course of a long life, nothing to get worked up about. No cause for a lot of overwrought religious speculation.

But the connection can't help but inspire quite alien ideas. Pastor Kummel had promised to do everything in his power. Smiling, he spoke of the miracles that a man in his position could hope for. Every cell in her body tells her that Pastor Kummel went to the foot of the throne and offered his own life in exchange for her son's.

For much of her adult life, the resources have been so meagre and the need in some cases so pressing that it seemed to her more and more that there was a fixed, inadequate quantity of things in the world. If someone comes up in the world and basks in the sun a bit, then that well-being and sunshine are denied someone else. It's the same way with things like joy and success. The sum total is paltry. If a little love and happiness come our way, someone else is deprived of them. Envy, which is such a stone in our path, derives from this insight, as does our reluctance to reveal our good fortune to others.

She has now regained her son, while Mrs Kummel has lost her husband. The thought is childish and shameful, unworthy of a well-educated, rational adult. It's a passing impression, the result of two shocks one right after the other. Of course that's all it is, and she needs to remind herself of that fact force-fully. She must resist, establish some distance from the rational woman scientist who finds herself weeping by her teacup. Half the night before the funeral of Pastor Kummel, whose stiff, frozen, dead body she can picture all too clearly. She weeps, too, for the care and attention she knows this body is being shown, in contrast to the countless labour-camp prisoners, her husband perhaps one of them, whose bodies are disposed of like so much offal. And alongside them, her son, risen from the dead. Behind him and Pastor Kummel are millions of people born and died, without meaning, suffering unfathomable pain. How can the Christian church call its God good?

She manages to prevent herself from falling on her knees and thanking God for her son's rebirth and asking him to receive Petter Kummel's soul. It's a good thing that she doesn't have to attend his funeral, she who in her present state would disgrace herself by weeping uncontrollably.

Chapter Twenty-Six

BEFORE THE FUNERAL CAN BEGIN, they must pass all the stations of the cross — rising; washing quickly at the washstand; dressing, which is no small matter considering the cutting wind outside; making the beds; building a fire in the tile stove; carrying out the chamberpots; waiting in line for use of the outhouse; breakfast. Frightening to see Mona, white against black, utterly self-controlled. "Eat!" she commands. "It will be a while before we get anything else!" Sanna in a dress and a cardigan, quiet. Lillus in everyday clothes on Gramps's arm. Unreal, the guests think as they eat their oatmeal. This is not happening. None of us are here.

But here they sit, like terrified hares in the path of a harvester. Let it stop. Don't let it come. But there's a knock on the door, the proper front door, and it's the organist and the verger who enter. Black suits, white scarves, white faces. "Good day to the house of mourning. We will bring in the coffin now. Maybe some of you would . . . ?" Frej and Ragnar and Uncle Richard galvanized. "Yes, we're coming." Quickly into their outdoor wraps, stumbling out the door with unbuttoned coats, down to the boat shed. The verger has the carrying straps from the sacristy and says it might be a good idea to practise before people arrive. There are now four of them, counting the verger. There will be six at the actual burial, but that's more for form's sake than because it will be too heavy for four. It is an honour for representatives of the parish to be among the pallbearers.

It appears that Frej, despite his youth, has the most experience carrying coffins. He organizes and instructs, excusing himself with "There were quite a few during the war." He avoids the expression "wooden overcoat". It's good to have something to do at last. They walk in step, the coffin swinging slightly as they carry it up the incline. A pause in front of the tall steps, then all together, the organist behind to catch it if it starts sliding backwards. Into the parlour. The coffin placed on the trestles.

Mona refuses permission to open the coffin. Petter's relatives have to bend to her wishes, although they remember the opening of Göran's coffin, the body already putrefying, and his mother's relief that it was done. Now it's Mona who is Petter's next of kin, and she has declared that they will remember him alive, what lies in the coffin is only a body. They have to give in, but even around a closed coffin, they all fall apart. It is the last time the family will stand gathered around Petter. They've decided to sing "Into Thy Mercy, Gentle Lord", but they are unable to bring it off. The organist gives them all a note in a strained voice but has to stop. They burst into tears at the very first words and, wailing, throw themselves down into any empty chair and sob in desperation. All except the dry-eyed Helléns, most notably the unconsolable widow.

Almost a little disdainful, unseeing, she stands there avoiding them all, at a safe distance from anyone who might possibly try to embrace her. She holds Sanna by the hand, a slightly cold and sweaty hand. She is quiet, Sanna is quiet and good these days and all the following days, and Mona can take her along to church with confidence.

Skog and Berg avoid looking at each other, but they do check their watches. The noise of motorboats can be heard in Church Bay, where the Coast Guard has broken up the ice. People are already walking past the house, glancing through the parsonage windows. The verger and the organist look at each other, the verger clears his throat at length, blows his nose in a large handkerchief. "I'll go on ahead. Give me a signal when you're ready to start." On his way out, he runs into Elis Bergman and Brage Söderberg, who've been chosen to be pallbearers. They're walking around wondering if they should go in. The verger waves them in. "Yes, at least into the hall. Skog will tell you what to do."

And sure enough, as Berg notes, Skog takes the first opportunity to give orders and take charge. As soon as he hears the newcomers in the hallway, he goes out and starts to confer in a loud whisper. "Yes, it's almost time. I'll get the family moving. Tactfully, of course. One needs to use psychology on these occasions." Deliriously self-satisfied, he is convinced that nothing will happen unless he makes it happen. In fact, the organist is already talking to Frej, and the three pallbearers from the family move out to the hall to meet those from the Örlands. "We'll take out the coffin now. We'll manage. The steps are the worst. Careful you don't slip in your leather shoes. The verger sanded, but it's still treacherous."

There are teachers and office workers in the funeral procession, and even they are looking at their watches. Mona is helping Sanna into her coat and cap, then she reaches for her hat, her veil still thrown back, and puts on her own coat. "Now we can go," she says, impatiently, in the direction of the parlour. And it's suddenly crowded in the front hall, sweaters and coats and hats, five fluttering veils, burial wreaths in hands. "Do we have everything? Come, Sanna. I'll hold your hand."

Sister Hanna watches them go with Lillus on her arm. Although everyone wants to attend the funeral, someone has to make the sacrifice and stay home with Lillus. Crying hard, she stretches out her arms towards them when she sees they're leaving, but not even Sanna cares, they just close the door and disappear. Outside, Mona nods to the pallbearers and, solemnly, they take their place around the coffin. They give it a trial lift and look at each other—yes, we're ready. The organist raises his hand towards the bell tower. The pallbearers start to move. The bell-tower bays are open, and the bells start to swing, the first stroke of the clapper against the side of the big bell muffled and stiff with cold. But then the speed picks up, both bells together, dark and light, the little bell scrambling above the weight of the big bell's authority, together the preponderant bright tone that is the distinctive sound of Örland church. The people up on the crown of the hill stop to let the funeral procession pass, those in the churchyard turn their faces towards the parsonage, the first hats and caps come off.

This is what they see: the coffin white, the mourners black, the little girl hidden behind the wreaths. A collective gesture as the women sweep their veils forward over the brims of their hats. The pallbearers coax the coffin down the steps and begin their steady pace. One more priest leaves the Örlands. The widow with her daughter, the parents, the siblings, the in-laws, Uncle Isidor. The organist wrings his hands to keep them warm enough to play. Nothing is spared them, every stone on the path, every grain of sand on the ice, every gust of wind, every freezing degree of chill, every peal of the bells, every second—they must suffer all of them, one by one.

The gates to the churchyard stand open, but in keeping with local custom, the coffin is set down on the coffin stone outside. The bells go silent, the two visiting priests and the organist meet the procession. When everyone has gathered around the bier, they sing, with the courage of despair, "Into Thy Mercy, Gentle Lord", and when the first verse is finished, the bells ring, the bearers lift the bier, and, singing, the people follow it across the churchyard and into the church.

By local tradition, funerals are to be conducted at the grave, but on this occasion, because of the many speeches and the considerable crowd, and because the dead man so loved his church, they are adopting a more modern custom and holding the funeral inside the building. The first pews are reserved for the immediate family, but otherwise the church is full to capacity and well beyond, the pews crowded, people standing at the back and on the stairs to the loft. The whole parish is here, and they surge to their feet when the coffin enters, escorted by Berg and Skog. The relatives take their places, the organist pushes through the crowd to the organ. The pumper is ready, though the whoosh of air cannot be heard over the rustling down in the church. The organist put his icy hands on the keyboard, hesitates, strikes a chord. The verger in his place. Skog in command by the coffin.

And now the congregation sings the way the dead man liked to hear them, for the last time, it seems to them. From deep down, broken by tears, but always some of them carrying the tune. They bray and drift, embroider and slip, fall behind or rush ahead, drag the organist with them, run out of breath on the high notes, gasp in unison for more, go silent when the words in the hymnal come to an end.

Skog full of importance, Berg uneasy, unseeing, in the first pew. Skog in the pulpit. "The Lord makes no mistakes," he proclaims, and Mona's heart stops beating in her breast. "Does he not say himself that we do not comprehend what comes to pass, but that later we shall do so? When we stand face to face with the Divine. Here on earth, our life is divided. We belong to two kingdoms. A kingdom of sin and death. But we belong also to the kingdom of forgiveness and of life. Everything in life is marked by corruption. These walls are thick, but they will nevertheless decay and fall to pieces. All those who lie in their beds outside in the churchyard are dust. Human life is like a flower — it thrives in the morning and dies in the evening and our body is destroyed.

"As I stand here and look at you, I know you all. But I also see that you have the mark of death in your faces. It is stamped on your features. But as the forces of decay do their work, it is good to remember what my successor has said to you from this very pulpit about the power of life and forgiveness. Now he is gone. He was taken from you just when everything seemed at its best. Weep! But not as they weep who have no hope, rather as they who have hope and know they will meet again on Judgment Day."

After Skog's homily, the church choir sings "Nearer My God to Thee" from the loft. They've been deprived of their most beautiful soprano and their deepest bass, and in the course of the hymn some voices break off completely and are replaced by deep sobs. "Still all my song shall be" is dreadfully shrill, a harrowing depiction of the defencelessness of anyone who has no other hope but God's uncertain mercy.

For Fredrik Berg, it's not as hard as expected to stand up and take his place beside the coffin with paper and prayer book in hand, look at Mona behind her black veil, Sanna a white smudge, and begin. "Anyone who ever met Petter Kummel will always remember the deep and powerful joy that he conveyed. He was open and accessible, and his piety was as honest as his firm handshake and as unaffected as his unpretentious simplicity. He loved his congregation and saw service to all of you as his mission in life."

Well on his way, his voice steady and clear, the acoustics superb despite the high humidity from the large gathering, he speaks about how much Petter would have liked to live with his family and in his parish, and he describes the night of the death struggle and the spring morning that dawned when the tragedy was complete. In the same way that Easter morning comes to us with its message of the resurrection after the dark night of Good Friday. His warmth and sincerity are no pretence as he turns towards Mona and Sanna and lets his eyes dwell briefly on the weeping parents and siblings.

"Lift up your eyes and cry out to God—and God's love, which passeth all understanding, will carry you in the eternal arms of the Father. Petter Kummel, whom we now consecrate to the peace of the grave, is also encompassed in God's love." An ancient ceremonial, words polished down to their absolute core. "Earth to earth, ashes to ashes, dust to dust, in sure and certain hope of the resurrection unto eternal life, through our Lord Jesus Christ." Three handfuls of the thin, greyish soil of the Örlands form a cross on the coffin's white covering. A hesitant hymn: "Our Years, They Flee Away".

Silence in the church. Mona rises, folds her veil back over her hat, takes Sanna by the hand, the wreath in the other, walks forward on steady legs, looks out over the congregation and speaks, while the whole church holds it breath. The child stands quietly by her side. She thanks them for the good years she and Petter had in Örland parish. She thanks Petter for the happy years granted her. She remembers his words to the grieving parents of the child they buried only one week ago. They were his words of farewell to her as well, though she did not understand it at the time. She lays the wreath on the coffin, adjusts it a little — good. Takes Sanna by the hand and returns to her pew. The church breathes out.

Then the parents and siblings, shaky and uncertain, broken voices, deep breathing. They are followed by other friends and relatives, and Uncle Isidor speaks for the entire family. "Petter Kummel followed his calling without expectation of success," he begins, in an old man's quavering voice, then takes heart and continues. "But success came. Those who heard him were open to his simple but profound message. Almost unnoticeably, all eyes turned to him. His naturally unassuming character and his honesty in both word and deed drew people to him. He struggled with his own sins as much as he did with those of his fellow men. On his travels, he faced storms and heavy seas without fear, but he trembled like a child before the sin and the temptations that carry many a priest to his spiritual grave. Yet that struggle ended in victory. During his years as a spiritual guide, the young priest grew more and more intimate with the power that flows from the gospel of the crucified Christ.

"My dear nephew, whom we miss so much," he went on, a little less firmly, with many pauses. "You have accepted the call to service in a new temple and need no longer tremble in the face of strong waves of temptation. The sea and its perils will not confront you there." He is unable to continue and gropes his way back to his seat.

Adele Bergman, deep in grief, hears the organist walk past her down the middle aisle. He is to speak on behalf of the parish and the vestry, but how will he manage, emotional as he is, and devastated by this death?

The vestry's large wreath in front of him, unembarrassed by his tears, his speech in his breast pocket. Amazingly collected.

"Dear Petter, our good friend and spiritual guide. Last Sunday when you laid to rest a little songbird from the east villages, you carried us metaphorically into God's heaven on a bridge of light. When you headed home that evening, little did you dream that you yourself were stepping onto the bridge of light you had described. You have left us and entered God's heaven. Your importance for the spiritual life of this community extends far beyond the few invaluable years we had you here. Now as we look forward, we pray, dear heavenly Father, give us again a shepherd who understands us."

His wreath placed, the local council next. Sörling and Fridolf, sombre, bow towards the coffin and the family. Berg and Skog come forward with the wreath from his clerical colleagues, Adele Bergman, weak with tears, lays the wreath from the Health Care Centre. Sörling reads the council's memorial and a special message from Doctor Gyllen. Then he reads a mass of condolences and memorials from a great many people who've been touched in some way by Petter's life and death, foremost among them the bishop and the assessor.

In conclusion, with fearless courage and one hand on the keyboard, the organist sings "A Precious Thing to Thank the Lord", all the way, across a bridge of light, safely ashore.

And then, no turning back. The church goes silent. No voices, only the rustle of people who have been crowded together too long and need to stretch. A pause, and the pall-bearers step forward, raise the straps to their shoulders. Now. Berg and Skog start walking, the coffin follows, then the immediate family from their pews and then the congregation, row by row.

Digging the grave was no easy task, they can be grateful that the ground wasn't frozen all the way down. It turns its dark maw towards the procession with its defenceless casket. For the Örlanders, the climax of the funeral is the moment when the coffin is surrendered to the earth. There is then no longer any need for self-control, they weep, they cry out, they kneel and stagger, grief, at this moment, need know no bounds.

All through the long funeral service they have stared at Mona Kummel's veiled head and shoulders. No trembling, no bowing of the head, no leaning to the right or the left to get support from mother or mother-in-law. She sits with Sanna beside her as if they were alone in the world, condemned to endure and survive. Ever since the death, the widow's unnatural self-control has been a source of collective concern on the Örlands. Everyone knows that open mourning is a good thing, everyone hopes that something will call forth the sobbing that wholesome grief requires.

Now all of them move towards the grave. Pushing and crowding are permissible at such times. No one thinks about priorities and status. When the coffin is lowered, which those standing farther away cannot even see, a wail goes up like a flame. The crowd surges, cries are heard above the weeping, people grab hold of one another, women call out, "No! No!" Those standing close to Mona try to save her, they sob loudly and try to draw her along, but even in the tightly packed crowd at the grave, she manages to parry their efforts and withdraw. Stiff and cold, she stands there and refuses to cooperate on their terms, strives only for distance.

Higher up in the churchyard, where she can see, is Cecilia. Why can't they leave the pastor's wife in peace? Don't they understand that she's not like them? Why can't they respect the fact that she needs air between herself and the world? The one she feels sorriest for is Sanna, who is small and short and can't see a thing among all these large, black people crowded around her. She is scared to death and is crying out loud with open mouth. Cecilia can see Mona saying, "Quiet, Sanna!" She moves towards them, but then Grandmother Hellén works her way through the crowd and takes Sanna's hand. No one hears, but what she says is, "Don't be afraid. This will be over soon and then we'll go home."

But it doesn't go that quickly, because on the Örlands the custom is to fill in the grave while the widow stands at its edge and watches the coffin disappear beneath the soil of the church-yard. So thin it is, she thinks again. A miracle that anything can grow in it. Almost laughs out loud—a miracle, yes indeed. Sanna cries loudly, pushed dangerously close to the hole. Soon they'll throw her in and shovel dirt on her until she dies!

Maybe I shouldn't have brought Sanna with me, Mona thinks, distractedly. She floats a little, loses contact with the ground a bit, hears nothing even though they're all making so much noise. The veil is good. She'd like to wear it always. No one can see you, it doesn't matter that you're not here. She feels nothing, everything slips and slides away, and just then her mother takes her under one arm, Sanna is still screaming, and her mother gives her a little shake. "Mona! They're starting to go! What an ordeal! Poor Sanna!"

Through her veil she sees that several of the women curtsey to her before they turn to go. The men bow reluctantly, the way they do at the Communion table. She nods back, as is proper. "Goodbye. Thank you." Quite clearly. Petter's family stands by the grave, their arms around each other. Skog is with them, Berg by himself, near Mona and Sanna and Mrs Hellén. Sorrow or just fear? What is it he's supposed to say? What should he do? Adele Bergman knows. She works her way to Mona. "Dear heart! God give you strength! We are all crushed. Such grief."

"Yes," Mona says. "Thank you." She extends her hand in its black glove. Goodbye. Adele: "You'll stay here with us! We can talk more later. Dear girl!" She walks away, bent over, black hat with veil among the women's shiny black silk shawls. The men in black below their freezing heads, only putting on their fur hats after passing through the churchyard gate. While they were inside the church, the wind freshened and then steadily increased out in the churchyard. The dry grave soil whirled up into people's eyes, and now the wind is whistling ominously and the wreaths are flapping and rustling, the soil left over from filling the grave is being swept away like smoke. Everyone needs to get home while it's still light, and the sacramental wind cuts right through their coats!

It exceeds even Mona's ability to treat five hundred people to funeral coffee. The refreshments are for family. Even the very dearest Örlanders leave. The organist takes her hand at the grave, unable to say anything at all, but she thanks him in a clear voice for his wonderful singing and lovely words, which she would like to have a copy of, and for his beautiful playing during the whole, long ceremony. The verger's dignity has never suited him better as he says, "The funeral was a great tribute to you both. And this evening, Signe and I will do the milking." "Thank you," she says again. "Thank you for all your trouble. The duties of a verger are no easy task under these circumstances!" He moves on and says goodbye to the Kummels and the priests, while Signe, waiting down by the gate, doesn't think she's capable of walking up and taking her leave.

It is dreadfully cold, the gale cuts right through bone and marrow. In order to survive, they must abandon the dead priest to the earth and move towards the parsonage as quickly as decency permits. Hellén, a practical man, speaks for everyone. "Now we should go. It was a fine funeral, but the longest one I've ever seen. Look at Sanna! Poor little thing is blue with cold!"

Everyone looks at Sanna, half dead. Grandfather Hellén lifts her up and starts walking, and Mona follows. Sanna is what she still has, and now she lives for the sake of Sanna and Lillus. And then the whole group, nearly trotting as soon as they get through the churchyard gate. They struggle through the wind, and there is hope. Hot air welters from both chimneys, and they can see that Sister Hanna has put more wood in the kitchen stove. Now she greets them in the hallway. "You poor dears, you're frozen solid. Come in. Come in where it's warm. I've made coffee and tea."

Mona adds her own, "Come in, come in." Quickly, she hangs up her coat, and now that her icy outer wraps are off, Lillus can come up in her arms. Everyone is now concerned about Sanna, who gets wrapped in a blanket and placed in a chair where she falls asleep of exhaustion and distress before she's had even a sip of hot currant juice or had time to bite into a raisin roll. "Poor little darling! Dreadfully thin!" says Grandma Kummel, and Mona hears the criticism — can't she see to it that Sanna gets enough to eat? Lillus, on the other hand, still has her baby fat, she's had a good long nap and is wide awake and happy, tries sitting in everyone's lap and likes Frej's best. When the mawkish Kummels see her enthroned in his arms, they get tears in their eyes. Quite clearly, she chooses the person most like her Papa!

Hanna has set the table and made everything ready, even warmed the rolls in the oven. "You've saved our lives!" they tell her, thinking but not saying: but not his, irretrievably dead. They look stealthily at Mona, who sits at the table drinking coffee and eating a roll as if it were a job. Poor, poor Mona, how can they reach her? How make her see that she's not alone, that she's surrounded by people who want nothing more than to support and comfort her?

There are many burning questions they need to discuss before they have to leave the next morning. Father Leonard, who has been quiet far too long, begins to discuss the funeral — the splendid speeches that warmed the soul and were comforting in a wonderful way. The fantastic flowers, in the middle of winter, way out here on the Örlands, an absolute miracle. The gripping expressions of sorrow from the Örlanders, the hymns they sang straight from the heart. The sheer number of condolence messages, greetings, letters and telegrams. Moving and touching, every one of them. They lie in great piles on the sideboard . . .

"Yes, please have a look," Mona interrupts. "Feel free to go through them and read them. There are so many we'll have to put a thank-you notice in the newspapers. It will be impossible to write a personal note to all of them. Although I mean to write to many of them, when things have become a little quieter."

And then Martha Kummel can no longer control herself. "What are you actually going to do? Eventually, you'll have to think about moving. Where will you find the strength?"

Mona is no frail little widow, and there is a gleam of triumph in her eye when she answers. "There's no hurry about that. They probably won't send a new priest until next summer. Until then, Berg will come out from Mellom now and then. He says in any case that I have the right to a year of grace and that I can live in the parsonage until February next year. So I think I'll stay here, at least over the summer."

Sensibly and rationally reasoned, and no problem talking to Mona as long as you stick to practical, concrete subjects.

Martha Kummel goes on. "That sounds sensible. You'll have time to think things over and look around for a job. You're lucky you have an education. But don't be hasty, you maybe have more immediate things to think about."

ICE by ULLA-LENA LUNDBERG

Fishhooks out, but she doesn't bite. What Martha Kummel is referring to is what's being discussed in every home on the Örlands and by many well-informed people on the mainland — what if the widow is with child! It's not unthinkable. If the child is born in the summer or the autumn, that would put two years between the baby and Lillus. In fact, it's not only possible, it is more than likely, and in many homes they already know that it will be a boy and that his name will be Peter. Mona knows very well what Martha is thinking, and she doesn't intend to honour her with a reply. "Of course there's a lot to think about!" she says, ready for a fight. "How else am I supposed to get through this?"

Silence, but Mrs Hellén, who is experienced at filling awkward pauses, smiles pleasantly. "No, there is really no rush about making decisions. I've already told Mona that of course she's welcome to come live with us while a decision crystallizes as to what she's going to do. She can take her time looking at the teaching positions that are advertised, and then we'll see how it goes."

Naturally, Martha Kummel will take the first opportunity to waylay Karin Hellén and ask her whether Mona is pregnant, and naturally Mrs Hellén will look at her blankly, express astonishment, and say, "At least she hasn't said anything to me." Mrs Hellén is content to say no more, whereas her old friend Mrs Kummel has already expressed her suspicions, bordering on certainty, to a number of the funeral guests who discreetly asked her the burning question.

This wall of resistance that meets every effort at a more intimate relationship with the disobliging widow creates despair among the in-laws — near panic when they realize that they leave tomorrow without a breakthrough having taken place. It comes from the heart when they say, "You can always turn to us!" And "Don't forget that the girls have a Grandma and Grandpa Kummel!" but their words bounce back at them like platitudes and empty phrases. Ringing hollow to a heart that is closed, frozen to the core.

The verger comes into the hallway, not wanting to come all the way in, just to report that he and Signe are going to do the milking. "Thank you. I really don't have the strength this evening. It's been such a day." Mona stands there isolated from everyone, from the girls who must be put to bed, from the funeral guests who must be fed, from tomorrow's breakfast that must be prepared. The sandwiches that must be made for their journeys. How could you leave me so? Thinks, very quickly, of the frozen dead body in the wood coffin beneath a layer of cold soil, in the storm that blows and blows. How cold it is, although they feed the fires steadily.

Chapter Twenty-Seven

WHEN SANNA WAKES UP, it is only to be sent to bed. But first she gets hot soup and the warm juice and bun she didn't have time to eat before she fell asleep. Then she falls asleep again, and when she wakes up in the morning, everyone is still there. She knows that Papa is dead and that there's been a funeral, which is why everyone has come, but she remembers nothing of the funeral except that she wondered how Papa, who is so big, could fit into the little chest on the floor. She can't remember Papa either, except as a flash when she looks at Frej.

Much more than about Papa, they're all talking about *Valvoja*, the pilot boat that will take the funeral guests to Mellom. From there they'll travel on towards Åbo or the main island of Åland. First they need to eat, and Mama warms up the fish soup. The stove warms the whole kitchen if the door is kept shut, and Sanna sits on a stool in the warmth while Lillus is carried from window to window by Uncle Frej, who deplores this unending wind that makes poor Ingrid so seasick. If Sanna says nothing, people stop talking to her, and if she sits still, the cat comes for company.

There is then no end to their departure. They say goodbye and goodbye and goodbye, and instead of going they start talking about something else and then they say goodbye and goodbye all over again. Mama dresses Lillus and Sanna and herself and goes down to the church dock with them to get them to go, but the whole time, those in front come running back because they have something else on their hearts. Only Mrs Hellén stays steadily on course, and Sanna walks beside her. Lillus has deserted and gone over to the Kummels, who repeat delightedly that she and they are birds of a feather. This makes Sanna angry. Lillus isn't a feather, although she's certainly a bird, a chirpy little bird! The Coast Guard is at the dock to take everyone the short distance to the steamboat pier, where the *Valvoja* lies waiting.

Now they have to hurry, but oh, it's awful to see poor Mona and her fatherless girls standing alone and abandoned on the dock. How will they manage? What will become of them? If only the distance wasn't so great! If only there was something they could do! But the widow has made it clear that it's unnecessary for her in-laws to stay longer, and when Martha Kummel asks Karin Hellén if she ought to stay anyway, Mrs Hellén, with her impenetrable smile, says no, if she understands Mona correctly, she needs time to collect herself and regain her balance.

"But isn't she *afraid* of being alone here?" Charlotte wonders. She herself has not dared go out after dark, what with the churchyard so close and the howling wind that sounds like she doesn't know what. "*I* wouldn't want to," she says, and no, they can all see that, but Mona isn't like Charlotte. She would be happy to see the dead rise and walk again. To set him down at the table, brush the soil from his clothes, serve him tea and buttered bread, wonder how everything got so crazy — how would that be frightening?

There is something about farewells, boats putting out, that makes you want to cry with regret even though it's a relief when the group is finally on board and no longer has to be provided with meals. There they stand, three small, dark figures in the fading February light. Mona and Sanna wave, Lillus, in Mona's arms, cries loudly and stretches out her arms towards Frej, wouldn't hesitate to leave everything behind and go with him. Everyone on the boat is crying, except Mrs Hellén and the Coast Guardsmen. Brage waves energetically and calls out cheerily, "Just let us know if you need anything, and we'll be here in a jiffy!"

Goodbye and goodbye and whew. If she herself turns to go, the guests can go into the cabin and get out of the wind. On *Valvoja* they'll be comfortable and can lie down flat so they don't get seasick, Mona explains to Sanna as they walk. Up on the steps they forget to look towards the churchyard, and Mona opens the weather-beaten door. Inside it's like an abandoned gypsy camp, the air thick with Frej's and grandfather Hellén's tobacco smoke, but at least it's peaceful. "Oh, how nice," says Mona, perfectly serious. "I have to start cleaning up, but first let's sit down and have some coffee. And some bread and butter would taste wonderful! And the buns were good, weren't they?"

"Yes," Sanna says, feeling a little happier. Everything is more like usual. Mona has retained the Hellén custom of really enjoying the refreshments only when the guests have gone.

Mona spends two days getting everything in order. The verger comes the first evening and offers his help, but now that the guests are out of the house, Mona can handle the milking perfectly well by herself. She puts Lillus in her playpen where she can toddle about without hurting herself, and Sanna is so sensible that she needn't worry about her. It's fortunate that the girls can keep each other company. It would be harder with only one.

420

It's especially lucky that Lillus has Sanna. As long as the house was full of people, no one noticed that she could no longer talk. In the midst of all the people, no one paid attention to the fact that she just waved her arms and squealed and babbled and shrieked. There is nothing left of all her many words and complete sentences, and Sanna has to start from beginning and teach her what everything is called. There is a lot that Lillus has lost. One day Sanna notices that she has also lost her good baby smell. That's why Mama doesn't like her as much any more, for she's stopped calling Lillus her rosebud but just says she's a filthy little piglet. And it's true, because nowadays Lillus just smells like a grubby child and nothing else.

Nature loves Lillus. It comes running up with a wet kiss and a hug the moment she comes down the steps. Big embrace — little piglet! And Lillus loves nature back, mud and water, grass and cow shit. A horrible child, the way she looks.

Nature tries different strategies with the parsonage girls. Sanna stretches out and grows taller and thinner, as if nature is determined that she not weigh one unnecessary gramme while at the same time giving her perspective and control. In Lillus's case, just the opposite. She stops growing in height but increases in girth, as if nature's plan was to see that she'll never have far to fall when she's knocked down.

Later in the spring, when they can spend more time outdoors, they are often seen on Church Isle — tall Sanna followed by her short, stocky satellite. They chatter constantly, for it's Sanna's responsibility to teach Lillus to talk. It's an entertaining process. Whenever she learns a new word, Lillus laughs and takes a little jump so the knowledge will distribute itself evenly throughout her body. Lillus is fun because she's surprisingly cheerful so much of the time, considering how little she's able to do and how little she knows. That doesn't seem to bother her much, and although Sanna sees it as a duty and a job to look after Lillus and keep her busy, she often thinks it's great fun to be with her as she plays.

Mama has a lot to do. Writes letter after letter to thank all the people who have written letter after letter. She has the animals to take care of and all her household chores. She goes back and forth in the kitchen and is angry at everyone who asks about her future plans. But mostly people do their wondering in the villages, for there aren't many who come to Church Isle now, except to services, which are held every other week. Then everyone looks at her, top to bottom and back up again. Mama is so vexed she turns red in the face. It's the reported pregnancy that's behind it, the posthumous son, a phantom that never takes physical form no matter how much they look. It's the loose-tongued Martha, her busybody mother-in-law, who has started this groundless rumour, which has leaped like wildfire from the Örlands to every Swedish-speaking community in Finland, where this son is already born and christened.

It's an assault on her person to expose her to gossip this way, and it's typical of Martha to elicit oh's and ah's from people while at the same time pretending to give Mona something to live for, as if it were the Son of Man himself she carried in her belly. For she will never let Martha know how she grieves and eats her heart out. On account of her rheumatoid arthritis, they decided to wait a little. They were planning a new baby for the late winter or early spring of 1950, and she had been looking forward with all her being to the intense love life of the coming spring and summer. Now there would be nothing, never anything more, all spoiled because of exaggerated consideration and caution.

Although Mama works and runs about all day long, Sanna sometimes sees her late in the evening sitting quite still at the table, her letter paper in front of her. But she isn't writing, and her eyes stare into empty space. The bedspread is still on her bed, maybe she'll never move again. But in the morning she's off to a flying start, and they all have to be ready fast, fast, as if it were the most shameful thing in the world for anyone to come before they're all dressed and their beds made.

Fredrik Berg comes with Post-Anton every other week to conduct services and confirmation classes. He stays for a few days, and while he's there Mellom has to make do without a priest, which, as Fredrik acidly explains, they do not find at all difficult. The little girls at the parsonage greet him joyously and Mona feels a stab of rancour, jealousy, God knows what, when she sees how ready Lillus is to trade the father she no longer remembers for Fredrik Berg, to whom she gives her unconditional love. She sits on his knee smiling benignly, her head on one side, all the words she knows pouring seductively from her mouth, with accompanying gestures. Sanna stands alongside, jealous for once of her little sister, and doesn't give up until Fredrik Berg has put Lillus down and picked her up, while Lillus leans against his leg and gazes up at him with passionate, tear-filled eyes.

She can grow really angry seeing them like this, as if there was something so special about being a man that even little girls, as soon as they have a specimen within reach, go all slinky and fawning and signal eternal fealty and show an entirely different kind of love than they're prepared to show their mother. Lillus is absolutely insufferable, gives him her undivided attention, sparkles and beams at the dinner table and engages him in a conversation that excludes everyone else. She behaves exactly like a Kummel, as if she'd never been raised to a stricter standard of behaviour, and Mama lifts her down from her highchair and tells her that's enough, Mr Berg is here to work, with the church's books and correspondence and the confirmation classes, and he doesn't have time for a lot of clingy children. She practically drives him to the office and closes the door behind him, for the girls' enchantment just emphasizes how much harder everything is for her.

It's too painful. She can hardly stand to have another priest at her table and feel the enormous difference but also the degrading desire to try so hard to be pleasant, as if in maleness itself there was something so irresistible that it must at any price be courted and idolized. Ugh, the way a person can behave sometimes! And yet Fredrik is her friend and the closest thing she has to a confidant, Petter's friend and colleague. The only one she can discuss her future with, and the only person who loyally keeps her informed about the discussions at the cathedral chapter about the Örlands' clerical needs. The first person to make an entry in the church record in a different hand, under Deaths: Pastor Petter Leonard Kummel, deceased by drowning at an age of 31 years, 4 months, 15 days.

The teacher in the west villages is about to retire, and people on the Örlands think it natural that Mona should take the job. She has thought about it, but no. How can she live here and be constantly reminded? Among people who are naturally moving away from him and the memory of him, people whose attention is focused on new people and new events, new tragedies, while she herself, never. No, it's too hard. Better to return to the mainland, she tells Fredrik Berg, where she has relatives and colleagues and isn't automatically associated with the tragically dead priest, at whose name people glance sidelong at her and go silent.

Fredrik Berg thinks this very sensible. He doesn't want to influence her one way or the other, only to support her in the choices she is eminently suited to make for herself. He admires her decision to stay at the parsonage for half her year of grace so she can manage the move as carefully as possible and avoid doing anything hasty. "I hope they don't send a new priest too soon," he says quite honestly. "I have nothing at all against coming out to the Örlands now that spring is on its way and it's all so beautiful. And you'd be left in peace here at the parsonage."

If only the cathedral chapter were equally insightful, but they feel that the best thing they can do for the Örlands is to find them a new priest quickly. For the bishop and the assessor, with their lively memories of the new vicar's heart-warming installation the year before, Örland parish is a particular favourite. No stopgap solutions, no half measures — it needs to be a proper priest, and right away. However, it turns out that all the men who have warm feelings for the Örlands and found their visits to the place unforgettable have pressing reasons to remain on the mainland. Among the younger guard, priests who have not yet passed their pastoral examination, there seems to be an actual fear of the appointment. They have children who must go to school, elderly parents who need support, important duties in their new positions. If only they were younger and not so bound. If only they were older and not so bound . . .

No, but there is one established middle-aged man, married but childless: Andreas Portman, ordained at a mature age after earning a laborious Bachelor's degree in Theology. High points for persistence, but a dubious pass on his exams. Raised in an agricultural community and thus able, presumably, to speak to the Örlanders as a fellow farmer. In need of an appointment, which arrives along with an enthusiastic introduction by the bishop himself: a singing congregation in an enchanting island landscape, everyone's mind open to the Christian message after the tragedy the parish has suffered. A rich domain, a wonderful opportunity to make a lasting contribution. A brand-new bridge facilitates communications between the church and the community — no risk of a repetition of the recent tragedy. The widow and her children are still living in the parsonage but will move out before the autumn. They have a right to live in the house, but some arrangement can certainly be worked out for the summer. There are attic rooms, for example, and the new priest and his wife can undoubtedly be accommodated there.

Portman, slightly suspicious, looks up the Örland Islands in his atlas, where they are not found. Too far out to sea from the perspective both of the mainland and of Åland. Hmm. On the other hand, a place where he can count on being left in peace from academic sophistries for much of the year. A place where the priest is an absolute, unquestioned authority, the obvious leader of the parish. A private little kingdom. A sphere of operations entirely under his control.

Not worth raising objections, much wiser to accept the appointment humbly from the bishop's hand. Grant me, Lord, to be thy obedient servant, a shepherd according to thy commandments.

* * *

And on the seventh of May, when Berg has confirmed his candidates and completed his duties on the Örlands, acting pastor Andreas Portman arrives with his wife and his goods and chattels. Both over fifty, with heavy bodies and stiff limbs. I feel sorry for them, for it

426

won't be easy to stand comparison with the young couple that came ashore here three years earlier, slim and smiling, the dead man already a legend. It will never be like it was with the Kummels, people are saying already, in advance, and there is distrust and antipathy before anyone has seen even the tips of their noses. They don't seem to be unaware of all this themselves, for they look unhappy, morose and shivering in the morning chill. "Well, well," he says when I show him the church when it appears. "Cold," he says. "Like a desert." He doesn't say that it's beautiful, and never reflects that it's the gateway to heaven.

You can't help thinking back. The reception committee back then, eager and expectant. The arriving couple delighted. Today, the dead pastor's wife has made breakfast, and the organist and the verger have come to welcome them and help them store their things in the shed, where they'll remain until the widow has gone. Those meeting and those arriving look at each other while we dock. Laboured goodwill, a sense of loss that strains the smiles of the organist and the verger. She, the widow, has her little girls with her and she occupies herself with them, but then she walks over to the railing and wishes them welcome, quite heartily.

Goodwill, but such distress. The verger starts to say something, but Portman interrupts. "Later! Right now we need to be a little methodical and get these things ashore. Careful there!" Like ordinary day labourers, Kalle and I and the organist and the verger stand there taking orders and lifting and carrying. "Careful!" comes from Mrs Portman as well, as if Kalle and I hadn't spent half our lives loading and unloading freight. It's the sort of thing that gives you a malicious desire to put down a box just a little harder in hopes of hearing the faint tinkle of broken glass. We're happy when everything's unloaded and we can start the engine and get away. But we're there long enough for me to hear that it's the dead vicar's wife, not the Portmans, who thanks the organist and the verger for their help.

427

ICE by ULLA-LENA LUNDBERG

And when she invites them all in for breakfast so they can get to know each other, Portman says, "Oh, we'll have time for that later. Right now, what's important is to get ourselves inside and get our bags unpacked." The organist, who has already taken several steps towards the parsonage, turns around, looking hurt and uncertain. Then he says, "Goodbye, then," to the widow and goes towards his dinghy pulled up on shore.

The verger remains where he is, almost choking on all his unused words, but he's then ordered to carry up two suitcases before he goes home. I can see from his back how deeply wounded he feels, and I wonder how in the world their collaboration is going to work. Although I don't often go to church, I know that things go badly when the priest and verger don't get along. The numbers on the hymn board squeak more than usual, and the gate in the altar rail sticks when the priest goes in and out. The weathervane on the roof of the church already squeaks so loudly we can hear it all the way down on the dock, and what that means you can work out for yourself.

Chapter Twenty-Eight

WHAT WAS TO HAVE BEEN their fourth summer on the Örlands becomes their first. For Mona, the first in a long life of perennial loneliness. For the girls, the first they remember, in an existence where Papa has always been dead.

This summer, too, there are a quantity of guests, people who feel sorry for the widow, who must do everything by herself and needs company and comfort. This means that in addition to her preparations for the move, she must also feed and house visitors. With the Portmans in the parsonage, this is no easy task. She no longer has the use of the attic rooms or the office, and in the kitchen she has to make space for Mrs Portman to prepare meals. They have worked out a schedule that keeps them out of each other's hair as much as possible, but all the extra coming and going accentuates the Portmans' feeling that they're in the way, and consequently they're consumed by ill will and rancour and wish to heaven that Mona and her crowd were all out of the house.

Lillus is afraid of them. Mama has taught them just to say hello and go on about their business, but Lillus can't manage that. "Waah," she howls the moment he looks at her, for Portman is in direct touch with the abyss in Lillus where the howling lives. Sanna looks pained, curtseys, and says "H'lo" and at the same time, "Quiet, Lillus!", dragging her along through the kitchen and out onto the steps. Outside they can live, if they stay away from the paths the Portmans use. They never appear near the cow barn, so they can hang out there, and in the cow pasture. It's a relief to be out of the house, but even though Sanna is wise far beyond her years, she has a hard time figuring out the Portmans' movements in order to keep them from looking at Lillus. Because she howls as soon as they do, and then Mama gets angry.

Mama is always angry. She has so much to do and never has time for everything she's planned, even though she's at it from dawn to dusk. They're going to move to the Helléns, but not yet, so Sanna doesn't have to think about that. Mama gets everything done that needs doing, but there's so much to think about, and it's good that Sanna can help by keeping an eye on Lillus!

Apple and her calf will go to slaughter in August. Goody will go with them to the Helléns and live in the cow barn there. The sheep and the chickens will be auctioned, along with the equipment from the cow barn. The congregation has divided the haymaking, which has now been hauled away from Church Isle. The barn is empty, and may never be filled again, for the Portmans do not intend to keep cows. They will buy milk from the parsonage crofters and rent out the pastureland. It's a crying shame, but perhaps it's only right that the vicar's animal husbandry should be eliminated now that he himself is gone and his survivors are about to live out their loss in another place.

A thousand things to think about. With a light heart, Petter broke up the moving crates and used the boards to build bookcases; now the verger has to tear apart the bookcases and nail together packing crates. She can pack the books, but there's much of the other stuff she'll need access to right up to the day they leave. First she gathers together everything to be auctioned. A lot of people cast sidelong glances at the furniture, because they know she's going to live in an attic room at first, but of course eventually she'll have a house and home again, so the furniture will go with her.

Best not to think about the joy with which she unpacked everything and arranged it all in the parsonage. It's a feeling she'll never have again, but she can still have order and method in her life, and perspective. It's a job, a project, a duty, and it can be done effectively and without a lot of sloppy sentiment. If she has to blow her nose, it's because it's been cold and raw all summer and because dust gets in her nose when she roots around in cupboards and sheds.

Now that the Portmans are here, there's a service every Sunday again, and they sit there all three, farther back than before. Mona and Sanna greet everyone, Mrs Portman, for the time being, no one. The congregation's reservations are clearly visible. Portman can't sing the Mass, so the organist sings the responses a little against his will, and the congregation joins in half-heartedly. The sermon is well prepared but dry. Kummel's sermons were always full of life and spirit even when he wasn't all that well prepared. But even then it was a pleasure to follow along and wonder how he was going to bring it ashore with the rather slender thread he was using as a lifeline. And the way he could sing! Everyone talks about it very openly so the Portmans will hear.

After the very first service, the organist is criticized for his slow tempos. That the congregation like them slow is no excuse. It is obviously the cantor's job to teach them to adopt modern hymn-singing styles! And the verger . . . Well, the verger should be more obedient and not constantly plead local custom. Young, uncertain priests lean on customs, but experienced people prune and select and introduce new practices where they're called for.

Now neither the organist nor the verger stop in at the parsonage after the conclusion of High Mass, and only occasionally can they talk openly with Mona. How will this all turn out? They both wonder, the verger more openly offended than the organist, who is struggling to achieve a more friction-free collaboration with his superior. He fears for the next meeting of the vestry. It's difficult to prepare an agenda for a priest who doesn't care in the least how things have always been done on the Örlands. He just invokes the excellent practices of his home parish in northern Ostrobothnia.

"It was hard enough", the organist says, "when we had to become Protestants in the fifteen hundreds. The church needs to be a rock, steadfast. We don't like all these changes. There's enough of that in society as a whole."

And the verger can only agree, especially since every normal person can see that the traditions on the Örlands are beautiful as well as functional.

Within the congregation, the customary division into two camps has asserted itself quickly. In this instance, the east villages are first with their attacks, the organist notes a little maliciously. But in addition, the formidable Adele Bergman tries to take the Portmans under her wing. For the first time, a slight coolness has found its way into the relationship between the Co-op's manager and the chairman of its board.

"It's not easy for him in the beginning," Adele explains. "So we have to keep open minds and welcome him without reservation. We must respect his calling and give him our confidence. We haven't yet seen how he means to work among us."

"Oh, I don't know," the organist says. "We've seen some ominous examples. He certainly hasn't kept an open mind towards us."

"So much the more reason to be encouraging and understanding. If the core of the message is sound, the outward forms don't matter so much."

"How do you get to the core of the message if the outward forms drive us away?"

"Now you're being too quick to judge him. 'Judge not, that ye be not judged.'"

"Dear Adele, I'm talking about our collaboration, which is going to be hard."

"It takes two to make a quarrel."

"If you say so."

"Now I've offended you."

"It doesn't seem that the confidence you talk about extends to me."

"Of course it does. I have complete confidence in you, and I'm trying to gain confidence in him. I'm defending him because it isn't easy to do. I don't want the priest we've been given to be disliked and persecuted. People are merciless, you know that yourself. But what if the ways of our Lord are such that he chooses a less popular and less radiant person to complete the revival that Kummel didn't have time to accomplish. What if even Kummel's death is a part of God's plan for us?"

"Then I have a bone to pick with Our Lord."

"This is not a joke. I'm saying we should be open to the possibility that Portman is God's instrument, sent to us for our salvation."

"Forgive me, Adele, but you're the only one of us who thinks that. The priest is also a public official, and what's happening here is a hopeless clash. And now I have to go. Thank you for the coffee."

A brief handshake is all, his dark, imposing features a little too dark at the moment. Out of the house, he walks straight down to the dock, doesn't look up even once as he cranks his Wickström into life and heads out. Sitting motionless in the boat, he turns away, as he must to be able to drive south. There is no light around the cup he drank from, the minutes he signed are lifeless. A wedge driven invisibly between her, who works to come closer to God, and him, who follows the ways of the world. Between her, who loves, and him, who doesn't return that love.

※ ※ ※

It was Mona who saw to it that Adele and the Portmans got acquainted. She invited Adele and Elis to coffee one Saturday afternoon when the shop closed at one, and she invited the Portmans as well. "The church has a real friend in Adele," she told them. "She's on the vestry, and it would be nice if you got to know each other."

It is as pleasant as always at Mona's table, and the food is good. The Portmans are dignified and austere, with courteous smiles. Adele is in her element. Goes straight to the need for revival and a deeper faith among the Örlands' lukewarm Christians, says how pleased she is that the venerable bishop has sent them a steady, experienced priest, hopes and believes that he will be a blessing for the parish. Unctuous and teary-eyed when she speaks of the work their former priest did not have the time to complete. Puts her faith now in the hope that he, Portman, has been guided by God to this isolated island parish.

"A demanding task," Portman agrees, and Mrs Portman nods. "A shot in the arm is undoubtedly called for. What's needed out here is a firm hand. The people are like big children."

Mona laughs happily, to everyone's astonishment. "You can't imagine!" she says, a remark worthy of Mrs Hellén, her mother. She passes the cake plate and then rushes out to say something to her little girls, whom she's been watching through the window. They're playing a game Lillus has invented. She yells, "Potman's coming!" and then they both scream and run and hide. When Sanna yells "He's gone!" they come back and start the game over again. "Stop screaming like that, good heavens!" Mama says. She hurries back in and interrupts the conversation once again. Small talk, a little of this and a little of that, until it's time to say their thank-yous and go.

Adele's heart breaks when she sees Mona active and brisk, at full speed, but without the dash and ardour that were characteristic of her as Petter Kummel's wife. Now she's the mother of these little girls, and it will take many years of work until they can stand on their own two feet. How will she manage? It's the question everyone asks, and Mona gives always the same answer. "I'll *have* to manage. That's all there is to it."

* * *

Mrs Portman has no children, and therefore Lydia Manström is counting on her to be an asset for the Marthas as well as for the work on public health. New energies and talents are always a good thing, so she bids Mrs Portman a hearty welcome. Now, in the beginning, she is a little aloof and makes no promises. It's understandable that she doesn't want to play a visible role until Mona Kummel has gone, but it can't hurt to pave the way and welcome her into the community of women in the east villages.

Arthur Manström's attitude towards Portman is, on the other hand, both prejudiced and dismissive. He regards him as a crashing bore, an unimaginative cretin, a self-important little pope. "You need to hear him only once to realize that he has nothing to say," he declares after the first church service. He used to go to church now and then to show his friendship for Kummel, and he had a very high opinion of the social gatherings at the parsonage, but now he goes on strike. No one so utterly without a silver tongue can possibly value it in someone else. So there is no point in wasting his eloquence on Portman, our sounding-brass prelate, as Arthur calls him. This makes it harder for Lydia to cultivate Mrs Portman's friendship, but by no means impossible, for who is it who sits on the vestry? Arthur or his better half? And who is chairman of the Marthas? Not Arthur. You need perseverance and patience while you wait for the parish to regain its even keel after the heart-rending events of the past year. Then it will become clear where people stand, and where the strengths and talents of the newcomers lie.

* * *

The little girls cannot imagine that the summer will end. For Mama, it passes at a dizzying speed. Their departure date at the end of August is already fixed, transport to the slaughterhouse for Apple and her calf has been arranged. Before she knows it, it's time to milk her for the last time and ferry her to the steamboat pier, pursued by Goody's anxious bellowing from the shore. From the steamboat pier, she is chased on board and down into the open hold of the freighter that will carry the Örlands' wretched autumn beasts to the abattoir in Åbo. It's all done harshly and mercilessly. For a person with Mona Kummel's background, there is nothing unusual about sending animals to slaughter, and among all the cows she's milked in her day, the obstinate and haughty Apple is not one of her favourites, but nevertheless. Her cow. Her life. Now over. And it's awful to see how lost Goody feels, even though she's had to put up with a lot of hard bumps from Apple and move out of her way all her life. Looking at Goody now is like looking at Lillus if Sanna were sent away.

Silly thoughts, as if cows were human beings. They're not, and she has to get Goody under control and lead her into the cow barn and tie her up so she doesn't rush around Church Isle bellowing all night.

The girls are nearly as unaware as the cows about having to leave. Sanna knows they're going to move, though she doesn't know what that means, but she has started to worry and sleeps badly, and Lillus, now two years old, is getting more troublesome. In order to get anything done, Mama has to hire Cecilia for a few weeks. Cecilia is calmer than Mama, and everything gets easier. Above all, Cecilia is Sanna's friend, and whoever Sanna likes, Lillus likes. And with Cecilia in the house, Mama has to control herself and try to seem cheerful. She doesn't mind that the girls are much happier in Cecilia's company than in her own, for all that matters now is getting through the next few weeks, whatever the cost.

* * *

The days fly by. The sheep are sheared one final time and the wool packed away. On auction day, they stand on display in their sheepfold, naked and trembling. The cat is allowed to

ICE by ULLA-LENA LUNDBERG

stay with the Portmans once Mona has told them about the mice, but the four hens are too much trouble and will be sold. On the day of the sale, all three of them go to Sister Hanna's by boat—not because she couldn't stand to be present, Mona assures them, but because she thinks the auction will go more smoothly if people don't see her and grow depressed. The organist keeps the books for the auction. In light of all that's happened, there is no reason to cry over the sale of the sheep and chickens, the milk cans and the farming equipment. "So what?" she says defiantly.

Yes, so what? She packs and organizes. Like a machine. Has to stop when the vestry appears to pay their respects. The organist speaks for them all, thanks her for the hospitality of the parsonage, looks back at the past three years as an unusually happy time in the life of the parish, hopes that the bonds between them will never be broken. He wishes Mona and her girls good fortune in the future, wants them to know they will never be forgotten on the Örlands. "Don't forget us, either," he admonishes her—and to help them to remember, he removes the brown paper wrapping on a lovely painting of Church Isle commissioned from an artist in Mariehamn.

The vestry in tears, the widow self-controlled, as she was at the funeral, but slightly less so now as she thanks them for the painting, for their friendship, and for the best years of her life. Turns quickly away, puts more wood on the fire, has a bit more colour in her face when she looks at them again and glances around the parlour. Packing crates stand in rows on the floor. Some have already been nailed shut, others will be filled with last-minute items. Her china has also been packed, so she doesn't know if . . .

No, no, of course no one expects her to give them coffee in the midst of moving. They are leaving, but nevertheless they want to thank her, officially, on behalf of the parish, for everything, even though every one of them has thanked her personally as well. Adele Bergman in tears, Sörling clearing his throat and uncharacteristically quiet, Lydia Manström concerned, hoping they can leave without any further outbursts of emotion. The organist so tense that he can't bring himself to suggest a verse of "Shall We Gather at the River" now that they must say farewell.

The vestry out onto the steps, for the last time. Everything packed except the most essential things, which will go into a suitcase in the morning. Cecilia is to go home this last evening. Mona doesn't want a farewell committee on the shore, she wants to say goodbye in an orderly manner. "Thank you, Cecilia, for all your help, we've been so happy to have you here." An envelope with her payment is put in her hand, real money. Sanna is allowed to go with her all the way to the bridge and then come straight back home.

Lillus cries when they leave, just Sanna and Cecilia. The evenings are already a bit chilly in late August, and Sanna shivers. Cecilia holds her hand and tries to be cheerful, but she cries when she says how awfully sad it is that they have to move. But Sanna shouldn't be sad, she'll have fun with Gram and Gramps and all the animals, and when she gets bigger she can come to the Örlands for a visit. "And I'll write letters to you," she promises, "and Mama can help you write back."

All too quickly they arrive at the bridge. It still doesn't have a railing, but it stands on solid pilings. Now that it's there, no one need drown on the way to Church Isle. This is where Sanna will turn back and Cecilia continue on. But they stand where they are and hold hands. Cecilia cries, and tears run down Sanna's cheeks and the tip of her nose. Anxiously, Cecilia realizes that because she's older, she must decide when to go.

She lets go of Sanna's hand, feels how reluctantly it is withdrawn. Cecilia can't look at her when she says, "Now I have to go. And you have to go straight home, otherwise Mama will worry. Goodbye, Sanna. Run home now."

Sanna is frighteningly wise and sensible. She doesn't ask even once if she can go with Cecilia a little farther. Nor does she beg Cecilia to stay. She doesn't say she's scared to walk home alone. Dusk comes quickly in August, and now they both have to go. She dries her eyes with the sleeve of her sweater and starts to run. Cecilia walks out onto the bridge and stops and looks around. Sanna is so little and slim that she quickly disappears among the junipers and shadows. The path is empty, as if she had never existed.

But Sanna has no way to leave her own life. She's in it all the time, and she's afraid. Although she and Cecilia came from the parsonage, she can't know for certain that it will still be there when she gets back, for the path is different from when they were together, goes uphill where before it went down, zigs where it used to zag. She works herself up so badly she forgets to cry, and then the parsonage is there, oddly crimson in the twilight with white trim that seems to sail out ahead of the red. She stops and starts buttoning her sweater, otherwise Mama will scold her and tell her it's her own fault if she catches cold. It's hard. The cardigan is tight and there are lots of buttons and buttonholes and they're small and she can hardly see the top ones at all. She furrows her brow and squints and has to do it all over again from the beginning when it doesn't come out even. Maybe Mama will come out on the steps and say, "Come, Sanna," but the house is completely quiet as if no one lived there. She goes up the steps and pulls hard on the door to get it open. It's dark in the hallway and she stumbles over a box and hurts herself. Then Mama comes out the kitchen door.

"So there you are!" Behind her, Lillus has been crying but hops with joy now that Sanna has come back. It's like Mama says to everyone — how fortunate that Lillus has Sanna.

* * *

It's unexpectedly difficult to get the cow aboard. I've seldom seen such a bewildered beast. She's lost her leader cow and has no idea what to do, throws her head about and bawls and foams at the mouth and can't stand still when we finally get her tied up. She's on her way to Åbo, where they'll force her into a truck and drive her someplace near Helsingfors. There they'll lead her into a cow barn with ten gigantic Ayrshire cows she'll have to live with. The concentrated feed and ensilage they'll give her will be way too rich and you don't have to be a dairyman to realize how much gas that will produce, and what godawful diarrhoea. She may get through her first calving, but then she'll get milk fever and be slaughtered. Better if she'd been sent to slaughter right away, with Apple. Poor, pathetic parsonage cow.

The widow doesn't want to give her up, she's all she has left of everything that flourished on Church Isle. Well, the children of course, but they're as bewildered as the cow and just as scared. A perfect disaster now that they're on their way. She made it known that she didn't want a farewell committee, so it's only the verger and Brage who are there to carry crates and furniture and help Kalle and me get it all stowed. She's in a terrible rush. It all has to go quickly, and she runs back and forth directing the loading and the little girls run after her, crying. She screams at them, tells them to stay where they are and just wait, she'll be right back. "Quiet, Lillus!" she commands, and the girls stand deathly silent on the dock while she runs up to the parsonage one last time.

I don't know but what somewhere deep inside she still imagines that everything will be all right. That she'll open the door and see him

441

standing there in his everyday clothes, happy, wondering where she's off to in such a hurry. That all the rest of it has been a long illness, bouts of heavy fever with restless nightmares. Now finally over.

In any case, something drives her up to the house one final time. In the hall, she collides with the Portmans, who have come down a little too soon, they can't wait to take possession of the house. "Oh, excuse me!" she cries, "I was just going to . . ." She has already said goodbye to them and runs past them into the parlour, nothing, the bedroom, empty, as if they'd never, hurries on, dining room, kitchen a final survey, got everything, back down the steps, no glance towards the churchyard where the grave is groomed and the rosebush blooms, back down to the church dock. There we wait, loaded. The men in the machine room as usual, in the saloon, several women on their way to Åbo, Brage and the verger at a loss on the dock.

The cow moos on deck and the widow Kummel comes running down the hill. She shoves Sanna on board, the little one is lifted across the railing. "Hold tight," she calls, and they hold on as tight as they can. And when I say to Kalle, "Okay, then we're off," they hold on for dear life. He pulls in the gangplank and closes the grating. The verger stands by the rail. Maybe he was more attached to her than anyone else, and he has the most to lose by the change in priests. She can't ignore him. He says, "Mona! I won't say goodbye . . ."

"No!" she says. "We've done that." She sounds angry and remote, but he goes on.

"I'll say 'Until we meet again!'" He covers his large honest face with the whole sleeve of his coat, and she, small, the tip of her nose white, says, "Good!" She sweeps the girls with her down into the saloon, and when she decides, no one dares grumble. There will be no teary-eyed looks at the church and the parsonage and the sea and the land. The saloon is under the deck, and from there you can see nothing unless you press your nose against the portholes, which I must admit have never been washed.

442

Once the engine is going, you can't hear a thing, and when you can't hear, it's harder to see. I can't even say if the verger and Brage waved or just stood there. The women told me that the widow greeted everyone and was careful not to look out. The girls were as quiet as mice, and neither one cried.

It was a great disappointment to the women that Mrs Kummel had chosen this particular time to travel. When there are several of them, and they've got hours to kill, they really open up and talk away as if they were drunk or ecstatic. Anything at all, and in whatever order, and the unspoken agreement is that no one will be held responsible later for what she says in the frenzy of the moment. They talk about the living and the dead and friends and enemies, urge each other on and get obscene, laugh and interrupt, start over and exaggerate and turn themselves inside out like wartime clothing. Most of all they love scandals and horrible accidents. The worst of all is still the death of the vicar, and here sits his wife, so how can they?

Here sits his wife, and they have to talk but restrain themselves and watch what they say. The whole pleasure of the trip is gone when they have to be so careful, and although they gossip about much and many, the absence of all the other things they might have said is great and vivid. The remaining subjects are dry and the hours stretch on.

Human beings are made to live on the surface, and for long periods at a time they can forget what lies underneath. Some things sink to the bottom and other things rise up instead. What has happened in the past moves steadily away from the real world, precisely the way the priest grows more and more unlike the man he was when he walked among us, and more of a stranger. This is as it should be, for everything flows and shifts and changes. It's the way of the world, and on the Örlands the priest is already a story, which people are happy to embroider. As long as his widow and his little girls stay put, the flow is interrupted, and depression and sorrow cling to the discussion, although new currents ought to wash them away.

There they sit, the widow feigning interest and the little girls unnaturally well-behaved. They produce a dejection among the women that feels like shame. Their sympathy has been exhausted, and people don't like to look their own inconstancy in the mirror. On board the steamer, they get through the night sighing, and in the morning they watch as a truck backs down to the edge of the pier and the poor cow is dragged ashore and furniture and packing crates are reloaded. Goodbye, they say, with relief, as they start towards the city, goodbye and goodbye. When they've rounded the corner, the truck disappears from view along with the vicar's widow and children, and when the women come back in the afternoon, the surface is clean and unruffled. It was best for everyone that they left.

THOMAS TEAL, TRANSLATOR

Thomas Teal is best know for his translations of Tove Jansson's novels and short stories, beginning in the 1970s with *The Summer Book* and *Sun City* and, more recently, *Fair Play* (2007, winner of the Bernard Shaw Prize for translation), *The True Deceiver* (2009, winner of the Best Translated Book Award), *Art in Nature* (2012) and *The Listener* (2014). He has also translated Fredrik Sjöberg, Maj Sjöwall and Per Wahlöö, and Theodor Kallifatides. He lives in Massachusetts.